Praise for Charlotte Butterfield

'Hilarious, thoughtful and so cleverly plotted. I wept buckets toward the end and it makes life feel much warmer'
JESSICA RYN, author of *The Extraordinary Hope of Dawn Brightside*

'A tender and poignant novel that taps into the "what if" in all of us, *By This Time Tomorrow* is filled with clever twists, humour and heartbreak. This thoughtful story about second chances is a life-affirming, magical read'
HOLLY MILLER, author of *The Sight of You*

'Hilarious, heartbreaking and unputdownable – I loved it'
DEBBIE JOHNSON, author of *The Moment I Met You*

'A delightful story of 'what ifs' and new beginnings – warm, funny and hugely relatable'
FIONA GIBSON, author of *When Life Gives You Lemons*

'A truly magical book that had me laughing one minute and crying the next – magnificent!'
EMMA COOPER, author of *It Was Always You*

'A perfectly magical mix of hilariously funny and heartbreakingly emotional – I adored it!'
RACHAEL LUCAS, author of *The Telephone Box Library*

'Thought-provoking, heartwarming and snort-out-loud funny – I adored *By This Time Tomorrow*. We'd all like to turn back the clock on occasion, wouldn't we? Charlotte Butterfield has created a story full of sensitivity, imagination and warmth'
FIONA LUCAS, author of *The Last Goodbye*

'Warm, witty and the mother of all what ifs for weary women!'
LAURA KEMP, author of *Bring Me Sunshine*

About the Author

A former magazine editor, Charlotte Butterfield was born in Bristol in 1977 and studied English at Royal Holloway. She moved to Dubai by herself on a one-way ticket with one suitcase in 2005 and left twelve years later with a husband, three children and a 40ft shipping container. She now lives in the Cotswolds, where she is a freelance writer and novelist. Her first novel won a Montegrappa award at the 2016 Emirates Festival of Literature, and she went on to publish three romantic comedies with One More Chapter (previously Harper Impulse), and *By This Time Tomorrow* with Hodder & Stoughton. *You Get That From Me* is her fifth novel.

You Get That from Me

CHARLOTTE BUTTERFIELD

First published in Great Britain in 2023 by Hodder & Stoughton
An Hachette UK company

1

A CIP catalogue record for this title is available from the British Library

Paperback ISBN 978 1 52935 374 7
eBook ISBN 9781529353754

Typeset in Plantin Light by Hewer Text UK Ltd, Edinburgh
Printed and bound in Great Britain by Clays Ltd, Elcograf S.p.A.

Hodder & Stoughton policy is to use papers that are natural, renewable and recyclable products and made from wood grown in sustainable forests. The logging and manufacturing processes are expected to conform to the environmental regulations of the country of origin.

Hodder & Stoughton Ltd
Carmelite House
50 Victoria Embankment
London EC4Y 0DZ

www.hodder.co.uk

To Team P, je t'aime, ti amo

You Get That From Me

1

Stella

Hello, person reading this in the future, my name's Stella Fairbrother. Stella means Star. It is 1995 and I am 12 years old and I like Boyzone, Chinese takeaways, watching Neighbours *and chain letters. When I grow up, I am going to be a marine biologist, or a lawyer, or a scriptwriter for movies. I live here with my Mum, Bonnie and Grandma Florence. Write your message next to mine for the next person to see or you will have twenty years bad luck, even though Granny says you make your own luck. Bye.*

I run my hand over my writing. God, I was a precocious child. The i's have little hearts over them and my y's and g's have extravagant loops that I always forgot to do, then would have to rub out the boring tails to make these more exciting ones. I vaguely remember writing this on the wall before Mum papered over it with the grey and pink diagonally striped wallpaper I've just spent ten days every morning before work stripping off.

I pick up the brush and dip it in the wallpaper paste to consign my words back into the time capsule once again by papering over it. I stop, and pause, brush poised in mid-air. Even though it's the words of an overconfident twelve-year-old, considering my current life situation, I can ill afford another twenty years' bad luck, so on a complete whim, and in spite of not really believing in luck, I reach into my bag for a permanent marker.

> *Hi, person reading this in the future, which, let's face it, will probably still be me. Stella Fairbrother here. Again. It is 2023 and I am 40 years old and I rarely listen to music, still like Chinese takeaways, watching Netflix, and I have over 3,000 unread emails in my inbox. I have grown up and I'm not a marine biologist, lawyer, or screenwriter, but I'm the assistant manager of a nursing home. I am also mortified to confirm that I still live here with my Mum, Bonnie, and my grandmother, Florence. By the way . . . there's no such thing as luck; good, bad or indifferent.*

I quickly paste the first strip of wallpaper on the trestle table to cover up both of these notes on the wall while trying to swallow down the resentment that keeps threatening to drown me. I honestly thought that by the age of forty I'd have a fabulously fulfilling and financially lucrative career, a supportive and not unattractive husband who did both his and my ironing on a Sunday afternoon while watching *Countryfile*, and a couple of cheerful and wholly acquiescent kids. It wasn't an unreasonable expectation I don't think, not like inventing the new internet or marrying a royal, or the deluded ambitions of my twelve-year-old self. I just wanted a nice partner and kids. That's all. Yet here I am, single, in my childhood home. It's like the last two decades have never happened.

I didn't have to move back in here with Mum and Florence after I rented my flat out. Kate and a few of my other friends offered their spare rooms too. But their houses have fridge doors covered in star-of-the-day certificates for 'sitting on the carpet nicely' and 'taking turns with the glue sticks' and that's not really what I want to see every time I take out someone else's milk to add to my coffee in someone else's Best Mummy Ever mug. So now I'm back behind the green door, hoping Mum doesn't catch me writing on my bedroom wall while I wait for my octogenarian grandmother to finish using the loo before I can have a shower and go to work.

'Sorry, darling, you should have knocked, I was doing a sudoku,' Florence says, twenty minutes later as she wafts out of the bathroom wearing a long kaftan.

'It's OK, no rush. My shift doesn't start until ten, I've got ages.'

'Come downstairs and have a cup of tea with me then.'

I don't need much persuading. Wallpapering looks a lot more fun than it actually is.

If inanimate objects could talk, the pine table in the middle of my mum's kitchen would never shut up. I think about the thousands of bowls of cereal I've had at this table, the amount of Sunday roasts, the pages and pages of maths worksheets, history coursework and university applications. I carved my initials into its leg before being angrily exiled to my room when I was about seven, despite my initials sitting next to the B.F. carved by my mother's hand when she was a child. The tell-tale grooves and felt-tip marks of two childhoods are etched into every part of its well-worn surface. Endless ring marks from endless cups of tea, glasses of wine, celebrations, commiserations, homework, hard work, heart work: like finding the perfect father for your unmade child. The trouble is, much like low-fat Chinese takeaways and 'all the taste but none of the caffeine' coffees, the perfect father doesn't seem to exist. And I should know.

I look gratefully up at my grandmother's lined, smiling face as she puts a mug of steaming hot tea in front of me.

'How's it going?' Florence asks, nodding at my laptop, which I've just opened out of habit, and am mindlessly scrolling through the donor database for the millionth time. 'Have you found a suitable spermatozoa for my great-grandchild yet?'

When I first mentioned the idea of sperm donation, eight years ago, my proclamation was met with a rousing 'But you're only thirty-two! Plenty of time to meet a real man,' so I set about trying to find him. Luke looked promising for a while, until he confessed that he 'doesn't like kids' – incidentally, he now has three under five. Then, two years later, after Billy had decided that monogamy wasn't for him – six months before getting engaged to someone else – I'd mentioned the idea of a donor baby again, this time with the casual breeziness with which one might float the idea of a weekend drive in the country. Once more, there was a chorus (and I'm absolutely certain that I wasn't imagining that this time it was a little lacklustre) of 'But you're only thirty-five, the man of your dreams could turn up tomorrow!' But this year, on my fortieth, when I announced to all my friends and family that this was the year that I was definitely going to get pregnant from a sperm donor, the response was that it wouldn't hurt to research it a bit. So that's what I've been doing. Every minute of every day. When I'm not working, when I am working, and even, annoyingly, when I'm sleeping – back in my childhood bed, because it turns out that making babies without making love doesn't come cheap.

I let my head fall onto the table. 'No, and I don't know if I ever will. It's so confusing.'

'What's confusing about it?' Florence says, pulling a chair up alongside me. 'You're not marrying the man, you're buying one of his best swimmers.'

'But the baby will be half him, so I need to pick a good one,' I say, sitting up and slouching back in my chair.

'It can't be that tricky. Come on. Let's look at the questions.' She peers at the screen. 'Height. Let's start with an easy one. Over six foot.'

'But I'm only five foot six; I don't need someone that tall,' I protest.

Florence shakes her head. 'Any man over five foot eight says he's exactly six foot. Someone who says he's six foot two is probably telling the truth.' For a woman who has been widowed for almost half a century, she's pretty clued up when it comes to the male of the species. She puts a tick next to 'Six foot and over'. 'Occupation.' She doesn't even wait for my answer and ticks 'Professional', which seems completely ridiculous. The odds are that they are, quite literally, professional wankers.

I have actually put quite a lot of thought into my ideal donor's job for quite some time, and it's amazing how picky you become over really good professions. I was tossing up between a criminal attorney and a chemical engineer last week before eventually coming to the conclusion that law trumps particles, and serial killers are much more interesting than scientists – as dinner-party topics, not dinner-party guests. I also tied myself up in knots over the donor's nationality. There were two contenders: one was Cuban-Egyptian-Welsh, the other German-Turkish-Irish. That was a tricky choice, intriguing cultural heritage on both sides. I ultimately plumped for the former, only then to read more of his profile and learn that he'd put down 'small bird' as his favourite pet, and atheism as a hobby.

I need to be more specific, I think, filter out the dross. I go back into my preferences and place a tick next to 'plays a musical instrument.'

'So you think you can tell that this donor is a good man by whether he plays the piano?'

'Musical ability is very important to me,' I say.

'You can't even play the recorder,' Florence reminds me.

'Exactly. So the baby's not going to get any from me, are they?'

Florence leans closer to the laptop. 'I think you're over-complicating things. Go back to the list of them all. OK, close your eyes and I'll bring that mouse thing up and down until you say stop. Ready? Go.'

'Stop.'

Florence puts on her glasses, which are on a purple string around her neck, and peers closely at the screen. 'Oh bingo, here we go, six foot two, Finnish-South African, model, actor, charity worker, tech CEO—'

My eyes widen as I grab the mouse from my grand-mother's wrinkled hand. 'Where? I didn't see that one?'

'Like someone like that is going to be pleasuring himself into a pot for twenty pounds.' Florence laughs at her completely unfunny joke.

'Thirty-five pounds actually,' I pout, sitting back with my arms crossed petulantly across my chest.

'Oh right, the big bucks. Look, whoever you choose is going to help you make a baby that is going to be the best baby in the world, and that's got nothing to do with what fancy degree this donor man has, or whether his favourite pet is a flamingo.'

'A flamingo is not a pet,' Bonnie, my mother, says as she comes into the room, shrugging her coat off and draping it over the kitchen chair. She kisses me on the top of my head and grazes her mother's cheek with her lips. 'Are you getting anywhere?'

'No,' I groan.

'Shall I make a new pot then?'

'I keep telling her,' Florence says as if I'm not here, 'that it doesn't matter what the man likes for breakfast, it matters what he's like as a person, but none of these profiles say anything about how kind he is, or how much he loves his family; it's like those type of values don't count anymore.'

'I think they still count, but it's not particularly sexy, is it – to say how kind and generous you are,' I say.

'I think kindness is incredibly sexy,' Mum says. 'Anyway, why do you want the donor to be sexy? You're not making the baby that way. You don't need to fancy him; just being a decent human being is good enough.'

The three of us sit around the laptop screen for the next half-hour, me dismissing each of their suggestions out of hand until Florence shouts, 'Enough. This is madness. Just pick one. Anyone. It doesn't matter. It's going to be the best baby in the world because it'll be raised by you, and your mum, and me too, if you get a goddamn move on having it.'

'But what do I tell them?'

'Who?'

'The child! How do I explain this?' I sweep my arm out in front of me at the screen of potential baby-daddies. 'How do I justify which one I chose for them to be half of?'

Florence shrugs. 'I've come to realise that the way babies come into the world is far less important than what you do to them once they're here.'

'But how will they know who they are? Where they came from? How can I look them in the eye and tell them that I have no idea about half of their history? And that's not accidental, that's a deliberate choice I made?'

Florence takes her time answering, as though she is carefully selecting the words out of a dictionary one by one. 'You choosing this path, this way, however . . . unconventional, shows how much you want them. And as for only knowing half their history, well, we've just got to make sure that we tell them as much as possible about the half we do know about.'

'I'm glad you said that; I've got something for you both. Stay there.' I run upstairs to the spare room which I'm staying in while I redecorate mine, grab a carrier bag I'd stashed in the wardrobe and run breathlessly back down to the kitchen, reminding myself on the way to add 'athletic ability' to my donor's must-have list, because I sure as heck don't have any. I place the parcel in front of them on the kitchen table, and nod at it grinning. 'Go on, open it.'

They exchange glances before reaching for it, humouring me the way they have for the last four decades. Inside the bag are three notebooks. Not the spiral-topped reporter pads you buy in packs of three at the newsagents, these are expensive hardcover journals I had to order from a stationery specialist on the internet, each one embossed with their name in fancy swirly letters. Florence is the first to speak, flicking through the empty lined pages with a confused expression. 'These are lovely, but I don't follow?'

'It's like what you just said, about making sure that we tell the baby as much as we can about the half of their history that we do know about, and so I thought that we – you, Mum and me – could all spend the next nine months, until the baby's here, writing to them. You know, like a long letter, or a collection of stories about us: our pasts, things we've done and seen, and people we've met that have been important to us, the things we've done that have made us who we are, who they are.' I can hear the excitement building in my voice, and hope that it will be infectious. 'It'll be like one of those celebrity autobiographies, so they have books all about where they came from!'

Florence doesn't seem as excited as I hoped she would be, but in some way this could actually be cathartic for her; I've never heard her talk about her parents much, so maybe there's some skeletons she needs to dig up and de-bone. And, at her age, keeping your brain active is a good thing anyway; otherwise it's a slow decline into watching reruns of *Murder She Wrote* all day. I see it at the nursing home every day.

'So, Flo, Mum, will you do it? For the baby?' I widen my eyes in the exact same way I've done to these two women thousands of times in the past, pleading for a later bedtime, just one more biscuit.

'Of course,' they say in unison, before putting the books back in the bag.

'Now please, pick a donor right now before I pop my clogs and your little bairn never has the chance to listen to my wisdom,' Florence says.

'Fine. Here goes.' I close my eyes, yo-yo the mouse up and down on its mat, and open my eyes on Babydaddy 333. A greyhound fanatic from the North of England who likes amateur musical theatre and crab cakes.

Florence wrinkles her nose, closes her eyes and puts her hand on top of mine. 'Best of three, eh?'

* * *

Dear Baby,

Writing to you seemed like a really good idea when I bought the notebooks. I've always been a sucker for a nice notebook. Perhaps in this day and age, it really should have been an online book – I'm sure there's software for that. But then technology moves so fast, what I'd be typing this on now might not even exist when you're reading this, so old-fashioned paper and pen is probably better. Except then you can see when I change my mind about what I write, or make a spelling mistake, which I have to hold my hands up to now, and admit may well happen quite regularly. Except if the occasion arises for me to write onomatopoeia, because I've always mastered that one. The key is to break words like that down, so ono-mato-poe-ia. But I'll probably teach you that in person once you're here and bringing your spelling book home from school, so you'll probably already know that. Argh, I'm waffling. This was meant to be a book of life, of love, and insightful thoughts, and all I've done so far is talk about tech-trends, give spelling tips, and prove that my brain works at about a million miles a minute. By the way, a mile is 1.6 kilometres.

I'm Stella Martha Fairbrother. Stella means Star and Martha was the name of my grandmother's landlady, don't ask, I don't know why, but apparently Mum said Granny Flo could pick my middle name, and that's what she went with. I have no intention of naming you after anyone I've rented a house from, so don't worry. My surname used to be Morris, until my parents got divorced, and Mum changed our surname back to her maiden name to erase my father completely from our lives after he left, leaving no forwarding address. Crikey, that got deep pretty quickly. A seamless segue between inane waffle and the darkest truth of my past. And there you have it, the reason, I suppose, why I'm taking so long to find you the perfect biological father, so that you don't end up a total screw-up and his half of you balances out mine. I know that you'll never meet the donor, or perhaps you will, the law changed recently so that once you're eighteen you can look for him, if you want to, and I'll help you if you do. But I wanted to make sure that the donor that helped me make you is decent, and kind and intelligent, and a good, good man, so that you won't feel, as I often have, that half your genes are crap ones.

Love,
Your Mum

2

Stella

The words in my childish scrawl on the bedroom wall that I papered over haunt me as I sit on the bus on the way to work, imagining a parallel life where I'm on my way to the other careers I could have had. *Should* have had. Sitting in the back of a black cab as I head to the Crown court to give the closing arguments in a high-profile trial; the whole courtroom poised for the eloquent words soon to trip off my tongue. Or sitting in the departure lounge before catching my flight to a remote archipelago in the South Pacific where a new species of finless porpoise has been spotted and they need my expertise urgently.

My phone pings in my bag. It's one of the nurses at the nursing home.

Hi Stella, 10 boxes of incontinence pads have just arrived, no room in sluice. Have put them in your office.

There is a really good reason why I ended up working in a nursing home, and it had nothing to do with the glitz and glamour, if you can believe it. It was the steel-clad guarantee that I wouldn't be around babies. For most of my life, I've had to smile politely while making life easier for other women and their offspring as my own womb is desolately holding a TO LET sign with no potential renters in sight. I move tables in cafes to make room for impossibly large three-wheel, off-road buggies that are more spacious and expensive than my first car. I hold little Harriet so Mummy can have a me-time manicure when I'm sitting next to her having a pedicure. I crawl under clothing rails for lost dummies in shops because Mummy's got another baby strapped to her chest and can't bend down. Not to mention the hundreds of pounds I must have put into assorted A4 envelopes over the years while working various office jobs for Karen's / Nina's / Lucy's / Olivia's / Teena's / Janet's / Gail's / Verity's / Zoe's / Poppy's / Katie's / Anna's / Simitra's / Angela's / Kirsten's / Claire's / Lena's baby showers, none of which I could attend, if only I didn't have a wedding / funeral / christening / bar mitzah / bat mitzvah / moving house / helping a friend move house / house sitting / house hunting / just really busy, sorry. But if there's one thing worse than actually attending someone else's baby shower, it's hearing about it on a Monday morning. *'So you had to guess the flavour of the baby puree while wearing a blindfold?' 'No way, that sounds hilarious, sorry I missed it.'*

So working at a nursing home and training your nose not to notice the combined odour of bleach and urine is a small price to pay for not having to contend with the output of other women's ovaries. Or so you would have thought. Except, Aisha, my boss, the care home manager, is currently four months pregnant and lets out a small groan every time she stands up or sits down. She sits at her desk on her giant inflatable ball in the tiny office we share, keeping tabs on her bladder activity on a little notepad next to her in-tray. It's bad enough she writes it down, but she also thinks it's absolutely acceptable behaviour to tell me every time she walks past my desk as well. Imagine doing that when you're not with child, just merrily telling an employee, 'That's the fourth pee of the morning, I'll need another one soon, just watch.'

I don't begrudge her; well, not really. I just thought that it would be a lot less painful to be in an environment where I wasn't reminded all day every day that other women seem completely able to find a mate and, well, mate. At first, before Aisha got pregnant, and apart from the weekly weekend visits by grandchildren bringing in their latest offspring all wrapped up in cosy rompers with bunny ears on their hoods, the nursing home seemed the perfect place to avoid other people's winning wombs. And I actually enjoyed my job – incontinence pads aside. I loved chatting with the residents, listening to the saucy stories of Elsie and trying not to look too shocked, or helping Douglas polish his medals for Remembrance Day. I felt useful, needed, and – apart from the well-intentioned enquiries into my private life – I felt that my lack of partner, or child, really didn't matter. But eight years ago, Marjorie became really ill.

I know looking back, I should have anticipated it; it's a nursing home, not a holiday park. Call me naive, or just plain stupid, but it hadn't really occurred to me that the longer I worked there, the more of my friends I'd have to see leave in an ambulance or a funeral directors van.

After her bleak prognosis, in Marjorie's final week, she was never alone. Her family set up a rota system around the clock. When one of her children left, an adult grandchild took their place, tag-teaming holding her hand until her last breath. She died on a Tuesday during the lunchtime weather report on the TV in the corner. It seemed wrong they were discussing the clear skies and sun when Marjorie's light was snuffed out. Her daughter was one side of her, her granddaughter the other, and watching this scene from the doorway made me imagine Florence's last days, with me and Mum each side of her, stroking her hair, running an ice cube over her lips. The scene then shrank in my head to Mum's deathbed, where it would just be me tending to her. Then to my own last moments, where I'd be completely alone. There would be no relay of relatives making sure I was never left by myself. The flowers in my room would be ones I would have bought myself. My will, if I even needed to make one, would name my godsons and a suitable charity.

'I didn't realise you were so close to her,' Mum said to me a few days after Marjorie's packed funeral, when I was still withdrawn and quiet. 'It's not like you to get so attached.'

I *was* sad, of course, that someone I'd had hundreds of conversations with and liked had died, but I wasn't just grieving Marjorie. The truth was, I'd had a glimpse of the perfect death if that's not too much of an oxymoron, and I was now facing the fact that I could never have it. Not unless I made some immediate, and fairly drastic changes. And that's how I became a mastermind-level brainbox on all things fertility related.

Just yesterday, my consultant turned to the student doctors behind him and said, 'There isn't a lot that Stella Fairbrother doesn't know about sperm.' Others may have winced at this unusual introduction, but I just felt a little rush of pride. He's right. I do know a lot about it. I know that in Slovak it is, rather endearingly, called 'spermie', as though each one has a little woollen bobble hat pulled down over its ears and a satchel slung diagonally across its body as it meanders its way through snow and sleet up the fallopian tubes. I even know that in the African language, Igbo, they call sperm 'spam', which really must have confused anyone from South-eastern Nigeria visiting England in the seventies if they were offered a sandwich.

Florence thinks I should get a less strange hobby. Which is a bit rich given she recently bought an inflatable paddleboard on eBay despite living forty-five miles away from the coast, being a month away from her eightieth birthday and currently on the waiting list for a second knee replacement. But I can't expect her to understand; not when she is the proud parent of a sixty-two year-old woman (my mum Bonnie) conceived by around seventy-five million of her husband's *spam* making their wiggling way all the way to her ovum after a romantic night out and a couple of gin fizzes.

Of course, I know I have that option up my sleeve. Mum's said it, Florence has insinuated it, and I'd be lying if I insisted that I haven't considered it. Any night of the week, I could put on my heels, head for the town, laugh at a few bad jokes, toss my hair about a bit and take home an unsuspecting real-life donor. It's what all my friends have done, albeit with a couple of years and a wedding in between the initial meeting and the conception.

But let's say, for the sake of argument, I did lure a potential donor back to my flat, what then? After the awkward clothes removal had taken place and the deed was done? I'd be faced with co-parenting with a stranger for the rest of my life. I want a child, not a complicated rota system tacked up on the fridge.

'You don't have to tell the man when you get pregnant, you know,' Mum said once, surprisingly out of character. But that's not an option because a giant cesspool of guilt would open up like a sinkhole on a wet road and consume me. So it has to be done this way. Anonymously. Solo. Completely, and terrifyingly, alone.

'I don't understand why it's taking you so long to pick one?' Kate says when I meet her after work at the wine bar on the high street.

'It's a massive decision!' I say, dipping a chunk of bread in her melted Camembert before remembering that I'm trying to cut out all the things that you're not allowed in pregnancy to get my body ready, so I spit it out in a napkin. 'When you meet a man in a bar and decide that he's the one for you, it doesn't really matter whether his hair is straight or curly or whether he passed his maths GCSE, because you've fallen in love, and you can overlook the unicorn tattoo on his forearm with the name "Pauline" underneath because he's just so amazing in other ways. But when you're faced with a database of hundreds of potential baby-daddies, it does matter. It matters a lot.'

'True, what if they're really ugly?' Kate asks, tipping a handful of peanuts into her mouth. 'They could sound great on paper, but they might be gross.'

'They don't have photos of the donors on the site, because of privacy and stuff, but many of them have put photos of them as children on their profiles, so you can kind of guess what their child would look like.'

'I think this is the right time for me to remind you that you had a Frieda Kahlo monobrow for the first sixteen years of your life.'

'So?'

'So, if the circumstances were reversed, and a bloke was picking potential mothers for their child, a young Frieda may not be top of the list, and now look at you. You're quite pretty, and she's an icon.'

I cast my mind back over all the potential donors I've dismissed out of hand over the last few months for exactly that reason. Considering the range and affordability of hair removal products on the market nowadays, I really should have been able to overlook a caterpillar perching on a ten-year-old's upper lip, or particularly overenthusiastic eyebrows that seemed to be walking across their face on a Sunday stroll. But why should I have to compromise on anything when there are another four hundred other men waiting for me to pick them? This might also explain why I am still single. I've been accused of being 'too picky' for the last twenty years, but I honestly can't understand why that's a bad thing. Surely having a set of criteria met when it comes to spending literally every day with someone until you die requires a certain level of pickiness. Sorry, but I'm not going to listen to someone sniff continuously regardless of the weather or season (Billy), or watch them lick their plate after eating at home or in a restaurant (Jonathan), or listen to a really loud, grating laugh that sounds like peacocks mating (Mark), or genuinely liking country and western music in a non-ironic way (Jake) just because they're attractive, wealthy and, in Mark's case, one of the leading figures in paediatric heart surgery. Limits are limits.

'Anyway,' I sigh, 'the countdown's on. The doctor wants to do the insemination on my next cycle. I start the injections next week.'

Yesterday, when he asked the question, 'Have you picked a donor yet?' he'd said it in that breezy way one might ask, 'Tea or coffee? Thick crust or thin crust? Movie or dinner? One digestive or two? Sperm donor 352 or 426? One will mean your child grows up to be clever, kind and stunningly attractive, the other means they'll spend their sixteenth birthday injecting heroin between their toes while waxing their unibrow.'

'Um, almost,' I told him with an apologetic smile. 'I've narrowed it down.'

He wasn't fooled; I've been procrastinating for months. 'I don't think that I need to remind you that time isn't really on our side, Stella,' he said, with more than a hint of disappointed head teacher about him. 'Every month that goes past, your eggs are deteriorating in quality, and so we really do need to move quickly on this. I'd like to harvest your eggs next month and we'll freeze them ready for when you pick a donor. But please pick one soon.'

I sigh and look at my friend. 'I need to find the perfect dad pronto.'

'Right.' Kate raises her full glass and taps it against my empty one. 'To the search for the perfect dad.'

'Perfect dad.'

3
Florence

Dear Little One,

Hello. Actually, hello seems woefully inadequate as the first word I say to you. I could easily rip out this page and choose a different word to start with, but then again, what could possibly be the right first word out of the 171,146 words currently in the English language? I've just googled that, by the way. I'm smart, but I don't have immediate access to facts like that in my brain. And I say 'currently' because new words are being added all the time. Like hashtag. Twittersphere. Neither of those were in the 1943 *Oxford English Dictionary*. I've just had a little look, on the internet, and actually new entries in the dictionary in 1943, the year I was born, were 'escape artist' and 'irritable bowel syndrome'. I can't for the life of me work out how in the very first letter to my new great-grandchild I've managed to shoehorn in the term 'irritable bowel' but I have, and here we are.

Stella, your mum, my granddaughter, thought this would be a good way for you to get to know us – the three women in your life. To tell you a bit about ourselves – 'what makes us us,' was how she put it. But that's impossible really, isn't it? To have that level of self-awareness to understand exactly why you behave, talk, walk, sit in a certain way? So I'm not going to enter into any grand self-assessment here, I'll leave that to the celebrities to do in their autobiographies. I'm just going to tell you a bit about myself, while I still have access to moveable joints in my fingers to enable me to hold a pen, and a fairly workable brain in my head to be able to remember.

I've been wondering where to begin, and then I thought that I should do what the King said gravely to Alice in Wonderland, 'Begin at the beginning, and go on till you come to the end: then stop,' so that's what I'll do. Feel free to skip the boring bits, which, amount to the first sixteen years of my life, so I'll whizz through that part for you, aside from saying that I was born on 17 May 1943 to Dorothy and Jack Weston at No. 17 Alderton Close, Chiswick. Don't bother looking them up, they're long gone, and the house is now under a Lidl superstore, or rather the bottom left-hand side of its car park, near the recycling bins and the nice Romanians who wash your car by hand. I had a brother; he died of measles when I was ten. His name was Stuart. No one ever called him Stu; my mother wouldn't let them. But I did, when she wasn't listening, and it really suited him. I don't really know what else to say about my childhood. I rose with the sun, did my chores, went to school, where I learned nothing useful in life apart from how to make a good scone and the length of the longest river in the world: the Amazon, 4,000 miles. Then I came home, helped my mother with the housework, and went to bed with the moon above my head.

But then came the summer of 1959. And everything changed.

I recall feeling as though everywhere I looked, everyone in the world was living a more exciting life than I was. I watched women wearing white capri pants swinging their legs over the back of roaring Vespas, laughter coming out of their pale pink lips as they tucked their arms around the waists of their

Brylcreemed boyfriends before whizzing through the park, past the signs that said in capitals, NO MOTORISED BICYCLES. I remember sitting there wondering how a roll of life's dice meant that I was a bystander to this fun, this frivolity, this breaking of rules. Why was I wearing sensible brown lace-ups instead of ballet pumps? I was annoyed that it never even crossed my mind before to even want ballet pumps. Or ride on a Vespa. And, truth be told, I'd always thought that a Brylcreemed head looked rather sticky and unnatural. But right then, at that exact moment, there was nothing I wanted more than to run my hands all over one. I bought a pair of ballet pumps and pale blue capri pants that afternoon. I even shaved my legs for the first time too – well, from the knee down, no need to do the tops – bit of grooming advice for you. Unless you turn out to be a boy, in which case, sorry for giving you too much detail, but it's always good to be informed.

You hear people saying, 'Oh, the sixties were the best years to be alive' – well, I don't know if you will ever hear that; by the time you're old enough, most of us will be dead. But honestly, little one, it was like no other time before or since. When Elvis wasn't making us swing our pelvises, Chubby Checker was making us twist them. My bra was pointy, my eyelashes could easily have airlifted me should I blink, and I walked everywhere in a shroud of eau de toilette from the local chemists.

I have to be honest with you. I had no idea what to do in between leaving school and getting married. I wasn't clever enough to be a teacher; I did like the idea of nursing, but my mother wasn't keen, and so when my friend Hazel showed me a job advert she'd cut out of her father's evening newspaper, I felt it was the sign I'd been looking for.

Attractive, personable waitresses wanted for discreet Westminster member's club. Must be single, no children, and have teacher's references. Ten pounds a week.

We would never have described ourselves as attractive, you didn't back then, but we were personable, if that meant polite and reasonably friendly, and we were definitely single with no children, and that was enough to get us the jobs.

I'd been working there for about a week and I loved it. On this particular day, a Thursday I believe it was, the club was quieter than usual. There was a big debate in the House of Commons apparently, so there wasn't the usual buzz of ministers swirling their amber liquid around their crystal tumblers and fogging up the lounge with blue smoke that used to make my eyes smart. There was still a smattering of suits and silk pocket handkerchiefs dotted about the warren of rooms though. I liked the spotty hankies the most; they denoted a certain joviality the plain ones didn't. They were an odd thing, pocket handkerchiefs – a lovely little splash of personality. Before my first day at the club, I'd never even heard of pocket handkerchiefs, let alone seen them in action. My father was smart, but stuffing a hanky you weren't allowed to use in your top pocket was not something he'd have gone in for.

I spotted a raised finger an inch off the arm of a Chesterfield to indicate a brandy glass needed a top-up. I scurried over, decanter in hand, poured the liquor in and nodded to the man with a bottle-green spotted triangle poking out of his breast pocket.

'Quiet in here today,' he said.

I nodded.

'Must be a nice respite for you.'

I nodded and smiled politely again, taking a step back.

'What's your name?'

'Florence,' I said, waiting for the predictable 'Nightingale?' that was about to come.

His reply was unexpected. 'Like Florence R. Sabin.'

'Who?' I asked.

'She died recently,' he said, his words coming out slowly, as though he was rolling them around in his mouth for size before saying them. 'Five or so years ago, I believe. She was a pioneer of medical science in America. The first woman to be voted into the National Academy of Science. Tuberculosis research, if I'm not mistaken.'

'Oh,' I said, standing a little taller.

'Do you like science, Florence?'

He was the first customer to say words to me that didn't contain a drinks or food order. I'd also never really thought about science beyond the nature studies I'd done at my secondary modern. Rubbing bark on paper with crayon, and growing cress seeds in the back of the airing cupboard, that's all I remembered about science. I knew that you breathed in oxygen and breathed out carbon dioxide. I racked my brain for more science-related knowledge I might have lurking in the back, but no, that was it.

I shrugged. 'Um, yes, I think so.'

'It's impossible not to, I suppose, isn't it,' the man said amiably, 'when the whole world around us is made up of infinite chemical compounds, and the physical properties of matter and energy.' He flung out his arms to really hammer the point home that he was indeed talking about the whole world, and nearly caught the side of the glass carafe on my tray.

'Yes, absolutely. Impossible not to. Excuse me, sir.'

I was trembling so much when I got into the kitchen, I dropped my tray and had to spend the next ten minutes brushing shards of glass out from under the ovens and cupboards. Since Stu had died, I hadn't been around any boy or man, and his intense stare and scrutiny caught me off guard. He was quite a bit older than me, and had a quiet self-assurance that came back then with wealth, and age, and being a man.

'Did I say something to upset you before?' he asked as I wiped down the table next to him a few minutes later. 'I thought I heard some crashing and banging.'

'No, I-I . . . tripped and dropped my tray.'

'I suddenly thought that perhaps you thought I was being a little too talkative. I do that when I get nervous, terrible really, has always happened, even at school. Why use two words when you can use ten? Apologies though, if I put you on the spot before, I didn't mean to be nosy, I just thought perhaps you might like to talk to someone, it must get terribly boring when it's quiet in here, or maybe you like it, when there's not dreadfully dull scientists like me bothering you every thirty seconds.'

'You're doing it again.'

'I'm sorry, what?' he looked taken aback.

I smiled at him. 'Talking too much.'

The man laughed and scratched the side of his face, 'You're right. I am. Sorry. Again.'

My manager called me then. My shift had ended and the new girl had arrived to take over. But I knew that this man was going to be special. That was the first time I ever spoke to your great-grandfather.

Henry came to the club every Tuesday and Thursday afternoon for the next two months. I even started swapping my shifts so that I could always be there. Sometimes, when the club was busy, we never even spoke, bar me asking for his order, and him placing it. But I knew that wherever I was in that room, his eyes would be on me. If I caught him by surprise, turned around, or looked up unexpectedly, he'd blush from the roots of his hair to the nails on his toes and look away. I couldn't explain it, but I liked it.

It was a Tuesday, eight weeks since I first met him, when he finally plucked up the courage to speak to me properly. He'd been nursing the same pot of tea for about an hour – I only found out afterwards that it was because he could only afford one pot but didn't want to rush it and leave without talking to me. I went over to his table and said, 'Can I get you anything else, sir, or perhaps just the bill?'

'Henry.'

'I'm sorry?'

'My name is Henry Fairbrother.'

'In here, you're sir.' I said, parroting what the manager had drummed into us.

'And outside of here?'

I suddenly blushed, mortified, that wasn't what I meant at all.

'Oh cripes, now I've made you embarrassed. I'm making a right pig's ear of this, aren't I?'

'Of what?' I asked, uncertain.

'I wondered if perhaps, you might permit me, one early evening, the light's best then, Victorian lamp posts, you see, give out more light than the modern ones, all down to refraction, if just maybe you'd like to take a stroll along the Thames with me? Perhaps along the South Bank on the other side of the river? Probably not, don't mind me. Forget I said anything. Foolish plan.'

I wondered if maybe, just maybe, once we were out of this stuffy member's club, when he wasn't the customer, and I wasn't the waitress, and I didn't have a doily on my head, he might relax and let me get a word in edgeways. So I said yes.

I laughed through my entire first date with your great-grandfather. We met outside the Festival Centre at 5 p.m. and had a bit of a stroll, and then walked down to the beach.

'Best of three, eh?' he said, picking up another pebble from the tiny patch of sandy grit on the bank of the Thames and raising his arm to skim it across the water.

I laughed at Henry's optimism. 'You are never going to do it,' I teased gaily, the wind whipping my hair around my face.

'Oh ye of little faith, just watch, this one will do five. At least.'

The pebble flashed through the air, hit the water and sank without trace. I couldn't hold back my giggles at seeing his downcast bottom lip protruding out. I bent down and found another flat stone and handed it to him. On a whim, I kissed it for good luck, immediately blushing as I handed it to him.

His eyes met mine as he took it from me and he smiled. 'Well, this one simply can't fail now.' He lifted his elbow out to right angles with his body and flicked his wrist. The pebble did a graceful arc and skimmed across the river's surface gracefully touching it seven, eight, nine times. 'Whoop!' Henry cried, lifting me off my feet in delight and twirling me round. 'We did it!'

I flung my head back and laughed a deep throaty laugh, batting him playfully on the head with my handbag, and telling him to put me down. My feet touched the sand again, our faces alive with fun and laughter. He didn't let go of me immediately, instead, our faces remained mere inches apart. Our lips met only for a second or two, but his mouth was soft, gentle, and I felt a fizzing inside my stomach I'd never felt before, and then it was over. Henry's neck sported the familiar pink rash I'd seen before, and this made me like him even more.

'Sorry, that was incredibly forward. I do apologise,' he said, running a hand through his sandy-coloured hair. He used to do that a lot when he got embarrassed.

'Not at all. I think we were just both very excited about the triumphant stone skimming.'

'Ah yes, absolutely, an instinctive hormonal reaction to sporting prowess.'

I loved the way he talked. *Instinctive hormonal reaction*. Who said things like that? Henry Fairbrother did. And not in the way the other men at the club did. He didn't have an arrogant bone in his body; he was just very clever.

After we left the beach, my arm tucked happily into the crook of his, he asked me as we wandered along the Embankment why I was working at the club. I explained that I wanted to experience life in London before getting married and having children. He grew quiet then, as though he didn't quite fully understand what I meant. 'But what are your dreams?' he pressed. 'Where do you see yourself in five, ten, fifteen years' time? What will people say about you after you die?'

I shrugged. 'In five years' time, I'll be twenty-one, hopefully married, with a baby on the way.'

'And then?'

'What do you mean, and then?'

'And what about for the other fifty or so years in your life?'

Was he making fun of me? I couldn't tell. He looked so earnest, so sincere, but what was he not getting?

'You can do more than just be a wife and mother, Florence. It's 1959. Things are changing, you have so many more options now, you don't have to just be a housewife.'

I could feel my heart beating a little faster and the hairs on my arms started to bristle. 'You make it sound like having children is a fate worse than death.'

He faltered then, his voice apologetic as he spoke, 'I didn't mean that, I think having a family is a wonderful thing, something I very much would love for myself too, but I would absolutely not expect my wife to give herself over entirely to the task of raising our family and running the home. I don't think of it as "fate" – I believe you make your own luck.'

'Perhaps you do if you're born with male organs,' I said airily, trying to shock him into silence with my coarseness.

'Tell that to Florence Sabin,' he retorted, barely missing a beat.

We'd gone for tea then, a cute teashop just off the Embankment. He hadn't ordered for me, like other men had, like my father did for my mother, but waited for me to choose my own pastry before choosing a different one for himself. It was a small thing, but nice. He talked of his love of science, of making things make sense. He had a cat called Winston, referred to his parents as Ma and Pa and smelled of a mixture of soap and leather. He had a dimple in his chin and left cheek but not his right, and a small recent cut near his right ear, which I assumed was a shaving mishap. He didn't ask me what my parents did for a living, or what film I'd seen lately, instead he asked me what made me laugh. What was my happiest memory? My biggest regret? I had no idea what to say, having never been asked these things before; I'd never even stopped to consider them. But after we said goodbye, it was all I could think about. It was neither here nor there to him whether I'd seen *Cat on a Hot Tin Roof*, but of course it's of consequence that I like to remember the moment my father returned from war and walked in the front door wearing his khaki military uniform. I couldn't have been more than three or four, but I remember the house filled with noise and laughter, neighbours, friends, family all crowding into our tiny front room, the air thick with smoke and the smell of sausage rolls fresh from the oven. I'm sure that memories like that would surface over time, as you get to know someone, but for Henry to dig them out on our first date was quite something. *He* was quite something.

Henry didn't come into the club the day after our walk along the Thames and the stone-skimming, or the day after that, but on Saturday morning as I arrived at the club, the receptionist handed me a little parcel wrapped in brown paper, simply addressed to Florence Weston, no postmark, no return address, nothing. I turned it over in my hands and carefully ripped along one of the parcel's seams. It was a photograph of a bronze statue cut out from a magazine and mounted onto a small piece of card. The inscription on the bottom of the statue read *Florence Rena Sabin 1871–1953 Doctor of Medicine*. I got the significance of it straight away.

A handwritten inscription on the back read:

Dear Florence, I came across this photograph in one of my medical journals, it seems that your namesake had a statue made of her and put in the Capitol Building in America. I thought this might serve as a reminder that one makes one's own luck in life. Henry

I held the card to my chest before remembering that I was standing in the entrance hall of the gentleman's club. My heart was in my mouth as I watched for the receptionist to leave her post at the front desk. As soon as the hall was empty, I leaped behind the desk and opened the heavy leather-bound ledger with all the members' details in it. I ran my finger down the list of surnames beginning with F until I found Fairbrother, Henry. Next to it was an address in Fulham. I scribbled this down on a notepad and slammed the ledger shut excitedly, stuffed the paper in the front pocket of my apron and calmly walked back to the dining hall to begin lunch service.

I took more time getting dressed into my own clothes after work in the female changing room than usual, giving my long brown hair twenty extra brushes, pinching my cheeks to give them some colour, and reapplying my eyeliner and lipstick. If I got the number 52 bus, it should stop near his house. I honestly had no idea what would happen then. If he was there, I'd thank him for the photo – and then, what, an evening walk? Dinner? And if he wasn't, I'd leave him a thank you note with my home telephone number on it. I wasn't being forward, I told myself. I was just doing what he said, and making my own luck.

4
Florence

Sixty-four years earlier . . .

On the way to Florence's job interview at the member's club in Westminster, she met Kenny Buck at the number 19 stop in Hammersmith where she had to change buses. All the places inside the bus shelter were taken thanks to the rain, so she pressed herself up against the wall to avoid being drenched by passing cars and buses. They started chatting, she mentioned the job interview and he dug into his pocket to present her with a dirty sixpence, 'for luck', he explained. It was this lovely gesture that made her say yes when he asked her out for a drink the following night – well, that and the fact that her parents had a Bible study meeting planned, and Kenny from Peckham seemed a more fun option than Moses from Galilee.

Florence wasn't used to boys asking her out; she wasn't like other girls, who swung their pelvises in time with Elvis, or twisted them at Chubby Checker's instruction. Her bra wasn't pointy, and her eyelashes were entirely her own. She smelled of soap and Oil of Ulay moisturiser not cloying eau de toilette bought from the local chemist's.

Kenny was a mechanic who smelled vaguely of diesel and aniseed balls. Due to the laxative quality of his favourite sweet, he also needed the bathroom at least four times during the three dates they'd had, which ruled out long walks completely, which was a shame because she loved nothing more than a wander along the Thames as the lamp posts were casting their glow on the water, but instead they had to stick to pubs with a nearby restroom. She tried not to look at his filthy fingernails, or the smattering of dandruff that embellished the shoulders of the dark shirts he wore, 'ironed by me mum' he proudly told her, but she couldn't judge, the pleated blouses she wore were crease-free because of Mrs Weston's dextrous ironing, not her own. Florence made sure to concentrate instead on the sprinkling of freckles over the top of his nose and the way his eyes danced when he spoke about cars, which was, to be fair, most of the time.

Kenny was well-mannered and could strip a Morris Minor's engine in under eight minutes. Which was, Florence assumed by the pride in his voice, really fast. More to the point, he never once peppered his chat with references to chemical compounds, and wouldn't know a cognac from a Calvados if his life depended on it.

Florence thought back to earlier in the day, how she had angrily slammed the dirty glasses into the sink at the club with such force the stems snapped clean off and she had to spend ten minutes brushing the shards out from under the ovens and cupboards after that scientist man had shown her up. She hated it when they did this, these men, when they dropped words into sentences like 'chemical compounds' and 'properties of matter' to prove how clever they were. It happened all the time; snippets of snatched conversations she heard in the time it took to pick up an ashtray overflowing with cigar and cigarette ends and replace it with a new one. 'Fiscal calendar', 'Radical Republican agenda', 'machine politics', the pomposity drove her absolutely mental. Even in her interview for the job, Mr Withers, the manager, spoke to Hazel and her about the need for 'absolute discretion', that she would be privy to some of the country's top political and intellectual minds discussing deeply confidential matters. 'Not that you'll understand most of it,' he'd said, 'that's why we only employ female waiting staff.' She and Hazel had nodded along, not realising at the time the incredible insult just casually hurled their way, crossing their fingers behind their backs, hoping he liked them enough to give them a job that paid in a week what these men spent on brandy and cigars in a day. But Florence was not sure how long she could last in this job; it had only been a week and already her frustration was mounting. Every reference to 'import tariffs' and 'twenty-four-hour filibusters', whatever the hell they were, just made her feel more and more ignorant until it actually made her chest feel like it was going to explode. Admittedly, she hadn't got a clue what all these words meant, but they shouldn't assume she didn't just because she was wearing a white pinny and not a bloody pocket handkerchief. Who invented those anyway? A little square of silk to give the impression that its wearer was much more fun and colourful than they actually were.

She didn't know why it bothered her so much. This divide: the 'them and us' mentality, men and women, upper class and whatever she was. Even getting this job in the centre of London, no one could understand why she wanted to do it. Her parents had looked at her as though she'd suggested moving to the moon. 'Westminster?' her father had said incredulously. 'Westminster?' her mother had repeated, because original thought wasn't permitted at 17 Alderton Close. Her mother had quickly followed that up with, 'Well, at least I suppose there's a better selection of potential husbands in Westminster.' As that sentence had hung in the air, punctuated by the staccato beat of the grandfather clock in the hallway, Florence could hear her parents' minds changing.

Florence and Kenny kissed at the end of their third date, standing in the doorway of the pawn shop next to the bus stop. Brief, aniseed-tasting, locking of mouths, which felt neither unpleasant nor pleasant, just unusual.

Annoyingly, the scientist was still hanging around the club all the time, at least twice, sometimes three times a week. Staring, always staring, with some pretentious textbook open on his lap. Florence had heard about men like this, posh upper-class types on the lookout for girls like her to add a bit of colour to their marriages. Well, she wasn't going in for it. She'd also decided that she wasn't going in for Kenny either. He might not shine a spotlight on her ignorance by peppering his sentences with long words, but actually he barely peppered a sentence with short words. Or any words in fact.

'Is he the strong and silent type, do you think?' Hazel suggested when Florence voiced her concerns over the lack of content in Kenny's chat.

She resolved to give him one more chance, and that night laboured through a spaghetti bolognaise and ice cream sundae with just the restaurant's jukebox for company. Due to Kenny's inability to converse, Florence had time to listen to the lyrics of each song, and as each new record dropped onto the turntable, her certainty mounted that Kenny and she were in no way compatible. He was not, nor ever would be 'a big hunk o' love', nor was she a 'teenager in love', and should he ask her to 'put your head on my shoulder', she shuddered at what might be attached to her hair when she lifted it up again. But it was

Lloyd Price's 'Personality' and his insistence that that's what mattered the most that really clinched it. ''Cause you got Personality, Walk, Personality, Talk, Personality, Smile, Personality, Charm, Personality'.

So by the end of the meal, Florence had categorically made up her mind to try to let Kenny Buck down as gently as possible. Except, of course, Florence had never let anyone down before, gently or otherwise, and had no idea how to go about it. She tried saying it, but the bill arrived and he insisted on paying it and she thought it bad form to do it directly after he'd bought her dinner. Then she'd brought up their differences again as he walked her to her bus stop, him gallantly walking on the outside getting his trousers repeatedly splashed from cars gaily traversing through puddles on the road. She was about to categorically state that their relationship wasn't working, and she really must concentrate on her job and leave him free to meet the woman of his dreams, which absolutely was not her, when the plug was pulled on the clouds and the heavens opened. He pulled her down an alleyway, canopied from the rain by scaffolding on the side of a building, where they stood laughing, catching their breath.

'You're shivering,' he said, taking off his coat and draping it over her shoulders.

'I'm fine, honestly,' she replied, trying to work out whether she could break up with a man whilst wearing his coat. Probably not.

'I could warm you up,' he said, leaning in closer, so her back was against the wall under the planks of scaffolding above their heads.

'I really think that we probably should be getting back. Not we. *I*. I should be getting back. Without you. You should be getting back to yours. And that's probably where we should stay. Me at mine. You at yours. That's probably for the best, wouldn't you say?'

Kenny made a murmuring sound into Florence's neck that sounded rather non-committal. His hands snaked round her waist as he pulled her closer. His breath on her neck was actually rather warming.

'I mean,' she started, trying to ignore the goosebumps forming on her neck from excitement as he nuzzled into it, 'I think we can both agree it's been a lovely few weeks, hasn't it, but at the end of the day, when's all said and done, in the long run, when push comes to sho-oooove.'

Kenny's hand had somehow found its way into her tights, and while it was very unexpected, the feeling was certainly rather pleasant. He seemed to be taking their break-up rather well. Florence wondered, as her legs buckled as she reached her very first climax, whether she would always associate the feeling with the smell of aniseed, but pushed the thought out of her mind as Kenny unzipped his trousers. Florence realised this categorically was not the right time to let him down gently.

For the next two days, Florence wasn't entirely sure what had passed between her and Kenny, and the spots of blood on her petticoat made her worried that she might have inadvertently hurt herself. She shouldn't have let him touch her like that, but he was so kind just paying for dinner, and she supposed that she just lost herself for a moment, sheltering under the scaffolding in the torrential rain. And it was actually very nice.

But then on the walk home when she'd tried to engage him on topics like recent films they'd both seen, he said that he swerved both *The 39 Steps* ('don't like politics') and *Some Like it Hot* ('don't like Americans') in favour of *Carry on Nurse*, which he declared 'bloody brilliant', while Florence omitted her (rather different) opinion on it. He had no idea the Soviets were planning to launch a rocket at the moon, shaking his head and said, 'not really bothered about the news', and even when Florence dug down to the depths of conversation starters and recalled that Burnley were currently top of the First Division, he declared that he didn't follow football.

'So there's nothing else for it,' she confided to Hazel the next day, at work as they both stood polishing the cutlery, 'the next time he phones and asks me out, I'm just going to have to say thanks but no thanks.'

'Especially when you've got the next one lined up.' Hazel nodded over to where the scientist was eyeing them from his armchair. He'd been nursing the same pot of tea for nearly an hour, and it must be stone cold, but he hadn't made any attempt to pay and leave and other people must want his table.

Florence strode over and asked him if he wanted anything else, or perhaps his bill. It would have been impossible for anyone to turn a deeper shade of beetroot than that man, his skin blending with the maroon swirls of the carpet as he stammered that his name was Henry.

Florence had no idea why she said yes to his suggestion of taking a walk the next day. Possibly, looking back on it, had he suggested tea or dinner or a drink, she'd have said no, but because he floated the very thing that Kenny could never do, she found herself nodding and agreeing that, yes, a walk along the Thames was exactly what she wanted to spend her afternoon off doing.

To her complete surprise, he was good company, albeit a little supercilious and pompous when he scoffed at her wanting a family and saying that she should follow her dreams. But where Kenny lacked in conversation, Henry made up for it, picking and poking at buried memories until she found herself sobbing in a teashop just off the Embankment. Henry didn't come into the club the day after their walk along the Thames and the stone-skimming, or the day after that, but on Saturday morning as Florence arrived at the club, the receptionist handed her a little parcel wrapped in brown paper, simply addressed to Florence Weston. She turned it over in her hands and carefully ripped along one of the parcel's seams. It was a photograph of a bronze statue cut out from a magazine and mounted onto a small piece of card. The inscription on the bottom of the statue read *Florence Rena Sabin 1871–1953 Doctor of Medicine*. She frowned, not understanding what it was, and turned the photograph over to see a handwritten inscription on the back.

Dear Florence, I came across this photograph in one of my medical journals, it seems that your namesake had a statue made of her and put in the Capitol Building in America. I thought this might serve as a reminder that one makes one's own luck in life. Henry

The nerve of the man! Of course he could dare to dream whatever he wanted, he'd been given every opportunity going since he could walk. He even called his parents Ma and Pa for goodness' sake! He hadn't grown up under the stifling expectation of rigid conformity with the prize at the end a loveless marriage with someone from youth church. *One makes one's own luck in life*. What elitist tosh.

As soon as the receptionist left her post, Florence leaped behind the desk and opened the heavy leather-bound ledger with all the members' details in it. She ran her finger down the list of surnames beginning with F until she found Fairbrother, Henry. Next to it was an address in Fulham. She scribbled this down on a notepad and slammed the ledger shut angrily, stuffed the paper in the front pocket of her apron and walked back to the dining hall, still seething, to start lunch service.

After work, Florence quickly changed into her own clothes, ignoring her make-up bag and hairbrush. If she got the number 52 bus, it should stop near his house and she could post the picture back through his door. That would teach him to keep his arrogant ideas about luck and life to himself.

She'd barely walked twenty feet down the road towards the bus stop when she became aware of footsteps behind her, matching her pace more or less perfectly. She turned once, twice, and was sure a dark figure darted back into the shadows. She crossed the street, deliberately keeping to the more well-lit side of the road, when the footsteps behind her quickened their pace, catching up to her. A hand grabbed her shoulder. Florence swung around, her handbag raised to pitch it at her assailant's head when she gasped. It was a petite young blonde woman, only a year or two older than her, carrying a small sleeping child in her arms.

Florence's arm dropped down and her brow furrowed in confusion. 'Who are you? What are you doing following me?'

'My name's Laura Buck. I'm Kenny's wife.'

Florence's mouth gaped open like a goldfish.

'And this is Peter, Kenny's son.'

Florence looked down at the sleeping tot, feeling ever so like she was about to throw up on him.

The woman added, 'I know Kenny's been seeing you, and

I'd like you to leave him alone, please,' she shifted the baby up on her hip, 'he has a family.'

Florence shook her head in disbelief, 'I'm . . . I'm so sorry, I had no idea.'

'It's not your fault, it's him, he never tells 'em. Just, you know, now you know can you not see him again?'

Florence nodded, resisting the urge to take the woman in her arms, which, she realised, would be odd.

The child started to stir, and Mrs Buck gave Florence a not unkind tight smile and disappeared in the darkness in the direction she came from.

Florence was left alone in the pool of light from the lantern over the doorway of a snooker hall, looking at her retreating back. She felt sick with guilt. She debated whether to go straight home, and not try to find Henry, but if she did, the suffocating silence of Alderton Drive would make her thoughts so much louder.

It wasn't her fault. What happened that night in the alleyway was a complete blip on an otherwise clean white slate, the result of too much cheap house wine and a desire not to offend, and there was absolutely no way she'd have even talked to him that first night at the bus stop if she knew he was married and had a child.

Throughout the bus journey to Henry's neighbourhood, Florence's guilt had turned the corner into white-tipped rage. How dare he treat his wife like that? His child? Her? What a despicable excuse for a man. She felt like going to find him right now to tell him exactly what she thought of him, but then she'd be breaking her promise to his wife.

She hesitated outside Henry's house. Her anger at him had been replaced with anger at Kenny. She shouldn't have come. Lights were on in every window. It was a tall, narrow townhouse, at least four storeys high, windows stacked one above each other. Which one was his, she wondered as she stood on the street, indecision stopping her from raising the door knocker. What if not all men were like Kenny? What if all men didn't fall into two categories? Boring, rigid and sanctimonious like her father, or charming, deceiving philanderers like Kenny? What if there was a third column for decent, honest men like Stu would have been? And just maybe, Henry Fairbrother? What if his intention was not to condescend, but to inspire?

It was ridiculous coming here. She was sixteen years old and had allowed herself to be seduced by a mechanic's apprentice with dandruff from Peckham with a wife and child. And now she was about to tell off a science scholar with five times her intellect and a hundred times her money? Stupid, stupid girl.

Florence turned and started to walk away before Henry could look out of his window and spot her—

'Florence!'

Henry was waving madly at her from the other side of the road. 'Florence! It's me!' He added unnecessarily, 'Henry!'

She couldn't help smiling at his enthusiasm. He was like an excitable spaniel. She waited for him to cross the road, apologising to a car and a bicycle as he weaved between them.

'Hello, you!' he panted when he got to within a couple of feet of her.

'Hello, Henry.'

'Were you coming to see me?'

She could lie and say that she was visiting a friend that lived nearby, or that she was just passing, but with Kenny's flagrant disregard for honesty fresh in her mind, she nodded.

'Sorry I wasn't there, but I'm here now, have you eaten? There's a lovely pub round the corner that does decent nosh?'

He swapped sides with her twice on the short walk to The Red Lion so that he would always be on the outside of her; he held open the door, pulled out her chair and stood up when she got up to use the ladies. Florence was delighted to note that the shoulders on his dark shirt were flake-free and he only used the lavatory once, and that was after two pints of Mild, which was completely understandable. He even came back to the table wiping his hands on his trousers after washing them, which suggested a level of hygiene Florence wasn't sure Kenny ever had as his hands always had streaks of black engine oil on them and the same telephone number written in biro on his palm for days.

One conversation topic flowed into another: next week's general election, the recent breakthroughs at the laboratory Henry worked at, the customers at the club, books he'd read. Florence found herself searching her mind for interesting observations to make about her day. She wanted to make him laugh, to intrigue him.

'What are you doing on Saturday night?' he asked. 'A friend of mine works at a theatre in Charring Cross, and can get me a couple of tickets to *A Streetcar Named Desire* if you fancied it?'

Growing up, every December, Florence and her family would get dressed up and go to the pantomime, eat intermission ice-creams from little pots and shout as loud as they could that someone was 'behind you!' But theatre trips stopped as soon as Stu died. She hadn't set foot inside one in five years, and although she always looked longingly at the bright musical theatre posters plastered outside every theatre she walked past on her way to work (and there were loads of them) she couldn't help feeling that if Stu couldn't see the shows, she shouldn't either.

Henry took Florence's hesitation as indecision over whether she wanted to see him again, and immediately blushed in mortification at being so forward.

Florence, thankfully, was becoming very adept at reading his variations in skin tone, and immediately garbled, 'No, it's not that I don't want to see you again, it's theatres, my brother died, you see—'

'On stage?' Henry said horrified. 'Did something fall on him?'

'No,' Florence replied, momentarily wrong-footed, 'of measles. But he used to love the theatre.'

Henry thought for a moment. 'Did he also love cake?'

'What?'

'What about biscuits?' he asked.

'I'm not sure what you're getting at?' Florence asked, confused.

'Did he ride buses? A bicycle? Eat sandwiches? Did he wear clothes?'

'No one likes a smart alec, Henry,' Florence said, realising what he was getting at.

Henry smiled, 'The very fact that he liked the theatre so much says to me that you ought to enjoy it again too. What's your brother's name?'

It wasn't just that Henry had asked the question, but also that he hadn't used the past tense – what *was* his name – that made Florence realise that she actually didn't mind Henry Fairbrother. In fact, she might actually quite like him.

5

Stella

I would never tell her this, but Florence's comments about me focusing on the wrong attributes of the donor keep replaying on a loop in my head. I have to keep reminding myself that I'm not designing the perfect boyfriend or husband, I literally just need his healthy sperm. There's no way of knowing whether he's a nice guy or not, he could donate thousands to charity but only as an act of guilt for being a horrible person, or as a form of tax relief. There should be some sort of morality test the donors need to take too. Or a multiple choice: You see a homeless person shivering on the street outside your house, do you a) walk past muttering 'get a job', b) give them your coat and make them some soup. That would be much more useful than knowing whether they did their 100m swimming badge and like spaniels.

My thoughts are driving me crazy; I need some air. It's my day off, the sun is shining, so I head to the little park opposite the house. Our vivid green front door sticks out amongst its gentile Farrow and Ball neighbours along the Victorian terraced street, all of whom have plumped for greys called things like Elephant's Whisper, or Touch of Teal. But Mum and Florence are adamant that the green stays; I don't know why.

Two teenagers sit down on the bench next to me. They don't acknowledge me, but then I doubt I'd have seen a forty-year-old woman when I was sixteen either. They start kissing, unnecessarily noisily as though they're sucking the saliva out of each other's mouths with a pipette. How long can I wait before standing up and leaving? I don't want them to feel embarrassed, as though what they're doing is wrong. It's flipping loud and almost certainly a little too enthusiastic on the tongue front, but it's not wrong. No one's kissed me like that in over a year. Actually, no one's kissed me like that in about twenty-four years, thank Christ.

A man and woman walk past wearing matching black trainers with pink Nike swishes on the side, the woman is holding their French bulldog on a lead with one hand, while the other hand is deep in the back pocket of the man's jeans. The dog squats and relieves itself right in front of me and the woman looks annoyed she has to stop caressing her partner's bottom in order to pick the mess up, such is the intensity of their love.

Across the path is the children's playground. Three-, four- and five-year-old examples of what happens when a single sperm fertilises a single egg run around shrieking. They're all so happy, these egg-sperm hybrids, with their birdsong laughter, runny noses and parents who don't know how lucky they are, with their successful conventional conceptions.

One mum sits on her heels in front of her toddler – at least I hope it's her toddler – as, after rummaging through her massive nappy bag and all her pockets, she finally proffers her sleeve to the little one to wipe its tiny leaky nose on. The teenagers see this too and make retching noises. I think it's lovely. I wish that was me. I want a snotty sleeve.

All these lives, these physical reminders of love and sex, make my head spin. I'm not actually sure I'm living the life that was meant for me. Somewhere along the line someone else's fate got confused with mine; the grand puppeteer in the sky got the strings knotted up and untangled them in the wrong way. I was a house captain for goodness' sake. Voted by the rest of the sixth form as the person most likely to win a Nobel Peace Prize and marry a film star. I received my first engagement ring at nineteen (thanks Elizabeth Duke at Argos), second at twenty-six and turned down the lead cellist in London's Philharmonic orchestra at twenty-eight. He had incredibly dextrous fingers but slept wearing gloves, which, call me shallow, I really couldn't handle for the rest of my life. I was the first of my friends to get a mortgage. I've been to America. South and North. Eaten kangaroo and crocodile (they both tasted like chicken, if you want to know). I should be the one currently extracting my hand from her husband's back pocket in order to get a poo bag out to clean up after her pedigree mutt, or offering my sleeve to my child to blow his nose on because I've forgotten the wet wipes (again) or snogging someone on a public bench so vigorously it feels like I've just spent an hour with a newly qualified dental hygienist. So how the hell have I ended up forty, alone and about to choose a random stranger to make a baby with?

'Are you OK?'

The teenagers are looking at me with abject horror on their faces, as I realise that I got so lost in my thoughts, ugly trails of salty snot are running down my face in torrents. 'Oh God, sorry,' I say, hastily wiping my face on my jacket. 'Sorry, no, you don't have to leave. God, stay, honestly, I'm fine. Come back!' And just like that, my wish has come true. I do have a snotty sleeve. Hurrah.

My phone buzzes in my pocket. I take it out. It's Florence.

'There's a cup of tea with your name on it currently sitting on the kitchen table once you get bored of sitting on that bench sobbing your eyes out,' she says.

I look up at the house, where Florence is waving from the first-floor bedroom. 'Can't a girl just sit on a bench, in a park, enjoying the sunshine?' I ask her.

'If that's what the girl's doing, yes. But if she's sat there because she's overthinking her life choices and feeling unnecessarily sorry for herself and scaring off the local youth, then she should probably get up and come and have a cup of tea with the two women who love her most in the world. I did suggest something stronger, but your mother reminded me that it's only twelve o'clock on a Tuesday. Every party needs a pooper.'

Mum and Florence are doing what can only be described as 'pretending to be busy' when I walk through the green door and down the hallway into the kitchen at the back of the house. Mum is wiping the already spotless kitchen worktop with a sponge, while Florence is refolding a pile of already folded tea towels and placing them back in the drawer I assume she's just taken them out of.

'Hello, darling!' Mum says as though my entrance is a complete surprise, despite there being three full mugs of tea on the table.

'Hey.'

'Come and sit down, love,' she says, sitting down and patting the chair next to her.

'We're a bit worried about you,' Florence says.

I give a small smile, and shrug, 'I'm OK, lots on my mind.'

'Has anyone else died at work?'

If you didn't know that I worked in a nursing home, that would be a very odd question. 'No, not since Trevor.'

'It can't help that you spend your entire day dealing with undertakers and staring out of your office window at the walls of a prison,' Mum adds.

It's true, my office does look out over the walls of the men's prison next door, not the best view for the residents' last days, but I think the land was cheap. I'm well aware of the irony of spending my days mere metres away from three-hundred virile men when I'm so desperate to find just one virile man. It would save quite a lot of money and invasive procedures if I just popped next door to ask one of them to provide a quick sample into a pot. It would, of course, be illegal and highly unethical, neither of which I have any intention of ever being. I also really don't want my future child to be half felon. Which is why it is so important to do the due diligence – like a house survey before you buy. The photo might look smiling and trouble-free, but underneath, there's a ton of subsidence and an incurable case of dry rot.

'I do a bit more in my job than that, thanks, Mum. And it's not like you're surrounded by green fields and daisies, is it?' I raise an eyebrow at her, an ability I'm forever pleased I have for situations just like this one, particularly as she can't do it. I make a mental note to check if any of the donors mention this under the Talents and Skills section, it would be good to have this ability on both sides to double the chances of the child inheriting it.

'A science laboratory is hardly the same as a jail, Stella.'

'No, you're right, there are no similarities at all between a place with no natural sunlight, things living in cages and 99.9% of the people within its walls having penises . . . and a prison.'

Mum tries to raise an eyebrow back but can't, so ends up just distorting her face, which makes me laugh.

'Stop it,' she says, 'you're always teasing me.'

'It's just too easy.'

'Did you ask Aisha about taking on a bit more responsibility?' Mum asks.

'I'm not sure now's the right time. More stress at work right when I'm trying to get pregnant isn't ideal.'

'But you haven't had a pay rise in two years.'

'But now I'm back here, I don't need as much money.'

'No, but it'd be good to start putting a bit by. You know, for when the baby's here and you want a place of your own again.'

'She's only just moved back in, Bonnie!' Florence says, rolling her eyes at me in solidarity. 'Don't go planning her exit quite yet!'

'I knew this would happen,' Mum huffs, 'you two always gang up on me. I'm just saying, it's never the wrong time to be ambitious. To want to be the best version of yourself. To plan ahead.'

'Why don't you go and have a bath after you finish your cup of tea?' Florence says to me. 'Try to relax.'

'I think I'll need it after that little motivational talk.'

This is officially the world's most uncomfortable bath and a hideous colour. At what point did a bunch of bathroom designers sit around a table and say that avocado was a stylish colour? It's not even a very nice vegetable. Fruit. Which is it? Tomato is a fruit, but you wouldn't put it in a trifle. So, anyway, a bunch of men, and it was bound to be men, made the massive leap from enjoying eating guacamole to wanting to lie in it. Madness. As soon as I have some money, I'll replace it with a nice white bathroom suite with a bath that's long enough to lie down in without your knees getting cold. If I am going to be injecting sperm into my womb and making a baby, there's no way I'm going to fit in here in nine months' time. I'm not actually going to inject it, for the record. It's a myth that something resembling a turkey baster gets shoved up your tuppence; it's a catheter, a thin tube, all very medical and not at all culinary. Although I saw a documentary once about a town in America where a man in a van literally pulls up to women's houses, has a fiddle with himself in the back and then hands over a little pot of his produce on the doorstep. It's one way to bypass the waiting lists, although you do run the risk of your child being related to everyone in its class when it starts school.

School. The place where bullies bloom and individuality is inconvenient. I stroke my empty belly, the vacant home soon to be filled with a lodger. What will school make of their story? The mother who couldn't find a mate, and the father who pleasures himself for money. Am I setting my child up for a life of ridicule and isolation? Should I just call the whole thing off and forget about it? Throw myself into a new career instead. I could retrain in law; it's not too late to honour my childhood dreams. I could become one of those hotshot barristers who charge five hundred quid an hour. But I couldn't do that with a child. Well, I could, if I was one of those high-flyers who breastfeed in court, paving the way for every other working mother to *have it all.*

This is why choosing the right donor is so important. All this research and energy and time that's going into making this baby as close to the perfect collection of cells as a human is possible to be is all going to be worth it when I'm in the audience when they get awarded an OBE or standing at the NASA launch site as they set out on mankind's first foray to Jupiter.

Look at Mum – her father was a mathematical genius and single-handedly shook up the world of biochemistry. Then Mum turned out to be the only woman to graduate from her six-year degree in genetic science (there were three women on her course at the start, but two got married and dropped out before the end apparently) and then she was the only female in the faculty for nearly ten years. Good genes, that's what that is. Then she goes and picks an out-of-work layabout writer for half of my genetics and see where that gets you. A forty-year-old daughter living back at home, in the same job I've been in for the last eight years in a company I only chose because old people can't get pregnant.

The water's cold now, but I don't want to get out of the bath. Once I do, I need to pick my child's DNA and I still have no shortlist. I thought I'd found the perfect one a couple of days ago, but when I went back online this morning to choose him, he'd disappeared from the database. I called the agency, and they said that he'd already reached his ten-family limit, the UK's ceiling for sperm donation. So ten other families got to him first, bagsying him like you would a seat on a bus, 'sorry, this one's saved, get yourself another, far more inferior option'. Ten other families now have babies with half the DNA mine should have.

I'm a little ashamed to admit this, but I even tried to find the donor on the internet, based on the information on the website, which is absolutely not stalking in any way, shape or form. I figured that if I could slot together the puzzle pieces – age 28, Latin American-Scottish heritage, six foot two, architecture graduate, likes golden retrievers and historical houses – then I could find him, ply him with alcohol and make a baby the old-fashioned way, saving a lot of paperwork and money. But all the architecture practices I researched annoyingly didn't have their employees' cultural heritage listed on their staff pages, nor could the National Trust provide me with a list of their members, along with their age and height. Surprisingly, The Kennel Club was equally protective over their database of pedigree dog owners. Closed doors at every turn.

It's not just me who's waded knee-deep into internet research. They think I don't know, but Mum and Florence can also now cite 'sperm-hunting' as one of their hobbies too, along with 'thinking about paddleboarding' for Flo and cryptic crosswords for Mum. I don't think they know I'm here in the downstairs bathroom out the back of the kitchen; the walls in this house are like cardboard, so when they start to speak, I can hear them as clearly as if they're in the bathroom with me. Mum seems to have widened her search to America, 'more expensive but more choice,' while Flo is enjoying investigating the offerings from Scandinavian sites: 'they're awfully tall and who doesn't like a Viking?'

'It doesn't matter though, really, does it?' I can hear Mum say, along with the thud of her closing her laptop. 'They're all blending into one now, she just needs to pick one and be done with it.'

'I get it though, she wants to give the tot its best chance in life,' I hear Florence reply. 'People spend months researching hotels to spend a two-week holiday in, you wouldn't just turn up to a travel agency and say, "book me into the one on page thirty-five, second one down", would you? Goodness, most people don't even eat at a restaurant without spending an hour trying to find a better one, so why should we expect her to just pick a donor, cross her fingers and hope for the best?' *Thanks Gran*. 'Have you written anything in your notebook yet?' she adds.

I feel bad for eavesdropping, but they know how thin the walls and ceilings are, and they're making no attempt to speak quietly.

'I don't know what to put. I honestly don't know why we said we'd do it,' Mum says. 'I hate stuff like that, soul-searching, writing grandiose statements about your life. There's nothing special about me.'

I debate hauling myself out of the bath just to go and argue with her, but Florence gets there first. 'As your mother, of course I'd have to strongly disagree with that statement, but I thought the same as you, but when I started, I actually quite enjoyed remembering your dad and being young. I couldn't stop once I'd started.'

'I can't understand her sometimes,' Mum says, 'I really can't, she's fantastic, I mean, what is wrong with all the men in this world that they can't see that, and she has to do this?'

There is a moment's silence and I can picture Florence cocking her head to one side before she speaks, 'It doesn't matter what you think though, does it, or me, come to that, she's decided that this is the way she wants to do it, so that's that. I decided to have you, and I was only sixteen, she's forty.'

'That's different, you were in love, married, supported.'

'She's loved and supported.'

'You know what I mean.'

'And you know what I mean.' I hear a kitchen chair scrape on the floor tiles, and Florence saying, 'Right, you should make a start on that notebook. Do you know what you're going to write yet?'

There's a low murmur, which I can't quite catch, but I can guess the flavour of Mum's reply. If she wasn't so strait-laced, it would have been extremely rude.

6

Bonnie

Dear __________ (tbc)

I don't really know what to write if I'm honest. Give me a calculator over a keyboard any day. I've always been like that: numbers over words, symbols over letters. Apart from the ones in the periodic table. I don't know why I'm finding this so hard, I could write a 10,000-word report on single nucleotide polymorphisms in a day if I needed to, so why is a letter to my future grandchild proving so unbelievably difficult?

I've been putting this off, but your mum, Stella, wanted me to write down a bit about me and my history so that you know where you came from, but, in all honesty, there's not much to tell. I'm as ordinary as the day is long.

I'm writing this letter to you in the exact same room that I was born in, which rather proves my point about being boring, wouldn't you say? I was born in 1960, on the day of a royal wedding. My mother, Florence, always said that she didn't know if the cheers and applause from downstairs and on the street were for the Princess or for me. It was definitely for the Princess.

This used to be a boarding house My mother and father rented a room from a lady called Martha, who then left it to them after she died, and they ran it as a guest house. So I grew up in this house, along with a steady stream of lodgers and colourful characters passing through. The house was filled with people coming and going, impromptu gatherings in the kitchen, the lounge, the hallway; little enclaves of poetry readings, record-playing, instrument-tuning, clothes-sewing, protest sign-making, batch food-cooking. It made me love my own company. There was never a moment's peace in this house, and if I'm being honest, I didn't like it very much. I looked for silence everywhere, even hiding in the bedroom wardrobe with a torch and a book for company while laughter and music echoed through every room. This makes me sound like a desperately miserable child, I really wasn't, but I was, and still am, very, very shy. Everyone was so nice to me, patting me on the head, asking me about school, offering a taste of whatever was cooking, putting a guitar in my hand to teach me a chord, but I'd retreat as soon as I could up to my bedroom where it was quieter and I could hear my thoughts again.

I got a university place at Bristol to study biochemistry and left home at eighteen, swapping one noise-filled home for another as I moved into my halls of residence. My first year passed by quickly. I loved the course, made a few friends who I'd eat my lunch with (my dinner I'd normally have in my room whilst studying, or it would be a sandwich in the lobby of the library – you quite rightly can't bring food inside, it would ruin the books) and I was content. It was customary to have a black-tie dinner in the final week of term, which I went to reluctantly, begrudgingly buying a lace black knee-length cocktail dress, which cost more than four textbooks. The girl in the room next to me did my make-up; I thought I looked ridiculous, with lurid pink blusher streaked across my face in a diagonal line on each side, blue eyeshadow and the bright pink lipstick I swear glowed in the dark, but finally I looked like every other nineteen-year-old girl there (and like some of the boys). After the dinner, we went to a tall narrow townhouse in Clifton village where there was an after party. I hadn't wanted to go, but my friends dragged me along. I only intended staying for as long as it would take me to lose them in the crowd so they wouldn't notice me slip away, but then I met Steven.

He was the only person there not in black tie. Instead, he had tight black trousers on, with three horizontal slits across them so you could glimpse his skin through them. He had a leather jacket on over a T-shirt and was leaning against the doorframe so I had to squeeze past him as I went in.

'Nice dress,' he said.

I think I thanked him, but I wouldn't have offered a similar compliment back; it wouldn't have occurred to me to. Perhaps it was the fact I didn't swoon at his feet, or giggle seductively that made him leave his post and follow me inside. He was so handsome. Roguish, I think you'd call it. While I was controlled with the left side of my brain, it was the right side of his calling the shots. I favoured logic; he owned his own set of tarot cards wrapped in a silk handkerchief. I dreamed of statistics; he thought in rhyme and iambic pentameter. On paper, we were opposites, repellent magnets, but somehow we fell in love.

I still have no idea why he chose to spend the evening talking to me that night instead of one of the other fifty or so girls at the party, but he did, and there we are, and here you are because of it.

Then one day, a few weeks before my graduation, a poem attached to a balloon was tied round the handle of my front door asking me to marry him. It even rhymed. I told you he was different. Everything about Steven appealed to me, which again is ironic, having spent the majority of my years trying my best to avoid the loud, creative types my mother collected like scarves, and he was the epitome of a struggling artist. He brought an edge to my life which it didn't have before, a sense of excitement, and he was all I could think about.

I knew I was quite young to get married, just twenty-one, but my mum was even younger, and she was desperately happy with my dad. After the wedding we moved in here, to this house. I remember thinking that this unimposing West London terrace was going to witness so much joy and love and laughter behind the shiny paint of the green front door.

Mum had the builders in to divide the house into two flats, the one upstairs for her and downstairs for us. The kitchen and lounge stayed where they were, there was already a downstairs bathroom put on the back of the kitchen, in the sixties I think, with a new electric shower over the bath which you didn't even need to put the immersion heater on for, and the dining room became our bedroom. Mum said it used to be their bedroom when she and Dad first lived here as lodgers after they married. I spent ages at the hardware store deliberating over the right shade for it, and eventually plumped for Peach Flush, which wasn't as feminine as Blush of Rose, but had more warmth than Apple Blossom, and I thought he'd like it. Before Steven moved in, I helped Mum move all her things upstairs, but as she didn't want to leave my flat looking too sad and sparse, she let me keep a couple of the cushions for the sofa and the odd picture – 'give me them back when you and Steven choose new ones of your own,' she said.

I cleared two shelves on the bookcase for his books, Mum and I spent a whole weekend sanding down and varnishing an old desk we'd found at a charity shop for him to write at, and I positioned it under the sash window of the living room, so he could look out at the street for inspiration and get lots of natural light during the day. I scoured thrift stores for more modern lampshades and rugs to replace the tasselled ones with swirly patterns on them, which provided the decor to my childhood, but weren't to everyone's taste.

To be honest, I've never had an idea of what's fashionable or not. I just looked down at what I'm sporting today for evidence of this fact and I have on a pair of grey cords I've replaced the zip on and patched up the back pocket of just because they're the most comfortable pair of trousers I've ever owned, and a black turtleneck. I'd be dishonest if I also didn't admit to writing this while wearing fingerless gloves because the boiler's playing up and it's really cold today. So, case in point. Not fashion-conscious at all. But comfortable in my own skin, which is far more important, and brings me back to my point about courage. Be fearless, because, God knows, at some point in your life, you're going to be grateful you are.

It's also important for partners to have the same hobbies and interests. Otherwise you'll be spending a lot of time apart. It's fine to have a different taste in books or solitary pursuits like crosswords or jigsaws, but for pastimes that involve other people, golf for instance, or badminton, it's always better to play with your own partner. I think that's when my own marriage started to show some cracks, when one of us got a hobby the other had no interest in participating in.

7
Bonnie

Forty-one years earlier . . .

Steven first brought up the topic of wife-swapping on a Monday. They'd just eaten a cottage pie on trays in front of the telly. Bonnie had followed the recipe in *Women's Weekly* to the letter but had used tinned steak and powdered mash and was still wondering whether he'd noticed when he casually mentioned his colleague Micky and his wife were having a party on Saturday night that he'd already said yes to.

'I think it's one of those "throw your keys into a bowl" type of parties,' Steven said casually, exaggerating the level of his breeziness by running his finger around his plate to not waste the last dregs of gravy.

'And you said yes to this?' Bonnie asked, her forehead furrowing in confusion.

Steven shrugged. 'We've got nothing else on.'

'So the fact we haven't decided what we're doing on Saturday night means the obvious choice is sleeping with someone else's spouse? Surely the cinema's an option?' she said.

'You don't go all the way with them, just a bit of a kiss and a cuddle, that's all. Anyway, everyone's doing it.'

Bonnie wished she could raise one eyebrow; now would have been the perfect time for that response. 'Everyone?'

'It's just a bit of fun, isn't it?'

'Define fun.'

'Look, we could just go along, have a few drinks, and see what happens, we don't have to do anything, do we? Have a bit of a laugh, let our hair down—'

'Have some stranger stick their tongue down my throat, yes, sounds really fun.'

'Oh loosen up for God's sake, Bonnie. You're twenty-two, in your prime, you're never going to look as good as you do now, make the most of it, woman.' He felt a bit cheated, if he was honest. The night he'd met her, she'd poured her body into a black lace dress and was the picture of mystery and intrigue. He'd asked everyone at the party who she was, but no one really knew. They thought they recognised her, but couldn't recall her name or any other detail about her, Holly? Polly? Binky?

Bonnie had one of those forgettable faces, which was neither so beautiful to stick in the memory, nor so unappealing to prompt a reaction. She'd been a bit heavy-handed with the make-up that night, but once the lurid hot pink lipstick had worn off, Steven thought she looked much better. Her hair was short and the colour of a muddy puddle, tucked neatly behind her ears.

He'd certainly never seen her before, although after dropping out of his English literature course two terms in, it's not as though he'd exhausted the campus and all its facilities, but if she had been in one of the many bars around the university, he'd never seen her there. Something about Bonnie intrigued Steven. It wasn't until he saw her leaning against the wall checking her watch and giving a barely concealed yawn while watching the room jump around pretending to be highwaymen to Adam Ant's 'Stand and Deliver' that he realised what it was. She was naturally as nonchalant as he was trying desperately to be. Every inch of her oozed disinterest and apathy, and he loved that. When he heard that she was from London, it was decided. She would be perfect.

It didn't take much to chip away at her icy armour. A red rose left on her doormat, a hastily edited poem swapping the name Connie for Bonnie, and an Oscar-winning performance feigning enthusiasm for her dissertation on the benefits of mapping the sequence of the entire human genome – 'Wow, that really does sound incredible.'

He was onto his last twenty pounds with no real idea of how to multiply it further when Bonnie was offered a highly paid job post-graduation with a research laboratory in central London. He asked her to marry him the next day.

If she was being honest with herself, Bonnie knew that she probably wasn't the only woman who had said yes to such a well-worded, eloquent proposal. It was too slick, too polished for it to have been the first time Steven had ever said those words out loud. But who cared? The other ones hadn't ended in rings being exchanged.

She never expected someone like Steven to look at her twice, and within days of meeting him, suddenly every song about love made complete sense. But as Bonnie looked at him now, across the living room, his new proposal hanging in the air, things made a lot less sense.

'Surely if I'm as much of a catch as you say I am,' Bonnie said to him, hands on hips, 'why are you falling over yourself to spend the evening fondling one of your friend's wives instead of your own one?'

'Well, thanks a lot for spoiling this for me. I thought it would be a laugh, but no, you have to ruin it.' He stood up to take his plate into the kitchen.

'Hang on a second, Steven, you're making it sound like I said no to a game of after-dinner charades,' Bonnie said, following him into the kitchen with her own plate.

He put his plate in the sink, making no attempt to turn the tap on, correctly assuming Bonnie would do it later, because she always did.

'Steven. Talk to me.'

'You're making it sound like some sort of sexist pervert party, where we all wear lederhosen and pass our wives around, but you get to have some fun too.' He slammed the fridge shut and opened his beer, leaving both the metal beer cap and the bottle opener on the counter before wandering back into the lounge.

'I thought we'd established it wasn't my idea of fun?'

'Would it kill you to just humour me for once in your life?'

'Can you keep your voice down,' Bonnie whispered. 'Mum's upstairs.'

'Oh yes, of course, can't let your mother hear us disagreeing, I bet her and the Late Saint never exchanged a cross word.'

Bonnie folded her arms across her chest. 'Don't call him that.'

Steven gestured at the black and white photo on their mantelpiece of Florence holding a chubby two-year-old Bonnie's hand. 'The sixties were meant to be the decade of free love, I bet she'd have loved a spot of swinging.'

Bonnie's eyes flashed, 'Stop it.'

Steven lay back on the sofa, as comfortably as one could on a seat made of rattan and one-inch-thick foam cushions and lit a cigarette. Bonnie moved instinctively to open the big sash windows in the bay window, which looked out over the dark street.

'It's November, Bonnie, it's bloody freezing out there.'

'But if you're smoking, we need to open a window, house rules.'

'It's our house, our rules, and I'm making a new one to say that I can enjoy a fag in peace without getting pneumonia.'

'But—'

'If you mention your mother again, I swear I'm going to stab this cigarette right through her favourite Laura Ashley cushion. Why have we even got her things still down here anyway? This is our home now, not a time capsule from the era that style forgot? It's 1982 for God's sake. Gary and Penny have wallpapered the ceiling in their bedroom, it's French apparently.' He spread his arms open to take in the room, 'It's embarrassing living in this time warp.'

'I painted the bedroom peach before Christmas, and the new avocado bathroom isn't even a year old.'

'Peach, avocado, it's like I'm living in a bloody salad drawer.'

'Well, feel free to suggest some decor ideas of your own if it bothers you so much?'

Steven stubbed out his cigarette in the ashtray on the rattan coffee table, but not completely, so a thin wisp of blue smoke still meandered up to the ceiling from it. Bonnie stared at it.

He yawned. 'Just buy a magazine or something, get some ideas of how to bring this place up to date, God knows it needs it. Right, I'm heading to bed, I'll lock up while you tidy round. Don't be too long.'

As soon as he left the room, Bonnie stubbed the cigarette out completely and moved to the window to let some of the smoke out, leaning over the desk she'd prepared for him, which he never used. For a writer, he didn't seem to do much writing. He didn't seem to do much of anything actually, quite often being in the same horizontal position when she left for work as when she came back from it. He started working a few shifts at a theatre last month, moving scenery about, fixing broken chairs, climbing up lighting rigging, that sort of thing. She found out from his mother, Valerie, not him, when she phoned and said how proud they were that his dream to be a playwright had come true and he was finally working in a theatre.

Married life certainly wasn't working out the way Bonnie thought it would. She lifted up the creaking sash frame in the bay window looking out over the street, noticing the peeling paint on the sill as she did, making a mental note to sand that down and paint it before Steven pointed it out. 'See,' he'd say, 'the whole place is falling apart around our ears!'

She stood for a minute or two breathing in the icy air, face turned upwards to the starless sky, the street silent save for a pair of angry cats fighting near the entrance to the park, and thought that as first wedding anniversaries went, this wasn't the best one. The card she'd written him still stood unopened on the mantelpiece. She quietly picked it up and threw it into the dying embers of the fire. The grey ash turned to flickering red flames as it hungrily ate it all up until there was nothing left.

Bonnie didn't own much make-up, so she had to go upstairs to borrow Florence's on the afternoon of the party. She didn't want too much, just something to stop her eyes looking so puffy and red. If Florence noticed the need for the foundation her daughter was lathering on her face like soap on a dirty dish, then she didn't say. She just made her a cup of tea and silently placed it down next to her at the dressing table, resting her hand ever so lightly on Bonnie's shoulder as she did.

She couldn't come straight out and ask Bonnie if she was all right, she'd just reply with a tight-lipped 'yes' and that would be that. So she had to do things like make tea, lend her cosmetics, make her dinner stretch to two on the nights when Steven had cooked for himself and not her. The partition between their two flats was not thick enough to conceal much, yet Florence rarely heard raised voices, but then again, she rarely heard the other sounds of marriage – the laughter, the chatter, the love. Instead, she heard the low hum of the radio or the television and short, clipped words batted back and forth, a three-word question, a one-word reply. And doors closing. A lot of doors closing.

'Are you sure?' she'd asked Bonnie when the wedding day was set for only six weeks after the proposal. 'Is there a reason for the haste?' she'd even said, her eyes flitting downwards to Bonnie's flat stomach.

'No!' Bonnie replied. 'We love each other, that's all, and if you love each other, then you get married.'

'Not necessarily,' Florence said. 'It's 1981, you could live together for a while, test it out for a bit.'

'Mr and Mrs Morris would never allow that!'

'They're not the ones getting married at twenty-one. You are. I'm just saying, there's a lot you don't know about someone until you're with them all the time.'

'Well then, we'll have lots to talk about when we do, won't we? You married Dad without knowing him very well. And you had me straight away. Why is there one rule for you and another for me? You were happy.'

Bonnie got up from Florence's dressing table, positioned in the bay window of her bedroom, where it had stood for as long as she could remember, and looked at her watch; they'd be leaving for the party soon. She felt sick.

'Are you OK, darling?'

Bonnie gave her mother a smile. 'Of course, you know me though, not really a fan of parties.'

'Marriage is all about compromise though, isn't it.'

Bonnie grimaced, recognising that this advice wasn't necessarily applicable in every situation.

'You're wearing trousers?'

Bonnie looked down at her legs before confirming, that, yes, she was indeed wearing trousers.

'But I told you what this party was going to be,' Steven said.

'You told me you wanted to kiss someone else's wife, you didn't tell me there was a dress code,' Bonnie replied coldly, pulling on her coat.

It hadn't escaped Bonnie's attention that Steven had purchased not only a new shirt for the evening, a rather shiny pale blue one, but was also wearing a grey tie, the first time since their wedding he'd done so. Bonnie narrowed her eyes. Actually, she thought, that *was* his wedding tie.

'I just thought you might make more of an effort,' he said.

'Oh, you mean like at a cattle market where they line up all the prize heifers for the men to bid on?'

'I thought you were on board with this?' Steven spat angrily. 'They're expecting us in half an hour, we can't be late.'

'Why? Because only the specimens with mange and one eye will be left?'

'This isn't about that, Bonnie, it's a party, a completely normal party. I told you, we'll go, meet some new people, have a few drinks, and then leave, if we want to.'

'You promise? If I feel even the slightest bit uncomfortable, we'll come home?'

'Of course!' He pulled Bonnie into his arms, so close she could smell an unfamiliar aftershave on his neck, which must be new as well. 'Right, let's go.'

The house was a 1930s semi with a touring caravan parked in its driveway and a garden gnome holding a fishing rod on the front step; if there was a competition for the unlikeliest setting for a swingers' party, this would be the winner, which cheered Bonnie up immensely. Tupperware parties, yes, wife-swapping orgies, no. They rang the bell. The door was opened by a man, early thirties, wearing a brown suit and holding a pina colada complete with umbrella and straw. Bonnie found the combination unsettling, but was very grateful he was fully dressed, one never knew what to expect from this sort of party, but it all seemed reassuringly normal so far. He ushered them in, complimenting Bonnie on her trousers, which made her turn to Steven and stick out her tongue.

'Come in, come in,' the man bellowed. 'Everyone's in the lounge, drinks table at the back, help yourself to whatever you want.'

There were probably twelve, maybe fifteen people in the lounge, some women (all in skirts) sat together on the sofas, while the men stood. Everyone turned to look when they walked in. Bill Withers was singing 'Just the Two of Us' loudly from the record player. Bonnie tried to catch Steven's eye to see if the irony registered with him too, but he had just taken a giant stride towards a group of two couples next to the fireplace and was shaking their hands, back-slapping one man with curly hair that flicked over his collar at the back. That must be Micky.

Bonnie chose alcohol over politeness, and headed straight to the table to pour herself a large white wine before making any introductions. She noted as she poured the wine into the glass that her hands were shaking.

'Hi there, I'm Peter,' a voice boomed behind Bonnie so loudly she spilled a bit of her wine down the man's tie as she swung around. He mopped it up with a piece of kitchen roll with tulips on it, then wiped the sweat off his brow. Bonnie placed him as easily in his forties, and more than a little overweight, hence the excessive perspiration. 'Sorry, about that, just saw you walk in, thought I'd come and introduce myself before anyone else got there first.' As he laughed, Bonnie counted four fillings in his molars. 'Haven't seen you here before,' he said, making her recoil a little.

'That's because I haven't been here before. Excuse me, I have to join my husband.' She hastily picked a bottle of beer for Steven out of a bright red kid's plastic bucket with a sticker of a dinosaur on the front of it. She gave the man a quick nod and left him standing by the drinks table rocking back on his heels as though having women walking away from him was not a rare occurrence.

'I got you a drink,' she said as she reached Steven's side, handing him the beer bottle and smiling politely at the two couples he was with. 'Hi, I'm Bonnie, Steven's wife.'

'So pleased you could make it, Bonnie,' Micky said. 'We weren't sure if you were going to come, Steven explained it might not be your thing, but we're glad you've changed your mind.'

Bonnie's smile grew tighter. 'I'm just here for the wine and the vol-au-vents, Micky. Aren't we all?'

They all thought that was hilarious. Bonnie didn't know why.

Everyone seemed to be having a wonderful time, if the empty wine bottles next to the bin and the sound of giggles echoing through the house were an indication. Bonnie, meanwhile, had decided to help the hostess (who she hadn't yet seen) by washing up the empty glasses and putting cling film over the devilled eggs before they dried out completely; you really shouldn't leave animal products at room temperature for too long. She must have been in the kitchen for almost half an hour and Steven hadn't once come to look for her.

By the time Bonnie wandered back into the living room, it had emptied out completely. Steven was nowhere to be seen. Her heart started thumping loudly in her chest and she blinked, trying to stop tears from forming. He was right, it was one of those parties, and he'd completely left her to it. She took a deep breath and exhaled slowly, trying to regain a modicum of control.

A cough sounded behind her, and she swung quickly round, seeing for the first time a man sitting in an armchair, a book open on his lap. One man. One woman. He must be the person she was supposed to be paired up with.

'I'm not going to kiss you.' She realised as she said it that it was the strangest, and rudest, introduction she'd ever made.

'That's a relief, because although you seem very nice, I do not want to kiss you either. I'm Oliver.'

'Bonnie.'

'Are you looking for a man in a grey tie? He said that if I see Bonnie tell her he's in the room at the top of the stairs, next to the bathroom.'

'That's my husband.'

'I'd go up there at your peril though. Just wait for them all to come back. I've learned that lesson the hard way. Some things can't be unseen.'

'I really want to go home. I'll be brave and shut my eyes.'

As she ascended the stairs, she was filled with a hope that Steven had changed his mind about this and just wanted to be with her, which is why he'd sent for her. This optimism was short-lived as she suddenly felt sick at the thought that he might not be alone in the room and this was just a ploy for her to get involved in something she didn't want to do. Her mum was wrong – there were some things she couldn't compromise on.

She listened for a moment outside the bedroom door at the top of the stairs. It was completely silent, unlike some of the noises emanating from the other closed doors along the landing, which sounded like nature documentaries were being recorded in each one. She gingerly opened the door to be greeted with a sight that made her gasp in horror.

Peter was standing in the middle of the bedroom. Navy socks pulled up to mid-calf, sky-blue Y-fronts just visible under a belly cultivated through years of saying, 'wouldn't hurt' to another helping of his wife's treacle pudding and a port and brandy nightcap. Apart from the pants and socks, he was completely naked, hands on hips, smile on face. Bonnie narrowed her eyes. That was odd. He only seemed to be able to grow chest hair on one side. His right nipple seemed to be lost in a forest, while the left was completely bare, like a sphinx cat. His beard seemed to be symmetrical though, so it wasn't a circulation issue.

'Have you tried taking Vitamin B supplements?' she said.

'I'm sorry?' he replied, his smile twitching slightly.

'To promote hair growth,' she pointed at his chest. 'You could always massage your chest with oil to stimulate the follicles.'

'I'd like to stimulate your follicles.'

Bonnie wrinkled her nose in disgust, 'Don't be vulgar. If I were you, I'd get dressed before you catch a cold, it's minus two outside.'

She shut the door quietly behind her, went downstairs to call a taxi and waited on the street until it came to take her home.

8

Stella

Strong, decisive and affirmative. That's what I need in a donor. Someone like Mum who knows their own mind and won't put up with any rubbish. But also caring, kind and helpful. If pushed, I'm happy to compromise on star signs. I've reached a stage in the research where even a Virgo would be considered if both his grandparents were still alive, he donated regularly to charity and could speak more than one language.

'But we don't have that information, Stella,' Jemima from the agency tells me, not for the first time.

I'm now on first-name terms with all four of the women and two of the men who work at the donor agency. Our relationship is very much one of estate agent and buyer who wants solar panels, underfloor heating, basement cinema room and ornamental pond with waterfall for the price of a Yorkie bar. They humour my almost daily phone calls, but I think they like me, however much I prevent them from doing their actual jobs.

'What about his IQ? Surely that should be the first thing you test along with genetic diseases and STIs?' I say. 'Do they have to supply their degree certificates or do you just take their word for it? Are they criminally checked? It wouldn't take long to run their fingerprints through the police system—'

'Most of our clients just want healthy sperm,' she says, pricking my conscience a little that surely having a healthy baby is more important than his ability to learn Greek.

'But you've seen some of them,' I remind Jemima, 'in the flesh, as it were.'

'I can assure you, that is not part of my job description,' Jemima laughs.

'But you've checked them in, or whatever it is you do when a man comes into the centre. So you know which ones are the really good ones. Are there any that you wouldn't mind having a baby with?'

'Stella, honestly, they all just blur into one, most of them are very pleasant.'

'Most of them? Not all then? OK, do it the other way, tell me which ones to avoid.'

'Stella—'

'I know, I know, the call may be recorded for training purposes. Just email me then. Or message mc, you have my number.'

'Stella—'

'Does the donor's profile start with a 2?'

'All of our donors have undergone a thorough health screening—'

'Yada, yada, yada. I know all that, but some are better than others, aren't they? My dad was a complete knob-end, so I need to pick a good one. Please, just point me in the direction of a good one. A pedigree if you will. Prize boar. A leading sire.'

'Goodbye, Stella.'

'If I tell you the donor number I was thinking of, cough once if they're good, twice for bad. OK? 324 . . . Jemima . . . Jemima?'

I throw my mobile onto the sofa and move over to the lounge window to look out on the street. This would make the perfect place for a desk. It would be lovely to sit here and work looking out at the world passing by. Admittedly, the view is taken up mostly by recycling bins and residents-only parking signs, but there is the park across the road, which is nice. I'll check with Mum and Gran to see if they mind if I put a desk here. I'll obviously move it at Christmas when we put the tree up.

There's been a nagging thought poking me from time to time that Mum had a point when she said I should be a bit more ambitious. She's never said it, well not to me, but I'm sure she feels a degree of disappointment that I inherited more of Dad's work ethic than hers. I'm not sure at what point I stopped wanting a career as a marine biologist or hotshot lawyer. There wasn't a defining moment, where I thought, no, dolphins have enough people worrying about them and wigs are too itchy; I want to spend my days ordering more incontinence pads and buying in easy-to-chew food in bulk.

I want my child to be proud of both her parents. Keen to inherit equal parts from both of us, not crossing their fingers that their maternal genes swoop overhead without landing while being so grateful their dad was an Olympic rower with a PhD in astrophysics. Incidentally, it's really annoying that 'Olympian' is not one of the categories on the filter list.

The front door shuts and there are voices in the hallway – one of them is Florence's; the other is a man I don't recognise.

'Hello?' I call out from the living room.

'Hi, darling,' Florence says, standing in the doorway. 'I'm glad you're here, come and meet Patrick.'

She's like a magpie collecting people instead of jewels. I wouldn't say that Florence brings random men home regularly, but she's instilled a definite open-door policy in the house. I've ceased to be surprised to find strange people sitting having cups of tea or, depending on the hour of the day – as long as it's after noon, she does have some standards – a glass of wine at the kitchen table with her.

Patrick pokes his head around the living room door, and rather than being a balding pensioner, my grandmother's companion is a smiling mid fifty-something with a full head of hair.

'Patrick's in my Italian class,' she says by way of explanation.

'Hi there, Patrick.' He stretches out his hand towards me.

I shake it, 'Stella.'

'Sorry for intruding, but the class finished and Flo said she had some home-made lemon-drizzle cake and invited me here to have some.'

If only it were that easy.

'Come and join us in the kitchen, darling,' Florence says, making her eyes really wide behind Patrick's back and nodding at him furiously.

'I'm OK for cake actually, but nice to meet you, Patrick.'

'I'm making tea for three, come on, kids,' Florence shrills as she walks down the hallway towards the kitchen, Patrick and me dutifully following behind her. 'Patrick's just moved up to intermediate,' Florence says, filling the kettle from the tap. 'He's a natural linguist.'

'Oh I wouldn't say that,' he counters.

'And he plays the clarinet, don't you, Patrick?'

'Oh, badly.'

'Hush, don't be so modest. He's a structural engineer, Stella, isn't that good?'

The penny suddenly drops as to why she's brought Patrick home with her. I really don't want to be dragged into this. It's one thing for Florence to take an interest in the online donors, but actually dragging one off the street with the promise of baked goods and making him a cup of tea in our kitchen is quite another. How does she think this is going to work? We have a brief exchange of CVs here in the kitchen before I give him a Tupperware and point him to the bathroom? Or is she thinking that we could go upstairs together for twenty minutes while she turns *Bargain Hunt* up in the lounge? Honestly, I know you should make allowances for old people, but she's gone too far this time. And he's at least fifteen years older than me, which makes him about twenty years too old to be considered by the agency. What's in it for him? Maybe he always wanted a child but just never had one? Did she have to convince him to come here or did he do it willingly?

'This cake is delicious, Flo,' Patrick says, licking his lips to prove his statement. Is that all she bribed him with? *'Come and have some cake and impregnate my granddaughter.' 'Oh no, I'm OK thanks.' 'It's lemon-drizzle.' 'Oh, well that's different, show me the way!'*

'What time did Bonnie say she'd be back?' Florence asks me, and I know why. Mum would be horrified that Florence is doing this, so she wants her out of the way for as long as possible, sneaky old goat. Oh, she's going to regret doing this.

'So, Patrick,' I say brightly, turning my body to face him square on. 'When's your birthday?'

A tiny blink-and-you-miss-it flash of confusion flits across his face before he answers, 'August.'

'Beginning or end? Leos are good, Virgos are not.'

'Beginning. I'm a Leo.'

'Well done, you're onto Round 2. How many countries have you visited?'

'I don't know, at a guess around twenty?'

'Not bad. Sports?'

'To watch – anything. To play – five-a-side football.'

'Can you ice-skate?'

'No.'

'Ski?'

'I used to snowboard. Sort of.'

'Are your parents still alive?'

'Yes.'

'How old?'

'Seventy-eight and seventy-nine.'

'Congenital diseases? Heart, lung, liver?'

'Um. No.'

Patrick looks towards Florence, who looks as confused as he is. That'll teach her. But I'm not finished yet.

'Have you ever been treated for herpes?'

The front door slams before he can answer. 'Hi, I'm home,' Mum calls out.

Patrick hurriedly gets to his feet, so fast his kitchen chair rocks backwards. 'I've got to go, thanks for the cake,' he garbles, before rushing into the hallway and past Mum, who hasn't even taken her coat off.

'Who was that?' she says, coming into the kitchen a minute later.

Florence purses her lips together. 'To be honest, I'm surprised you could see him at all through the smoke that came off his shoes as he ran away. That was Patrick, Bonnie, lovely, kind Patrick from my Italian class, the one I've been talking about setting you up with. He was really keen to meet you, but then Super Sleuth Stella here started asking him all these really inappropriate questions about genital warts, and the poor lamb just ran off.'

Bugger.

'I'll be upstairs if anyone needs me,' I say, gingerly edging out of the room.

Lesson learned. Not everyone is as preoccupied with my impending insemination as I am. Patrick seemed really nice as well. I wonder if I can entice him back with the promise of more baking and less intrusive questions about his sexual health. Mum's been single since Dad left; she deserves a nice man in her life. Especially a clarinet-playing, Italian-speaking Leo who doesn't have herpes. Although, I realise, he never actually answered that last question.

I sit on my bed and rub my face with both hands. I need to slow down. Or speed up. Either one, but this state of limbo, where no decision is being made is becoming really stressful. For me and everyone around me. I open up my laptop and log back into the fertility forum. I'm not sure whether this anonymous online donor community has kept me sane or driven me so far from the state of sanity that I wouldn't recognise it anymore. For every post that reassures me that many other women just like me are going through exactly the same thing, there's a post entitled LET ME GET YOU PREGNANT TODAY where a charming fellow offers to come round (as long as you're within the M25, he's not made of money) and NI you. NI is the acronym for naturally inseminate; I think you can see where this is going. And hats off to these men, why waste money on dinner and drinks on a Tinder date when you can offer to be a donor and get straight to the discarding of underwear stage?

Today's gem comes in the form of Paul. His message has the heading I AM YOUR DONNER. It takes every ounce of self-restraint not to make a kebab joke in the comments. Paul is a 'senor prodject manger with menny degrees'. He also writes u instead of you, is only available before six on Tuesdays and Thursdays, never at his house, only at 'yrs', would like the train 'fair' equivalent in Sports Direct vouchers and is especially looking for lesbian 'cupples' to give his 'seamen' to.

You can't blame him for trying. And he's already had fifteen replies. I can't imagine Paul would be anyone's first choice, but he is a lot of women's last hope. And that makes me sad. Thanks to moving back in here, I can afford the clinic, the sanitised insemination, but for many women desperate to conceive, Paul's their shining beacon. Their perfect donner.

For Christ's sake, Stella just pick one and be done with it, I tell myself. But for the love of all that's holy, don't pick Paul.

9
Stella

'Would you like a Polo mint?'

I shake my head at Mum.

'Aniseed ball?'

I screw up my face, 'I don't know why you like those, they're disgusting. And apparently they make you go to the loo lots.'

The waiting room at the fertility clinic is such an odd place. All these couples sitting around, and they are all couples. Even occasionally when you do get a woman in on her own, she makes sure she says in a loud voice, 'my husband's just parking the car' or 'my partner's stuck at work' as though it would be absolutely inconceivable to be doing this alone. On the other hand, I refer loudly to myself as Mzzzz, so as to annoy all the smug Mrs-es, and deliberately wedge myself between the couples, not leaving an empty seat beside me for a partner who couldn't be arsed to leave work in time, or to get here early to get a parking space. But as Mum's come with me today, to everyone else in the waiting room we look like a rather postmodern lesbian couple, one twenty-odd years older than the other, trying to embark on a shared parenting journey with the sperm of a gay friend called Marco who will *definitely* be involved every step of the way.

Every ten minutes or so, the receptionist calls a woman's name and she and her partner usually go in together, moral support and all that, then come back to the waiting room, holding hands, to wait. Then the man's called, and this part of the appointment is a solo job. Every man for himself. And we all sit there, knowing what he's doing behind the door everyone has to walk past to go to the ladies to pee in their own pot. No one makes eye contact with anyone else because if we did, we'd share the same thought.

There was a potentially disastrous moment earlier on when two men rose out of their chairs when the receptionist cheerfully called out the name Ian. One was white, one black, and the black Ian coughed good-naturedly and said, 'Well, it'd be obvious if they mix ours up,' to which the room gave polite chuckles, while every woman in there thought about the possibilities of receiving the wrong sperm.

They better not mix mine up, not when I've spent months finally finding him. Donor 203. I'm not going to lie, I've always liked the number 3, and he's a Libra. There's more to him than just that though, he's a pleasing mix of Dutch and Cornish: Van Gogh's talents and Poldark's looks. He's a six foot four law graduate, loves animals, the countryside and all four of his grandparents are alive and in their nineties, so there's some good genes there. The photo of him as a child showed a beaming six-year-old riding a horse, so I'm hopeful that some of his equestrian skills will rub off on the little one and I'll spend the next ten years hanging off a paddock gate watching them win gymkhanas and their bedroom will be covered in colourful rosettes. I'll have to get an estate car or a 4x4 so that I can pop the boot up and we can have our picnic sitting in the back on rainy days on the edge of a showjumping field. We'll need a big car anyway for the dogs.

And one of those metal barriers between the boot and the back seat so they don't jump through and get muddy paw prints on the upholstery . . .

'Stella Fairbrother.'

I nudge Mum, who puts down the magazine and anti-bacs her hands. 'We're up, come on, it's not every day mums are there at the moment of their grandchild's conception.'

'What a thought,' Mum replies.

'You're far too prim for your own good, you are.'

We go into the consulting room, and I introduce Mum to my consultant. 'Hello, Doc, this is my mum, Bonnie. Mum, this is my consultant. These are his students,' I add, sweeping my arm over the four girls and boys standing behind his chair like child bodyguards.

'Delighted to meet you,' the doctor's blue eyes shine above his grey beard. 'Dr Foster. And no, I have never been to Gloucester.'

Mum laughs appreciatively, while I shake my head, 'I don't know what that means.'

The doctor and Mum share an eye roll at my expense before he cracks on with business. 'Right, so today's the day. As I explained on the phone earlier, out of the six eggs we fertilised, we've got two viable embryos – one we're implanting today, the other we are freezing for possible use later. Up you hop.'

Every day for the last week, I'd prayed and prayed that the six would stay six, but every day, his nurse relayed a number which was one less than the day before, until yesterday's call confirmed that just two remained.

'You're not relaxed,' the doctor says in a tone of surprise a few minutes later, as though the sensation of cold metal being pressed against your cervix is second only to having a nice warm bath in terms of loosening up and winding down.

'Try and relax, Stella,' my mother echoes.

'I'd like to see you try to relax while a team of people are peering up your vagina. Actually, no I wouldn't.'

'You should be used to it by now,' Mum says, before realising how horrific that sounds, and immediately back-tracks, digging a hole so deep she nearly falls into it. 'In a medical way only, not in a sexual way. She hasn't had a boyfriend in years. Obviously. That's why we're here, isn't it?'

I cringe as the students collectively tilt their heads pity-ingly, now viewing me as the 40-year old virgin. 'Stop talk-ing, Mum.'

'Yes, absolutely.'

We both fall silent as we watch spellbound on the small screen as the doctor threads the thin catheter into place. A small bubble floats out of the end of the tube and gently bounces into my uterus.

'Is that the embryo?' Mum asks, wide-eyed.

'It is,' confirms the doctor smiling. 'First grandchild?'

'Yes,' Mum gushes. 'Well, all being well. I know the statistics.'

'Sometimes even scientists prefer faith and hope over statistics, Mrs . . .?'

'Doctor. Of genetics, not medicine. But I'm not married. My name's Bonnie.'

That was a lot of information for one question. I cough. 'I hate to break up this magical moment, but I've still got my feet in stirrups over here.'

'So, take it easy for a few days,' the doctor says, putting the tools in a silver tray and pulling off his gloves. 'Try to resist the temptation to take a test before fourteen days, it's a waste of money, but when you do, call the office and let me know the result. Good luck, Stella, I have hugely enjoyed our journey together. Bonnie, lovely to meet you.'

The door of the clinic swings shut behind us and I waste no time in singing, 'Mum and Doctor Foster sitting in a tree . . . K I S—'

'Be quiet! He was a very nice man, that's all, and obviously very highly skilled.' She narrows her eyes at me, 'Why are you walking like a penguin?'

'I'm worried it might fall out.' It's taken me so long to get to this stage; I'm suddenly overcome with protectiveness for this little bubble.

'It can't just fall out.'

'But it just went in, why can't it just come out?'

'It's not my area of science, but if I was to hazard a guess, it would be because the uterine cavity has a viscous lining which acts as a glue, and—'

'Mum, it was a rhetorical question, I don't actually want to know what the lining of my uterus is made up of.'

The house is quiet when we get back; Florence is engrossed in writing in her notebook on the kitchen table, which pleases me enormously. She looks up when we walk in, 'Well?'

'So I am currently with embryo,' I smile.

'Brilliant news! Now go and sit down in the lounge and I'll bring you through a cuppa.'

'No, I'll make it, I don't have to be on bed rest, the doctor said. The *eligible* doctor who incidentally, took a fancy to Mum—'

Mum blushes and swats the air, 'No he didn't, don't be ridiculous.'

'*Call me Bonnie, I'm not married*,' I impersonated.

'Is this true?' Florence asks, obviously delighted that after the Patrick debacle there's already a Plan B forming.

'No,' Mum says.

'Yes. He's a widower.'

'And I'm a very happy spinster,' Mum counters.

'Perfect combination,' I say. 'Once you dust the cobwebs off.'

The mention of dust makes my nose itch. I instinctively cross my legs, keeping the embryo safe inside me as I sneeze. My thighs stay clamped together for a few seconds before I release them just in case the tiny bubble we saw on the screen flies out of me and ricochets across the kitchen, bouncing off the cabinets before finally landing in the small gap between the cooker and the worktop and sliding down to the floor on top of a random piece of brown papery onion peel and the manual for the dishwasher, lost forever.

'On second thoughts,' I say, 'I'm going to have a lie-down.'

The forums say that this is the time for self-care. For doing what makes you happy. Destressing and decompressing. Which is excellent advice. A paint-by-numbers kit or maybe a nice jigsaw would absolutely take my mind off the fact that my chance at being a mother is currently deciding whether to cling on for dear life or have a nice swim through my cervix and out of my vagina.

* * *

Dear Baby,

I made you today. Well, me, and a whole team of very clever fertility doctors and scientists, and a lovely man you may one day choose to meet. I've done my best, little one, to find a man who will give you the best chance at being happy. I know people say that nurture trumps nature and a loving home is all that matters, and I promise you, my darling, you will have that, but sometimes it's good to have nature give a helping hand too. I hope you never think badly of me, doing it this way, making a conscious choice to bring you up without a dad in your life. I grew up without a dad, and at times I wished it wasn't that way, so I pray that you won't blame me for it. But I had no choice, darling, I couldn't wait any more, and so this was the way you had to be made. But if you do decide to look for him, Donor 203, I will help you, and I have absolutely no doubt at all that he will be everything you could ever want in a dad, and I will do my damnedest every day of my life to try to be the mum you want too.

10

Florence

Dear Little One,

I've been thinking about this quite a lot, so bear with me while I try to assemble my thoughts into a semi-literate order. I've re-read my first letter to you, and I fear I rambled on a bit too much. You see, I was dreading writing it, and then once I started, I just couldn't stop. It was as though the lid was sealed on my memories sixty years ago and then pop! Off it came and everything tumbled out. I doubt you really wanted to know about stone-skimming and sentimental statues of dead scientists, but if you're anything like your great-grandfather you'd have just nodded along anyway, humouring me, because that's what he did, always making me feel that what I had to say had value, even though his brain was five times the size of mine and a class or two above me. Those things mattered more back then. They don't seem to now. Love is love. And that's the way it should be.

I see his common sense in Bonnie, your grandmother, every day. The way she sits quietly and assesses things before jumping in with both feet, which is much more my way and your mother's. Leap first, think later, that's always been our motto. But your mum has definitely inherited Henry's compassion. She hides it well under a cloak of humour and funny one-liners, but she couldn't do the job she does without caring about people. I've seen her, sitting for hours hearing the same Blitz story, playing the same game of chess, long after her shift is up just because she knows that it matters. She's done it with me too, sitting in my room next to my bed when I had my first knee operation, sometimes through the night in the first few days, reading aloud from my book before audiobooks were really a thing. Holding my arm as I took my first tentative steps down the road, then around the block. She'd be making jokes the whole time, mind you, suggesting that we steal a sloth from London Zoo, and then open a book on who would be faster, and split the profits. I don't think she gets that kindness from me; I'm not a cruel person, but I know that I sometimes tell people what I think they want to hear, what will make them happy. I don't think that makes me dishonest. But Henry was different. He was honest to the core.

I'm starting to realise that I've filled my life with so many distractions because it stops me getting sad, but the funny thing is, now I have stopped, and am allowing myself the time and space to remember, I'm not sad. I'm actually not sad at all.

11

Florence

Sixty years earlier . . .

Henry had been carrying a pretty antique square emerald set in little diamonds around with him for nearly three weeks, just waiting for the right time. He'd already asked Florence's father for her hand, an exchange that lasted less than three minutes once the information was imparted that Henry's grandparents owned half of Rutland and his father played the organ in their local church on Sundays, as well as the occasional weekday weddings and funerals if his work at the university permitted.

'We need to choose a date,' Mrs Weston said, mere seconds after Florence skipped home wearing the ring, admiring how it shone under the tassels of the lounge corner lamp. She waited until her husband had left the room before she whispered to her daughter, 'When are your courses due?'

Florence was blushing almost as much as her mother. Aside from leaving a sanitary belt and napkin on her bed when Florence was twelve alongside a book called *Very Personally Yours* in which the words, 'certainly you can go to dances, but save the jitterbug routine for another time,' stuck in Florence's mind until this day, Dorothy had never referenced menstruation. Florence must have looked confused, as Dorothy added, 'Well, obviously, you'll be wearing white, and your wedding night will be an important moment, and so you need to pick a date when your monthlies won't ruin things.'

Florence had been a late bloomer, not getting her first period until she was fifteen, and she still hadn't got used to charting the dates in the Kotex calendar in the back of the book like she was meant to do. She definitely had a couple during the summer, once being caught unawares and she had to borrow a spare belt and napkin from Hazel when they were at the pictures, but that was back in June, more than six months ago.

Her heart plummeted.

'I'll think about the date, excuse me,' she said, and fled up to her room, shutting the door behind her and sinking onto the bed, where she just sat staring into space wondering how on earth this had happened. She and Henry hadn't done anything like what the books said could make a baby; they'd kissed, and he'd rubbed her chest a bit over her blouse, before apologising and stopping, saying that it wasn't long to wait until the wedding. She'd done more with Kenny, but they were standing up the whole time.

'But that's impossible,' Hazel whispered the next day as they stood side by side in the club kitchen polishing glasses, 'you must have something else wrong with you.'

'Like what?'

'I don't know, I'm not a doctor!'

'So what should I do?'

'Go and see one, I suggest.'

'I can't go to *my* doctor, he's in the same prayer group as Mum and Dad and I don't want to worry them if it's something serious.'

'There's a surgery on the road behind here, go there after work and say you've just moved to the area.'

It was relatively simple to register, everyone was very polite and cordial. Florence conversed for a few minutes with the elderly doctor about her work at the club. After he'd recognised her uniform, he tried to tease any names of famous politicians she might have served out of her, before pausing while writing down her symptoms in his notebook, his fountain pen hovering in mid-air above the pad.

'In my experience, there's usually only one explanation for missed menstruation, Mrs . . .'

'It's Miss. Miss Weston. I'm not married.'

A deep inhalation. A frantic scribble on the form. A steely glare taking in the damned soul sat gamely on the bed before him in a hospital gown that did little to disguise the fact to the trained eye that Florence was quite clearly about sixteen weeks pregnant.

An hour ago, Florence had been a respectable and respected member of society. On her way into work this morning, she'd offered up her seat on the bus; she'd brought her library book back a week early, spine intact, hadn't even turned the corner of a page, preferring instead to use the bookmark she'd embroidered herself, blanket stitch around the sides to prevent fraying and a daisy on the front. She'd dropped off an extra dress she'd run up on her old Singer sewing machine to Nancy at work to give to her sister – waste not want not – and she'd popped the half a crown she'd found on the pavement outside the doctor's surgery into the collection box for a new dialysis machine for the local hospital in the surgery's entrance hall.

But none of that mattered now.

She was sixteen, unmarried and pregnant, and that's all anyone was going to care about.

Florence left the surgery in a daze. A mind-numbing daze that meant she had no memory of the bus journey home, or eating the faggots and mashed potato her mother put in front of her at dinner, or what they talked about while she and her parents ate them. It wasn't even as though her brain was whirring over the situation; it was absolutely, completely blank. Sleep eluded her, but again, not because her mind was too busy, the opposite was true, it seemed to be on strike, completely unable to form even the most basic coherent thought.

As she got dressed for work the next day, pulling on the stockings and stepping into the black skirt, it hit her that the reason she'd had to move the button on the waistband a few weeks ago wasn't because of the rich food she'd been eating at the club, hoovering up the last slice of Black Forest gateau in the cake cabinet or whatever sponge pudding was left on the dessert trolley at the end of the day, but because she was growing a life inside her. Instinctively, her hand stroked her belly, immediately removing it when her mother's voice rang out from downstairs telling her she was going to be late if she didn't hurry up.

Mr Withers, the manager, was standing outside the staff entrance to the club when she ran in that day, putting up his hand like he was controlling traffic to bring her to an abrupt halt. 'My office.'

She followed him down the corridor, coat still on. Kitchen hands and pot washers looking up as they passed the open door to the kitchen, giving her consolatory looks.

He didn't offer her a seat, although he made a show of taking his own, smoothing down his jacket, lining up his hole punch and stapler on his desk before he spoke.

'I had a very interesting call this morning, Miss Weston.'

'Oh?'

'Indeed.'

Florence's eyes flitted around the room, taking in the bookshelves lined with leather ledgers, and a stuffed white owl on one of the top shelves. She never understood taxidermy; a picture of an owl in flight would be far more attractive than a stuffed dead one.

'Did I, or did I not, make perfectly clear in your interview that any fraternisation with any of our members would not be tolerated and would result in instant dismissal?'

Henry.

'Added to this, is the news I received this morning about your . . . situation, and I don't think that I need to remind you that this is a respectable establishment, based on over two-hundred years of history, and alignment with the most senior and respected political figures in the country. I am not going to let a teenage girl with loose morals cast a shadow over this business. Here are the wages owing to you. You have ten minutes to collect any belongings you have in the staffroom and vacate the premises. You can return the uniform by post.'

The fog returned, and Florence blindly left the building, emerging into the sunshine holding a small bag with the contents of her locker in it. She stopped statue-like on the pavement, completely at a loss where to go, or what to do. Terribly important suits carrying briefcases tutted at her blocking their path. A bus stopped with *Fulham* on the front, she let it pause for a few moments before it revved up its engine and went past. Across the road, another bus stopped, this one heading towards home. If she hurried, she could catch it, but her feet remained rooted to the pavement.

She just couldn't make sense of this. It must be a mistake, although the test in the surgery seemed conclusive. Someone needed to help her understand what was happening, and the obvious person was Henry, with his unparalleled intellect and calm and steady manner. Her mother had always said that babies were made when two people loved each other, but Florence couldn't fathom how that might be so, when no parts of their bodies had touched apart from their lips. Was love alone enough to make a child? There was talk in school, and the turned-down page in *Lady Chatterley's Lover* that was passed around talked about 'crouching loins', but to her knowledge, Florence's loins had never crouched. Nor had the 'curves of her flank' been stroked. She knew pregnancy had something to do with a man's *thing*, but she'd never even seen one!

Her thoughts kept coming back to that night with Kenny Buck under the scaffolding, that unusual feeling she had, down there, followed by the sharp pain and the spots of blood, but that was just a vigorous spot of petting, that couldn't possibly have led to this. Could it?

12

Stella

'I better get back, it's Mum's birthday today, and we're going out for dinner.'

'Hang on, there's a few more things in here you could take with you,' Kate says, her bottom sticking out of the hall cupboard. 'I have a bumbo if you want it?'

'I don't know what that is,' I answer honestly, feeling incredibly inadequate and underprepared that motherhood is filled with such foreign jargon. I've just said yes to a breast pump and a massive inflatable beach ball, both of which are now by the front door and have a purpose I'm yet to discover.

'It's like a little seat they can sit in before they can sit up by themselves,' Kate explains. 'It's wipe-clean.'

'Where was that type of seat when we needed them at university?' I reply. 'Keeps you upright and wipes clean: that right there is a business plan waiting to happen.'

'Can you hold Zeus a second?'

I swallow down the giggle that always bubbles up every time I hear Kate say her youngest son's name out loud. She even had a book of names, and this was the one she chose, after opting for Thor, the god of Thunder, for her first. I know I've already mapped out a life of pony trekking and holidays in North Cornwall for my unborn child, but to have such confidence in your child that they will be able to carry off a name like Zeus or Thor when they grow up is pretty remarkable. I've started making a list of names I like, once again thanking the gods (neither Zeus nor Thor) that I don't have to compromise on my favourite names because my partner doesn't like them – although, what were the chances that both Kate and Lee would say yes to a Greek and Norse god without hesitation?

Mum keeps telling me not to get my hopes up, not to buy anything or picture the embryo as a real person because it isn't yet. She keeps referring to it as a blastocyst, which is really winding me up. She can be as sensible and practical as she likes, but that's not me. As much as I normally try to avoid any link between me and Steven, my dad, I think that's where I must get it from, this dreamer quality. I don't even have to screw my eyes up to instantly conjure up situations that haven't happened yet. This embryo is as real to me as Zeus is (the child, not the god). And the stink emanating from his nappy, and the growing stain on my jeans is enough proof for anyone that he's pretty damn real.

'Hey, Stell,' Lee says, coming into his kitchen and wrinkling up his nose at the smell that is really ungodlike. 'Fancy a beer?'

'She can't, she's pregnant remember?' Kate says, coming back into the kitchen holding a purple plastic seat-thing, which I guess must be the bumbo.

'I'm not yet, it was only implanted a week ago, I can't test for another week,' I say, wheeling out the line I'm supposed to say, while there's no part of me that believes it.

'Oh yeah, I forgot you had that done,' he says, as though I've just had lash extensions. 'Isn't it a bit weird, you know, having a stranger's, you know . . . things inside you.'

'You make me sound like a lock-up storage unit.'

'No, you know, their . . . jizz,' he clarifies unnecessarily.

Kate clicks her tongue impatiently, 'What do you think actually happens, Lee? They don't just pour it in. It's done in a lab where they mix the egg and sperm together to make an embryo, then put that in.'

'Still a bit weird, isn't it?'

I clock Kate giving her husband narrowed warning eyes as though he's just repeating what he's probably told her without me there.

'The whole conception thing is weird, this isn't any less weird than the two of you making him,' I nod towards Zeus who's now having his nappy changed by Kate on the kitchen work surface. I make a mental note not to stay for lunch if it's offered.

'Yeah, but that's normal life, innit? This, what you had done, is science.' He rolls the word 'science' around his mouth like it's an offensive term.

'Not really. It's the same, just without the need for new bedding or a shower afterwards.'

Lee considers this for a moment and cracks open his beer. 'Anyway, good luck to you, I know I couldn't do it.'

'No, that would be physically impossible and a massive waste of money seeing as you don't have a womb.'

'Shame though, isn't it,' he adds, 'that you needed to do it this way.'

'She didn't *need* to do it this way, she *wanted* to do it this way,' Kate says, disgruntled on my behalf. I appreciate her backing, but I'm not sure he's wrong.

'My mate Neil's single.'

'There's a reason for that. You've tried setting me up with him before,' I remind him. 'We met for a drink and he was actually swiping on Tinder during the date, while I was sitting opposite him.'

Lee shakes his head sorrowfully, 'It's an addiction.'

'It's rude.'

'He wants kids.'

'Not enough to put his phone away and note that my name is Stella not Sophie.'

'I'm sure he'd definitely be up for seeing a kid on the weekends Chelsea's not playing at home,' Lee continues, like it's a sacrifice of heroic proportions.

'I wish you'd mentioned this before, Lee, it does sound like I've missed out on a really fantastic opportunity, but unfortunately I'm already growing a baby from someone else. Oh well.'

'Next time maybe,' Lee says merrily. 'It'd save you doing it this way.'

'Lee!' Kate berates. 'Stella's taking control of her life and eschewing traditional expectations of what motherhood means to the modern woman.' Kate turns to me, and seeing my look of wonder at her monologue explains, 'I've been reading up about it.'

'Thank you,' I say, 'and yes, I'd love the bumbo.'

'I'm putting it in the dining room,' I say before Mum can ask me where I'm going to put the pile of Kate's old baby things in my arms. 'We always eat in the kitchen, and so it's a room that's never used.'

'I thought I told you not to get ahead of yourself,' Mum shouts through.

'You did. And I thought I told you that a life without a bit of excitement is not a life.'

'But I don't want you to be disappointed,' Mum says, this time from the dining-room doorway, watching me pile up my haul.

'And I don't want to live my life in a state of flat-line because I don't want to get excited about things just on the off-chance it all goes wrong.'

'I don't do that,' she replies, disgruntled. 'I just don't always expect things to go right, that's not the same thing as expecting them to go wrong.'

If she thinks stockpiling baby stuff is wrong, then I know exactly what she'd say to my plan to take a test on Day 7, but she's not me.

The chemist on the high street is one of those really old-fashioned ones, not a modern chain. They stock things like shower caps, knee-high surgical stockings and foam rollers, which the customers love because their average age is about a hundred years old and they all smell of Parma violets and travel lozenges, which incidentally they sell as well, next to the till. For some reason, Mum never goes in there, and can't understand why I do; she prefers the Boots, but it's an extra ten minutes' walk, and, to be honest, there's something about this old pharmacy that I really love. I was really upset when they got rid of the old till for one whose keys don't stick when I was about seven or eight and ran home with Florence to tell Mum, trying to gasp the words out between sobs. I emptied my piggy bank, Florence emptied her purse, and we bought the old till from them. I played with that till for years, I have no idea where it disappeared to.

The price tag on the pregnancy kit is faded, and it has a layer of dust on it, suggesting it has been there a while, but it is still in date, just. The lady behind the till is one of those people who must have ended up in London by accident, because instead of silently packing up the kit in a bag and holding out her hand for the money, she says, 'Do we want the test to have two lines or don't we?'

If I were Mum, I'd have told her that was quite frankly none of her business. If it was Florence stood here, she'd have asked if they have a kettle out back, and if so, pop it on, there's a love, get cosy, it's a long story. I standing rather comfortably in between the two women in my life, so I smile and say, 'Definitely two lines.'

'Well, I'll keep my fingers crossed for you both.'

'Aw, that's so lovely,' I say, 'keeping them crossed for the baby too.'

The older woman gives me a good-natured smile, 'No, I meant for you and your husband.'

'Oh, I'm not married.'

'Boyfriend then.'

'I don't have one.'

The woman studies me for a moment over the top of her glasses, trying to work out if I might be one of those people who manages to get to middle age never having been told how procreation works. In which case, this is £7.99 down the drain.

'It's a donor baby,' I explain. 'From a man I've never met.'

'Never met?' her face crinkles in confusion, 'How do you know you like him then?'

'I don't need to like him. My egg just needs to like his sperm.' I've gone too far. I knew I'd gone too far as soon as I'd said it, and it doesn't help that I'm not actually sure whether I pronounced it right, or did, indeed, say spam.

Either way, she shoves the test in a bag, gives a loud sniff and announces the price, holding out her hand for the money.

'I didn't mean to be rude,' I say, trying to back-pedal, 'it's just what it is.'

'It's your business, madam, not mine,' she replies stiffly.

'Sorry,' I say, 'I shouldn't have said *sperm* out loud. But at the end of the day, it is just a bodily fluid like phlegm and I guess that gets said out loud in here loads.'

'Have a good day, madam.'

I can tell she doesn't mean it.

When I get home, Mum is coming down the stairs and looks at the paper bag I'm holding with the logo of the chemist's on it and gives a little frown.

'I know, I know,' I say, shrugging my coat off and putting it on top of Mum's anorak in the hallway, 'it's only day seven I'm not going to take the test, just buying it.'

'So why not buy it on day twelve?' she asks.

'Because I was passing the chemist anyway.'

'Going where?'

'What?'

'You've only got the one bag, so you didn't do any other shopping?'

'Jesus, Mum, I'm forty years old, I can take myself for a walk without needing a permission slip.' I walk into the kitchen and Mum follows me.

'I just don't want you to be disappointed, if you take the test now, it's going to be negative, and then you'll be upset, but if you wait a week, it's got more chance of having the outcome you want.'

'Doesn't it get boring always playing by the rules?'

'What?' she looks taken aback, but I can't help carrying on, even though I know I shouldn't.

'You're just always so sensible, don't you ever just want to do something completely wild and unexpected? You don't always need to do what people tell you to, you know; trust your instincts, fly by the wind. Have that cappuccino after three o'clock in the afternoon. Open the next bottle of wine. Go for a walk with no purpose.'

'I'm not you, Stella, I don't have to do those things to feel alive.'

'So what do you do to feel alive?' I press.

'I read books. I listen to the radio. I try to find genetic markers for unusual hereditary diseases. I look after you and Mum.'

I start to feel bad; she's right. I need to stop doing this, assuming that everyone is made the same, with the same needs and aspirations. I haven't picked up a book in a year, or listened to the radio, and I don't really understand what Mum's sentence about genetic markers even means, let alone do it to feel alive. And she does look after us. It's her salary that pays for the lights to work, for the bins to be collected, for the food in the fridge. She's the one who remembers to put the recycling out, and to put the lock on the bike, and to get the car MOT-ed on time. Doesn't she deserve a bit of a break? Especially on her birthday.

'I know I teased you about it last week, but Dr Foster is really nice,' I say, changing the subject, holding out an olive branch.

Mum shakes her head. 'He may well be, darling, but I'm not interested.'

'Why not?'

'I'm happy with life as it is.'

'Don't you want to be in love again?' I say 'again' because I'm assuming that at some point in her life she's been in love.

She married my dad after all, and people tend not to marry people they don't love.

'I am in love. I love you, and Mum, and part of me already loves that mass of cells inside your uterus.'

'*In* love. It's different. Don't you want to feel your heart beat faster when someone looks at you, or have butterflies in your stomach as you count down the minutes until you see them again?'

'And you think Dr Foster would make me have butterflies?'

'Why not?'

'I love your enthusiasm for your consultant, that's great; he seemed very good at his job. But in terms of him and me making each other's hearts beat faster, that's a bit of a stretch. Unless it's angina. Which at our age is quite probable.'

'You're so annoying,' I huff like a teenager. Being back in this house is clearly making me regress.

'Be a love and turn on Radio 4. *Woman's Hour*'s about to start, it's time for me to start feeling alive.'

13

Bonnie

Dear ____________ (tbc)

I was there as you were put inside your mother. Until then, you'd been an idea, but now you're real. Which makes this notebook slightly more important, doesn't it? I want what I write to be useful, to give you an idea of where you came from, but also perhaps pass on some advice gleaned from being alive longer than you. The trouble is, I'm not really an advice-giving type of person. I believe that everyone should do what's right for them, not follow the hollow words of people who think they know better, so you're not going to find much counsel or guidance in these pages. If I could hope one thing for you though, it would be courage.

Most people would probably say happiness, I'm guessing that's what your mother (and mine for that matter) will probably be wishing for you, so they have that covered. Of course I want that for you too, but also, I would hope that you turn out to be strong enough to follow your brain, because your head is always more reliable than your heart. But I'm a scientist, so of course I'd err on the side of thinking over feeling. Not that I've always followed my own advice, which is why I'm reticent to dole it out. Your mother came about purely due to my heart calling the shots, which is, I suppose, the way it's meant to be.

Today is my birthday. A day to celebrate coming into the world. Making it around the sun another time. But I always feel a bit subdued on my birthday; I'm not sure why. I've always had lovely birthdays, most of them in this very house. Friends from school crammed into the living room, all furniture pushed back against the walls so we could sit in a giant circle passing a parcel around until the music stopped, or all our kitchen chairs, and those borrowed from our neighbours either side of us, placed back to back in a line down the middle of the room for musical chairs. My dad would control the music, my mum running back and forth from the kitchen to the living room to see the games, wiping her hands on her pinny as she came down the corridor. I was the same when Stella had her birthday parties here: the same games, the same sandwich fillings, the same joy. And one day, we might celebrate your birthday in the same room too. I only knew the sound of laughter growing up in this house. Which is, I suppose, all you could ask for. And it's all I want for you.

Earlier on, your mum and I were talking about love, which got me thinking about the idea of monogamy, which our popular culture tells us is what we should all be aspiring to. It's a strange concept though, if you think about it, isn't it? The idea that somewhere around the world there is one person who is the right match for you. It seems unlikely, given the number of people in the world, that it's going to be someone in your class at school, on your degree course or working at an adjacent desk in your office, but these are some of the most common places people meet their spouses. Our ancestors, the primates, the Mammalian group, which we as people are part of, are completely polygamous, happily leaping from tree to tree mating with any other primate they come across. Chimps are renowned for mating with everyone else in their group, but we as humans don't tend to do that. We also don't pick nits out of each other's fur or eat woodlice from under rocks, so we can't assume our primate ancestors are the benchmark for behaviour standards.

I'm not particularly sentimental, but I read a quote once, I forget where I saw it, probably a card in a newsagents, but it said, 'A friend is one who overlooks your broken fence and admires the flowers in your garden'. I like that. Too many people in life will focus on your flaws, the things you get wrong, or aren't good at, but a true friend won't even see those things and will instead find the uniqueness in you. When you find that person, make sure you keep hold of them. Some people are really lucky, like my parents, and they find it in their partners who they're with every day. Others find it in a friend they might only see once a week, but know they are always there, admiring your flowers.

I had a friend like that once; they were a scientist, like me. It didn't matter to them that I was a little bit more serious than other young women my age and didn't immediately clap my hands together with delight when a certain song came on the radio or spend every moment reading women's magazines with the latest fashions. I couldn't see the point of spending so much time making the outside of you shine, when the inside of you doesn't. It's false advertising. And my friend thought the same. We'd talk for hours about things other people would yawn at, we'd stand in front of paintings in museums, not talking, just thinking, and we'd be the only ones queuing up for art-house subtitled films at the cinema, rather than the latest exploding blockbuster whose queue stretched out the door of the theatre. You know you've met a true friend when you can sit side by side not talking and not feel lonely.

14

Bonnie

Forty-one years earlier . . .

These wife-swapping parties happened every month, sometimes every three weeks if the urge to break your marriage vows was so compelling you couldn't wait another week. After the first party, Bonnie flatly refused to go to another one, standing firm to the resolution she'd made in the back of the taxi that night, even in the face of Steven's anger: 'you're selfish'; cajoling: 'the next one will be so much better'; guilt-tripping: 'if you were more fun I wouldn't want to do this'; anger again: 'for Christ's sake, Bonnie, lighten up a bit, humans are carnal beings!' but still she refused. She told him that if it was that important to him, he could go by himself, but apparently that was against the rules. Bonnie found it strange that a party with seemingly no respect for the rules society functioned on could be so prescriptive, but there we are, she thought, even anarchists have their own code. Seemingly, you had to come to the party as a couple, even if one of the couple didn't join in. 'You can't just have dirty old men turning up by themselves,' Steven said, completely oblivious to Bonnie's pointed look in response.

After all the above failed, at home he just pretended she wasn't there: filling the kettle with just enough water for one cup of coffee; taking just one portion of frozen haddock out of the freezer; turning the light off in the lounge while she was still in there, leaving her in the dark. His sulking lasted six weeks and five days, even over Christmas Day when he made a point of scraping his roast turkey into the bin and defrosting a frozen chicken kiev in the microwave. Florence had overcompensated for that, saying loudly how juicy the turkey was, how crunchy the potatoes, how clever of Bonnie to make both sage and onion stuffing and parsley and thyme. He'd refused to move his desk from the bay window for the Christmas tree to stand in the place it always had done since she was born, saying that he needed the natural light to write. He never wrote. So for the first time in twenty-two years the tree sat glumly in a corner, away from the window, looking wrong, while the desk stayed where it was, gathering dust.

On New Year's Eve, faced with the prospect of seeing in 1982 alone in front of the TV, Bonnie snapped and said to Steven, 'Fine, if it's that important to you, let's go to another damn party, but this time I'm bringing a book and we're home by midnight.'

The fact that she had relented, however reluctantly, was taken by Steven as acceptance, and even encouragement. The sound of the running tap in the bathroom ten minutes later, as the clock counted down to a new year, drowned out her sobbing, so he was none the wiser that she did care. She cared a lot. She couldn't understand why he'd want to fool around with any other woman when he'd picked her, but as was becoming more and more obvious, he hadn't picked *her*, he'd picked London, and her flat, and half her salary. He'd picked her life, but not *her*. She didn't even know whether he liked her very much; the signals were confusing. He would bring her a cup of tea when she was working, then call her a 'nerd', a 'geek', 'boring', 'dull'. He'd take the bins out, put the milk bottles on the doorstep before tenderly raising her nightie over her head under the bedcovers most nights, but then, he would also fly into rages that had her mother knocking on the door asking if 'everything is all right, darling?' He'd ignore her for days, making himself tinned soup for dinner and scraping what she'd prepared into the bin, while other nights declaring himself to be 'the luckiest man alive'. So while her heart was screaming at her not to do this, not to give in and be part of this, her head said that it was a sacrifice worth making.

In the week leading up to the party, Bonnie barely slept, and she carried with her a perpetual feeling of nausea. True to her word, when the night of the party rolled around, while all the other primates were upstairs picking nits off each other, Bonnie sat in an armchair downstairs in the lounge reading Salman Rushdie's Booker Prize-winning novel *Midnight's Children*, which was coincidentally hailed as a 'feast of sensations'. Even more brilliantly ironic was Oliver's book which he was reading on the sofa, another Booker Prize contender of 1981, called *The Comfort of Strangers.* They had a good laugh about that, whilst her husband and his wife were upstairs in Bedroom 3, which had Danger Mouse wallpaper and a set of bunk beds. When Steven and Janet came back downstairs giggling like children who'd eaten a whole bag of pick'n'mix, Bonnie and Oliver shared a look that was equal parts discomfort and disgust. Steven's tie was hanging out of his pocket, his shirt undone at the neck, and both their mouths looked like they'd been rubbed with a wire brush.

Bonnie slept upstairs with Florence that night. Florence didn't ask her why when she knocked on her door just after 1 a.m., she just silently put a new pillowcase on a pillow and squeezed her daughter's hand as they drifted off to sleep.

By April, possibly the fifth, if not the sixth party of this kind, Oliver had started bringing his own bottle of wine to share with Bonnie, preferring a nice Chablis to the tepid two-pounds-a-litre boxed wine the hosts invariably served at these gatherings, opting for alcohol content and price over taste and vintage. For her part, Bonnie started bringing her own snacks to share with him, delicate little morsels that travelled well in Tupperware: devils on horseback, brie and cranberry parcels, that sort of thing. It wasn't much, but it wasn't a dried-out defrosted sausage roll or a cheese and tinned pineapple hedgehog, which was the usual party fare which went untouched on the dining-room table. It was fair to say that Bonnie had actually started looking forward to these parties now (although possibly not as much as Steven and Janet). She cut recipes out of the women's magazines she now bought, put extra thought into the earrings she put in her ears, which scarf might work best with her outfit. Normally, she hated unnecessary fuss and earrings and scarves previously fell into that category but not any more. She'd also started cutting articles out of the paper which she thought Oliver might be interested in. Like her, he was a science graduate, but specialised in pharmaceuticals and currently worked in the local high-street pharmacy as the lead chemist. He loved the clipping she gave him about what a difference the new hepatitis B vaccine was going to make, and they had a really interesting discussion about the ongoing research into a drug to control cholesterol which was being tested in America.

They were deciding whether to open the second bottle of wine he'd brought with him, or whether he should go into the kitchen to put the kettle on, when Bonnie told him that as it was her birthday, they really should pop the cork.

Oliver's eyes widened, 'It's your birthday? Today?'

Bonnie shook her head, 'Tomorrow, but technically' – she looked at her wristwatch – 'it begins in twenty minutes, and even I would think I was boring if I ushered in my twenty-third year with a cup of tea in my hand.'

'In that case, give me ten minutes and I'll run to the shop on the corner and get a bottle of champagne,' Oliver started pulling on his coat.

'No, no, don't do that, stay here, this wine is fine.' She thought for a moment, 'Or, and this is very naughty, so don't judge me, but I'm sure I saw a bottle of Moët in the fridge when I went to put the chicken liver pâté back in there earlier.'

'Say no more.'

Oliver returned a couple of minutes later holding an opened bottle of cold champagne and two cut-glass crystal flutes.

'I do feel a bit bad about doing this,' Bonnie admitted, holding out her glass for him to top it up.

'I think, in the circumstances, in this setting, our loose morals are possibly forgivable. Now, may I be the first to wish you, Mrs Bonnie Morris, a very happy birthday.'

'Thank you very much, so far, being twenty-three is pretty good fun. Cheers.'

It was true, the first hour of it was, but then it started to go swiftly downhill after that.

'Is that our champagne?' a barefoot woman shrilled as she tucked her blouse back into her skirt from the doorway. 'We were saving that for the christening!'

'I'll pay for it,' Oliver said, standing up and reaching for his wallet in his back pocket.

'No, I will, it was my idea,' Bonnie interrupted, leaning down to pick up her handbag.

'You will not, it's your birthday!' Oliver took out a note and gave it to the woman, who was trying to look stern and affronted, her hands on her hips, but as her red lipstick had smudged around a two-inch radius of her mouth, it lessened the effect. She accepted the money regardless.

'It's your birthday?' Steven said, coming up behind the woman, moving her aside by her shoulders. 'You never said?'

'Shouldn't you know when your wife's birthday is?' Oliver said accusingly in a tone Bonnie had never heard him use before. She imagined that if he were ever mugged it would be the voice he would use.

Steven's eyes flashed, 'Who the hell are you?'

'Oliver Gillespie. I'm Bonnie's friend.'

'My wife doesn't have any friends. Come on, Bonnie, we're going.'

Bonnie mouthed 'Sorry' to Oliver, as she gathered up her things and followed Steven out onto the street, but not before he swiped a bottle of beer from the drinks table for the journey home.

The taxi ride was conducted in complete silence, but as soon as the green front door opened, Steven erupted, 'You made me look like a complete wanker!'

'*I* made *you* look like a wanker?' Bonnie laughed. 'And how exactly did I do that?'

'I bet everyone's still at the party now, thinking what sort of bloke spends his wife's birthday copping off with someone else?'

'Who indeed?'

He threw the empty beer bottle onto the tiled floor with such force, it shattered across the entire hallway, and Bonnie gasped as glass splinters fell on her feet. A giant crack now snaked down the centre of one of the 150-year-old Victorian tiles her mother had spent years on her hands and knees proudly scrubbing clean. Bonnie couldn't peel her eyes away from it, feeling a lump rise in her throat.

Steven followed her gaze downwards. 'Oh great,' he said, 'now I'm going to get the blame for that too. Honestly, you wind me up so much.' He stomped into the living room and poured himself a brandy from the decanter on the side and lit a cigarette, his hand shaking with fury. Bonnie still stood in the hallway, frozen to the spot in shock.

Upstairs behind her own front door, Florence stood with one hand on the handle, poised to fling it open and launch herself down the stairs.

Silence.

Hundreds of potential responses ran through Bonnie's mind. Cause and effect. Flight or fight. She could pour petrol or water on the flames. How she reacted could change everything. She thought of Florence upstairs, by herself, by no means an old woman, she was only turning forty soon, but she was alone. She'd tell him to get the hell out, Bonnie knew that. But then what? Steven wouldn't leave, this was now his home too. This house that had been a sanctuary to her mother for over twenty years, a place where Bonnie herself was conceived and born, the only home she'd ever known. He'd smash it up completely, until nothing was left but splinters from the floorboards she'd learned to crawl on.

She heard a familiar clunk as Steven put his shoes up on the coffee table, the smell of smoke snaking out into the hallway. It would set the smoke alarm off at the bottom of the stairs soon, which would bring Florence down, which would ignite the spark that once lit could never be undone. That decided it. Bonnie walked calmly back into the flat she shared with her husband, closed the door quietly behind her, opened the lounge window and went to get a dustpan and brush from the hall cupboard.

If there was a party the next week, then Bonnie and Steven didn't go to it. In fact, it was never mentioned. The broken floor tile was never spoken about either, and after a hasty run to the shops the next morning while Bonnie was having a birthday coffee upstairs with Florence – 'Yes, Mum, it was a great party . . . Yes, lots of fun, lovely start to my birthday . . . No, no trouble when we got in, must have been the cats outside you heard . . . Yes, such a nuisance. I'll call the council' – Steven even managed to make the rest of Bonnie's birthday as enjoyable as it could be. He conjured up fresh croissants, coffee, flowers, a card so hastily written the ink had smudged, and a plastic turquoise beaded necklace with matching clip-on earrings Bonnie knew she'd never wear, but proclaimed them 'lovely' nonetheless. A truce had been called: an unsaid agreement that life would go on.

'We should have Oliver and Janet round for dinner,' Steven said, apropos of nothing, one evening in May.

Bonnie stiffened. When she'd had a sore throat the week before, she'd deliberately gone to a different chemist's to avoid seeing Oliver, still so embarrassed at the altercation on her birthday. She thought that with the date of the next party coming and going without any reference that that chapter of their lives had closed. It was a shame in some ways.

She knew she had to tread carefully with Steven. 'Um, why would we do that?'

Steven shrugged, 'Well, I'm friends with Janet, you seem to get on well with Olly—'

'Oliver.'

He didn't hear her, 'And I thought it might be nice to get to know each other more, you know, have a proper chat over a nice dinner, you could do that lasagne thing you do, nice wine, might be fun.'

Bonnie shook her head, the idea of Oliver and Janet sitting here, in this kitchen, round her table, eating off her crockery and sitting on her sofa made her feel sick. 'I don't think they'd want to come,' she said weakly.

'Nonsense, Janet said they'd love to.'

'When did you speak to Janet?'

'Don't go getting your knickers in a twist, I just gave her a call and suggested it.'

Bonnie didn't even know he had their number. How often had he called her before this? 'You asked her before you'd talked to me about it?'

'I knew you'd say yes in the end.'

Bonnie crossed her arms on her chest and leaned back against the stove, 'Well, I'm not, Steven, I'm not saying yes, I don't want to do this. I have put up with so much this last year, but, honestly, I draw the line at anything like that happening in my own house, I couldn't bear it.'

'Anything like what? I'm suggesting we have another couple round for dinner, like most people do at weekends. There's nothing odd about that.'

'So no funny business at all?'

Steven rolled his eyes. 'No, Bonnie, no funny business. Just dinner.'

'Why wouldn't you want to do a bit of entertaining?' Florence asked her when Bonnie popped upstairs to borrow one of her mother's many cookbooks. 'Your flat is looking lovely now that you've spruced it up a bit and you're a fantastic cook.' Florence kicked off her flip-flops and climbed onto the kitchen counter to reach the books above the cupboards.

Bonnie could hardly tell her the truth, so just scratched her head and said, 'You know me, Mum, I just prefer a quiet life.'

'Everyone needs to let their hair down occasionally, love.'

Bonnie groaned. 'You sound just like Steven.'

'Well, do you like this couple? Here, take this Italian one, it has lovely desserts in.' Bonnie took the outstretched book from Florence and offered her hand for her mother to jump down.

Bonnie felt her cheeks flame, 'It's not that, I just, I don't know, I feel a bit funny about having people round, it's quite . . . intimate, you know.'

At the word 'intimate', Bonnie blushed even more furiously, frantically flipping the pages of the book to disguise her discomfort.

Florence smiled. Bonnie had always been a funny one.

On the day Oliver and Janet were due, Bonnie glanced around the house as if seeing it for the first time, through Oliver's eyes, not hers. She'd never noticed how threadbare the rusty brown carpet on the stairs was, nor how dated the plywood panelling in the living room seemed. Where would they sit? The painted rattan sofas surely qualified as the world's most uncomfortable things to sit on in the history of seating options, which is why she and Florence always used to sit on the floor, but the only other choice was the beanbag chairs, and that wasn't going to work at all. Seeing Janet's knickers as she got up from one would be the nail in the coffin of an evening that felt doomed before it even began.

At least the bathroom was fairly new. The salesman had corrected Bonnie when she'd called it green in the showroom. 'It's avocado,' he simpered, suddenly promoting it from ordinary to exotic. Bonnie really hoped they would need to use it while they were here. But she could hardly suggest everyone wash their hands before dinner, like you'd say to a group of muddy children fresh in from the park. She suddenly wished she'd spent the bathroom money on a new sofa now. Or a new dining table for the kitchen. She ran her hand over its scratched surface, they'd had this pine one since she was a child. It had marks all over it, including her own initials carved into the leg; she was such an obnoxious child. Thank God for tablecloths.

She looked at her watch. Half past five. They were due at seven. She was going to need some help if everything was going to be ready in time. Steven was nowhere to be seen, popping out mid-afternoon with a vague, 'just got to pick something up.'

'Are you serving the spinach dip in a bowl or a cut-out loaf?' Florence said ten minutes later over the blitzing noise of the Kenwood mixer she'd had longer than Bonnie. Thank God she'd been in when she'd run upstairs to ask for her help, Bonnie thought.

'Loaf. It's in the bread bin.'

They worked alongside each other in the kitchen amiably for the next hour, aided in no small part by sharing the sickly-sweet bottle of Mateus Rosé that was meant to be for dinner, and the sultry tones of Bob Marley and the Wailers drifting out from the record player.

'I do like reggae,' Florence said. 'My friend Nancy had a lovely boyfriend from St Lucia in 1964. He lived with us here for a while, do you remember?'

'I was four, so no.'

Florence smiled. 'Apparently he had a tattoo of a mermaid on his navel who was holding a fishing line that went all the way down to his—'

'Stop it, Mother. Stop it now. Right, I'm going to get dressed.'

Florence disappeared upstairs as soon as Steven came back smelling of The Coach and Horses, only five minutes before the doorbell rang. Bonnie placed the last napkin in the last wine glass, and replaced Bob Marley with a much more suitable Carole King on the turntable, which Steven promptly changed to The Clash.

Janet handed Bonnie a fuchsia-pink wrapped bouquet of chrysanthemums and flashed her a gleaming smile before also adding her coat into Bonnie's now full arms.

'Just go through,' Bonnie said, 'Steven's in the living room, to your right.'

'How are you?' Oliver said in a low voice to Bonnie as his wife strode on ahead, her heels clipping like a pony on the floorboards. Bonnie hung Janet's fur coat up on a hook in the hallway, over the top of her own anorak. 'I was a bit worried after the party.'

It had taken less than a minute for the parties to be mentioned, and it wrong-footed Bonnie completely. She mumbled something about needing to check on the soup, and she hurried off down the corridor into the kitchen. She'd spent the best part of four days planning this menu, disregarding Steven's suggestion of lasagne completely in favour of a three-course dinner. The starters were ready; the steaks for the Tournedos Rossini coming up to room temperature ready for grilling, the red wine sauce already made in another saucepan, and the tiramisu lay soaking in its own lovely booziness in the bottom of the fridge.

She'd splashed out on a new tablecloth and set of matching napkins with a scalloped edge to them and had lit candles that were dotted around the kitchen, dulling the bright turquoise of the kitchen cabinets they couldn't yet afford to replace. She gave it all a final once-over. It looked too romantic. She hastily blew out the candles on the worktops and windowsill and turned the bright white fluorescent strip ceiling light on instead. There. Much better.

Steven was on his A-game. He even deftly pulled out dining chairs for both Janet and Bonnie simultaneously, making him look more like a flamboyant matador than a suburban husband, and everything he did was to prove to whoever was watching that he really was absolutely brilliant.

An hour passed (and Bonnie knew it was an hour because her eyes kept flitting up to the clock on the wall, where the minutes were moving agonisingly slowly) and Janet had just told a deeply unfunny story about having gone to bed at 7.30 the night before because the light bulb in the lounge had gone out and Oliver was out working until 11 p.m. and she didn't want to sit in the dark all evening. Bonnie gave a tight smile at this and picked up the spinach dip inside the carved-out bread bowl and held it out to Janet, 'Don't hold back.'

'Not for me,' Janet said. 'I imagine there's rather a lot of calories in that.'

'I wouldn't know,' Bonnie said, ripping off a massive chunk of white bread and scooping a spadeful of creamy dip onto it, a little dripping onto her chin, 'life's a bit too short to worry about that sort of thing.'

'Janet does Callanetics,' Oliver said in way of explanation.

'Calla-what?' said Bonnie.

'Callanetics,' Janet replied, smiling with her teeth. 'It's a new type of muscle-toning exercise. From America. The body of your dreams is just a few hours away.'

'In Kent?' Bonnie replied innocently, taking another loaded shovel of dip. She knew that if she looked up, Steven's eyes would be boring a hole through her face, so once she finished chewing, she picked up her napkin and delicately patted around her mouth.

'So your mum lives upstairs Bonnie?' Oliver said.

'Yes. I've lived in this house since I was born, and when Steven and I got engaged, we converted it into two flats.'

'Steven said that your dad isn't alive any more?'

Bonnie took a moment before she answered, 'No. You'd have liked him though. He was a scientist as well.' Florence was always telling her how she got his brains.

'It was really funny,' Steven said, a little piece of spinach caught in between his two front teeth, 'when I told my parents I was moving in with a biochemist, they thought this was my way of saying that I was a poofter!'

There was Janet's high-pitched laugh again, 'Steven, you're so funny!'

'That's actually quite offensive,' Oliver said. 'To women and homosexuals.'

There was a strained silence.

'Are you planning on redecorating at all?' Janet asked, pointedly looking around the sixties kitchen, the Formica surfaces, open shelving and turquoise cabinets.

At the exact time Steven said, 'God yes, we're going to rip it all out,' Bonnie replied, 'Nothing's wrong with it.' She added, 'I mean, I've given it a lick of paint, freshened it up a bit. Perhaps a new carpet. I've just had the bathroom done,' she added a little too eagerly.

'And you'll need to get rid of that green front door as well,' Janet continued. 'Green's a very unlucky colour.'

Bonnie smiled brightly round the table. 'I was brought up to believe that you make your own luck.'

'I'll get these,' Steven said, clearing the table in record speed, while Bonnie was still eating, whipping her plate out from under her. 'How does everyone want their steak?'

'Well done please,' simpered Janet, making Bonnie hold her breath for Steven's familiar response of 'not really worth making it then if you're just going to ruin it by having it well done,' but instead he said, 'Coming right up.'

'How's work?' Oliver asked Bonnie, turning Bonnie's attention away from watching Steven pretend he knew where the frying pans were kept by opening every cupboard except the one they were actually kept in.

'Fine. Good actually.' Bonnie took a sip of the wine Oliver brought. 'We think we're getting really close to defining a genetic marker for Huntington's disease using DNA polymorphisms to map it.'

'That's incredible, if you can isolate that gene, that's setting an astonishing precedent for neutron recovery for all sorts of autosomal diseases.'

'I know! We're working on a theory that if we can identify chromosomal deletions or translocations by using chromosomal banding patterns, then we can establish links between specific genes and their corresponding chromosomes. The trials on mice should start in the next couple of months.'

'Just think of the disease-associated genes this could affect – how exciting!'

At some point during this conversation, without the two noticing, Janet had got up from the table and was helping Steven at the hob. Her 'helping' took the form of lightly touching his arm while telling him how clever he was for flipping the steak over at exactly the right moment.

Chromosomal chat ended when Steven and Janet rejoined the table, amid much fanfare and literal tooting of imaginary trumpets 'doo de doo' when the steak and red wine sauce, and Bonnie's carefully sliced roasted hasselback potatoes, were placed on the table.

'Bonnie, we are so lucky to have husbands who cook,' cooed Janet. 'Although even Oliver couldn't have pulled off a night like tonight all by himself, could you, darling?'

Bonnie looked across the table at Steven expectantly, waiting for him to correct Janet, to throw a soup-spoon-sized compliment her way. Something. The steak was only good because Bonnie had marinated it; hope you've all left room for my wife's spectacular dessert; the dip was home-made. Anything. But there was nothing.

'It's all really good,' Oliver said. 'Thank you so much, Bonnie.' He added, 'And Steven,' after a deliberate two-second pause.

'Just wait until you try Steven's tiramisu,' Bonnie said smiling. 'He's been working on it all afternoon.' The wine, and possibly the proximity to an ally were making her bold, 'What did you put in it again, Steven?'

Steven's eyes widened back at her, wondering why she was being so difficult. Tonight of all nights. He vaguely remembered seeing it in the bottom of the fridge when he went to get the mustard out. A big white thing in a bowl. 'Well, cream, obviously, and well, you'll just have to see if you can guess the rest,' he said triumphantly, pleased with his swift sidestep.

The four chairs, which Bonnie had set out earlier in the evening, had been equally spaced around the pine table at the start of the night, yet as the evening marched on, Janet's chair was so close to Steven's that another inch and she would have been sitting in his lap. Similarly, in order to hear each other over the David Bowie album belting out from the record player behind them, Bonnie had moved closer to Oliver, where he was sketching out his plans for the drop-in mobile clinic and pharmacy that he was planning to pitch to the council on a paper napkin. The first few times Janet let out one of her high-pitched squeals of laughter from the other side of the table at something Bonnie's hilarious husband was saying, Oliver's head snapped up, but as he got more engrossed in describing the plans to Bonnie, and answering her questions about it, he didn't seem to notice how raucous their spouses were being. Steven was now twirling Janet around the kitchen to The Clash's 'London Calling', picking a potato masher out of the utensil pot and strumming it like a guitar, giving Janet a spatula to sing into.

'We could go into the living room if you like,' Bonnie shouted to Oliver, who nodded his assent, topping up their glasses before following her out of the room.

'Didn't you say your mum lives upstairs?' said Oliver, lowering himself onto a beanbag. 'Won't she mind the noise?'

'She's working tonight. She's a nurse, so does shifts, and anyway, even if she was here, this is nothing compared to what we hear from her flat at all hours, she's a bit of a party animal.'

'Really?'

'You sound surprised.'

Oliver smiled, shaking his head, 'No, no, just you don't seem like that at all.'

'I'm not. I'm much more like my dad, he was quiet too. Apparently I'm the carbon copy of him.'

'I'm sorry I can't meet him, I think I'd rather like him.'

'I think you would too. And he'd definitely like you.'

'Would he like Steven?' Oliver saw Bonnie flinch and immediately apologised, 'Sorry, sorry, that was rude. I didn't mean that the way it came out, I just meant that we're always subconsciously seeking our parents' approval, aren't we, and it's so much harder when they're not around to give it. My mum died when I was fifteen, and I often wonder what she would have made of Janet, whether they'd have been friends or not.' He let out a deep sigh, crossing his legs, 'And, in all honesty, I don't think they would. I think she'd tell me that I was a complete fool.'

Bonnie nodded, 'I know what you mean. I think that too sometimes, I imagine Dad hearing how Steven talks to me, or seeing me at those bloody parties, reading my book downstairs with you, and he's just shaking his head at me at what I put up with.'

'So why do we?'

'Because we think that this can't last? That they'll grow up soon and start being more sensible and, well, niccr?'

'Janet's nice. Most of the time.'

'Yes, of course. Steven too, absolutely.'

Oliver let out a long sigh. 'Actually, you know what, Bonnie, she's really not, she treats me like a complete doormat, thinks I'm boring and wet and ruining her life by just existing.'

'Steven thinks I ruin all his fun.'

'Janet says I'm more like a pensioner than a twenty-six-year-old.'

'Steven only married me for my house.'

'I'm sure that's not true.'

'It is. And the irony is, he spends most of the time finding fault with it. The floorboards are creaky, the windows too draughty, the water pipes noisy.'

'I think it's lovely, Bon,' Oliver said, looking round him. 'Really lovely.'

A moment's silence. 'I think *you're* lovely,' Bonnie said.

Oliver's gaze settled on Bonnie, who instead of feeling embarrassed felt emboldened and completely sure of what she was about to do. Leaning forward, she moved closer to him until her mouth met his, softly at first, her heart beating so fast and loud inside her chest. His hand snaked up to the back of her head, pulling her closer into him. She felt a stirring inside her which she'd never felt before and just allowed her brain to switch off from everything except this kiss, this glorious, delicious kiss.

'Bloody hell,' came a slurred shout from the doorway, breaking Bonnie and Oliver apart. 'Janet, come and look at this! My wife and your husband are only bloody swingers! If you can't beat 'em, join 'em, eh?'

15

Stella

Nothing exciting ever happens in this house. Nothing against Mum and Florence, but some houses just have that aura about them, don't they? Solid, square boxes of normality. The seconds last minutes, minutes last hours, hours last days, and I swear this two-week wait has now been going on for about four and a half months. I'm becoming a little bit claustrophobic in here – it feels like I spend all my time with Mum and Florence, even though they both have their own lives. Florence is busier than God; at the last count, she had fifteen different social and sports clubs on the go, while Mum still contributes to scientific journals and speaks at conferences and taps on her laptop late into the night looking at comparison sites for cheaper home contents insurance or whatever it is she is doing. Meanwhile, the house's walls are slowly closing in on me.

Speaking of walls, as well as repapering my old bedroom, I've also taken it upon myself to give the rest of the house a bit of a spruce. Florence and Mum have lived in it for so long, they no longer hear the creaky eleventh stair, or the whistling pipes, or see the cracked floor tile in the hallway, or the wall in the kitchen with uneven plaster where some has chipped off, goodness knows how. I'm no plumber or plasterer, but I definitely can't sit here staring at cracked ceiling roses any more. Plus a trip to the hardware store would absolutely take my mind off the fact that I'm doing the conclusive pregnancy test tomorrow.

'I'm sorry, but do you mind carrying my shopping to the car? I'm pregnant, you see,' I flash a winning smile at the man in B&Q and try to stick out my stomach as far as it will go, which, bearing in mind the embryo is still invisible to the naked eye, isn't very far. 'The paint's really heavy.'

'Of course, love.'

'It's for the nursery,' I add, pretending he asked, as we cross the car park . . . 'For the baby.'

'Great.'

'I've gone for Golden Honey in the end. I really liked one colour, but then saw that it was called Dead Salmon, and you can't really paint a baby's room a colour called Dead Salmon, can you?'

The man doesn't appear to have an opinion either way on this, but I'm not letting him off that easily. Speaking to anyone that isn't Mum or Florence is such a novelty.

'There was one called Newborn Baby,' I continue, 'but it was pink, which would have been perfect if it's a girl, and I'd be fine about having it for a boy too, but I can already guess what my mum would say about that, she's pretty conservative, is my mum.'

'Hmmm.'

'I saw another one called Three Legs! Now if I asked you to hazard a guess what colour a paint called Three Legs was, what would you say?'

The man shrugs and looks longingly back at the safety of the superstore, whose electric doors are tantalisingly teasing him by opening and shutting of their own accord.

'Go on, guess,' I prompt, smiling.

'Purply brown.'

'Oh, yes, you're right. You must have cheated though, you do work here, so you must have seen it before.'

'Nah, lucky guess.'

I reach up to close the boot, 'I'd have said more of a greeny blue, or, and you're going to think I'm mad here, maybe a taupe.' I slam the boot down before I realise that the man has already hotfooted it back across the car park and is speed-walking through the electric doors back into the store.

No one's at home when I get back, so I leave the paint in the car. The calendar shows that Florence is at her photography class, and it's Mum's afternoon volunteering at the local Amnesty International Bookshop, which she says she does for the cause, but she also gets half-price books, and considering the average price is 50p, we have heaving shelves of 25p books in every room now.

I'm not really a fan of silence. I'm much more like Florence than Mum in that way. And Dad, apparently, who couldn't bear a room without life in it. 'He was always dragging your mum to parties,' Florence told me once when I'd asked her what he was like, knowing that if I had asked Mum the same question, she'd wave the question away. 'Life and soul of them,' Florence added. 'He'd get all dressed up, slick back his hair, I could smell the aftershave up in my flat he put so much on, and they wouldn't come back sometimes 'till the early hours. I'm not sure your mum liked them at first; she even went to one in trousers. I wouldn't have said anything to her, none of my business what someone else is wearing, but I remember your dad saying to her that she was a bit casual, but she didn't care, she's never been one for show, but he was. He was like one of those prize ponies with their mane plaited just waiting for a rosette to be pinned to him.'

Remembering this makes me think of Donor 203. Does he like parties? Half Dutch, half Cornish: a pretty laid-back combination of cultures, so in all likelihood he wouldn't be a social butterfly. If he's not surfing, he's probably cycling (his quads must be rock hard). Good job we haven't actually met in person, he'd think I was an absolute slob. I picture the blind date we might have had if we'd matched on Tinder, him reeling off his hobbies, and me telling him that I collect streaming subscriptions. He'd order a salad and something exotic with high nutritional value, like quinoa or bulgur wheat, and I'd have the pasta carbonara with extra cheese. He'd say a quick 'no thanks' if the waiter asked if we'd like to see the dessert menu, and I'd say that it wouldn't hurt to look.

Was I right in picking someone so opposite to me? I know he's not going to have a direct hand in raising our baby, but it will be half him. What if I have nothing in common with my child? What if it innately has all his traits and none of mine? What if the baby only wants to eat chips with mayonnaise and not ketchup (that's what they do in Holland). That's if the child will want to eat chips at all, being so sporty and aware of body mass indexes like their dad.

I wonder if Donor 203's parents know that their son's a donor? It's odd to think that my child could be standing next to their paternal grandparents in a sandwich shop on a summer holiday in Padstow, touching shoulders, neither side having any idea they're grandparent and grandchild. Besides, there might be half-siblings my child won't ever meet. If Donor 203 can be used by ten different families, then chances are I'm not the only one to have plumped for Mr Gymkhana.

I'm from a long line of only children; both Mum and Dad were, Florence was by default after her brother Stu died, and it is lonely sometimes, being the littlest adult in every room. I don't want this child to be lonely. The agency did say that many women choose to have a sibling from the same donor, so their children are complete siblings, which would be an option. I have got a frozen embryo I could use at some point in the future. Oh my God, look at me thinking about a second, when I'm only thirteen days pregnant with the first. Steady on Stella.

Speaking of pregnancy, no one has ever been pregnant before. I mean, obviously I know they have, but not like me. I'm also aware that I'm driving everyone insane. Even if I can't see them, I can sense their twitching mouths and eye rolls when I say something like, 'I can't have tuna mayonnaise sandwiches, it's the mercury and the raw eggs.' Even though it's Helman's and I'm pretty sure it hasn't got raw eggs in. Or, 'I can't have tea; it lowers my folic acid count. Oh, and we need to start listening to more classical music, it's good for brain development.' I don't even recognise myself these days. Even Kate says that I'm the most annoying pregnant person ever when I phone her to ask if it's true that if I look at ugly animals for too long my baby will look like them, because I watched an hour-long documentary on Golden snub-nosed monkeys without thinking and then couldn't sleep from worrying.

Maybe Florence is right; time does go quicker when you're not alone. This afternoon by myself is dragging indeterminably. I tidy up the living room; stack the magazines and books in neat piles; align the coffee table with the geometric lines of the rug under it and straighten the cushions on the sofa. I resist the urge to sink down on it, I'll never get up, it's the opposite to that hard-backed monstrosity of a settee we had growing up, which was so uncomfortable we had to sit on the floor. Which was also ridiculously uncomfortable because we didn't have carpet. God, the eighties were rough.

I wander into the dining room, which used to be Mum and Dad's bedroom when the house was divided into two flats. It's sometimes easy to imagine my dad here, and at other times incredibly hard to conjure up the silhouette of a man in this space, which seems by default so intrinsically female. Which way would the bed have gone? Leading down from the wall towards the fireplace, or facing the window towards the garden? I imagine him opening the wardrobe, which would have been here, in this alcove, getting a shirt out, probably ironed by Mum, getting dressed in front of its mirrored door. Did he like mornings? Mum does, she's always the first up. Did she have to shake him awake, or did he join her for a post-dawn walk around the block and a breakfast for two, or did he pour himself a cup of coffee from the Teasmade on his bedside cabinet because the fifteen paces between the bedroom and the kitchen next door was just too much?

I can understand why Mum's never told me any of this, never painted a picture of who he was. He left us both with no forwarding address, so of course she's not going to spend the next four decades talking about him. It was probably self-preservation. Mum's not like Florence, with armfuls of love to give anyone who looks like they want or need it. Mum loves rarely, but deeply. For all I know, she's still mourning Steven now, which is why she shuts down any hint of anyone else and won't talk about him. My child will know more about their dad from his 250-word donor profile than I know about mine.

The dining table's a mess. Florence has commandeered it as her workspace for whatever is occupying her at the time, so photography books with lurid pink and orange Post-it notes sticking out of them are balanced on a *Learn French in 30 Days* book and CD, two cookbooks, the manual for a new foot spa, and three reminders from the library to return overdue books. I'm about to leave it all exactly how I found it, when a flash of turquoise catches my eye. It's the notebook I bought Mum.

I shouldn't look. It's private. But it's for my child. And the child is in me. So if I read it, my brain will impart the knowledge to the baby, thereby carrying out the purpose of the book. Now, admittedly, in all my embryonic research, mother-to-baby knowledge transmission has never come up, but there is so much science just doesn't know yet.

I pull out a dining chair, and begin to read.

And one day, we might celebrate your birthday in the same room too. I only knew the sound of laughter growing up in this house. Which is, I suppose, all you could ask for. And it's all I want for you.

I don't know at what point during reading the entry I started to cry, but tears are now falling freely down my cheeks. It is more than just wanting to avoid dying alone and lonely, it is more than wanting to leave a legacy, it is about adding to the memories in this house. Of replicating the love and laughter I had, Mum had, Florence had. I will hand my child the tools myself to engrave their initials next to Mum's and mine in the legs of the kitchen table. I will studiously mark their height each year on their birthday on the kitchen door frame alongside ours, exclaiming with delight, 'Oh look, you're taller than I was at seven' (thanks, Donor 203 for your ceiling-skimming height). I will bake their birthday cakes in the same kitchen mine were made in, carry them up the same stairs, avoiding the creaking eleventh step, that I was carried up, that Florence and Henry carried Mum up. This house will wrap its welcoming walls around another new baby, and keep us all safe.

16

Florence

Dear Little One,

We are all so incredibly excited about your arrival in nine months' time. A new life brings with it so much joy. You should know just how much your mum has yearned for you, much more than I did for Bonnie, or Bonnie did for Stella. That's not to say that we weren't thrilled to be pregnant, but we did it because it seemed the natural order of life, not because we couldn't imagine our lives going on for one more minute without a child in it.

As soon as Henry and I started seeing more of each other, going on more walks, going to a few more dances, dinner dates, the pictures, the expectation was that we'd get married and children would soon follow and so it did. We had a wonderful wedding, at a local church, and shared the cost of decorating it with flowers with two other couples who were getting married the same day. At the end of every pew were little bouquets of lily of the valley and white carnations. We sang 'Lord of the Dance' and 'Sing Hosanna' and I honestly thought I would burst with happiness. My mother wore a navy suit with a pale blue trim and her hat was so wide, it's a wonder she could get through the church door. My father gave me away and you couldn't have found a prouder man in the whole of England, except maybe the man I was marrying.

Someone Henry worked with gave us the address of a boarding house, this house, where I'm writing this letter to you, and we moved in straight after we came back from a week in Cornwall where we had our honeymoon. I remember looking at the address on the little piece of paper, on our way here, thinking that this house, which I hadn't even seen yet, was going to be our first home. Henry tried to carry me over the doorstep, through the green door, but I wouldn't let him, but that's how we entered this house for the first time, laughing like the children we were.

Laughter wasn't really a sound I was used to hearing, if I'm honest with you. When a house lives through death, it changes, and after Stu's illness, the sounds of my childhood home in Alderton Drive were of objects in the house, not of people. Pots clanging together, taps being run, the television, when we got one, being on. That was a turning point, the day my father came home with the Radio Rentals TV, because then there were human voices in the house again. It didn't matter that they were coming from a little box in the corner and not from any of the three people who lived there, suddenly there was talking, and laughing, and occasionally singing, too, which was just brilliant.

So it was a massive shock moving straight in here, where every room had a different lodger in it, apart from the kitchen and living room, which were communal spaces. Henry was the first man to board here. Martha, the landlady, had always preferred to rent rooms to women, but he won her over immediately with his warm smile and his promise to fix anything and everything that would go wrong. The list she gave him went on for pages, but he never moaned about it.

We didn't have those fancy pregnancy tests when I found out I was expecting your grandmother Bonnie, we had to go to the doctor, who prodded our stomachs a bit and then told us. Men weren't allowed in with us either, babies were women's business, apart from the doctors, who were all men. Henry was so happy though, I think he had a smile plastered on his face for the whole nine months! We were young parents, but we were ready for it in our own ways. He made such a fuss of me as well when I was pregnant, everyone did really, always making sure I was drinking enough water and milk, that I was eating regularly, I felt like a right pampered princess!

As I grew bigger with Bonnie, I'd sit on the settee watching the other women in the house dance around to Chuck Berry records in the evenings, 'Roll over Beethoven' and 'Johnny B. Goode', swinging each other around the room, under each other's arms. I couldn't join in of course, Henry tutted if I so much as swept the kitchen floor, but I'd happily sit there tapping my toes and insisting that Henry do the gentlemanly thing and twirl each of them round and round until everyone's sides were splitting with laughter.

I saw Chuck Berry in concert in London, at Shepherd's Bush in 1972, and when Chuck started singing, 'You Never Can Tell', well, the crowd went wild and I stood still, in the middle of all the clapping and screaming, just listening to the lyrics, thinking of Henry and smiling.

'*It was a teenage wedding and the old folks wished them well . . . C'est le vie, say the old folks, it goes to show you never can tell.*'

17

Florence

Sixty years earlier . . .

It was Hazel's day off, and she seemed the only person in the world that might be able to make sense of this, so Florence hurried to her friend's house, just a few streets away from her own. Hazel's mother, Mrs Taylor, ushered Florence in with a wide smile, the same way she had for over a decade, telling her off for muddy shoes, asking after her parents, checking if she was hungry before saying, 'Hazel's upstairs, love, go on up.'

Hazel's bedroom was at the back of the house, next to the bathroom. Tiny blue forget-me-nots covered every inch of the wallpaper, floor to ceiling, while pink curtains matched the frilled bed covering Hazel was lounging on, reading a copy of *Jackie* magazine. 'Stupid Cupid' was playing on the record player.

Florence sat down on the bed next to her friend and nodded at the magazine, saying sadly, 'Is there anything in there to explain how on earth I might be pregnant?'

After the initial open-mouthed shock had worn off, Hazel was just as mystified as Florence was. She had a little bit more information as she'd recently managed to read a Harold Robbins novel of her mother's. 'Look,' Hazel said, unearthing it from under her bed and flicking through it until she got to the passage she was looking for. '*All these last months I was longing for you to take me – I wanted your child inside me under my heart.*'

Florence looked confused, 'Where did he take her?'

'I don't know,' Hazel tried flicking back through the book to find out, but she couldn't spot any other clues. 'Also, I thought babies grew in your stomach, not under your heart?'

Florence lay back on Hazel's bed. 'My parents are going to kill me.'

'But you're getting married soon, no one bats an eyelid at this happening to married women.'

'But what if the baby isn't Henry's?' Florence said, voicing out loud the nagging worry gnawing at her. She still didn't know exactly how this baby had been made, but she and Henry had only held hands and kissed on the cheek, which seemed an impossible precursor to pregnancy.

'But who else's could it be?'

Florence refused to meet her friend's eyes. 'Kenny's.'

'The mechanic? From months ago? You said you didn't do anything with him.'

'We didn't, well, not really . . . On the last night we saw each other, we were walking to the bus stop and it started to rain and we sheltered down an alleyway—'

'Oh good God, Florence!'

'No, it's not what you think, we had a bit of a kiss and a cuddle, but we were standing up the whole time, and I definitely didn't see his thing anywhere near me.'

'It must have happened then,' Hazel pronounced.

'But we were fully dressed! And standing up!'

Hazel shook her head, 'Look, I don't know any more than you do, but it sounds like it's Kenny that's done it.'

'But he's married!' Florence wailed.

'What?' Hazel's eyes were as wide as saucers. 'He's married?'

Florence covered her face with her hands, 'I didn't tell you because I didn't want you to think badly of me, I didn't know when I was seeing him, I swear to you I didn't, but his wife was waiting for me one day after work, with their child—'

'He has a child!' Hazel squealed.

'Ssshh, keep your voice down!' Florence darted her eyes towards the shut bedroom door. 'I promise I had no idea. Anyway, I'd already started seeing Henry by then, so I had no intention of ever seeing Kenny again.'

'What a mess,' Hazel sighed.

'You're telling me.'

'I think the most important thing is we have to keep it to ourselves while we work out what to do.'

It cheered Florence to hear Hazel use the word 'we', it made her feel less alone, but this moment of optimism was short-lived as Mrs Taylor rapped loudly on the door and shouted through the wood, 'Time to go now, Florence, your mother called and wants you home.'

The sound of Mrs Weston's weeping reached Florence before her key was in the lock. For a moment, Florence hoped someone had died, before silently reprimanding herself.

If Florence thought the volume was loud from the hallway, it was nothing compared to the noise her mother made when she actually clapped eyes on her daughter. Mr Weston was standing up behind his wife's armchair, one hand on her shoulder, the other holding a lit Woodbine. It looked like the scene of a Victorian portrait sitting, were it not for Mrs Weston's anguished wails and frantic handkerchief dabbing.

'Mrs Taylor just telephoned us. She heard you and Hazel talking. We know everything,' her father said coldly. 'You disgust us.'

'Oh, I—'

'There is nothing you can say to make this any more palatable. Just look at what you've done to your mother. What can you possibly have to say for yourself?'

Shock and shame pulsed through Florence, 'Well, I honestly—'

'We are not interested in any of your excuses.'

'But you just asked me —'

'How dare you answer back!'

Dorothy flung her head back on the headrest of the armchair and gave an anguished howl that Florence had only heard once before when a wild fox had got caught in the barbed wire at the back of their garden.

'Go upstairs now, and don't come out until I say so,' her father ordered.

When time ticked into the fifth hour of her confinement, Florence started to wonder if her punishment was actually death by starvation. In the time that she'd been in her room, the telephone had rung five times, the doorbell had gone three times, and there had only been a twenty-minute pause in her mother's sobbing, when, Florence assumed, she stopped to eat something. No one had thought of giving Florence anything so much as a glass of water, and although she didn't recognise the tone of white-hot rage in her father's voice, she thought it best to do as he said and stay out of sight.

It was starting to go dark outside. The road was filling up with husbands' cars back from work. Florence sat by the window for a bit next to her dressing table, watching each house as its front door opened, hats and coats hung up just inside, aproned wives visible in some, small children in others. The same story repeated in each one. Except theirs tonight.

Florence's stomach was growling, she hadn't eaten since breakfast and she was beginning to feel nauseous and faint, but she didn't dare go downstairs.

The door knocker sounded, echoing up the stairs, followed by low voices in the hall. Florence couldn't pick out who the visitor was, but whoever it was was being shown into the front room. A minute or so later, footsteps on the stairs made her sit up on the bed.

'Come downstairs,' her mother ordered from the doorway, as though stepping into the same air space would contaminate her.

Florence followed her obediently, matching her footstep for footstep down the stairs and across the hallway to the sitting room. She saw her father first, standing up by the fireplace, and in the high-backed armchair on the other side of the mantle sat an ashen-faced Henry, clasping his hands tightly together in his lap, as if in prayer.

Florence's blood drained out of her face.

Her father took a deep intake of breath. 'I've asked Henry to come here today so that we can sort this sorry mess out now, before anyone else hears of it. To say that we are disappointed that you couldn't wait until the wedding to do what you have both done is a gross understatement. It goes against every moral we have tried to instil in you, Florence, but the facts are the facts, and we can't change them now. I have called Father Philips and he will conduct a wedding ceremony tomorrow, so that, to everyone else, it will appear that the child is early when it is born, and if there's talk, as I'm sure there will be, then you will just have to weather it.'

Florence hadn't taken her eyes off Henry, who first seemed engrossed in the carpet, then his shoes, before eventually feeling the pull of Florence's gaze too much to resist, he met her stare.

'What time is the ceremony?' Henry asked, making Florence's mouth fly open in surprise.

'Henry, no,' she said, 'you don't need to do this.'

'Of course he needs to do this!' her father roared. 'It is exactly what he should do, considering the situation he has put you in.'

Henry gave her a tiny, blink and you'd miss it, shake of the head, telling her that he wanted to, that she shouldn't say any more. That he was prepared to swoop in and make everything better. That she should just stay mute and let him take the blame. It would be so easy for her just to nod and let the tidal wave carry her away, but this wasn't his mess to clean up. She'd always relied on other people to chart the course of her life for her, but suddenly she knew that the time had come to make her first decision completely, and terrifyingly, on her own.

'He doesn't need to,' Florence said firmly, ignoring the slight tremble in her voice as she spoke, 'because it's not his baby.'

The next few minutes passed in a blur. Henry stood up. Her mother fell down. Florence's scalp burned from where her mother had lunged for her, grabbing a fistful of her hair before dropping to her knees in agony. Her father used words she'd never heard before, which had Henry blushing from the roots of his hair down the back of his neck. He kept trying to interject, to calm things down, 'Mr Weston, please', 'Mr Weston, just listen', 'Mr Weston, if I could just—'

'Henry, just go,' Florence begged, the humiliation of her confession, followed by this horrific display of animalistic rage by her parents just meant that she wanted him as far away from here as possible. 'Please.'

'I can't leave you, not like this. I'll go through with it, Florence, I will. Tomorrow, I'll marry you.'

Florence shook her head sadly, 'I can't let you do that, Henry.'

'Think about it please. I'll be at the church waiting for you tomorrow. We'll never mention this again. It will be my child. I'll never think of it as anything but mine, I promise. Please. I love you, Florence.'

Florence pulled the small emerald off her finger and held it out to Henry, tears falling down her face, 'Please, Henry, just go.'

'No,' he said adamantly, 'I'm not taking it back.'

'Henry, I can't keep it. It's yours, to give to someone else, someone lucky enough to marry you.'

He brushed past her to the front door, leaving her hand with the ring still in it outstretched in the air.

The next day, the time of the ceremony came and went and Florence didn't leave her room. Her pillow was wet through with the deliberations over what to do. If she had only turned down Kenny Buck's invitation to go out for a drink, or got a different bus to work that day and never even met him she'd be planning her wedding to Henry with no worries in the world. But she couldn't marry him like this. She saw the disappointment in his eyes last night as he saw her for who she really was and she couldn't bear to marry him now and feel that weight of disappointment every day for the rest of her life. He deserved so much better. She must have fallen asleep that night at some point, because she woke up to her mother, pale and weary, opening her curtains and putting a suitcase at the end of her bed on her feet. 'Pack some things.'

'But where am I going?'

'You'll need a few nightclothes, your dressing gown, a towel, your toilet bag and some changes of clothes. We leave in half an hour.'

'But, Mum—'

'I am not your mother, Florence, until you have this . . .' Mrs Weston faltered and looked heavenward as if to get strength, 'this situation sorted out. Then we will see.' She turned to leave.

'But what do you mean sorted out? Where am I going?'

The door clicked shut behind her and Florence was left alone. She looked around her room, what could she take to a place she didn't know, for a length of time that was unclear? She'd only spent a few days away from this house, with cousins in Norfolk each summer, but she didn't think she was going there, her mother would have said.

She quickly packed the items her mother had listed, adding in a couple of her favourite books, a charm bracelet Hazel had given her for her sixteenth the year before, and as a last-minute decision, her stuffed teddy bear, which was imaginatively called Bear. It had moved from her bed to a shelf a couple of years before, and she didn't know why she grabbed it, squashing it down at the top of her case until she arrived where she was going and was beyond pleased that she had.

The car journey took almost two hours through the streets of London. Florence stared at the back of her parents' heads in silence the whole time. Her mother, exhausted from showing more emotion in the last twenty-four hours than in the last forty-four years, sat statue-still, her handbag on her lap, her hat an inch away from touching the roof of the car. It was only Mr Weston's white knuckles as he gripped the steering wheel that gave away his true feelings. He didn't look in the rear-view mirror at his daughter once, even though she barely took her eyes off him.

The pristine white facades of the houses of Queensway and Maida Vale gave way to the loud streets of King's Cross, and eventually the stacked grey terraces of Bethnal Green and Bow. Adverts on the sides of buildings were for tobacco brands; gone were the big department stores and canopied restaurants with pavement chairs and tables, and in their place stood pubs with Union Jacks draped on them, cafes called things like 'Dino's Caff' and blood-splashed butchers standing in once-white aprons in doorways. Florence shrank back as far as she could in the rear leather-look seat of her father's blue Rover.

There was no point asking any more questions, Florence had guessed where she was being taken. Not the exact name, or location, but the type of place. And she knew she'd in all likelihood be leaving it alone in just over five months' time.

She knew they were close to their destination when her mother swivelled round in her seat and said, 'Put this on,' taking off her glove, then her wedding ring and holding it over her shoulder to Florence. 'If anyone asks, he's serving in Malaya.'

Florence knew better than to argue, and slipped the ring on her finger. It was too loose. She felt in her pocket and pulled out Henry's emerald ring. She was hoping where they were going might be near his lodgings, and she could insist on returning it to him, but for now, it would help keep the wedding ring on her finger, and further cement the existence of a husband away in the tropics fighting for his country.

Mr and Mrs Weston didn't get out of the car when it pulled up outside the large grey building, nor did the woman looking out of the window waiting for them to arrive expect them to. The parents never did.

18
Stella

Sitting on the edge of the bath upstairs, holding the stick in my hand, I find myself chanting 'two lines good, one line bad' like I'm a brainwashed inhabitant of Animal Farm. The thought of the farm takes me back down a rabbit hole of how lovely it would be for my child to have a pony and a paddock, and a puppy, but, to be honest, I'd settle for none of those things, and just a heartbeat.

I have, of course, completely ignored my consultant's advice, like I knew I would the second my brain heard it, and I have done ten tests over the last week: one each morning (stronger wee) and one each evening (more hours have passed since morning) and all of them were negative. Even when I held them up to the light (natural and artificial) and tilted them at varying degrees. I'd done some in the downstairs toilet, and here, in the upstairs one too, just in case one bathroom was luckier than the other. But this is the magical fourteenth day. The fourteen days I was supposed to wait. The day my baby is going to miraculously show itself, giving a little wave in the form of a double pink line in the little window of the white stick.

I spoke to Mum the other day about love making your heart race, and butterflies flapping around in your stomach, but that was nothing compared to this; I've got a whole menagerie going on inside me.

I look at my watch. Another minute to go.

A soft tap on the door. 'Any news, darling?' Florence asks through the wood.

I get up and open the door, 'Thirty-two seconds to go.'

'Would you like company for those thirty-two seconds?'

'Twenty-four now,' I say, my eyes trained on my wrist.

'Twenty-four then.'

'Nineteen now.'

'Nineteen then.'

'Sixteen now.'

'Time goes faster when you're not alone.'

And then that's it, two minutes. I cover my face with my hands, 'You look, Flo, I can't.'

'So what do we want to see? I never did one of these when I was having your mum.'

'Two lines in the same box. Parallel lines. Like pink train tracks.'

Florence picks up the stick and squints at it. 'Hang on, I need my glasses.'

'For Christ's sake, woman, are there two lines?'

Florence puts her glasses on from where they were hanging around her neck and peers at it again. 'No, just the one.'

'There can't be,' I grab the test from her. 'It's the fourteenth day!'

'I'm sure it'll show up tomorrow,' Florence says like my baby is a parcel that was held up at the depot and rearranged for next-day delivery.

I take it to the window and hold it up. Then switch the flashlight on my phone on and direct it at the very definite single line.

'Darling, I'm so sorry, but there was always going to be a seventy-one per cent chance that it wouldn't work,' Mum says helpfully from the doorway.

'If you don't have anything useful to contribute, I'd rather you didn't,' I snap.

'I think Mum means—'

'No, Flo, don't stick up for her.' I round on Mum, still in the doorway to the bathroom, 'Would it kill you to be just a little bit supportive, and maybe not shout statistics of failure in my face?'

'I wasn't shouting, and I was just saying, that it was always going to be a long shot on the first go, you knew that. That's why I kept saying to not get carried away with the idea of success, then this wouldn't be such a big blow.'

'Right, yes, absolutely, let's all live our lives expecting the worst and then be pleasantly surprised when something more passable happens, shall we?'

Mum blinks in quick succession.

'Anyway,' I add, in a softer tone, 'just because the test is negative doesn't mean it hasn't worked, just that the hormones aren't showing up yet.'

'But by day fourteen—'

I hold my hands up to stop her from finishing the sentence, because I know. I know what she's about to say, and I don't need it. 'No. No. Just stop. Just let me have this, OK?'

'OK.'

I've got to get out. I've got to leave the house and get some air. Despite it being a Wednesday morning just a few minutes after nine, the park across the road is full, probably with people having just dropped off their older kids at the infant and junior school round the corner. I have to move out of the way of buggies and prams and drunk toddlers weaving across the path so many times I lose count. Groups of women laugh, coffee cups in hand, nappy bags on the back of prams, watching their kids ignore each other in the sandpit or idly pushing the swings with one hand, while the other checks their phone. Some sit under trees, some on blankets with thermos flasks: a planned coffee in the park. Others lounge on the grass: an impromptu pit stop. No one else feels the same disappointment as me this morning. None of these people woke up with the same sense of excitement as I did, booking the day off work to spend the day celebrating. Bounding out of bed with an anticipation of how extraordinary the future is going to be only to have their whole world fold in on itself like a melting ice-cream cone. Look at them all. Not a single care in the world.

'You're so lucky.'

The woman's voice takes me by surprise, and I look up, a little startled. A woman around my age, maybe a little younger is standing, hip thrust out to one side to provide a nice shelf for an ice-cream-covered toddler to relax on, while a newborn is attached to her front with an intricate-looking wrap contraption. She reminds me of one of those donkeys that scale the Nepalese mountain ranges laden with luggage.

My face must look as blank as I feel because she follows that up with, 'I'd give anything to sit on a bench in a park by myself for five minutes,' she laughs, 'or just be able to go to the loo without spectators.'

I smile along with her because, well, you have to really, don't you? I don't want her to tell her husband later on as they peruse the Vietnamese food delivery menu that she was 'only trying to make conversation with the lady on the bench, there was no need to use that type of language'. So I nod and smile, and say that it certainly looks like she's got her hands full, to which she nods and says, 'Not half!' I don't ask her the kids' names or their ages, even though she looks like she's poised to tell me anyway, because it's what I'm meant to say next. But it's not going to alter my life, is it? Knowing that Thomas is two and Esme is four months, but they're both very big for their age. Just like it's not going to alter hers if I tell her that an hour ago I thought I was pregnant, and now I'm not, and I've just wasted £6,000 chasing a dream which I should have known would fail because life's like that. Nothing I plan works out. So instead I look at my watch, make a fake gasp of surprise and say that it was lovely talking to her, but I really have to head back.

As I turn back towards the house, I glimpse Mum in the top window, looking out at me. She ducks behind the curtain when she sees me looking. Her heart's in the right place, I know that. I can't expect her to change her personality and be all glowing with optimism when she's spent her life dealing with statistics and hypotheses. Every day of her career, she has done research and experiments based on success rates, on probability, this is what she knows; what's ingrained in her. I need to give her a break. But also, she needs to recognise that where she sees statistics, I see hope. And surely, there's still some hope.

My period comes at around seven that night. No fanfare, no *EastEnders*-style duf-dufs, no melancholic orchestral music, just an ordinary monthly period, coming on the wrong day at the wrong time. I left the Tampax box on the side of the basin in the bathroom and only remember when I hear someone open the top drawer in the vanity and gently place it back inside. A few minutes later, I hear the front door shut.

At eight, whoever left comes back, evidently from the corner shop with a clinking carrier bag. A few seconds later, a knock on my door.

'I'm really sorry,' Mum says quietly, earnestly, 'truly. I was praying more than anyone that it would work, and I know how devastated you must feel.'

'Thanks,' I mumble, unable to say much more.

'I've made a chicken fricassee, your favourite, and I've got lots of wine, and you can eat with us in the kitchen, or up here on a tray, whatever you like. And we can talk about it, or not talk about it, whatever you want to do.'

'I want to change into my pyjamas and eat my dinner in the living room in front of the trashiest TV possible and drink all the wine.'

'That we can do. Three TV dinners coming up.'

Mum and Flo both changed into their nightwear too to keep me company – Florence floated downstairs in a multi-coloured kaftan, and Mum reduced the cost per wear of her M&S flannel pyjamas down to pennies.

'Am I allowed to say that there'll be a next time?' Flo says tentatively as she balances her tray on her lap.

'You're eighty, you're allowed to say whatever you like,' I mumble with my mouth full.

'But you still have a frozen embryo, haven't you? You could try again with that?'

'We don't have to talk about that tonight though, do we,' Mum says brightly, shooting Flo a warning glance. 'Plenty of time to think about next steps.'

'I'm not doing it again,' I say. 'It's a sign that I'm not going to be a mother. No point going through it all again.' As I say the words even I'm surprised by them. In all truth, I've put no thought into what happens next because I hadn't envisioned this scenario ever happening. I'd imagined the celebratory dinner, the whoops and the cheers, not the pyjama pity party with mum and Flo tiptoeing round me like I'm a fragile invalid. I'd done everything right. I'd sent out the positive messages to the universe manifesting a baby, and it had never crossed my mind that the universe wouldn't listen. So that was that.

'Sign schmine,' Florence scoffs. 'The only thing that it's a sign of is that it didn't work this time. Next time could be completely different.'

I shake my head. 'Or it could be exactly the same. I'm forty. It was always going to be a long shot, like Mum kept telling me. It's my own fault for running away with the idea. If I was more like Mum, and didn't get emotionally invested in anything, and just be a bit detached, then I wouldn't be so disappointed when things don't work out.'

Over on the armchair next to the fireplace, Mum stops eating and puts her knife and fork down on her plate. 'I know you think I'm quite pessimistic, Stella, but I'm actually not. I have dreams and hopes just like you do. I have wished harder for this embryo to take probably more than you have, but the difference is that that's all it is, hope. I don't let myself start living the dream until it's actually happening because sometimes the despair when something doesn't turn out the way that you've rehearsed in your head is just too damn difficult to live with. You don't have the monopoly on disappointment you know Stella. Yes, this is a horrible, horrible situation, but we've all been there in one way or another, we've all poured our souls into hoping something would work out and then—' she clicks her fingers, 'Poof, it's gone, leaving you feeling desperate and alone. I know only too well the feeling of having to piece your life back together again after the crushing disappointment of your life not turning out the way you'd planned it . . . Excuse me—' she chokes out a sob as she flees the room.

Flo and I look at the closed lounge door after Mum has run out of it with our mouths open. I had no idea she felt like that. She's never really talked about Dad leaving, not like this anyway, never framing it as a 'crushing disappointment'. It was always a string of small facts pulled like colourful handkerchiefs from a magician's sleeve: 'He always wanted to travel'; 'Our life was too small for him'; 'We stopped loving each other'; 'We grew apart'; 'He was a free spirit.' She's never before given an indication that she's been carrying with her this deep well of despair barely buried beneath the surface.

'You don't need to say it,' I tell Flo, sticking a forkful of tepid fricassee in my mouth.

'If you're sure.'

I wait to finish chewing and then swallow, waving my fork in her direction, 'You can't deny that she's pretty negative sometimes.'

'Realistic is not the same as negative.'

'It is when it comes to my life.'

'I'll allow you a little self-pity today, Stella, considering what's happened, but not indefinitely. You make your own luck in life, remember that.'

'How exactly do I make myself pregnant, Flo? Tell me that? That's purely down to luck, and not of my making.'

'True. But you have to be in it to win it.'

Ah. The old lottery cliché. And this is a lottery isn't it? And right now it feels like my chances of winning are just as miniscule.

Florence's words float alongside me for the next few weeks, poking me in the shoulder should a minute or two pass by without me thinking about it. If I were looking for omens or signs of what to do next, I'd have found them everywhere. I was even stuck in a traffic jam getting out of Morrison's car park behind a Range Rover Evoque with the number plate IVF yesterday. But as I'm making my own luck, not believing in fate or destiny or whatever, it barely registered with me.

'I get it, I do,' Kate says when I video call her to talk it through. We were meant to be meeting in person, but Lee had five-a-side and the babysitter never turned up. 'But honestly, Stell, I would trade lives with you in a heartbeat. Thor and Zeus are being absolute buggers.'

She says this without even the tiniest hint of mirth, and it takes every ounce of self-discipline, and God knows that's not an attribute I have in abundance, not to ask if they've been chucking thunderbolts at each other again.

'I know that this probably isn't what you want to hear, but honestly, having kids is pretty shit eighty per cent of the time.'

'Eighty per cent? Really?'

'OK, maybe that's a bit harsh. Seventy-eight per cent. Absolute shite seventy-eight per cent of the time. You have this fantastic life where you just can leave the house whenever you want, without a bag bigger than the one I took to Thailand for a month. You drink hot beverages while they've still got steam coming off it. You have a poo without an audience. You can still jump on a trampoline or laugh out loud without Niagara Falls happening in your pants. You can begin and end a conversation with someone without the word "SNACK!" being shouted in your face. You can pick any item of clothing out of your wardrobe and put it on fairly safe in the knowledge that it doesn't have another human's excrement or vomit on it. You need to set your alarm for the morning because without it, chances are you might just sleep right through it until lunchtime. You can literally fly tomorrow to a yoga retreat in Goa if you want to, while I think an hour by myself at a supermarket is a massive treat. And then, sometimes, when I've finished my shopping, I sit in my car in the car park and look at Instagram for ten minutes knowing full well that the sodding mini milks are melting in the boot and I'm probably going to give the boys salmonella if the frozen nuggets reach room temperature, but do you know what? I don't care, because those ten minutes are the best ten minutes of my week. And, and,' Kate's voice had now reached a pitch only dogs could hear, 'you can still have sex without a crippling fear that a tiny sperm might find its way to an ovary and make another one of the little fuckers.'

Silence.

'Oh God, Stella, I'm sorry, I didn't think about that last bit. I'm so sorry. I'm just having a bad day.'

'Look, try to find some clothes that don't have excrement or vomit on them, it's Thursday night, and the big Asda is open until ten tonight, I'll be right round to look after the boys. Go on; treat yourself to a couple of hours me-time. Sit in your car for as long as you want. Or go crazy and sit in their nice warm cafe instead.'

'Are you serious?' she asks, like I've just offered her a two-week cruise around the Med.

'Of course. If what you say is correct, then surely an evening in with your kids will put me off motherhood for good and we can all move on with our lives. Either way, you get to leave the house, which I think we can both agree is a good thing. I'll be over in twenty minutes. If you can change Zeus's nappy before I get there, that would be ace.'

* * *

Kate doesn't even wait for me to take my coat off before grabbing my face in two hands, kissing me on the lips, and slamming the door behind her. She's left no instructions, no pointers, or even told me where in the alarmingly quiet house the two boys are.

'Thor?'

The lounge is empty. Well, no, that's not correct. The lounge is empty of humans, but every inch is filled with piles of stuff: toys, cars, plastic food, real food, clean clothes, dirty clothes. It's giving me palpitations and I'm hardly the poster girl for clean living. I mean, I ran the vacuum round my flat every Saturday morning for two years without realising that I didn't have a bag attached.

'Thor?'

A pile of laundry on the sofa shifts slightly creating a small avalanche of pants.

'Thor? Are you under there?' At this point, boy / rat have equal probability.

I cautiously poke the pile and a little giggle escapes from inside it.

'Zeus? Are you in there too?' I flex my fingers and start tickling all over the heap to a building cacophony of snorts and screams.

Half an hour later, once the boys are settled on the sofa in clean pyjamas (I sniffed them), one with milk the other with hot chocolate, I set about clearing the detritus of the day. I put a wash on, pile the laundry into four stacks to be taken upstairs, and scoop handfuls of toys into the wooden hamper. The house has never looked in this state when I've visited before, and Kate has certainly never said any of those things before, or at least not in that way. She may have laughingly referred to the front row applauding her bowel movements, but never in the head-in-hands way she spat it out earlier. Is parenthood really that bad? Have I actually really thought this through?

The fertility counsellor has asked me so many times why I want to do this, and my answer has always been the same, because I have to. But it's all a lie, isn't it? The joy of motherhood is a myth, perpetuated by people like Kate who hide what it's really like, making people like me think it's all Farley rusks and talcum powder. Mum must have had days like this when she was bringing me up alone. Days that didn't end when night began. Days when whatever she did, I wouldn't stop crying. Days when my fever wouldn't break with Calpol. Days when she looked at me and wondered if it was worth it. If I was worth it.

Kate returns carrying five Asda bags and a grateful smile. 'It's not all bad,' she says as I put my coat on in her hallway.

'I know,' I reply.

'It's more like forty-eight per cent shit.'

'That's better odds.'

'Some days, it's like thirty-five per cent.'

'Even better,' I smile.

'I think you should give it another go.'

'Really?'

She nods. 'For the thirty-five per cent days.'

'But you have Lee. I'll be doing it alone.'

'Stella, you are surrounded by people who love you. You are definitely not going to do it alone.'

'You'll help me figure it out?'

Kate nods. 'And for the ninety-five per cent shit days, I'll meet you in the supermarket car park. Just say the word and I'll be there.'

'Love you.'

'Love you.'

In the morning, I wait until Mum and Florence have just put large spoonfuls of cereal in their mouths before I say, 'I've just called the doctor and scheduled the next transfer.'

Mum's so desperate to speak, she can't chew quick enough. 'So soon?' she gasps as soon as she's swallowed. 'Why not wait a bit longer, give yourself a break?'

'Why?'

Mum flounders, 'Because, well you need, I don't know, a bit of downtime to process this.'

'It's processed. What I need is a baby. And I have another one currently sitting in liquid nitrogen in a lab in Basingstoke.'

'It's OK to be sad, Stella.'

'I was sad, and now I'm optimistic. So I'd like you to be too. I know it doesn't come particularly natural for you to see rainbows instead of clouds, but I need you to try.'

Florence has been silent throughout this, with an increasing look of confusion on her face. She says finally, 'Do they thaw them like mince? Or can you pop it in frozen like fish fingers?'

It's official. She's lost her mind. 'I'm sorry?'

'Some things don't need to be thawed, do they?' Florence continues. 'Like fisherman's pies, the ones with mash on the top, you can just whack them in the oven frozen, but other things, like quiche, you need to thaw first. Which one's the embryo?'

There's a couple of seconds of silence where we all process what she's said and then Mum starts to giggle. Seeing her laugh makes me break into a chuckle, until both of us are clutching our sides. It's not helped by Florence saying,

'What? What did I say?' every few seconds. 'It was an honest question! I don't know why you two find it so funny.'

'Flo,' I gasp, trying to catch my breath, 'you just compared my embryo to a fisherman's pie.'

'And a quiche,' Mum wipes her eyes.

'Honestly, you two are like little children. I was just interested in the scientific process, that's all.'

I smile, 'They thaw it. It only takes an hour to thaw before they transfer it.'

'Next she'll be asking if they use the microwave or just leave it out at room temperature.'

'Even I know that you should never defrost anything at room temperature, I'm not stupid,' Florence huffs. 'So they must use a microwave.'

'So when's the next transfer scheduled for, and I'll put it in my diary?' Mum says before Flo can add any more.

'Wednesday the fourteenth of June.'

Mum smiles and says something that's both cryptic and entirely out of character. 'I've got a good feeling about that. I've always liked Wednesdays.'

19

Bonnie

Forty years earlier . . .

They decided Wednesday would be the best day. Halfway between weekends, it would break up the week nicely. There were other rules too, the most important one that it was only one day. Nothing could happen on other days. No contact, no letters, no phone calls, just once a week where all four of them could check out from their marriages for twenty-four hours. The other six days they were plain old Mr and Mrs Morris, and Dr and Mrs Gillespie.

It was Steven and Janet's idea. Floated initially with trepidation a week or so after the fateful dinner party, while *Terry and June* were bickering on the television in the background. 'We were thinking,' Steven cleared his throat, 'that is, Janet and me, whether, you know, because of the thing, between you and Olly, whether you might think about an idea we had, of sort of making this more of a regular arrangement, a sort of hall pass if you like, of, you know, having a night a week where we could, you know, meet up, me and her, and you and him, you know, like a date or something.'

'An affair?' Bonnie asked.

He looked shocked. 'No, not at all, not an affair, absolutely not, I love you, how can you think that I want an affair?'

'Because you just said you wanted to meet up with Janet once a week for a date.'

'Hang on a second, you kissed Olly.'

Oliver. 'We had far too much to drink that night, that's not the same as the months you've been fooling around with Janet.'

'So you don't want to spend an evening with just him talking about chromosomes or whatever it is excites the two of you?'

In truth, Bonnie couldn't get Oliver out of her head. Since their kiss, he popped into her head a few thousand times a day. Every task, thought, action was punctuated with his name, his face. But Steven didn't need to know that.

'No,' she said, 'I don't. because I'm married to you.'

'Surely *we* can define what that means though? Our marriage doesn't need to be governed by the same rules as everyone else, we can make up our own for what works for us.'

His reasoning appealed to Bonnie's liberal tendencies, but the idea of breaking the oath she'd made in church little more than eighteen months before was weighing heavily on her mind. Could it really be that easy? Surely if everyone just made up their own rules, then society would eventually collapse, taking with it all sense of propriety and order?

'How would it work exactly?' she asked finally.

She'd deliberately not changed the bedding in the bedroom she shared with Steven, or shaved her legs, or put on nice underwear. Steven, meanwhile, had the longest shower he'd ever had, cut his nose hair, and invested in a peppermint breath spray he had to visit three different chemists to find (not including Oliver's). To say that their plans for the evening were different was an understatement.

'So, I'll see you tomorrow then,' Steven said, picking up his overnight holdall containing tomorrow's clothes, two bottles of wine and no pyjamas. He hoicked it over his shoulder, making the contents clink.

Bonnie looked up from the food processor, where she was making a coleslaw to go with the baked ham that was roasting for her dinner with Oliver. 'OK,' she said, over the noise of the blades. She deliberated for a moment whether to finish the sentence with a cheery, 'have a nice time!' because that's what one would normally say if your spouse was going away for the night but then remembered where he was going, what he would be doing and so chose to say nothing, merely turning up the speed on the side of the mixer. This still felt really wrong, and as much as she kept telling herself that she was merely having dinner with a friend, who was going to sleep on the fold-out camp bed she'd already made up with clean sheets complete with folded white bath and hand towel on the end of it in the living room, Bonnie couldn't shake the feeling of guilt and anxiety. Not least because she had to ask Florence if she could get the camp bed out of the attic, the hatch being in her flat, and then stumbled her way through an explanation as to why she needed it.

'My friend Oliver, our friend, is staying over tomorrow night, in the living room, and so, yes, I just need it.'

As expected, Florence didn't ask her to elaborate further, she just smiled, and said, 'That's nice,' but Bonnie felt that a lie by omission was still a lie.

Steven stalled, standing by the kitchen door, looking like he wanted to say something else. 'So I'll head straight to the theatre from Janet's, so I won't see you till tomorrow evening. Can we have that chicken fricassee thing you do? With the rice?'

'Yes, sure,' Bonnie replied. 'Although some of this ham will be left, so we could have ham sandwiches.'

Steven curled his lip up, 'I'd prefer the chicken.'

'Can you remember to book the car in for its MOT tomorrow as well?'

'Sure thing.'

Still he didn't go.

'Was there something else?' she asked, taking out the blades from the food processor and running them under the kitchen tap.

'I just, you know, I understand that this is a big deal for you, and just wanted to say good luck.'

'I've made coleslaw before.'

Steven scratched his nose, 'You know what I mean. Just try to have a bit of fun with someone who can speak to you on your level and has the same interests as you.'

Bonnie tried to keep her expression neutral as she stared out of the kitchen window at her mother's old vegetable patch which she'd let the weeds take over. Since Florence had moved upstairs, with the only access to the garden through Bonnie and Steven's flat, the garden had grown wild. 'It's just dinner,' she replied.

Bonnie changed the music three times; lit and blew out the candles; tried a skirt, jeans, trousers and then jeans again; had both wine and beer chilling and made ice cubes and cut up lemons in case he wanted gin and tonics. Her hair was up, then down, then up again; she wore heels, then sandals, then bare feet, contemplated her house slippers, then wore sandals again.

Oliver brought flowers with him, which at the last minute he left in his car outside, and was wearing a blazer he wished he hadn't when he saw Bonnie's jeans and sandals.

'Uh, hello,' he said, ducking his head slightly to kiss her cheek. They had an awkward moment as she turned her head too quickly and he got a faceful of hair. 'Sorry.'

'Come in, come in, you can put your bag in the living room where I've set your bed up.'

If Oliver was surprised by the sleeping arrangements, he didn't show it at all. In fact, he made himself quickly at home by unpacking his pyjamas and placing them under the pillow on the camp bed next to the fireplace and setting aside his toilet bag and toothbrush for later. He debated whether to put his slippers on in an attempt to make his outfit more casual, but thought it might be interpreted as presumptuous, so didn't. He'd visited Japan as a student and now wished that English people had the same custom of removing their shoes when they entered a house so that he could walk around in his socks. They were a good pair after all.

'Drink?' Bonnie asked brightly, ignoring the butterflies swarming around inside her.

'Do you know what,' Oliver said, 'I could murder a cup of tea.'

Bonnie smiled. Tea would be the perfect nerve-settler.

After dinner, Oliver stretched out his long legs under the kitchen table, and ran his hand along its pitted top, 'Is this the same table you had when you were a child?'

Bonnie smiled, 'Yes, Mum said that when she moved in here, it was a boarding house, you see, and Mum and Dad rented a room in it. There wasn't a table and they ate their dinner on trays in the living room or up in their bedrooms, which felt all wrong, so one Christmas they got this.'

'The things it must have seen.'

'I know, I often think that, the conversations, the fights—'

'The things people have written on it, signing cheques, birth certificates—'

'Death certificates,' added Bonnie, remembering her mother hunched over the table after leaving her father at the hospital.

Oliver reached across and placed his hand over Bonnie's. 'Sorry.'

She shook her head, 'Don't be. It was a long time ago. But you're right, if it were a person, it would have a very interesting autobiography to write. I used to do my homework on it alongside Mum, who was studying for her nursing exams, alongside a lodger called Larry who wrote protest songs to sing at marches, so he'd be scribbling away, moaning, "Nothing rhymes with nuclear!" while I was memorising pluperfect French verbs and Mum had her nose in a textbook about osteoporosis care in the elderly.'

'Sounds busy.'

Bonnie nodded, pleased now that she hadn't put a tablecloth on it. 'It was.'

They played two games of canasta after that, possibly the two thousand and something card game the table had hosted, and one of the best. The tea had grown cold in the pot in favour of the chilled wine from the fridge, and they were having so much fun Bonnie forgot entirely about the Viennetta ice cream dessert in the freezer until she saw it there as she put a Tupperware with the leftover ham in it as they were going to bed.

'Have you got everything you need? Glass of water?' Bonnie asked.

'I'm grand, thanks, I've had a really super evening,'

'Me too. Well, I'll say goodnight then.' Bonnie hovered by the door to the living room, unsure what, if anything, the protocol might be for this situation. 'If you're up before me in the morning, then there's teabags and coffee in the cupboard above the kettle, and there's bread in the bread bin.'

'Got it. Night then.'

'Night.'

Bonnie carefully undressed and put on her nightie, tying the bow at her neck and rubbing in her face cream before slipping under the covers. She tried reading for a bit as she listened to the sounds of Oliver preparing himself for bed, the tap running at intervals signalling his teeth were being brushed; the flush of the toilet followed by the tap again, his standards of hygiene pleasing her. A cough. Then the sound of the light cord being pulled in the bathroom signalling the end to his ablutions. Soft footsteps padding back to the living room, the gentle thud of the door closing, then a creak from the camp bed as he lowered his body onto it. The pipes were awake and whistling a jig long after the living room had succumbed to silence.

Bonnie lay in bed staring out of the dark window. Steven liked the curtains closed, but Steven wasn't there. A couple of stars were out, and the moon was full, casting a white glow over the garden. She was aware of Florence asleep the other side of the ceiling, and a man who was not her husband asleep the other side of the wall.

Should she have kissed him? Why didn't he kiss her? Did he just want to be friends? Why did she agree to this ridiculous situation anyway? What was Steven doing right now? Don't think about that. Flick it away. What was she thinking? It was such a lovely evening. Why didn't Oliver kiss her goodnight? Did she even want him to? Of course she did. If her husband was doing it too, did it make it a sin? Why should sin come into it when she wasn't even religious? Why did they get married in a church then? Because Mrs Morris insisted on it. What would she think about this? What would Mum think about this? She should have served the Viennetta.

A hot drink. That's what she needed. She'd have to be quiet though. She padded barefoot down the corridor to the kitchen, and gently closed the door behind her, the light of the hallway shining through the glass panels in the door. She turned a lamp on in the corner, and slowly filled a saucepan with milk and flicked the hob ring on. It had barely started to heat when she saw a flicker of a shadow in the hallway through the frosted glass. For a moment, she thought it was Steven, but this silhouette was taller, slimmer. The door handle turned and Oliver stood in the doorway in light blue pyjamas with smart navy pinstripes; he wasn't wearing his glasses. His hair was unruffled from sleep, which was obviously eluding him too.

'I'm making some hot chocolate if you want some?' Bonnie asked.

'Lovely. Thanks.'

'Did I wake you?' she said.

'No, not at all, I can never sleep in new places the first night.'

'How many new places do you sleep in?' she asked teasingly.

'In boring pharmaceutical conference hotels, lots; in this type of situation, none.'

Bonnie got two mugs out of the cupboard. 'Pleased to hear it.'

'I think I need to apologise,' he said.

She turned her head and looked at him quizzically, 'For?'

'For not thanking you properly for dinner.'

'You did, you even complimented me on the way I buttered the Hovis loaf, so I definitely felt thanked.'

'I mean, I didn't, *show* my appreciation.'

It was taking longer than it should have done considering the level of natural intelligence Bonnie possessed for her to join the dots and fully comprehend what Oliver was trying to say.

'Oh,' she replied, her cheeks flushing, 'yes, well, I'm very pleased that you thought you should remedy that.'

'Are you?'

'Yes.'

He moved closer to her, pinning her up against the hob, just as the milk boiled over behind her, spilling a little onto her nightdress.

'Oh god,' she gasped, turning the heat off and moving the wet patch of fabric away from her skin. In two deft movements, which completely contradicted his awkwardness from a moment before, Oliver untied the bow at her neck and whipped her nightie over her head, swiftly followed by his own pyjama top. Bonnie ran her eyes over his smooth defined chest. He picked her up and set her down on the edge of the kitchen table, kissing her lips, her neck, her breasts. And, just like that, a new chapter in the life of the kitchen table was written.

Wednesdays were definitely the highlight of everyone's week. Yet, somehow, and Bonnie thought a lot about why or how this might be, the very existence of Wednesday made the rest of the week so much shinier than it ever had been. She'd started singing in the shower before work; Steven made her breakfast in bed at weekends. They now spent their Sundays, not glowering at each other over the papers, or alone, he at the pub or football and she reading or with Florence, but together. They visited the street market in Portobello or Camden, had pub lunches, or even, admittedly this only happened once, visiting the Renoir exhibition at the South Bank Centre, followed by a walk through Jubilee Gardens and along the Thames, stopping to skim some stones on the little beach in front of the gallery.

Wednesday. This one day, this mutually agreed step away from their daily lives, had injected a different perspective on their marriage. They weren't trapped any more, they were liberated. And it felt wonderful.

20

Stella

I go alone to the doctor's for the transfer this time round. Mum wanted to come, but she came last time and it didn't work. Not that I think she's the reason, but I want everything to be different about this time. I take the bus, I wear a different outfit, I had toast instead of cereal for breakfast, and I make sure I salute at a single magpie and mutter, 'Hello, Mr Magpie and how's your wife?' to avoid impending sorrow. I must have said it too loudly because the chap next to me moved seats at the next bus stop.

'On your tod this time?' Dr Foster asks.

I nod. He must be able to sense the mood has altered this time because he does the transfer in silence, just patting my knee when it's done. I watch the little black and white bubble on the screen, willing it to swim, urging it to bed in, cling on, to stay.

I haven't been inside a church recently. By recently I mean not since my foreign language exchange to Florence where a visit to the Duomo was compulsory, but the same blanket of reverence seems to be in this white box of a consulting room. The same complete silence, where everyone is just hoping their thoughts are loud enough to be listened to. This is literally my last chance. I'm forty. The injections and hormones and tests and drugs and hopes and failures and prayers and disappointment and faked optimism and tiredness, bone-aching exhaustion, is too much. I can't do it again. It has to work this time. It has to.

The nurse squeezes my hand and I close my eyes. A little tear escapes out of the corner and runs down my cheek.

I still walk like a penguin down the corridor to the exit instead of doing lunges – some things just can't be different. As the electric doors slide open, I see Mum and Florence, leaning against their car.

'We hope you don't mind, but we couldn't let you go home on the bus,' Mum says.

I fall wearily into her arms, feeling Florence's hand on my back, not needing to say a thing because sometimes thoughts, it turns out, can be heard.

I take two weeks of holiday days owing to me, and I barely leave the house for the next fortnight. Every forum, both of the medical and hearsay variety, agrees that embryos can't be dislodged by walking out of your front door, but I'm not taking any chances. I've even started doing Flo's sudoku to pass the time. I'm pretending that I'm really blasé about this second transfer, but I'm really not. Everything I'd bought before the last time taunts me that I've tempted fate. The cans of paint go unopened. No due-date calendars are filled in. I don't ask anyone to carry my not really very heavy shopping, and I resist the urge to kick-start a conversation with the pregnant cashier in Costa Coffee (I did have a decaf though, you know, just in case) on my only venture out of the house. I haven't opened the door to the dining room in over a month, so I don't need to see the Mount Etna of baby supplies Kate gave me, and unlike the first time when I told anyone and everyone who would listen that I was 'with embryo', this time, just the three of us know. This isn't like last time though, when I knew that I had an immediate back-up plan. My eggs are, quite literally, in this one basket.

Exactly fourteen days later and not a minute before, the pregnancy test is sitting comfortably under the tea cosy on the kitchen table. So it's understandable that Mum's a little confused when she comes into the kitchen to see me rooted to my chair staring at a knitted rainbow.

'Everything OK?'

'There's still a minute left,' I say, my eyes not moving.

'Can I just say,' Mum pulls out the chair next to me, 'before we know what the result is, that I'm so incredibly proud of you for doing this.'

I look sideways at her. 'Really?'

'Really. You're not waiting around for life to happen to you, you're taking control, and I think it's fantastic. I wish that I was half as strong and capable as you are when I was pregnant with you.'

'I'm not pregnant yet.'

She puts her hand on top of mine, 'Like I say, whatever the result is, I'm proud.'

I look at my watch. 'OK, time's up. You look.'

I'm expecting Mum to resist, and insist that I look myself, but she whips off the tea cosy, picks up the test and says, 'Yes. There's definitely two lines.'

'What?' I grab the test from her. Two bright clear lines wink back. 'Oh my God. Oh my God.'

Hearing the commotion from the living room, Florence rushes in to the kitchen. 'Is it positive?' she gasps.

I can only nod, unable to do anything but smile as she flings her arms around me. The three of us press together in the kitchen, tears of joy streaming down each of our faces.

Florence starts doing the conga around the ground floor of the house, 'We're going to have a ba-by, we're going to have a ba-by, do do do do oh, do do do do', her hips swinging underneath her kaftan. Meanwhile, I just sort of sit there lamely, my mind numb, in total disbelief that all these months of planning, these years of wanting have come to this. Two pink lines on a little piece of white plastic.

It sounds ridiculous after all the planning and imagining I've been doing, but all my thoughts were about getting to this point and then what happens after the baby's here. I honestly hadn't really thought about the middle bit; the bit where it's growing inside me, and I'm entirely responsible for it. I've never even had a pet to practice on, and there are so many rules and regulations and do's and don'ts. I had two plants on the windowsill in my flat, one I killed through under-watering, the other one through over. I'm suddenly gripped with this fear that I'm going to inadvertently harm the baby somehow. This is going to be a long nine months if all I'm doing is googling things like, 'Can pregnant women eat pistachios?' (Answer: apparently only twenty-four in one sitting, which I feel is very precise.) I need something to occupy my mind or I'll go mad. But more than that, I need to show my child that I may not be able to provide them with a daddy, but look at this shiny new bike Mummy's bought you. I need to prove to my child that I'm someone they can rely on.

21

Stella

Dear Baby,

I am officially twelve weeks pregnant with you today! Whoop whoop! I saw you on a scan for the first time, doing your thing, swimming about . . . Actually, you weren't really swimming, more lazily flopping about, but then again, you are my daughter. Or son. But probably daughter. The sonographer (I just learned that term today, now look at me throwing it casually about like I've swallowed a dictionary), was non-committal when I asked her if you were the cutest baby she'd ever seen, but I could tell she thought it but was just too professional to confirm it out loud just in case the other couples waiting outside heard her and felt bad when it was their turn.

She asked me if I wanted two sets of photos, one to give the father, I said yes, just to be polite. Then I felt guilty for the rest of the day that I didn't own what I was doing and just say, 'I will take two sets, yes, but not for the father because I only know his number not his name.' But I didn't, but it made me think about what you're going to tell people when they ask who your dad is. I don't want you ever to feel uncomfortable or different. Families come in every shape and size these days, you don't have to live within the rules like my mum and gran did, we're doing it our way, the way that works for us, and that's OK.

Mum

* * *

I've been waiting until this scan to buy any baby paraphernalia this time around, call it superstition, call it tempting fate, whatever, but I have. And now I have two sets of scan pictures to prove that the baby's real and on a one-way ticket out of my womb, it's time to go shopping. And against all of my better judgement, my mother is tagging along.

'And the handle is height adjustable, so it'll be comfortable for your partner too if he's taller than you.'

'I don't have a partner,' I say, 'so is it cheaper if I don't get an adjustable one?'

The lady in the baby section of the department store smiles politely back at me and says, 'All our prams are height adjustable.'

I smile back, 'Of course they are.'

'You don't need to tell everyone about being single, you know. It costs nothing to just smile and say nothing,' Mum whispers once the saleswoman has walked away.

'It costs the price of an adjustable handle I don't need.'

Mum wanders off to look at the cots, while I try not to scoff at a Babygro that says *Daddy's Little Princess* on it. Why is everything so geared to co-parenting? I reach up to take a cute flamingo mobile off a shelf and knock a wooden sign off. Stooping down to pick it up, I read that it says, 'There's no buddy like Daddy,' and feel an urge to smash it. It's as though every sodding item in this sodding shop was designed and manufactured purely just to taunt me with my life choices.

I strike gold with the next shop: two possible prams with handles firmly welded in place, only problem is they're both hot pink; but the lovely shop assistant is on hand – 'let me look out the back for you.' Everything is looking good. I've also found a nappy bag that looks exactly like one of those designer Hermès Birkin handbags, and despite the not inconsiderable price-tag, it's perfect. I have it in my hands, turning it over, inspecting it from every angle, when a heavily pregnant woman sidles up alongside me and says chirpily, 'Don't get that one, I made that mistake with my first, and my husband felt a right idiot carrying it round whenever he took the baby out, so buy a bag Daddy will like too.'

'Daddy won't be using it.'

She laughs, 'Oh we all think our husbands are useless, but honestly he'll surprise you by how involved he is once the baby's here.'

'It really would surprise me, because I have no idea who he is,' I say with a smiley shrug, revelling in the woman trying to disguise her shock with a red-faced giggle.

'Will you stop doing that,' Mum hisses behind me as we watch her hurriedly waddling out of the shop.

'What? It was her that brought Daddy up, not me. Anyway, it's funny seeing people's reactions. What do you think of this bag?'

It turns out the prams only come in pink, not the grey I want, and although I am 100% sure it's a girl, I'm not sure that she, nor me, are particularly pink kind of people. I haven't had it confirmed that she's a she; she's not playing ball in that department, definitely not an exhibitionist in the scans, showing her wares for anyone to see. In fact, I'd go so far as to say the baby's a bit of a prude, obviously taking after my mother. The baby always twisted away at the vital moment, or, comically, crossed her legs as though she was at a tea party holding a parasol. I really hope we have something in common.

I buy a little grey teddy bear to put in the crib. Florence has given me a well-loved, if rather age-worn, teddy called Bear, which has pride of place on the nursery shelf ready to watch over the baby when she arrives.

So I have a lovely new nappy / handbag and soft toy, but am pram-less and exhausted when we arrive back home to find Florence sitting in a deckchair in the garden, writing in her notebook. She closes it as she hears us open the back door and step out onto the patio. I wish I knew what she's just written. I'll just have to wait for her to go out again before finding out.

'Successful trip?' she asks.

Mum says, 'No, Stella got annoyed about handles.'

'Handles?'

'Don't ask.'

'It was a perfectly legitimate reason,' I say. 'Every time I push the damn thing, I'd be reminded that I'll never need to use a function on it.'

'I never use the defrost button on the microwave, it doesn't mean that I shouldn't use it for jacket potatoes,' says Mum.

'Anyway, I've got another six months to go, so there's plenty of time to find the right pram.'

'That'll go so quickly,' Florence says, 'won't it, Bonnie?'

Mum nods, a little distracted, probably still thinking about the shopping list we left with and returned with still intact. She hates it when best-laid plans go awry.

22

Bonnie

Dear _______ (tbc)

I've always been a planner. Maybe it's the scientist in me, but I love a good list and the feeling you get when you cross a line through each item, or put a little tick next to it. But you can't really plan for every twist and turn life takes you on, and sometimes it's a real test of strength to make a Plan B when Plan A goes to pot. There's a saying isn't there, about making lemonade when life gives you lemons. But for lemonade to taste good, you also need sugar. And sometimes that's in short supply.

* * *

Forty years earlier . . .

'It's off,' Steven said, matter-of-factly, as if he was talking about a pint of milk. 'Janet's pissing me off, and so we've decided to call it a day.' It was a Thursday evening, late in September, the house was spotless, all traces of Oliver removed from the night before, as per the agreement. A beef casserole was in the oven, and a new BBC drama circled in the *TV Times* ready to watch after dinner.

'What do you mean, it's off?' Bonnie said, her heart both thumping and sinking simultaneously, her hands wrist-deep in oven gloves.

'It's not fun anymore, so we've decided to stop it.'

'But, but . . . you can't, not just like that, we need to all agree, to talk about it.'

'That wasn't what we said at the beginning,' Steven said, slamming the fridge shut and opening his beer. 'It was actually your rule remember, that this only carried on if everyone is happy with it. Well, me and Janet aren't happy with it any more. So it's done.'

'But—'

Steven angrily threw the beer bottle at the kitchen wall, chipping a bit of plaster off, which fell to the floor along with the bottle, miraculously intact, beer staining the wall and floor. 'It's done, Bonnie. Finito. Kaput. Are there any more beers anywhere, that was the last one in the fridge? That bastard's not been drinking my beer as well as banging my wife, has he?'

Bonnie recognised this mood, despite not seeing it for months, and quickly pulled on her coat, stepping over the chalky inch-square bit of plaster on the floor next to the new Welsh dresser. 'I'll just pop down to the shop and get some more, I'll clean that up when I get back.'

Collar up, she hurried down the darkening street to the corner shop but kept walking until she'd reached the chemist's. The CLOSED sign hung on the door, telling her cheerfully that it reopened at 9 a.m. the next morning and to remember to take her multivitamins. She peered through the glass, hopeful of seeing a light on in the back, some sign of life, but nothing. Stuffing her hands in her pockets, she half walked, half ran to the telephone box a little way along the road, she didn't have long.

She waited with tapping toes for a teenage couple to stop fogging up the glass. She rapped on the glass, springing the pair apart, who then shuffled past her, wishing death upon her with their eyes. Her fingers trembled as she dialled the number.

'Yes?' Came Janet's curt voice from the receiver.

There was a split second where Bonnie considered hanging up, but instead said, 'Janet, it's me, Bonnie.'

'What do you want?' she asked tersely.

'Is Oliver there?'

'Yes. But you can't speak to him.'

'Please, Janet, I just need to—'

'He's my husband, just leave him alone.' The phone went dead.

Bonnie sank back against the glass of the phone box, a couple of prostitutes' calling cards falling on the floor as she did so. She tried to control her breathing, which was fast and ragged, and closed her eyes, only opening them when an angry knock on the door made her jump. 'Sorry, sorry,' she said, pushing past the man counting coins in his palm and hurrying back to the corner shop to buy Steven's beer.

Later that night, Steven's snores came quickly, but sleep didn't for Bonnie. He had been rough and unloving, and mechanical, all the things that Oliver was not. In one moment, every ounce of happiness had been snatched away from her, and they were propelled back in time to an era of brusque exchanges and resentment. The pipes whistled their melancholy tune well into the night, when Bonnie must have finally drifted off to an uneasy dreamworld.

Oliver was waiting outside the house for her the next day, sitting in his Vauxhall Astra, the engine off, so as not to add unnecessary pollution to the thick London air and not to draw attention to himself as Steven left the house ten minutes before. Bonnie didn't see Oliver's car at first, tiredness blinding her as she hurried past on her way to the bus stop.

'Bonnie, wait!'

She swung around, and her heart leaped. She took in the dark circles under his eyes that matched her own, his shirt collar open with no tie, creased from two days' wear.

'Bonnie, can you sit in the car and talk to me?'

He was going to tell her that he was in love with her; he'd hinted at it for weeks, throwing out endearments like 'increasingly fond', 'I really, *really* like you,' and the clincher, murmured only two nights before: 'I'm really falling for you.' She didn't know how it would work; Steven wasn't going to leave their flat easily, and he'd fight her for everything in the divorce, but she'd give him whatever he wanted. It wasn't ideal of course, no one wanted to be a divorcee at the age of twenty-three, but she also couldn't have foreseen that the love of her life would turn up just two years after her wedding.

She sat in the passenger seat and turned her body to face Steven's, her face expectant.

'Janet's pregnant.'

Bonnie felt punched in the stomach.

'It's not mine, but she told Steven last night, and he wants nothing to do with it, or her, and she's in a complete state.'

On the road in front of them, two pigeons vied for a day-old kebab curling up on the pavement. Bonnie watched as the bigger one attacked the other one with a vicious peck whenever it got too near.

'Talk to me, Bon,' Oliver pleaded.

'I don't know what you're saying,' Bonnie replied weakly.

'I can't let her go through this alone,' he said softly.

'So that's it then. Us. We're done because my husband impregnated your wife.'

'Bonnie, I—'

'You don't have to be so bloody decent all the time, Oliver,' she shrieked. 'They got themselves into this, it's nothing to do with you.'

'I can't leave her, Bon, we've been together since school, she was my first love, me hers, I can't abandon her now.'

'But you can abandon me?' As she said it, she could hear the childish tone to her voice.

Oliver slammed the heel of his palm on the driving wheel, 'What would you have me do?'

Bonnie turned her head to the passenger window so he couldn't see the tears forming in her eyes. 'Nothing. You're doing exactly what you're supposed to do, being a kind and loyal man.' She felt the bile rise in her throat as she rounded on him, 'But, right now, I wish you were more like Steven, and tell her that it's her problem and you're in love with someone else. If that's how you feel.'

'I am in love with someone else.'

This should have buoyed Bonnie, the affirmation that she wasn't imagining that this was real. That he did love her. But his tone was so wistful, so hopeless, that it was no consolation. 'But that doesn't matter, does it? You're still going to do this. You're still going to put your happiness, and mine, way behind Janet's. You're going to bring up Steven's baby as your own, pretending that you're one big happy family, knowing that just around the corner from your sodding chemist is a woman who loves you more than she ever thought possible!' Bonnie wiped her nose on her sleeve.

'Please try to understand, Bonnie—'

'I don't know what you want me to say, Oliver, congratulations? I'm so happy for you both? This isn't fair,' she shook her head in despair, 'this isn't fair.'

'Bonnie, please—'

'Just leave me alone now, Oliver, I can't understand what's happening, I just need to be by myself.' Bonnie slammed the car door and, instead of going to work, walked the other way, back to the green door, let herself in, and flung herself face down on her bed and wept.

She left it a fortnight before trying to talk to him again, thinking that two weeks would be enough for him to realise that this wasn't his mess to clean up. Two weeks for Janet to realise that Oliver's happiness was as important as her own, that she could release him and could raise this baby alone. Two weeks for Steven to come to the conclusion that he'd made a terrible mistake and his future actually lay with a woman who couldn't change a light bulb, thought him hilarious, and was carrying his child.

No call or letter came from Janet nor Oliver, and Steven showed no signs of remorse or any type of mental conflict either: he drank, he watched football, he ate freezer meals for one on his lap in the living room, while Bonnie ate alone at the kitchen table, trying not to think about the story she'd helped write for it.

On the fourteenth day, Bonnie walked down to the high street. A lady she'd never seen before was in a white coat up on the pharmacist's dais under the three-dimensional mint-green PRESCRIPTIONS sign, checking prescriptions against the little white bags lined up in front of her. Bonnie's eyes darted around for Oliver.

'Excuse me,' she said to the lady, 'is Oliver Gillespie here?'

'No sorry, madam, he's left.'

'Left? What do you mean left?'

'His wife and him have left the area.'

'What?' No. No. No. Not that.

'They're having a baby,' the woman continued, smiling.

'What?' Bonnie just stood there, numb.

'I'm sorry, madam, was he helping you with something? Do you have a prescription?'

Bonnie slowly shook her head, trying to take this in. 'No, I'm . . . I'm a friend. Sorry, um, this is a bit of a shock, I didn't know he was leaving.'

'Your name isn't Mrs Morris, is it?'

Bonnie nodded sadly.

'Hang on a second, there's a letter for you, in the back. Won't be a tick.'

She reappeared half a minute later with a white envelope, with her name handwritten on the front in Oliver's distinctive capitalised print. 'I think it comes from looking at doctor's scrawls all day that I've developed this ridiculously neat writing,' he once laughed self-consciously as they did the *Telegraph* cryptic crossword together in bed.

Bonnie went next door to a cafe, chose a table away from the window in the back and waited for her coffee to be set down on the table before opening it.

Dearest Bonnie,

If you're reading this, then you came looking for me, and if that's the case, then I hope by now you understand why I had to do this and stand by Janet. She's terrified and heartbroken and, like us, had really thought that a new life with a partner that really understood her was just around the corner. I know this seems terribly unfair. You and I were dragged along on this adventure of Steven and Janet's and now, once again, we're suffering because of their actions. But I won't let this torment you every day, so I have resigned from my job, made Janet do the same, and we have left the area for a new life somewhere else. It wouldn't be fair for you to bump into Janet in the supermarket with the baby, or walk past my chemist's and see me. I'm not being a martyr about this; it's as much self-preservation for me, as for you. I couldn't bear the idea of catching a glimpse of you and always knowing that what could have been would be so much better than what is.

I know I am in no position to say what I am about to, please believe that this comes not from a former lover with biased intentions, but a friend who has only ever spoken the truth to you. Steven isn't right for you, Bonnie. You deserve someone to light up when you enter a room, to gaze in awe at you when you speak, wondering how the stars have aligned so that they have the sheer luck of being your husband. I thought I might be that person for a while, but life had other plans. But that person is out there, Bonnie, and I am certain with every fibre of my being that that person is not Steven.

Please forgive me for everything, I'd like to say that if I could rewind the last year and do things differently I would, but actually, I wouldn't, because all the pain has brought me such incredible joy too. I wish nothing but happiness for you, Bonnie, and hope that with time, you would wish the same for me too.

Oliver

* * *

Bonnie's period didn't come on the fifteenth. It was marked as the fifteenth in Bonnie's diary, so it really should have come on the fifteenth. There was only one reason why it wouldn't have. She didn't need to waste her money on a test. She knew. She just didn't know whose baby she was carrying.

23
Stella

'Aisha, can I have a word?' I've deliberately waited until she'd emptied her bladder for the third time that morning, and eaten her hourly cereal bar so all the key bases are covered for a positive outcome. 'You're due in four weeks' time, and I wondered if you'd thought about what was going to happen when you go on maternity leave?'

'I'm glad you've brought this up. I've actually drafted a job description that I was going to put online this afternoon for a new manager. In all honesty, I don't think I'm going to come back after my maternity leave, and so I thought it best to advertise for a permanent replacement.'

'Um,' I shift my weight from one foot to the other, 'would you consider me?'

'You? I didn't think you had any ambition to manage the place? It's a lot of responsibility.'

I feel a little deflated by Aisha's reaction. Was that the impression I give? That I'm not ambitious or responsible?

'You've never shown any desire to do the budgets, or recruit care staff, my job is more than just making the residents laugh, you know, a lot goes on behind the scenes.'

'I know that, honestly, Aisha, I do, I've really thought about this and I want to be more than I am at the moment.' Ever since those two lines appeared on the stick something inside me switched. I've done everything I can to choose a

Grade A father for the baby, now I just have to make sure that I measure up too.

She studies me briefly. 'I'd be lying if I said that I didn't have concerns. Don't get me wrong, the residents love you, but managing a care home with forty-five residents and fifteen staff is a massive undertaking.'

'Do I have to manage the undertakers too?'

I see her eyes narrow.

'Sorry. Just trying to lighten the mood,' I say. 'Look, I know you think that I float around here telling jokes and chatting about the war, but I see all the cogs turning in this place to keep it open, I see how hard you work, and everyone does, to make this a place you'd want to spend your last days.' I take a deep breath. 'There's something else. I do have to be completely honest with you, I am pregnant.' I see a fleeting look of concern wash over Aisha's face so I quickly follow that up with, 'I'm twelve weeks, but I will work the whole pregnancy, and I'll definitely come back after the baby's born too, but I want this, I want the challenge, and to step up and to do this. I want my child to be proud of me. I want to be proud of me.'

I can't read Aisha's expression; her face is still and she looks as if she is studying me, but then she smiles, 'I'm so happy for you, Stella, truly. I'll redraft the job advert to be for a new assistant manager and I'll put it online today, then you can start interviewing next week.'

'Me?'

'Of course. You *are* the new manager after all. Congratulations. We'll tell the residents at tea time. They'll be thrilled.'

I wasn't expecting Aisha to mention the pregnancy in her speech, I hadn't explicitly told her not to, but I thought there was a code between expectant mothers that if it's not your news to share, don't share it, but there it was, bundled up in the same package as my promotion. It catches me off guard and I'm not prepared for it. To be fair, the residents are thrilled, lots of clapping and cheering, most of them because they genuinely like me and are delighted for my good fortune, a few of them because everyone else is doing it and it looks like fun. They swarm around me, clamouring to have their questions heard: 'You kept that quiet!' 'I didn't even know you had a husband!' 'What's his name?' 'What's your name again?' 'Can we meet him?' 'How long have you been together?' 'What time's dinner?' 'Where did you meet?'

The horrified face of the woman in the chemist's flashes into my mind. These residents are old, much older than she was, and they wouldn't understand the idea of sperm donation. I'd hate for them to look at me the same way that woman did. I know it was probably the way I packaged it, comparing sperm with phlegm, loudly, in the middle of a pharmacy, but it's hardly conventional what I'm doing and they wouldn't understand. If they weren't shocked, they'd be pitying, and I don't know which is worse. So I say, 'His name is Sam, we met in a park, we're not married yet, but planning to combine a wedding with a christening. He works away a lot so I don't think you can meet him, but we're both delighted. Now who's for another biscuit?'

* * *

Dear Baby,

I got a promotion today! I am now the general manager of the care home! I know it's not a worthy job like a pro bono lawyer, or a clever one like a scientist, but I'm good at it, and I like it. It was really lovely, the current manager is going off on maternity leave and she practically begged me to take her job, saying all these wonderful things about how I was wasted as an assistant manager and how I am ready for the big job, and there was no way that I could turn it down after that speech!

Then there was a bit of a party for me with all the residents, and everyone was clapping. I'll take you in there when you're here, they will absolutely love you. I think we may well drown under a mountain of knitted garments, but everyone is so happy for us.

Granny Florence and Mum don't know it yet, but I'm going to be using my promotion money to have the garden redone as a surprise, ready for summer. Every time one of us comes back from the supermarket with a herb in a pot, or a big leafy lettuce, Florence tuts and says that we really should be growing our own, like she used to in the little patch of grass to the side of the kitchen under the dining-room window.

I've often thought of her and Henry there, kneeling in the dirt, trowel in hand, while Mum sat nearby in a large Silver Cross pram wearing one of those old-fashioned knitted bonnets – like the ones I'll force you to wear when we visit the nursing home! The vegetable patch had long gone by the time I was the chubby-cheeked toddler, riding my tricycle around and around the patio, which is currently hiding under forty years of dirt and grime. Mum used to chalk out little roads and zebra crossings for me to cycle around, using the little horn attached to my handlebars to warn pedestrians (my teddies) that I was coming through. I think I'd like to get a sandbox for you to play in as well.

I've got next door's gardener coming round at eleven to quote for the job. He's about ninety, and whenever I see him out of a window up a ladder pruning their hanging baskets, I instinctively hold my breath and hope for the best, but he seems a cheery soul.

Mum

⋆ ⋆ ⋆

The gardener is five minutes early and wastes no time imprinting muddy footprints all the way from the front door down the corridor through the kitchen to the back door by the bathroom. He walks around the garden, which considering it's probably about the size of one of those pocket handkerchiefs Flo wrote about in her notebook, doesn't take long. He stoops down a couple of times to let the earth run through his fingers, and then says, 'Yep, this'll be fine for veg.'

'Great, and can you put a bit of lawn in over there? And clean up the patio a bit?'

'Yes, no problem, I can even build a little barbecue area for the man of the house if you like?'

For a moment, I think we may have stepped back in time a few decades, which gets my back up. 'I'm not married. But I do like barbecues, so why not.'

He takes out a packet of cigarettes and I immediately say, 'Can you not smoke please, I'm pregnant.'

He looks down at my belly, which, to be fair, just looks like I've had a big lunch, and says, 'Thought you said you weren't married?'

'I'm not. The two aren't related. They don't inseminate you at the altar.'

'Fair play.'

'So how much will it be?'

'Probably three days' work, so three hundred through the books, two fifty cash in hand?'

'Two fifty it is then. Start Monday?'

'Grand. Bye then.'

That was easy. I put a line through 'Garden' on my to-do list for the house. I've had new carpet put in the back bedroom, which will be the nursery, the old carpet looked like it had never been changed since the sixties, and it had these funny white spots in the middle of it, like bleach or something. I've also got a quote to replace the cracked Victorian floor tile in the middle of the entrance hall that's been there forever, and the plasterer is coming on Monday to repair the chipped plaster in the kitchen. I did get a quote for a painter to paint the front door and get rid of that awful green, but his fee was too high, so I might do that myself, I'll see. Noisy pipes are also crossed off, and next on the list: Smash the avocado.

24

Bonnie

Forty years earlier . . .

You could hardly see the far wall of the downstairs bathroom through the steam. Even if she could, there's no way Bonnie would have been able to focus on it. She wasn't a drinker at the best of times, and this was the worst of times.

She stepped into the water, wincing as her foot stung with pain before turning completely numb and an angry red. Then the other foot. Her head spun with the effects of the searing heat and the quarter of a bottle of gin she'd just drunk neat. She had to lean forward, bracing her hands against the cool tiles, a momentary relief. Slowly, she lowered her body until her bottom was touching the scalding water. A red-hot pain shot through her making her gasp. Ignoring every part of her brain that was telling her to wrap a towel around herself and open a window, she pressed on, until the whole of her body was submerged in the green bath and her skin was slowly turning crimson.

The torture was a relief, numbing her thoughts, allowing the blackness she'd craved for the last few weeks to take over. She closed her eyes, and gently allowed her head, then her face, to be enveloped in the burning water, her nose the final part to sink below the surface. The first minute was easy, then her lungs started to hurt as much as her body, every part of her burning. With pain. With shame.

A crash of the door. Two arms pulling her up. A gasp of air. The cold tap on full. An icy blast of air from an open window. Then everything went black—

A switch clicked inside Florence, swiftly shifting her from mother to nurse: her fingers feeling for Bonnie's pulse, her ear to her daughter's mouth listening for her breathing. Relieved to feel and hear both, she cradled her daughter's head in her lap as they sat slumped on the bathroom lino.

When Bonnie awoke, she was lying on Florence's bed, naked under a blanket, her skin slightly mottled, but pale once again. The curtains yet to be drawn showed that it was dark outside. Florence was sitting on the bed beside her, stroking her hair.

'I'm sorry,' Bonnie croaked.

'No, I am. I should have known something was wrong. This wasn't the way to fix it, Bonnie.'

Bonnie started to cry. 'I feel so foolish.'

'Sshh . . . we'll make it right.'

Florence didn't ask any more then, just quietly placed toast with honey next to Bonnie on the bedside table a while later, along with a cup of tea, before getting back into bed alongside her. Her mind taking her to a time when a tiny Bonnie had crawled into bed next to her, her daughter's small bed at the foot of her own wet through. Another time, when the house shook with laughter and music, the noise too much for her sensitive six-year-old ears. And another, when the house rang out in silence, the rooms empty once the mourners had gone, their black clothes lying on a heap on the floor, the two of them, once again, alone together.

'He's gone,' Bonnie finally croaked out.

It took a moment for Florence to leave the last memory and register the present. 'Steven?'

'Oliver. He's gone, and I think I'm carrying his baby.'

Florence bit her lip, as a wave of recognition and sadness washed over her.

'I love him, Mum, I love him so much.'

Florence didn't say anything, just rhythmically stroked her daughter's head. She'd met Oliver a few times, always on Wednesdays, always when Steven was away somewhere. It was none of her business what happened downstairs, not if no one volunteered the information, and she never asked. But she could see by the way her daughter's eyes danced when she spoke about Oliver, the way her cheeks were gently flushed and her voice an octave higher, that he wasn't just 'my friend Oliver', he was much more.

Bonnie hadn't even realised she was doing it half the time, dropping his name into conversation just to hear what it sounded like out loud. It was as though she was denied of saying it at any other time, and when it was just she and Florence, she'd pepper their conversations with mentions of him. 'I was thinking if Saturday is sunny,' Florence might say, 'I was going to go to Kew Gardens if you fancy it?'

'My friend Oliver has the most incredible sunflower in his garden, it's over eight foot tall!'

'Remind me that I need to stock up on Lemsip for the flu season, Betty's already down with it.'

'I'll tell my friend Oliver to put some aside for you at the chemist. He gets a staff discount.'

'When you get the chance, can you ask Steven to help me move the wardrobe in my room to the other bedroom? I want to change things up a bit, and it's a three-person job.'

'I'll ask my friend Oliver to help, he's popping round on Wednesday.'

That was the first time Florence had met Bonnie's friend Oliver, when he happily rolled his sleeves up, bent his knees and took the majority of the wardrobe's weight on his back along the landing while the two women guided it at the other end. He'd stayed for a cup of tea upstairs in Florence's flat, the three of them amiably sitting around her little bistro table in the back bedroom, which she used as a kitchen, with a two-ring hob and small sink newly plumbed in. Unlike Steven, who never took his eyes off the door the two or three times he'd been upstairs, Oliver even said yes to a refill and a Garibaldi.

Before it came to this, if she'd asked Bonnie outright how her marriage was or how she knew Oliver, Bonnie would probably have told her, but that would have been far too intrusive and would definitely have made Bonnie feel uncomfortable. Florence heard Henry's voice in her ear, as she so often did, telling her to give Bonnie some space to figure everything out herself. She always listened to him, but this time, he was wrong.

'Where has he gone, darling?' Florence murmured into Bonnie's hair.

Bonnie shook her head sadly. 'I don't know. His wife . . .' when she said this, she tilted her head up, to look for signs of judgement in her mother's face, but found none. 'His wife is also pregnant.'

Florence bit her lip.

'It's Steven's.'

Florence closed her eyes. The house shook as the front door slammed downstairs, then echoed with Steven opening and shutting every door in their flat, yelling Bonnie's name into each one.

Bonnie shrank back into her pillow, 'Please, please don't tell him I'm here. Don't tell him anything.'

Five rapid angry knocks on Florence's front door at the top of the stairs made Bonnie pull the bedcovers up to her chin. Florence straightened her trousers and jumper and closed the bedroom door behind her.

'Hi, Steven,' she said, opening the door, refraining from commenting on the racket he'd made downstairs.

'Have you seen Bonnie?'

Florence shook her head, 'Not since early this morning, I think she got called into work.'

'Her car's outside.'

'Maybe she got the bus?'

'Did you see anyone pick her up?'

Florence shook her head, 'No, I don't think so. Why are you looking for her?'

'Can't you just mind your own bloody business for once in your life?'

'You're the one standing at my front door asking questions, Steven, not the other way around.'

In her mother's bedroom, cowering under the covers, Bonnie couldn't believe how confident her mother was, how completely believable her lies sounded, completely defiant in the face of the hateful scowl she was certain Florence was receiving from her husband.

'If you see her tell her to come home straight away.'

'Is anything wrong?'

'Just tell her.'

Florence didn't close her front door completely until she was absolutely sure that Steven had shut the door to his.

'I'm guessing you heard all that,' she said, going back into the bedroom.

'I can't go down there, Mum, not like this.'

'It's fine, darling, you can stay here for as long as you like.'

'But he's going to start drinking soon,'

'I think he already has, to be honest.'

'So it's only going to get worse, the longer I stay away.'

'Has he hurt you?'

Bonnie shook her head, remembering the night of her birthday in the hallway when he broke the floor tile, she thought he was going to then, but it was as if he knew that it would definitely be the end of their marriage if he did. No, he was too calculating, too manipulative to cut short their cat and mouse game early. He took pleasure in opening her post 'by mistake'; deliberately changing the television channel when she said that she liked a certain programme; asking her for a specific meal for dinner and then not coming back until the wrong side of midnight, turning the main overhead light on in their bedroom, ensuring she would stumble through her next day at work in a bleary haze; getting up and leaving the room when she was in the middle of speaking, or turning the volume up on the stereo to drown her out. All these things in isolation would be nothing more than mildly discomforting, but the everyday drip drip of feeling invisible in the home she loved was slowly and systematically breaking her heart.

'What happened between him and Oliver's wife?' Florence asked.

Bonnie shrugged, 'The same that happened between me and Oliver – she loved him more than he loved her.'

'The few times I met Oliver, he seemed pretty smitten with you. And a decent sort of chap, is he really leaving you to go through all this alone?'

'He doesn't know. He moved away before I found out I was pregnant. Anyway, I don't know for certain it's Oliver's.'

'So it could be Steven's?'

'A tiny chance, yes.'

'Does he know, about it?'

Bonnie shook her head.

'And how far along are you?'

'Three months.'

'OK then,' Florence let out a sigh of relief, 'so you still have some options, proper options, not what you tried earlier.'

She was wrong, Bonnie thought, there were no options as far as she could see. If what she had tried to do earlier had worked, then she'd have merely exchanged one heart-twisting agony for another; the guilt would have slowly eaten away at her until nothing was left. But then, she thought of bringing a baby into this world which was half Steven, who might grow up to look at her with the same disdain and contempt he did. Or worse, if it had Oliver's wide eyes which narrowed in understanding as they read her thoughts. There were no options.

'You could go away,' Florence said quietly, making sure with every syllable that her suggestion was different to the one forced on her twenty-three years before. 'You could have the baby and if after that you decide that you really can't do this, then there are many families that would be very happy to raise the baby as their own. But please know that if you decide to keep this baby, then you're not alone, I will help you every day of its life, to raise it together. I know I'm not as handsome as Steven or as intelligent as Oliver, but I'm here, and I'm willing, and we can do this.'

Bonnie was silent in the face of two new paths, her logical mind immediately calculating the likely hypothesis of both. Could she give her baby up, regardless of which man it was half of?

The loud punk strains of The Clash suddenly pushed through the floorboards and quite clearly the lyrics 'Should I Stay or Should I Go Now' filled the house. It took a moment to register and then Florence gave a little snort. Bonnie followed a second or two later with a little chuckle, then the two women were in fits of laughter, tears falling down Bonnie's cheeks in a messy hybrid of mirth and sadness.

Should I stay or should I go?

'You should answer the poor man,' Florence said.

'He's not a poor man, he's a selfish bully.'

'Well, that's your answer then.'

'He's not going to go quietly.'

'But he will go. If you want him to.'

'I can't do this by myself, Mum.'

'Yes, you can. I didn't think I could, but I did.'

'No you didn't, you had Dad.'

Florence's mouth twitched. She'd always told herself that if it came up naturally, if it was ever questioned, or necessary to tell the truth, she would. Telling Bonnie about Kenny now would show her she really did understand, Bonnie would see that Florence had been in exactly the same position but with fewer options, that she wasn't giving her empty words of sympathy, she could actually empathise entirely with her, but would that outweigh the crushing realisation that her whole life has been based on a lie?

'I keep thinking about what Dad would have said about this,' Bonnie added, puncturing Florence's resolve to retell the past truthfully. 'He'd have hated Steven on sight and would love Oliver.'

'He'd have liked whoever you liked.'

'He'd have made a good show of pretending to, like you do, but I can tell you think Steven's an idiot.'

'He just needs to grow up, that's all. Maybe a baby will do that, if you give him a chance.'

'But what if it's not his? I pretend? I couldn't do that, not to him, or the baby. I couldn't live a lie forever.'

Florence remembered thinking this too once, but it was much easier than she thought it would be. 'Just take each day as it comes.'

'Do you think Oliver will ever come back?' Bonnie asked.

There was no mistaking the desperately hopeful tone to her question, making Florence answer the only way she could have done, 'Things have a way of working out the way they were meant to.'

Bonnie tiptoed down the stairs an hour later, making sure she opened the front door silently from the inside and slammed it shut loudly, adding a cheerful, 'I'm home!' for good measure.

Upstairs in her flat, Florence poured herself a large brandy and sank into an armchair in her lounge, staring at the sofa opposite her where her and Henry's bed used to be. The sofa slowly disappeared and Henry was sitting up in bed wearing his striped pyjamas. His book was open on his lap, and his eyes smiling over his glasses. 'You did well there, old girl.'

Florence tipped her glass to him and smiled gratefully back.

The music suddenly turned off downstairs, and voices too low for Florence to make out individual words took its place, but at least there was no shouting.

Bonnie had chosen not to mention Oliver at all when she told Steven she was pregnant. There was no point: he'd gone and wasn't coming back, so there was nothing to be gained by bringing him into this. It was a simple choice for Steven to make, like the words of the song said, stay or go? Stay and raise a baby with her, or go and be free.

'So,' she said, bracing herself for his answer, and hoping her voice didn't have a tremble to it when she asked, 'which will it be?'

'I'll think about it,' he said.

25

Stella

'I have no idea who the father is. This is a donor baby.'

The midwife clearly hasn't read the email I sent her ahead of tonight's NCT class explaining my situation, otherwise she wouldn't have asked if we were waiting for Dad or whether we should make a start. I figured there was no point telling a lie to this group of strangers, like I did to the residents in the nursing home. I only did that because they wouldn't have understood what it meant. With this group, either they'll be horrified and I'll never see them again once this class is over, or they'll be fine about it and we can all move on.

The midwife blinks a couple of times and smiles brightly, 'Fantastic. Good for you.'

'It's a what?' I hear the male half of the couple to my far right whisper to his wife.

'Sshh, she said it's a donor baby.'

'Oh,' comes the whisper again. 'That makes more sense. I thought she said doughnut.'

'I think that's really brave,' simpers the woman immediately to my left, who I think is called Fleur. She emphasises quite how brave she thinks I am with a tilt of her head and sticking her bottom lip out. Thanks Fleur, appreciate it.

I can feel the six couples appraising me like I'm on the *Antiques Roadshow*, looking for visible flaws and cracks, date stamps and misuse by previous owners.

Fleur's husband coughs, then says, 'I hope you don't mind me asking . . .'

I already do.

'But what made you decide to do that?'

I smile sweetly back, 'Probably the same reasons as all of us here. I want a baby.'

'But by yourself?'

'Yes. By myself. And my army of fierce women that I have around me. What made you decide to have a baby – sorry, I didn't catch your name?'

He looks embarrassed, 'Michael. And, um, well, we felt the time was right, I've reached the top of my career, our mortgage is paid off and the school fund is looking pretty healthy, so here we are.'

God, I hate them, with their solvent successful lives and their planned-to-precision pregnancy. 'Yes, like I said, the same reasons as you. Minus the career and the house ownership.'

'Are you a lesbian?' the woman opposite me wearing a turquoise maxi skirt asks with, and I'm sure I'm not imagining, a little twinkle in her eye.

'No, no, not a lesbian. Just a single woman wanting a baby.'

'How do you know the donor's not a psychopath?' Fleur asks, her eyes wide with curiosity and drama.

'How do you know Michael's not?' I counter.

Michael shifts uncomfortably in his seat.

'It's always the quiet ones you have to watch,' I add, with a raise of my eyebrow and a knowing nod.

'Shall we make a start?' the midwife says, but no one pays any notice, finding my situation far more intriguing than the plastic uterus with detachable cervix that she's holding in her hand.

'How did you pick one?' the woman opposite asks.

'That was the toughest part,' I say honestly. 'It took months to find one that felt right.'

'There must be so much choice,' says one woman wistfully.

'I bet they all lie, like on Tinder,' says another.

'Do you know what he looks like?' the midwife asks, letting curiosity get the better of her and joining in.

'No, but I know he's tall, he's half Dutch, half Cornish, blond hair, blue eyes, law graduate, loves animals, horse riding.'

'He sounds bloody lovely,' says a woman with red hair to my left. The man next to her glares at her and moves a little away from her. 'What?' she says. 'He does. I'd have picked him too.'

Most of the women nod in agreement, and I clock a couple of them sneaking a sideways look at their own sperm donors seeing how they measure up to mine. It makes me feel rather smug if I'm honest.

The midwife coughs. 'We've only got an hour left, so we really should talk about the labour—'

'Aren't you worried though? About doing it by yourself?' Fleur asks.

'What time does Michael leave for work?' I ask.

'Just after six,' she answers slowly with a look of confusion on her face.

'And get back?'

'Eight-ish.'

'So I could ask you the same question.'

'But . . . but . . . he'll be there for the night feeds,' Fleur stammers, while Michael looks like this is news to him.

'I was raised by a single father,' says the red-haired woman's partner. 'You don't need two parents, just one good one.'

I could kiss him, except his wife is my main ally in the class and so I won't.

'Did you have to have sex with him?' the maxi skirt lady asks and this time I do not mistake the lascivious lick of the lips.

'No. No I did not. It was all medically managed.'

'How much did it cost?' Fleur probes.

'I'd rather not—'

'Was it thousands?'

'It was . . . an amount.'

'If it was a movie, you'd bump into him in a supermarket and fall in love,' says one woman wistfully.

'The thought has never crossed my mind,' I lie. And it's not a supermarket I intend to meet him in, it's a train station. In the rain.

'OK everyone,' says the midwife, trying to pull what's left of the session back together, 'Who'd like to see a uterus?'

After the class, the red-haired woman is waiting outside the toilet when I come out of it. 'Sorry,' I say, 'here you go,' and hold the door open for her.

'I was waiting for you actually. I just wanted to properly introduce myself. I'm Eve. And I think what you're doing is awesome.'

'Um, thank you.'

'Take no notice of what some of them said. They're just jealous that your baby's going to have better genes than theirs.'

'That's the plan,' I laugh.

'Look, you seem really nice, so you've probably got enough friends, but if you ever wanted to meet up for coffee or lunch, I've written my number down here.'

I take the scrap of paper from her; she's written her number on the back of a KFC receipt, so I know we'll get on.

'Can you thank your partner for standing up for me too?' I ask.

'Oh we're not together. We're co-parenting. Two people who like each other enough to share a child, but not enough to share a house or a bathroom.'

'Wow. OK. It's just you didn't correct the midwife when she referred to him as your husband.'

'After seeing the flak you got? No chance,' she laughs. 'And sometimes it's just easier that way, isn't it? Look, I've got to go, I've got a date with a hot Welshman, but I'll see you next week?'

I nod. I like meeting people who make me feel conventional and boring.

One of the trashy showbiz magazines I wasted my money on yesterday had a tour of a film star's house, including their new nursery that cost £25,000. Now I love a new cushion and oversized rug as much as the next person, but twenty-five grand? For a baby's bedroom? I realise I'm not an expert in this field, but I really can't see how much nicer their baby's room would be than the one I've got ready for my baby. Are rich babies any happier or healthier than ones born to parents who are still paying for their sofa in monthly instalments? (I really should have added that cost to the rent seeing as I'm not the one sitting on it any more.)

The words of Fleur's husband Michael at the NCT class have stayed with me over the last month; his smug proclamation that they delayed getting pregnant until their mortgage was paid off and he'd reached the top of his career ladder. Should I have held out another year or two and saved up more? Or waited for a partner to arrive in my life to do this journey with me? Even though they were much younger than I am, both Mum and Florence waited until they had a home and a husband they loved. Doing it alone would never have crossed their minds.

I literally have nothing to offer this child except love and a barmy army of women around it. Is that selfish? What would Donor 203 make of me? His reasons for doing this couldn't have been financial, being a lawyer, so he must have done it for altruistic reasons, to make families complete. Would he be disappointed his sperm ended up inside me? I'm almost certain I'm not what he had in mind when he made the decision to do this. But am I any less worthy than a couple who have tried and failed to make children of their own? Surely me, Mum and Florence are as tight as any couple. Tighter even than some of the couples in my NCT group, who don't even seem to like each other very much. Me, Mum and Florence might not be a conventional set-up, but I couldn't have been more wrong when I thought that I'd be doing this solo, completely and terrifyingly alone.

The baby kicks in agreement, making me smile and stroke the spot on my stomach she kicked. I'm certain she's a she. How can she not be? This house hasn't had masculine energy in it for decades.

'We'll be OK, little one. I haven't got twenty-five grand to spend on your curtains, but we've got a roof over our heads and enough love in these walls to make a good go of it.'

'Speaking to yourself again?'

I turn around to see Eve standing in the open doorway to the nursery. 'Your gran let me in,' she explains. 'She's also just spilt soup all over the sofa, but wouldn't let me help clean it up.'

I shake my head, 'She's awful, she loves eating on the sofa whenever she can, but it does mean it's looking more and more like it's got patchwork upholstery.'

'I heard what you were saying, before,' Eve says. 'I didn't mean to, sorry.'

I shrug, 'Honestly, it's fine, just feeling a bit pensive, that's all. It's all becoming quite real now.'

'I know what you mean. Ben's just got a new girlfriend, and it's made me realise that this co-parenting business is going to be a bit more complicated than either of us really realised. We both just wanted a child so much, it just seemed such a simple decision, and now we have all these other things to consider.' She picks up Bear from the shelf and smiles as she turns him over in her hands. I pray he doesn't disintegrate into sawdust. 'I actually envy you doing it alone, I just didn't think I could.'

'Why not?'

'I don't know really. Social conditioning, I guess? Two parents better than one. Also, I didn't really want the responsibility of being the only one to keep it on the straight and narrow. I thought I could share the blame if it all goes wrong,' she laughs. 'I thought Ben was as clean-cut as they come, but he's only recently told me about an uncle who's in an open prison in Gloucestershire for selling counterfeit Filofaxes, so criminal activity is in the blood, which he kept quiet about until now.'

I laugh, 'Fake Filofaxes? That is the very definition of a white-collar crime. At least you can unearth the demons in Ben's DNA over time. I have no idea really about my baby's dad. Or my own dad come to that.'

'Well you've turned out OK.'

'I'm not too sure about that.'

Eve looks around her, 'And this house is a lovely place to grow up.'

'I never thought I'd be still living here with my own child. It's really strange to think that I was a baby here, and my mum. So much for spreading my wings.'

'I think it's great. It's got a lovely feel about it.'

I unfold the blanket at the end of the cot and fold it again, just to give my hands something to do. 'Are you ready for all this?' I ask.

'Not in the slightest.'

'Promise you're not just saying that to make me feel better?'

Eve laughs and holds up three fingers, 'Brownie promise. Anyway, is anyone ever ready?'

'Fleur and Michael?'

Eve scoffs, 'Absolute rubbish. I guarantee his whole "we waited until we were mortgage-free" bollocks was just stalling for time because the idea of parenthood scared the bejesus out of them. Like it does everyone.'

I'd like to think she's right, but I can't imagine Florence or Mum being scared or unsure about anything. I'm usually relieved I've got two such capable role models, but right now, when I need someone who's been through the quagmire and come out the other side, I just wish they were slightly less perfect.

26

Florence

Dear Little One,

All this preparation for your birth has made me reflective and took me back to that sunny morning in May 1960 when your grandmother Bonnie arrived into the world. Princess Margaret, the Queen's sister, was getting married that day, resplendent in white (a bold choice, said some, including my mother to anyone who would listen). As she stepped down from a glass coach outside Westminster Abbey in front of two thousand guests, crowds of half a million well-wishers lining the streets waved miniature Union Jack flags. Front rooms across the country were packed with friends and neighbours, all eyes trained on tiny wooden television sets flickering black and white through the foggy haze of Rothmans King Size.

Martha, our landlady, had made the front bedroom lovely for the birth, even renting another small black and white TV so I could watch the wedding upstairs to take my mind off the labour. There was a vase of fresh daffodils on my bedside table, and crisp white linen on the bed. It smelled beautiful and fresh. I wanted that to be the first thing that Bonnie smelled so the rest of her life would be like that. Henry couldn't be in the room with me when Bonnie was born, the midwife was adamant about that, but he didn't leave the house the whole time, and as Bonnie was a stubborn little thing, he was sitting on the landing outside the room for nearly eight hours, silly man! He even had his sausage rolls and bits from the buffet on a paper plate on the top step. Martha brought me in a plate of party food too, to keep me going, I don't think I'd have been treated any better if I was giving birth in Buckingham Palace.

Honestly, you should have heard the cheers from downstairs, when the midwife opened the door to tell Henry and he shouted it down the stairs, 'It's a girl!' Everyone completely forgot about the royal wedding then, all toasts were for Bonnie, and the party carried on until the early hours. Henry slipped downstairs for a small glass of beer with everyone, to be polite, but he was back before I knew it, he wouldn't leave my side.

I knew of babies that slept in chests of drawers, and I'd have been fine with putting Bonnie in one for the first month or so, but Henry wouldn't hear of it and came home one day with the most marvellous walnut crib, which rocked back and forth. Her bed was better than ours! 'Only the best for our Bonnie,' he would say. Honestly, you couldn't have found a prouder husband or father if you'd have scoured the whole of the country. It was a bit embarrassing really. 'Knock it off,' I'd say, as he'd sneak up behind me while I was washing up or something and he'd plant a massive kiss on my neck. 'People are looking!' But I liked it really, and no one was looking. That was the wonderful thing about this house, everyone's business was their own.

27
Florence

Sixty-two years earlier . . .

Six miles away from Westminster Abbey, on a heavily stained mattress in a second-floor bedroom of the St Philomena's Crusade of Rescue overlooking an East End street, Florence pushed her baby into the world. The newborn's first screams were drowned out by an impromptu rousing rendition of 'God Save the Queen' from the street below, which was adorned with Union Jack bunting and trestle tables heaving with platters of pork pies and luncheon meat gently curling in the sun.

'Just in time for the party,' the nun smiled, handing Florence the infant wrapped in a towel. 'I'll go and make up a bottle for it.'

Florence looked up from where she was studying her baby's chubby hand in awe, which was clasped around her finger. 'Her name's Bonnie.'

'Sorry?'

'You said "it", but I'm calling her Bonnie.'

The nun's kindly smile wavered, 'It's best not to name it. In all likelihood, they'll want to change it.'

'Her name's Bonnie. And I'm going to feed her myself,' Florence added. 'So no need for a bottle.'

If it had been the chubbier one, the one with hairs growing out of the mole on her chin and an uncanny ability to slip the words 'sin', 'shame' and 'damnation' into every sentence – even the seemingly innocuous phrases that you'd think were hard to pepper with casual condemnation, like announcing that supper was ready: 'Jesus fed sinners, thus so shall we'; not leaving windows open: 'That's all you need, pneumonia on top of eternal damnation' – she'd probably have slapped Florence around the face with the afterbirth cord for such rudeness. But as luck would have it, and Florence wasn't so drugged up on pethidine not to recognise that in this instance she had been uncharacteristically lucky, the nicer nun who had been by her side for the last three hours just gave her a sad smile and said, 'It's really best not to. It's harder for you and confusing for them in the long run.'

Ten minutes later, the midwife placed a lukewarm bottle of evaporated milk down on the nightstand next to her.

'It's for the best,' she said.

'Yes,' Florence agreed meekly to the nun's retreating back, before unscrewing the lid, grimacing as she gulped down the sickly-sweet liquid while sticking her large milky white breast into her baby's hungry mouth, 'it is.'

Four weeks later, the last of the rice was still clinging to the cracks in the gutters outside the cathedral. Flags were yet to be untied from the some of the nation's lamp posts. The princess and her new husband were having to remember to rotate every hour or so to ensure their bodies had an even golden bronze tan whilst aboard a yacht meandering around the Caribbean and Florence left the mother and baby home unseen under a blanket of darkness.

The church clock just struck eleven, an hour after the bearded nun had declared lights out with a cheery, 'Go to sleep so you'll be one day closer to your day of judgement.'

It had to be this way. Bonnie and Florence were on borrowed time with every day that passed. Almost every baby born at St Philomena's was destined for a home in an unspecified place 'in the countryside', fresh air apparently being so much better for it than maternal love. Florence saw it happen every day. A 'doctor's appointment' or a 'nice walk around the block' a baby doesn't come back from. It would be Bonnie's turn soon and she wasn't taking any chances. Her parents organised the whole thing, the only thing left was to sign the form which had been waved in her face every morning that week.

In one hand, Florence held a bag containing a nightdress, a rosary and a selection of terry towelling cloth nappies and once-white Babygros one of the other young mothers in the home had no need for any more, while in the other hand, she clutched a piece of paper with an address in Wandsworth on it. Grace, the girl in the next bed to Florence, had surreptitiously pressed this address into her hand a few days before, her red-rimmed eyes silently begging Florence to do what very few of them were able to.

Florence had never been outside alone after dark in the East End before. Laughter spilled out from the public house on the corner, and reflections pooled in puddles on the road from the windows of the houses she scurried past, still ablaze with light and life. People eating late dinners, families talking round kitchen tables, even a man and woman kissing on a sofa, which made Florence blush and walk faster. She thought of her parents, sitting in adjacent armchairs, sleeping in adjacent beds, living adjacent lives. Mr and Mrs Weston would be asleep now. Eleven o'clock was not an hour that appeared twice a day in their semi-detached in Chiswick. They'd be in their nightclothes under starched white sheets – *always buy white, Florence, anything else is commo*n.

A drunk suddenly stumbled out of an alley in front of her, tucking his shirt in his trousers as he rebounded off a wall, and Florence instinctively pulled her coat around Bonnie so she'd be safer. She'd tied Bonnie to her front using strips of the frayed bedsheets from St Philomena's. She'd always thought that motherhood started at the moment of birth, the point at which a baby, covered in all manner of bodily fluids, was handed over, and she definitely had felt a flash of something then. And when her breast was pumping food like fuel into Bonnie, there it was again, but this, this feeling of being her sole protector against the whole city of London, this fierceness, this is what motherhood felt like.

The night bus was quiet. Unnervingly quiet after the sounds of the streets. Florence was on high alert for anyone from the home chasing after them, constantly checking behind her, holding her breath every time the bus stopped in case anyone got on and took them back. Bonnie slept the whole way; Florence felt down more than a few times to feel the reassuring staccato beat of her pulse against her finger. After frequently checking the piece of paper during the journey, she got off at the bus stop Grace had told her to, and turned left, towards a darker terraced street with fewer lamp posts. This street was asleep. Curtains drawn, doors double bolted for the night, lights off, cereal boxes and bowls already on kitchen tables ready for the morning. One house, halfway along the road, on the left, had a lantern glowing over a green front door.

Florence wasn't expecting it to be green. It wasn't as though she pictured it as any other colour, but the fact it was green threw her a little. Green was the colour of the ill-fated Ford Zephyr her father had been forced to return to the dealership after finally saving enough to buy because her mother insisted that 'green is unlucky'. He'd had to wait another four months, taking the bus to work every day until a different colour had become available, so in some ways, her mother had been right, that was quite unfortunate. It was also the same green of the emerald Henry had offered her when he thought she was someone different. It was also the same green as the fields she had been promised Bonnie would grow up surrounded by as long as she signed the form earlier that morning.

Sign the form.

Sign the form.

They could shove the form up their— *Florence!* Oh God, she couldn't even curse without hearing her mother's horrified voice and imagining her crossing herself.

Florence raised the door knocker and rapped it three times against the wood. If she stayed here for a while maybe she could convince the owner to paint it a luckier colour.

A woman Florence guessed to be in her fifties opened the door on a chain, gave her an appraising nod and invited her in by unhooking the chain and opening the door wide enough for Bonnie and Florence to squeeze through. They stood in a warm narrow hallway wallpapered in a vibrant pattern of orange concentric rings. Florence had no idea what to expect, what would happen now. Until a minute before, this was a scribbled address in pencil, now it was Florence's only chance at a future, even if it did have a green door.

Florence unbuttoned her coat to give Bonnie some air, making the top of her head visible.

'What's her name?' the woman asked kindly.

Florence could kiss her for using a pronoun that wasn't 'it'. 'Bonnie,' she said letting out a breath. 'Her name is Bonnie.'

'Pretty. Come on, follow me, you must be tired.' The woman led the way up the staircase to a landing with three doors off it, reeling off the house rules as she walked. 'No overnight guests of either gender without asking first. If you smoke, open a window and before you sleep, close it. If you cook, wash up after yourself. The rent is whatever you can afford, and we look after each other, no judgement, no gossiping, and no blethering about anything that's not your business. All right?'

Florence nodded, not entirely sure what blethering was, whilst at the same time being resolutely committed never to do it. She was so grateful she could cry but settled for an appreciative nod and a dozen quick blinks.

Martha, the landlady, anticipated her every need, right down to the blanket-lined bottom drawer of the walnut chest, which Florence carefully laid Bonnie in.

Florence didn't know whether she should stay upstairs and go to sleep, or go downstairs. It wasn't a hotel, not that she'd ever been in one. But if she went downstairs, should she get changed? Her mother would get changed. *'If we let standards slip in the home, what hope have we got outside it?'* Florence never understood the lengths her mother went to in order to pretend to be something she wasn't. Did her father really think that she did all the housework, childcare and cooking in a white blouse and pleated skirt smelling of Yardley's English Lavender all day? And why would he care if one day she did decide to greet him in her pinny smelling vaguely of lard? The world wasn't going to end if she hadn't lacquered her hair into place.

'Knock knock,' Martha said, preferring to say the words rather than do the action, as she opened Florence's bedroom door a little, half an hour later. 'Don't want to disturb, but I made some Irish stew earlier, and there's some left if you're hungry? It's ready when you are.'

As Florence padded down the stairs, she could hear music coming from the record player in the front room that was as far from the melancholy organ music of her childhood as it was possible to be. Her eyes widened as she stood in the doorway. Three girls were lounging on different mismatched armchairs, more limbs than she had ever seen before were stretched out on the floor or flung over the arms of chairs. Florence was slightly jealous of the ease at which they could just relax, having never done that in the home she grew up in, let alone a communal living room in a boarding house belonging to someone else.

'Hello, I'm, um, I'm Florence,' she said from the doorway.

Everyone offered their hands for her to shake: one girl got up to do it, the other two just elongated their bodies upwards to make their hands meet hers. Two of them looked a similar age to Florence, the other one was slightly older, all three were smoking. Florence resisted the urge to cough and looked towards the sash window to check it was open. The fact it was made her relax; she could definitely settle in a place where rules were followed.

'Take a pew,' Martha said, bustling into the room and handing Florence a steaming bowl.

She looked around, not understanding what it was exactly she was supposed to be taking, before realising Martha just meant sit down. She'd never eaten a meal not sitting at a table, or in the living room. She balanced the bowl on the arm of the sofa, and greedily gulped down the stew – the nicest thing she'd ever tasted. Martha and the other girls were chatting amiably about something, but Florence wasn't really listening, it was the first time in a month that she'd been apart from Bonnie and it was unnerving.

As soon as her bowl was empty, she said, 'I should, um, go back up to . . .' Her voice trailed off, then nodded up at the ceiling rose, as though the rest of the sentence was written on it.

'Of course. See you in the morning. Help yourself to anything in the larder.'

As Florence climbed the stairs, she listened out for whispers, the kind that always follow someone leaving a room, where the gaps are filled in by those that want to share the fact they know more about them than everyone else: '*his wife left him for a man she met at the post office*', '*they said it's reached his liver*', '*she arrived with a baby under her coat!*' But all she heard was one of the girls, Rosemary, she thought her name was, ask if anyone minded if she had a bath.

28

Stella

'You're going to set a bath up?' Mum asks. 'In the living room?'

I lick my finger and casually turn the page of my magazine. 'It's better than the front garden.'

'Why can't you use the bath in the bathroom?' Florence asks.

'Oh Flo, so many reasons. One, because it doesn't fit all my limbs in at one time. Two, it's puke green.'

Mum folds her arms across her chest. 'It's avocado.'

'It's 2023,' I reply in the same nasally tone. 'Anyway, I don't want the first thing my child seeing when it opens its eyes is that colour. It's going to think it's swapped my womb for a bowl of guacamole. And it's not going to be a bath, it's more like an inflatable paddling pool.'

'In the living room?' Mum repeats.

'Yes mother. In the living room. And I'll set up a couple of deckchairs and a tiki bar next to it for you and Flo to get the full holiday feeling. You could drink pina coladas and wear bikinis.'

Florence actually looks like she's considering this. 'I haven't worn a bikini for ages.'

Mum scoffs. 'You're eighty, there's a reason for that. What about the carpet, it's cream?'

'Mum. Can you please, for one minute, stop being so bloody sensible and embrace a new experience?'

'But why does it have to be the living room? What if the neighbours see?'

'If they're able to see, then they're standing in the middle of your flowerbed trampling your roses, and you should really go out and have a word with them about boundaries.'

Mum is pensive for a moment, then claps her hands together in delight, 'I've got an idea!'

Florence and I trade a glance that says, *oh god.*

Mum says excitedly, 'Why don't you use my bedroom, that's the room I was born in wasn't it, Mum? That would make a lovely continuity, wouldn't it?'

'Do you know what, that would be really nice,' I say slowly, the idea of past and present melding together. I turn to Florence. 'But didn't you tell me once it was the front bedroom where Mum was born?'

'Was it?' Mum asks, peering at her mother. 'I always thought it's the one I'm in. I've often lain in bed thinking about life going full circle, it being the room I was born in and will probably die in.'

'Jesus, Mum!' I gasp.

'Bonnie!' Florence scolds.

'What?' Mum shrugs, looking at each of us, 'It's not maudlin, it's a fact of life. So which one was it, Mum?'

Florence scratches her head, not looking at either of us in the eye. 'Oh crikey, it was so long ago, I've forgotten.'

Florence doesn't see Mum narrow her eyes at her in concentration, trying to see if this memory loss is a glitch or the start of a long road to eventual complete neurological collapse. She's always on high alert for signs of degenerative decline, thrusting a crossword in front of Florence and ordering her to 'do that' or asking her, apropos of nothing, what the capital of a random African country is out of the blue, just to check on her cognitive function. Though it might have been more helpful if Mum had asked her the capital of Spain or Portugal rather than Gabon (FYI it's Libreville, but I had to look it up, after I looked up where Gabon is). I can't blame mum though, I've been a bit worried too. Recently Florence has been mixing things up a little, particularly about the past. I wonder if the notebook is making her confused.

When I stripped the wallpaper off the small back bedroom in order to paint it Golden Honey – a much harder job than I first thought, as layer, after layer came off, like peeling an onion – Florence commented from the doorway, 'I remember when I papered this room for Bonnie, when she was about two, I got myself into such a muddle with it, I had to use my week's wages to pay for a man to help me.'

'Didn't Grandpa help?'

'Oh, he didn't live here then.'

I narrowed my eyes at her, and she quickly said, 'I mean, he wasn't here then, he worked away a lot during that time.'

Then, a few days ago, the three of us were watching something mindless on television, a soap opera that none of us really followed, and two of the characters were getting married. 'Do you remember the first dance at your wedding, Mum?' I asked.

She shook her head. 'Your dad was in charge of the music. It was probably something loud and shouty.' She turned to Florence. 'Did you and Dad have a first dance, Mum?'

Florence smiled. 'We did. In this room! We had the reception here, after the ceremony, took all the furniture out and put it in our neighbour's garden, and everyone stood around the edges of the room as we twirled around to Elvis's "Can't help Falling in Love".'

'I didn't know that was your wedding song,' Mum said. 'I love that song.'

'Here,' I grabbed my phone, 'I'll play it.' I found it easily on YouTube and turned the volume up, muting the TV as I did. Florence closed her eyes and started swaying in time to Elvis's dulcet tones in her armchair. Mum and I shared a smile.

As I go to bed, something gnaws at me. I know I shouldn't have read their notebooks, but they were designed to be read by my baby one day, so it's not as though they were private thoughts, but I'm sure Florence wrote in one entry that she and Henry moved in here after they got back from honeymoon, so how could they have got married here?

An hour or so later, as I close down my apps on my phone before bed, I notice that Elvis's song only came out in October 1961, two years after their wedding. I sigh sadly; I see it at work every day, a blurring of recollections, tiny slices of memories dissolving and disappearing. But I can't bear that it's happening to Florence.

A few days later, the rattle of the letter box wakes me up. I've been meaning to throw the old wire basket attached to the back of the letter box in the bin because it's been my daily alarm call ever since I can remember. When I had the capability to just yawn, turn over and go straight back to sleep, I didn't mind it, but now I'm needing the loo every seventeen minutes during the night, any sound that wakes me up earlier than necessary has to go.

There are a couple of letters addressed to Mum, three handwritten ones for Florence, who has collected a motley bunch of pen pals from around the world. And at the bottom of the wire tray is one addressed to me, a thin white envelope, the address typed on the front. I almost put it into the pocket of my dressing gown, but something stops me, and instead I slide my finger along the seal. It's from the donor agency.

Dear Ms Fairbrother,

We regret to inform you that a highly unusual breach of protocol has occurred concerning the donor sample that was provided for your recent intrauterine insemination. It transpires that somehow you were provided with a sample from a different donor.

Please rest assured that all our donors undergo the same screening process to rule out genetic diseases and chromosomal abnormalities. All donors have tested negative for HIV, hepatitis B and C, human T-cell lymphotropic viruses and sexually transmitted infections. All samples also incur a 180-day quarantine process whereby they are retested for any new infections which may have developed.

Please find attached the information in your new donor profile, and as a gesture of goodwill, we are refunding the £950 via bank transfer, which should show up in your account within twenty-eight working days.

'That's nice of them,' Florence says, without a trace of sarcasm lacing her words.

'Which part?' Mum replies angrily. 'The part where they gave her some random sperm, or the fact they told her about it?'

'The refund, £950's a lot of money.'

Mum turns to face Florence, 'Mum, how are you not getting this? The baby's father is some *random bloke*.'

'He was always some random bloke.'

'But now he's more random!'

I haven't said anything yet. I don't need to, between the two of them they are voicing all my thoughts out loud anyway.

The three of us are sitting around the kitchen table, all still in our dressing gowns and slippers, a pot of tea, the antidote to all trauma, even apparently wrongful insemination, sits between us.

'Let me read his profile again,' Mum says, holding out her hand for the piece of paper which was attached to the letter and details Donor 302, the mistaken replacement of Donor 203. She picks it up, 'Donor 302, 34, five foot five, 58kg. Uses prescription lenses, allergic to rapeseed, shellfish and horsehair, no medical conditions or abnormalities. He has a bachelor's degree in Theme Park Engineering and is a qualified face yoga practitioner. He loves rollercoasters, comic books and body art.'

'What's body art?' Florence asks. 'Painting on people?'

'Tattoos,' I reply in a monotone voice, hearing his profile out loud was worse than reading it to myself.

'I once knew a man who had a tattoo of a mermaid on his navel holding a fishing line which went all the way down to—'

'Thanks, Mum, that's enough.'

'I don't know what you're both so fussed about, he sounds fun, who doesn't love a rollercoaster?' Florence says. 'And a good comic. And it's not as though the baby's going to come out covered in ink, will he? That's not genetic.'

'He's allergic to horsehair,' I say weakly, realising as I say it that the very last vestiges of my imagined life have completely evaporated along with all the rosettes my child will never win.

'But we don't have a horse,' Florence unhelpfully points out.

I start crying, 'And we never will.'

'What is rapeseed?' Florence asks.

'Those yellow flowers in every field you go past,' Mum replies.

'So now we can never live in the countryside either.' I rest my head on the kitchen table, trying to come to terms with a very different future than the one I've had plotted out.

Mum pats my shoulder, 'Just because Donor 302 is allergic to those things doesn't mean that your baby will be. Dad was highly allergic to shellfish too, wasn't he, Mum, and I love prawns.'

Florence nods and smiles, 'Yes, exactly. The baby's only half him, your half might cancel all that out. Like it did with me and Henry,' she adds.

'He's really short,' I say, looking at the statistics on the top of the page, which I'd skipped over earlier on seeing a mass of numbers. 'And much lighter than me. If we met in real life not only would we have nothing to talk about, I'd crush him.' I think about Donor 203, just going about his business, being six foot four and Viking-like, peeling mussels off rocks near where his parents live on the coast for his dinner, cantering through a rapeseed field on a horse without a hint of a sniff or the need of an EpiPen.

'But look,' says Florence, jabbing the paper in delight, 'he's a Gemini, you said that was a good one.'

'Whoop-de-doo. Like star signs are even real.'

'Well, we can't do anything about it now,' Mum says. 'Just got to make the best of it.'

'You're both missing the point,' Florence says, 'you wanted a baby, you got a baby. What does it matter if it was from a different donor?'

'I know that,' I gasp between sobs, 'but I really liked the Dutch-Cornish heritage.'

Mum tilts her head to one side, 'What would a Cornish-Dutch heritage look like? Were you expecting the baby to shoot out of you wearing clogs and eating a pasty?'

This is probably the funniest thing Mum has ever said, but I can't even smile. I'm completely numb.

29

Bonnie

Bonnie has been nauseous for days. She's felt this way ever since the letter from the agency came claiming their 'highly unusual breach of protocol'. Watching her daughter leapfrog from disbelief, to anger, to revenge, to sadness was too much. Bonnie had set aside an hour this morning to write in the journal, but after this news, she feels too numb to write anything. She feels absolutely lost. The look on Stella's face as her world fell apart and everything she thought was sure, solid, concrete just crumble away was heart-breaking and it took every ounce of strength she had not to cry with her.

She stopped herself just in time from telling Stella that she knows how she feels, but she does. She knows the aching guilt at not knowing whether to love or despise the baby growing inside. She saw Stella stroke her stomach and pull her hand away, Bonnie did that once too, one minute feeling this fierce rush of love and protection, the next anger and fear. She thinks she's done a good job of hiding it, as Stella will have to do when the baby comes. And somehow, the fear turns into love in the end anyway, it did with her and it will with Stella.

Bonnie wasted the first year of being a mother looking at Stella through narrowed eyes. Was that Steven's sneer she just glimpsed as Stella refused a rusk, or was that Oliver's quizzical assessment of the rusk before accepting it? Both men had sandy blond hair, like Stella's, but the slightly lopsided smile was pure Oliver, while Stella's eyes were lighter than Oliver's, a pale blue, like Steven's, and her own. She'd wished she'd spent time looking at the way Oliver's hairline grew, or whether he had one crown or two, like Stella. She'd never thought to study his fingers to see if they had the same curve to the index fingers as Stella and she spent weeks trying to conjure up the shape of his feet to see if he had a high arch too. Steven was flat-footed, always clomping around the flat.

It was exhausting and anxiety-inducing, and she lost the first few precious months of Stella's life playing detective, trying to decipher her DNA, when it actually didn't matter at all. But how can she say this to Stella?

'Knock knock,' Florence says, opening Bonnie's door a little.

'Come in, Mum, I'm just . . .' Bonnie tails off, realising that she was just sitting on her bed staring into space, and there's no way of hiding that.

Florence shuts the door behind her and sits down next to her daughter. 'I just wanted to see how you are?'

'Me? Oh I'm OK.'

'Are you though? I thought maybe this business with the donor was bringing it all back.'

Bonnie arranges her face into a smile. 'No, not really.'

'No?'

Bonnie sighs, 'If anything, it's making me question my job. Here we are, saying to her that genes don't make a person who they are, and that's exactly what I've been trying to disprove my whole adult life!'

'But common sense surely tells us that we can't be carbon copies of the people that made us, otherwise we'd never evolve, as a species,' Florence says.

'Not copies, no, but surely we inherit some of their

characteristics, physical and emotional. I have your hair that won't stay straight longer than three minutes, and I definitely have Dad's inquisitive brain, no offence.'

Florence thinks of Kenny's indifference to current affairs, and the fact that despite winning eleven Academy awards he would have dismissed *Ben-Hur* out of hand because history was boring. 'None taken.' Florence continues, choosing her words very carefully, 'If we follow your logic, how do you explain the fact that Stella has spent her whole working life until recently coasting through menial jobs because of what she thinks is her DNA when both her actual parents are hard-working professionals?'

Bonnie gasps. This is the first time Florence has mentioned the probability of Steven not being Stella's real father since she was born.

'It's learned behaviour,' Florence continues, knowing that every word she says is going to imprint itself on her daughter, but also knowing that it needs to. 'She knows what she's been told about him, and she's assumed parts of his personality for herself.'

'Was it a nursing degree you had or a psychology one?' Bonnie says nastily.

Florence ignores her. 'I think you need to tell her.'

'I absolutely do not.'

'She is down there right now, beating herself up about the fact that she, through no fault of her own, has made a baby with different genes than the ones she chose, and she thinks that these genes are going to make the baby turn out to be a completely different person.'

'Well they might.'

'And they might not. The child, like Stella ...' Florence pauses, adding *'like you'* silently to the sentence, 'can become whoever they like, unencumbered by who their parents are. If you can set her free from this mentality she has about her dad being a good-for-nothing, which she thinks means that part of her must be too, then she won't bring the child up with the same hang-ups. A month ago, she thought they were going to be a champion showjumper, now she's planning a savings account for their future laser treatment when they want their facial tattoos removed. She needs to realise that what your parents choose to do with their lives does not need to be your story . . .' Florence falters. She thinks, *Should I tell her? How can I sit here lecturing Bonnie on the right thing to do, when I'm not doing it either?* 'Just think about what I've said.' Florence gets up from the bed and pats her daughter on the shoulder. 'I'll put the kettle on.'

30
Stella

I have nothing in common with this new donor. Not that I did with the one I'd chosen, but Donor 203 represented everything that I would want in a partner, in a dad. This new donor wouldn't even be my friend, let alone a suitable father for my child. What grown man designs theme parks? Reads comic books? Moves his face around and calls it yoga?

I've spent every night this week mulling these thoughts over. Surely a woman that wanted a baby as much as I did would welcome any baby at all, so I hate myself for feeling this way. I can't have wanted a child as much as I thought I did if I feel like this. I go to stroke my bump the way I have hundreds of times a day for months and then pull my hand away, it feels different now. I feel like I have an intruder in my stomach, someone I didn't invite in, someone I don't know at all.

'Stop it,' Kate says, reading my mind, when she comes over the next day after Mum called her without me knowing.

'Stop what?'

'Your mind, running away with you. Your baby is happy and healthy and that's all that matters. You got so hung up on finding the perfect DNA for it to counteract yours—' I try to interrupt, but she holds her hand up, 'No, let me finish. You've always had this hang up about your dad being shit, thinking that that makes you half-shit, but it really doesn't, because you're not. I would not be friends with a half-shit person.'

'Neither would I,' Eve agrees. I'd introduced Eve and Kate weeks ago, knowing they'd get on, and when Mum called Kate, Kate called Eve, so now I have an even bigger tribe of women rallying around, trying to make me see sense.

'But what if she came from a donor whose parents died in their forties of a horrible genetic disease she's already carrying?'

'Stella.'

'Or they're both incarcerated in a maximum-security jail and when the baby comes of age, her father can track her down and force her to attend visiting times with him and she has to put her belongings in a little tray to go through a scanner and they check the inside of her mouth for heroin? Then they coerce her to join the family business and she becomes a mule for a Mexican cartel?'

'*Stella.*'

'Their grandmother is meant to live in a fishing village in North Cornwall making her own jewellery from sea glass she finds on the beach and their grandfather is a professor of environmental science and grows his own tulips.'

'That's very specific, was it on his profile?'

'No, I've made it up. But I'm sure it's close to the truth.'

'You definitely shouldn't let the clinic get away with it though, what if it happens to other women?' Eve says.

'Eve's right, don't let them think that you're taking this lying down, but you do have to face facts. You've chosen this path to get pregnant, which means that there is a lot you don't know about half of them, regardless of whether it was your Dutch Cornishman or this other chap, and that's just the way it is. Fretting about it now isn't going to change anything, is it? Just enjoy the last few weeks of pregnancy and look forward to holding your beautiful baby. Even if it turns out to be related to Kim Jong-Un.'

I do as Kate and Eve say when they leave, and just sit there imagining what it's going to be like to hold my little finger out for the baby to clasp their tiny hand around, and I try to put everything else out of my mind because It. Really. Does. Not. Matter.

I meet with a solicitor the next day, who says that I definitely have a case against the donor agency, and they're just waiting for me to give them the go-ahead to lodge proceedings against them.

Eve doesn't know what I'm waiting for, 'If you ordered a long red skirt from Next and it came and it was a hat, you'd ask for a voucher in compensation.'

'But what if it's still a skirt, just a different cut and pattern?' Mum asks when I repeated Eve's argument when I get home from having a coffee at her house.

'But what if I really, really, wanted a long red one?'

'Well then, I'd question how much you really wanted to wear clothes in the first place if you could be that prescriptive over what it looked like. How do you think the hat would feel if you didn't even try it on and you just got rid of it?'

'I'm not sending the baby anywhere, that's not even in question!'

'We're not talking about the baby. We're talking about hats.'

I'm confused.

'What would be the reason you would sue them?' Mum prods again.

'Because I trusted them, and they made a mistake.'

'I'd say a baby's a miracle, not a mistake.'

'I don't mean that *it's* a mistake,' I say quickly, horrified that she could think that.

'What would the baby think, in a few years' time, if they find out that you sued the agency because they weren't exactly what you ordered. That you were disappointed in them.'

This is so unlike Mum, this peck-peck-pecking.

'But they can't get away with it,' I say weakly.

'Do you, or do you not, have a baby inside you whom you love?'

'Yes.'

'Do you love it any less now you know it isn't quarter Dutch and quarter Cornish and is actually half a man who likes roller coasters?'

'No,' I say truthfully.

'So what would possibly be the point of dragging this through the courts when you've ended up with the very thing you wanted when you entered into this?'

I can't explain it, certainly not when she's in this frame of mind, but it's so much more than just getting the wrong donor. It's the fact that I'd built up a picture of who the father was. He wasn't a number to me. He was real. He'd been walking alongside us the whole way through the pregnancy. I'd pictured him there at the scans, pointing excitedly at the screen with me, counting the arms, the legs. He'd be there at the birth, whispering in my ear in his West Country drawl that I could do it, that I was strong, that our baby was strong.

I had a storybook when I was young about a little boy that sat on a bench drawing pictures and all his drawings start coming to life. Donor 203 was like that. He'd ceased to be a 2D profile on a webpage long ago and in my mind he now talks, and walks with long, purposeful strides with his long, purposeful legs. He loves mornings, always setting his alarm early to go for a dawn walk on the beach with his dogs – he has two, both rescues, one walked with a limp for months, but thanks to 203's patience and care, he runs in and out of the sea, jumping over waves with no trouble at all now. He's got a camper van which he goes away in at weekends, it's a bit of a squeeze as he's so tall and long of limb, and the dogs are quite large, but he doesn't mind, they keep each other warm. After a quick swim in the sea, his breakfast smoothie and a quick check of his emails, to see what pro bono legal advice he's being asked to give at the refugee centre he volunteers at, he heads to the stables, where he teaches horse riding to disadvantaged children for free. In the afternoon, he'll call his mum, check she's all right, before contacting the donor agency to see if anyone has chosen him as their donor, and if so, can he have their details, because he loves his life, but it would be so much better with the love of a good woman and his biological child in it.

So there it is.

Donor 203 wasn't just supposed to be my child's father; he was also destined to be my soulmate.

* * *

Two months later . . .

I wake up in the middle of the night and for a horrible moment I think I've wet myself. I call out to Mum in the next bedroom, who then hammers on Florence's door, 'Her waters have broken!'

I remind her that we're not using that type of language, which confuses her for a moment as she's never sworn in her life. 'My membranes have been released,' I say, repeating verbatim the terms I learned on the online hypnobirthing course I took, thinking as I say it that if I had met this version of me a year ago, I wouldn't recognise her and might possibly have punched her in the face.

Mum and Florence spring into action, boiling the kettle, collecting towels, because in every episode of *Call The Midwife*, that's what you do despite the fact that my doctor has vetoed my plans of a home birth due to being a 'geriatric mother' which made me feel just fabulous.

I'm not sure how I feel now it's all happening. If the donor mix-up had never occurred, I think I'd be more excited than nervous, and for the thousandth time I feel a flash of anger at the clinic that took the edge off the joy I should be feeling.

We get to the hospital in record speed, and as I'm the only woman in active labour, I can have the room with the pool in it too. It's funny how good luck often follows bad.

'Do you think Stella was joking about the pina coladas? I found some of those pre-mixed cans in Sainsbury's and brought a couple with me just in case.' I hear Florence ask Mum as they sit side by side on plastic chairs in the delivery room while the midwife examines me for about the twentieth time. 'I quite fancy one, but didn't know if it's poor form to be drinking cocktails while someone in the room is in labour?'

'Believe me, Stella would be the first to have one if she wasn't the one in labour, so go ahead. But have something to eat first to slow down the absorption of the alcohol into your small intestine.'

Florence groans. 'Don't worry, you've managed to take the romance out of it, I'll stick to tea.'

'Speaking of romance, I'm not sure how she's managed it, but Stella's turned this hospital room into a scene from an adult movie,' Mum whispers.

Hearing this makes me smile, and she's not wrong. About thirty battery-operated tea lights are dotted around the room; the pool in the middle of it now softly lit by the glow of the candles. It doesn't have the symbolism of bringing a fourth generation into the world in the same house, but at least the hospital floor is mop-able, unlike the carpet at home, which had I gone for the home birth would no doubt have every towel we owned rolled up around the pool like sandbags to protect it. Alexa is playing soft instrumental music in the background, interspersed occasionally with a soothing voice telling me that with every breath my cervix is opening like a rose in bloom.

'I don't know about you,' Florence stage whispers at the side of the pool, 'but I'm about ready to push.'

The midwife has evidently been to the same elocution trainer as the voice from the speaker, as she tells me in a sentence that takes much longer to say than it should do, 'On your next surge . . . breathe your baby . . . down . . . to meet you.'

I grab Mum's hand on one side, and Florence's on the other, as all three of us breathe the baby down to meet us.

You're not quite so chilled as you slide out into the water as if emerging from a shute at a water park, are scooped up out of the water and give an almighty cry. The three of us: grandmother, mother and daughter, all put our heads together, cooing over the newest member of our tribe, while behind me the midwife discreetly fishes something unsavoury out of the water with a kitchen sieve.

'He's gorgeous, well done, darling, and all that black hair, wow!' Mum plants a kiss on my head, and I close my eyes locking this moment in. Until they spring open in shock.

'He?'

'Yes, it's a boy!'

'It can't be!'

'It is,' Florence says gleefully. 'I saw his penis!'

In none of the scenarios I'd played out in my head did I imagine she'd be a he. Whether that came from only ever being around women, I'm not sure, but I don't think it ever really occurred to me that it was a possible outcome.

'But I don't even have a boy's name,' I say, panic rising in my voice. 'I didn't even open that section of the book.' I got all the way down to Zylina – Greek for Woodland – and called it a day, having narrowed my choices down to fifteen names. Fifteen girls' names.

'Plenty of time for that later,' says the midwife, placing my son on my chest. 'Little one wants a cuddle with his mummy.'

Despite my shock, as soon as his tiny body is placed on mine, a whoosh of happiness floods through me. This. This little person is my chance to get it right, to pass memories on, to make millions of new ones with, to love, to protect, to guide, to grow with. My eyes close as I try to lock this feeling in forever. Our family is complete.

'Does this bring it all back?' I ask, opening my eyes as I stare in awe at his tiny fingers. 'Does it remind you of having me?'

Mum nods and smiles, a glimmer of a tear making her eyes shine. 'That's just what I was thinking.'

31

Bonnie

Dear Thing,

I can't quite believe that I am addressing my grandson like that, but in true Stella fashion, your mother wants to make sure she gets it right when she eventually names you, so I'm afraid we've been calling you Thing for the past week since you arrived. I promise you that it is not going to stick, and if by chance, you are reading this at eighteen and we have just done a Toast to 'Thing on his Eighteenth', then you have my heartfelt apologies.

You may not have a name yet, but you have made an impact on all of us in every way imaginable. A new baby always brings with it tremendous joy, but we have waited for you for so long, which makes you all the more special. You have breathed new life into this house, filling every room with hope and happiness. I have no idea what we talked about before you arrived, because now you're the centre of our universe, much like your mum was with me, and I'm sure I was with Florence.

* * *

Forty years earlier . . .

'I'll stay, but I'm telling you now, I'm not changing any nappies, and if it doesn't sleep, then you have to stay upstairs with your mum.'

The way Steven phrased it, and the way his voice went up at the end, plus the pregnant pause, gave all the signals that he expected Bonnie to say thank you. Thank you for staying put and choosing us, rather than leaving. She could tell he was thinking, 'not you as well,' when she told him she was expecting. He'd rolled his eyes and gave a long sigh, as if she'd just told him that they were out of milk and could he pop out and get some.

He still hadn't told her that Janet having his child was the reason he'd stopped everything; she only knew that from Oliver. Steven had just shrugged when she'd cried, 'Why? Why are you stopping it now?' replying casually, arrogantly, that 'it was getting too serious'.

If he wasn't going to be completely honest, then neither was she. There was no need to spell out the role that Oliver may have played in her current situation. Bizarrely, the idea didn't even seem to occur to Steven. She correctly guessed why. How on earth could a good-looking creative be less virile than a high-street pharmacist? It simply wasn't possible.

Over the next few months, the bin bags grew heavier and clinked louder with the evidence of Steven's evenings when Bonnie took the full bags out of the kitchen bin and put new empty ones in before leaving for work in the morning. He slept in late and disappeared while Bonnie was at the lab to some indeterminate place, which smelled of perfume and cigarettes. The ideal father.

At work, Bonnie's white lab coat was a handy camouflage for the baby bump, which seemed as if it was growing by the day, which she supposed it was. Five months had gone by before her boss called her into his office and told her he'd 'noticed her predicament' and 'in the circumstances' would be handing control of her project over to Colin, who despite graduating with a lower degree, and having never managed a research project of this size before, 'was showing tremendous promise'. Bonnie tried to argue, telling him that she was intending on only taking the minimum amount of maternity leave, that she absolutely could complete the project from home, that she could combine motherhood with work without any detrimental impact on the project, but her boss just played with his stapler and cited the example of his own wife, who loved her job as a geography teacher, *really loved it*, and fully anticipated returning as soon as their children were born, but 'something switches inside a mother' and it was much easier for the handover of the project to happen now, when Bonnie can mentor Colin, rather than afterwards, when Colin's left all alone, 'bearing in mind his lack of experience'.

Bonnie had once overheard a colleague laughingly describe her to a new colleague as 'a ham sandwich', which perplexed her at first, unsure how a person could be a type of food. But then, as she ruminated on it more, she realised it was actually something of a compliment. You know where you are with a ham sandwich. It's the perfect lunch, an easy dinner and, if you're feeling continental, an interesting breakfast choice. It's got protein and carbohydrates, fat if you add butter, fibre and nutrients if you use brown and not white bread. The way her colleagues were laughing suggested this wasn't a good food to be, but Bonnie couldn't disagree more. Yes, it was perhaps not as flamboyant as a seafood risotto, but then it has less of the associated risks. It needed minimal prep, was easily stored, ready in seconds and was timeless. Her boss was a stuffed pepper: looked interesting, very modern, bit of a faff to assemble and actually fell apart very easily. No one would expect a ham sandwich to stand their ground against a stuffed pepper, which is why when Bonnie stood in the middle of his office and said, 'No,' every head in the lab outside the open door jerked up.

'I'm sorry, Bonnie, what do you mean?' her boss asked, looking completely perplexed.

'I mean no. I'm not handing my project over to Colin, or anyone else. I've been working on this for two years, I know every single thing about it, and the fact I am currently carrying a child inside me has no impact on my ability to see this research through to its conclusion.'

'I-I just thought it would be easier . . .' her boss stammered.

'For who?'

'Well, you, and the baby.'

'Thank you for your concern, but I'm absolutely fine. I am very happy to have Colin on my research team though, I need a few more assistants.'

Something switched in Bonnie that day. The speed at which her boss stuttered, 'Well, if you're sure,' and Colin had to shelve his grandiose ideas of moving to the bigger desk stunned her slightly. Was it really that easy? Bonnie recognised that a different manager might have insisted she step down. A different stuffed pepper might have turned the team against her, waged a war of contrition until she couldn't stand it any more. She'd seen and heard it happen to other women. But for her, on that day, it didn't. She'd stood her ground and the humble ham sandwich won. It might be unadorned and uncomplicated, but it wasn't to be underestimated.

As her car drew up to the kerb later that evening, she wished she was in the type of marriage where she could kick off her shoes at the door, put her stockinged feet in the lap of her husband and say, 'you won't believe what happened at work today,' but she wasn't. She knew that Janet was though. Right at this moment, Oliver was probably rubbing Janet's knotted shoulders and making her a nice cup of tea. Janet would be shrugging him off of course, telling him he was doing it too hard, or not hard enough, and asking if he left the teabag in for long enough, and complaining that he knew she liked honey not sugar in it, so why did he add sugar?

Bonnie could hear the sound of laughter and music from the road, and even though she didn't know for sure it was coming from the house with the green door, she guessed, and when her suspicions were proved right, her heart sank. As she put her key in the lock, the music was so loud, it was a wonder the neighbours hadn't formed a disorderly queue snaking down the street to complain.

Florence's front door at the top of the stairs was much more enticing than her own one, and Bonnie walked heavily up the stairs, exhausted from the day's confrontations and not ready for the night's one.

Florence opened her door warily but broke into a smile when she saw it was Bonnie, and ushered her in.

'How long's that been going on for?' Bonnie asked.

'Most of the afternoon.'

'I'm so sorry, Mum, you're on nights at the moment, aren't you?'

'It doesn't matter, love. I got some sleep this morning before he woke up.'

'It does matter. It's not fair. You're on nights, Gary next door is on nights, Mary and Keith the other side have young kids, it's not on.' Galvanised by what happened at work that day, Bonnie's had enough of the men in her life thinking they can steamroll over everyone else.

'Don't get yourself worked up, darling, it's not good for the baby.'

'The baby, the baby, all everyone ever talks about is what's good for the baby.'

'I just meant—'

Bonnie put her head in her hands, 'I know, I'm sorry, I don't mean to snap, I know you mean well.'

'You can stay up here if you like? I'll be leaving for the hospital soon.'

'It's as loud up here as it is down there. Anyway, that's not the point, is it? It's my home. I've got as much right as him to be there. More even.'

'It might just be a last hurrah before the baby comes and things settle down.'

Bonnie gave her mother a pointed look, 'I think we both know Steven has no intention of "settling down".'

Florence rubbed her eye. 'I can't give you any advice, darling, you need to do what's right for you and . . .' She stopped herself from adding 'the baby', but the unsaid words hung in the air anyway.

'Right then,' Bonnie said, standing up.

'What are you going to do?'

'If the music stops in a couple of minutes and you hear the front door go, everything's fine. If you don't, and you hear shouting, then call the police and report a disturbance. I'm not joking, Mum. That's what I want you to do, OK?'

'Bonnie, you're worrying me.'

'I'm fine. I'm not going to do anything daft, but that's what I want you to do.'

'I'll come with you.'

Bonnie shook her head. 'No. I'll do this by myself. Three minutes. Time it.'

The fug of smoke in the living room was so thick, it made Bonnie cough as she opened the door. No one noticed her standing there. There were two other couples she didn't know, one pair lying on the floor side by side on their stomachs looking through records, the other kissing on the sofa. Another woman was curled up in an armchair, the back of her messy blonde head to the door. Bonnie looked around the room through the nicotine haze for Steven and couldn't see him and almost turned around to look in another room, but then saw two legs and Steven's feet under the blonde woman, who was clearly sitting on his lap.

Bonnie walked to the record player, pulled the plug out of the socket, silencing the room, and strode over to the bay window, straining to pull up the heavy sash window.

'Hey!' the woman on the floor said. 'Who are you?'

'I'm Steven's wife, and you need to get out of my house.'

Steven roughly shoved the woman on his lap to one side and got up. 'How dare you? These are my friends.'

'You can join them if you like,' Bonnie said.

'Steven,' the woman who had been on his lap simpered, slipping her feet into her shoes, 'come on, let's go.'

'This is my home. I decide who to invite into it. Stay where you are, Kathy.' Steven picked up the wire of the record player and plugged it back into the socket. The room pulsed again with music.

'Steven, turn it off,' Bonnie shouted over it, aware that now the window was open, the whole street was encased in sound.

'Come on, mate, leave it, she's clearly upset,' the man on the floor said, getting to his feet.

'She's always fucking upset,' Steven spat, lighting a cigarette and throwing his lighter on the table, like a gauntlet.

Bonnie moved over to the record player, but Steven stepped in front of her, his face inches away from her own, his beery breath putrid.

'Leave it.'

She moved to the side, to go past him, but he mirrored her, blocking her. She moved the other way. Again, he blocked her.

'Steven, let's go,' Kathy said. 'I don't want to be here any more.'

'See what you've done?' Steven leered, his bloodshot eyes bulging. 'You've spoiled the party.'

A hand appeared on Steven's shoulder from one of the other men, 'Leave her alone, Steve, she's pregnant.'

'She was a boring cow before she was pregnant.'

'I'd like you to leave. All of you,' Bonnie said. 'Including you, Steven.'

'Me?' he sneered. 'It's my house.'

She shook her head, 'No it's not.'

Steven shook his shoulder free of his friend's warning hand and raised it to strike Bonnie, who was prepared for it and ducked out of its way. His fist struck the wall behind her. A crack. Followed by an anguished howl as he held his fractured knuckle.

Bonnie swiftly bent down to unplug the record player, plunging the room into complete stunned silence.

'Knock knock,' said Florence's voice from the doorway. 'I think you all need to leave now.' She opened the door as wide as it would go. 'You too Steven. And I'd get that hand looked at. I'm going to the hospital now if you'd like me to give you a lift?' she said brightly.

'Fuck off,' Steven said as he pushed past her, grabbing his coat from the hallway pegs and crashing out of the front door into the darkening street. His friends mutely followed him, one of the men giving Bonnie a small apologetic smile as they padded past her, one of the women saying, 'sorry about the mess,' as they left.

'You OK?' Florence asked Bonnie, who stood in the centre of the room like a statue.

She nodded.

'I'll call work and say I'm not going in.'

Bonnie shook her head. 'Don't be silly, I'll be fine.'

'But what if he comes back?'

'He won't.'

'He will eventually.'

'I don't think he will. I'll pack up his things now and call his parents to collect them. Then I'll call a locksmith and get the locks changed. And tomorrow I'll call a solicitor.'

'You look exhausted,' Florence said.

'I feel exhausted.'

'Have you got anything in for dinner?'

Bonnie thought for a moment. 'I have bread,' she said, 'and some ham. That will do nicely.'

Bonnie was right, Steven didn't come back. The divorce papers were drawn up and sent to his parents' house and the next month went by quietly, without any drama, but also without any real happiness or enjoyment. She was tired, heavy, lonely. Her waters broke one morning as she was making a bowl of porridge. She simply looked at the drips on the floor, put down the box of oats, gave a big sigh and heaved herself up the stairs to ask Florence if she wouldn't mind driving her to the hospital.

'Will Daddy be joining us?'

'No.'

'There's still time for him to come, you're about six centimetres dilated, so your mum can pop out and make a call and if he's quick he can still make it.'

'Look, I know you mean well, but as far as I'm concerned, this baby doesn't have a father, so can we just speed this up and get it over with so we can all get on with our lives?'

'Bonnie, the nurse was just trying to help,' Florence said after the nurse nodded meekly and fled the room, no doubt to tell her colleagues about the horribly rude woman in Delivery Room 2.

Bonnie lay back on the bed and closed her eyes. She didn't mean to be so curt, she just hated this whole sensation, hated Steven, hated Oliver, hated what one of them, both of them, had done to her. Hated the fact that she had a womb that could be so vilely inhabited by one of them. Both men were walking around, right now, when she was flat on her back, pains coming every three minutes, this living thing pulsing its way out of her one contraction at a time. These men were living their lives, years ahead of them blissfully free, completely unaware of what they had done to her. Trapped her. Incarcerated her. Tied her to another human who she didn't ask for.

'Would you like some water?' Florence asked, trying to smooth her daughter's hair out of her eyes, but Bonnie snapped her head away.

Florence pursed her lips. She was trying. She was really trying, but nothing she could say or do could raise Bonnie out of this. They hadn't talked at all about what would happen next. She assumed that Bonnie's indifference meant that she had decided on an adoption, which tore at Florence's heart like a wild animal, but it wasn't her choice any more than it was her own mother's to force an adoption on her either. She just hoped Bonnie would hold the little thing first, she knew she'd regret it if she didn't.

Bonnie didn't swear, or scream or shout throughout the whole labour. Her composure, her detachment, was unnerving. Florence could feel it and it was clear the two midwives felt it too. The moment of the baby's birth, normally heralded with whoops and joy, was curiously devoid of anything. Externally anyway. Florence's heart was beating against her ribcage with a tidal force, while Bonnie's trembling jaw made it clear she was just pretending to be calm and emotionless.

'It's a girl,' the midwife announced, choosing to make the announcement with a tone one might use to recite an interesting fact, rather than a life-changing proclamation. 'She's very pretty.'

'Do you hear that, darling?' Florence prompted, smiling. 'It's a little girl.'

Bonnie nodded.

'We'll just weigh her and clean her up a bit, then you can have a cuddle?' The midwife's voice went up at the end. It sounded unnatural, as though she'd never said it that way before, as a question not a statement.

Bonnie calculated that she had about three minutes to make the decision that could change everything. Three minutes to decide whether this baby should just be taken away without her seeing it, touching it, or whether she would risk it just to lock in the memory of what it felt like to hold her own child. Bonnie started silently counting down each second, never tearing her eyes away from the tiny red infant being wiped down, put on the scales, wrapped in a towel. 'You make your own luck,' her dad used to say. Did she make this? Was this a situation she had consciously chosen? No. But how she responded now was entirely down to her.

The midwife turned back to the bed, the little girl in her arms. 'Here she is,' she said, 'shiny as a new penny.'

Florence held her breath.

Bonnie turned her head to the wall and pulled the sheet up over her. 'You take her, Mum, I'm really tired.'

In the days and weeks after Stella's birth, Bonnie's thoughts, when she was lucid enough to have them, always meandered to Oliver. She hadn't opened the *Dr Spock's Common Sense Book of Baby and Child Care*, or glanced at the leaflets she left the hospital with. Instead she was obsessed, and even Bonnie herself would recognise that it had become an obsession, with finding Oliver.

There was no way that he would have stayed inside the M25, she thought, it was too close to her, and the way that his letter had said 'we've left the area', suggested that it was at least an hour away. Bonnie felt that she could also rule out small rural villages. Even if they had a chemist, there was no way that Janet would be happy living in a pair of wellies in the middle of nowhere. So that just left cities and towns. Bonnie remembered from school there were fifty-one cities in England, each one would have, what? Twenty or thirty pharmacies. Bigger towns would have one or two and there must be a hundred or so towns outside London, so a possible 1,400 chemists where he might be working. She could make a list and systematically cross them off once she'd phoned them. She did love a list.

A horrible thought struck her. But what if they'd gone abroad? More and more people were moving to France or Spain these days, even Australia. Maybe Oliver and Janet had gone to the other side of the world too? That would be right up Janet's street; she'd be one of those people who'd have an accent in minutes.

Bonnie shook herself, there was no point letting her mind wander into what-ifs, that wouldn't be useful. She had already crossed off Cornwall, Devon, Dorset and Hampshire, which meant that he must be somewhere north or east of Somerset.

'Knock knock. I think she's hungry,' Florence said, coming into the living room holding Stella. 'I've already changed her, so she's all ready.'

'You do it. I'm a bit busy. I've sterilised the bottle already.'

Florence didn't argue. There would come a time that she would, but six weeks after leaving the hospital wasn't it. She was just grateful that baby Stella had left with them, because in the hours after the birth, she wasn't sure she was going to. She reasoned as she boiled the water for the formula that there would be plenty of time to figure out the logistics of who did what later on. She'd taken unpaid leave from her own job while things settled down; Bonnie wasn't ready yet to be alone with Stella. She hadn't even wanted to name her; it was Florence who suggested Stella after the main character in the play Henry took her to on their first proper date. Henry would have liked that.

'Hello, can I speak with Dr Oliver Gillespie? . . . OK, sorry to bother you . . .' Bonnie put a straight line through the cathedral city of Wells, thinking as she did so, that once she found Oliver, they should visit some of these places, they sounded lovely. They could even take Stella with them, once she was on solids and able to be more than ten feet away from the steriliser. He'd probably insist on pushing her pram, not through any grand masculine gesture, like Steven would have done, but just to save her a job. Oliver would have been horrified that she had considered, however fleetingly, giving their baby away, but he never needed to know that.

Yesterday, Stella was Steven's baby and Bonnie didn't make any calls to any pharmacy. She refused to hold Stella all day, and left her lunch and dinner untouched. But today Stella was definitely Oliver's. The sun was shining, and she really enjoyed her prawn cocktail baguette she had for lunch. She might even take Stella to the park later, but only if she got through to all the chemists as far along as Swindon – that M4 corridor might take a while.

Just then, Florence started singing to Stella along the corridor in the kitchen. It was the first time Bonnie smiled in months. Maybe they could make this work.

32
Stella

The books say babies smile at six weeks, but Thing's been doing it since he was about a week old. And today, on his three-week birthday – he definitely raised one eyebrow, then the other at me when I tried to give him his first bottle. I can only attribute this to his father's penchant for facial yoga, which must have given him really fantastic muscle control. I'm yet to see any other signs of his paternity, but I've removed all permanent markers from the house just in case he wants to practise some body art.

I was worried that it would be a massive disruption having a baby in the house, the walls are so thin and you can hear everything, but Thing hardly cries. How different would Donor 203's baby be? Would he be just as placid and good-natured? I hate myself for doing this, constantly comparing the real with the unknown, the what's here with the way it might have been, but I can't help it. I literally pray every night, actually talk to a god that until now I was very dubious about, that I won't always feel like this. That one day I'll wake up, see Thing do something and not immediately regret that he got the wrong father.

My phone rings; it's Kate. I pick it up and say, 'Before you ask, no I haven't got a name yet.'

'It's been three weeks, Stella.'

'I know, but you had months to choose your boys' names,' *and you still chose Thor and Zeus*. 'It's a really big decision and

I had a lovely girl's name picked out, I honestly didn't even consider that he'd be a boy.'

'Would the girl's name still work for the boy?' Kate asks. 'There are loads of gender-neutral names nowadays.'

'It was Mia. So no.'

'Have you been reading the name book?'

'Every day. What I don't know about boys' names isn't worth knowing. For instance, did you know that more than 45 million boys have been named James and Cameron means crooked nose?'

'It'll come to you.'

'I hope so. Because I've started calling him Thing, and I really don't want that to stick.'

'Would you like me to tell you our back-up names? If the boys had come out and not suited Thor and Zeus?'

'I can't imagine the chances of that happening were very high,' I say.

'I loved the name of the Greek god Cronus, until I found out that he swallowed each of his children before vomiting them back up again.'

'I can see how that might be problematic.'

'So do choose wisely. Nothing that has unsavoury connotations.'

Later that night, Florence, Mum and I are sitting around the living room, and I'm feeding Thing again. The health visitor came earlier and weighed and measured him and he's in the fifth percentile for both, which is really small. 'Is Dad quite short?' she asked cheerfully.

I nodded and replied, 'Five foot five.'

'Really? Well, he might surprise us and be a late bloomer.'

Her words have spurred me into action and I've literally

turned my son into a foie gras goose, force-feeding him every time he opens his eyes.

'I think I've found a name I like,' I say.

'Oh yes?' Mum says.

'What do you think of Oliver? It was Flo who suggested it, and I actually really like it.'

Mum turns to Flo angrily, 'You? You suggested Oliver?'

'What's wrong with Oliver?' I say. 'I think it's a lovely name.'

Mum actually looks like she's shaking. Her face is pale and her voice trembles as she says to Flo, 'How could you?'

'Mum, chill out, it's just a name. If you don't like it, I'll choose another one.'

Florence speaks quietly, 'I think he looks like an Oliver. Kind, clever, loyal.'

I look down at Thing. I mean, it's lovely for her to say those things about him, but he is only three weeks old, so while it would be nice to think that these attributes are shining out of him now, even I recognise that it might be a stretch.

'I can't believe you,' Mum says to Flo, standing up and walking out of the room.

I shake my head at my grandmother, who looks like she's about to cry, 'I wouldn't worry, Flo, you weren't to know she'd hate it so much. I think she should just count her lucky stars that I'm her daughter and not Kate, after seeing her reaction to a normal name like Oliver, I can't imagine how she'd have felt having a grandson called Cronos.'

'I'd better go up and see her,' Flo says wearily, heaving herself out of her armchair.

'Rather you than me.'

I can hear the murmurs of their impassioned exchange through the floorboards. Not the actual words, but the tone and intent. Mum's clearly upset and Flo's apologising over and over again. I've floated names like Malachi and Ozymandias before and her only response has been a quiet 'veto', from the corner, so this is totally disproportionate.

Thing stretches and yawns, his tiny rosebud lips making a perfect O, balanced by the cute circular dimple in his chin, which I am intensely envious of. It must have skipped a few generations because Donor 302 didn't have one in his childhood photo, which I've spent hours poring over, and neither do I, but in the photo on the mantelpiece of a young Florence and Henry, my grandfather is clearly sporting a fine example of one. I do this a lot. Looking for clues. Thing's fingers are long and narrow, perfect piano-playing fingers Flo called them, whereas I have short stubby fingers that bend to the right, making them perfect for no musical instrument at all, except maybe bagpipes. His dark brown eyes still surprise me; mine are as pale blue as you can get – Touch of Cornflower, Dulux would call them, and Mum's and Flo's the same. Mum thinks Steven's eyes were hazel, but she can't be sure.

My phone buzzes. It's Eve. Her daughter Lara was born a week after Thing, and had a name before leaving the delivery room. She's sent me a photo of the contents of Lara's nappy next to a photo of her eating a Caramac. I send back a vomit emoji.

Eve: Is Thing sleeping better?

Me: What's sleep?

Eve: Good job he's cute.

Me: Question: What do you think of the name Oliver?

Eve: It's better than Thing.

Me: Naturally. But it doesn't make you angry?

Eve: ?????

Me: My mum stormed off when I suggested it.

Eve: That's odd. What did she do about Ozymandias? Break a window?

Me: He's going to be the first child at his school called Thing in the history of education.

Eve: You're overthinking this. What was your dad's name?

Me: Steven. But he was a knob. And if I call him Steven, my mum might actually start a fire and burn us all to death based on this afternoon's reaction.

Eve: Grandfather?

Me: Henry.

Eve: I like Henry. He looks like a Henry. Henrys are cool – Henry Winkler was the Fonz. A bit of a ladies' man – Henry VIII. Strong – Henry Cooper. Good businessman – Henry Ford. Literate – Henry James. I could go on?

Me: You know a lot of Henrys.

Eve: It'd be a nice tribute to your grandfather too – was he nice?

Me: Never met him, but the house is a shrine to him, so I guess so. Isn't Prince Harry called Henry? It could be Henry on his birth certificate, but I could call him Harry. I think you're on to something …

Eve: Start calling him it and see if it fits.

Me: It fits better than Thing.

Eve: That's a low bar.

Me: Right, best go and change Harry now … It works!!

I decide to keep this exchange between Eve and me a secret for a few more days for me to make sure it's definitely his name before telling Mum and Florence, who seem to have settled on an uneasy truce. This house hasn't seen much tension in my lifetime, but since Mum's outburst over the name Oliver, her mood seems different, more detached somehow, as though she has retreated inside her own head for a while.

33

Florence

Darling Harry,

I still can't believe Stella called you after your grandfather, he would be so proud. I can see him now, standing up a bit taller, smiling his bright beaming smile that used to light up a room. He'd have loved you to bits. He doted on Bonnie since the second she was born, actually even before that, making sure that I was warm enough when I was carrying her, asking if I was hungry, do I need another cup of tea? It wasn't really the norm back then, for the fathers to be so involved, but Henry took no notice of that. I think he changed more nappies than I did and I'm sure he would have breast-fed her himself if he could have!

It is so wonderful to have a baby in the house again; everything smells of talcum powder and fresh laundry. Babies put everything into perspective, don't they? Well, you wouldn't know because you are one at the moment. But they do. Nothing else matters when you're holding a baby, real life just ceases to exist and you can lose yourself for hours in the way their tiny eyelashes curl.

Bonnie's eyelashes were something to behold. All the girls who lived here used to coo over them, saying, 'She'll never need to stick hers on!' Honestly, it was like Bonnie had five mothers living in this house: Martha, my landlady of course, who was always up for a bit of babysitting whenever I needed to pop out, and the three girls who lived here too, Nancy, June and Rosemary. Of course, my own mother was smitten as well, what with Bonnie being their only grandchild, she was always sending little cardigans she'd knitted, or a ten-bob note for me to buy myself a treat. Not that I wanted for anything, Henry made sure of that.

* * *

Sixty years earlier . . .

The rattle of the letter box woke Florence up. Today was the first day in weeks that she hadn't bounded out of bed with the sound of it and rushed to see if her parents had replied to her letter. She'd thought that enough time had passed after leaving St Philomena's and it was the right time to reach out to them, tell them about Bonnie, reassure them that they were safe. But it had been three weeks since she had sent it and she'd resigned herself to not receiving a reply. The combination of this, and Bonnie's first tooth breaking through sometime between one and four in the morning, meant that Florence simply turned over in her bed and went back to sleep. When she came into the hallway a couple of hours later, a small white envelope was in the base of the wire basket attached to the back of the door. Florence's name was written in her father's neat uniform script on lines drawn in pencil with a ruler. She slowly tore it open.

Dear Florence,

We received your letter. Please do not write to us again, you have made your mother very unwell with this ghastly business.

Lawrence Weston

She couldn't believe it. She honestly thought that once the baby was here, they'd come round, who couldn't fall in love with a baby? A grandchild? Surely once their anger had worn off they'd relent. They couldn't just block her and Bonnie out of their lives, not after losing Stu. She and Bonnie were all the family they had. She read the letter again, this time taking every nuance in. Her father had signed his full name at the bottom, not Daddy, not Father, not even an initial, he actually used the official signature that he used for writing cheques. Not that there was a cheque in the envelope she was holding. Florence even gave the envelope a little shake, just in case it had done that thing where the white of the back of the cheque had blended with the white of the inside of the envelope, but nothing fluttered out. So that was it. A two-line goodbye. She and Bonnie were on their own.

It was all very well Martha saying 'pay what you can afford', but even Florence, with her limited experience of economics and bookkeeping, having left school at sixteen with just incredibly neat handwriting and an ability to recite all the words to Wordsworth's 'I Wandered Lonely as a Cloud' could recognise that as a business model, it was a really bad one. Martha did say magnanimously that you couldn't put a price on a clean house, after Florence had spent the last two months eliminating every speck of dust from every surface, every smudge from every wall, even cleaning the ceiling cornices with an old toothbrush, and she'd found out that the proper colour of the kitchen tiles was actually orange, and not brown. But even so, Florence was running out of ways to compensate for her lack of funds and there wasn't a Plan B – living at Martha's was the entire alphabet of plans.

'I need to get a job,' Florence announced to the other girls that evening. Once she overcame the ridiculousness of sitting on the floor – '*The floor? Like a dog?*' she could hear her mother say – she found it actually quite liberating. She even loved to eat her dinner on the arm of the sofa now too.

'Can you type?' June asked.

Florence shook her head.

The three girls looked back at her, heads cocked to one side, Florence was sure they must be wondering how she had managed to make so many wrong choices in her short life. It shouldn't be too hard, should it, following the route of womanhood. 1. Learn to type. 2. Get married. 3. Have a baby. Three things the modern woman needed to do. In that order. Definitely in that order, any other order counts against you. *Oh, sorry, silly me, I did do all those things, just a bit jumbled up*. Well, that doesn't count, you do not pass go, and you do not collect two hundred pounds. Two hundred pounds. How on earth could Florence ever get her hands on two hundred pounds? Or even twenty pounds? Twenty pounds would be all right.

The other girls weren't thinking that though – after all, judgement of any kind was against house rules. They were actually thinking about their own jobs, wondering if they could put in a word for Florence. Rosemary was a dancer in a newly opened revue bar off Piccadilly. Not the type of dancer who wore heart-shaped stickers over their breasts, thank you very much, although every art form had its merits. She even owned ballet shoes with blocks in their toes, although the revue owners didn't seem that impressed, or keen, on her wearing them, and instead gave her a pair of impossibly high heels at the start of her first shift, which made it nigh on impossible to do a pirouette.

June had started work in a travel agency in Chelsea, hired ostensibly for her seventy words per minute skill gained at the secretarial school her parents had paid for as a gift for her eighteenth birthday, yet a month in she was yet to type a single letter. She had, however, so far spent the day traversing the length and breadth of Oxford Street for presents for the boss's wife and girlfriend, taken his suits to the dry-cleaners three times (and picked them up), bought theatre tickets (unclear who for), settled hotel bills (very clear who for), restaurant bills, tailor's bills, rental car bills, florists' bills (having two women on the go was an expensive business). And while a job was a job, and money was money, this was not why June had spent hours with thirty other teenage girls blindfolded in a hot room with a tea towel over her hands. Florence baulked when June said that bit, before realising she was talking about leaning to touch-type.

Nancy, meanwhile, worked in an independent clothing shop on the King's Road, and despite 'the long hours, horrible people and crap pay', it was the career path that Florence felt her non-existent skills would be most suited to. Nancy promised she'd speak to her boss.

Two days later, Florence found herself in a borrowed twinset and mid-calf-length skirt of Martha's in the back room of the boutique. 'So, tell me about yourself,' the owner of the shop smiled and tapped the ash of her cigarette into a glass ashtray on her desk.

'So, um, my name's Florence, I'm eighteen years old, I have a daughter called Bonnie.'

'OK, wonderful,' the woman interrupted, rising to her feet, 'let me stop you there, I don't want to waste any more of your time, or mine. Thank you for coming.'

'But I haven't told you anything about what I can do. I'm a hard worker, I can—'

'Mothers do not make good employees, Mrs Weston, I'll only have to let you go further on down the line, so it's much better if we stop this now.'

Florence heard the assumption but didn't say anything, Nancy had warned her not to. 'But—'

'Goodbye, Mrs Weston.'

'It's Miss actually,' Florence said loudly over her shoulder, taking in the delighted mouth drop of horror as the door slammed behind her.

Florence's fleeting moment of wonderful defiance was short-lived when Nancy also joined her on the pavement, clutching her handbag and her owed wages.

'I'm really sorry,' Florence said, horrified.

'Don't be. She was an old bag anyway.'

'But even so. I shouldn't have been rude to her.'

'You weren't rude. You were honest. But it's probably best not to be though, huh?'

At the interview at June's travel agency the following week, Florence was more prepared. So when June's philandering boss asked her the same question, Florence was ready with the answer, 'My name is Florence Weston, I am eighteen years old, and I'm from Surrey.' She got the job.

All was well for three months until Martha called her at work to say that Bonnie had a temperature and could she pick up some medicine from the pharmacy on the high street on her way back. Her boss, a father himself, overheard the conversation and told her she could leave early if she liked, following his kind offer up with, 'You kept that quiet that you had a family, what does your husband do?' and she replied without thinking that she hadn't got one. It was a shame, she quite liked working there.

Devoid of other options, and exhausted from circling job adverts in every newspaper and magazine she could convince the other girls to buy for her, Florence begrudgingly auditioned at Alma's Revue Bar where Rosemary worked. They'd called it an 'audition' rather than an 'interview' in the job advert to make it appeal to aspiring actresses, of which Florence definitely was not, she just needed a job, any job. Their smoke-and-mirror wording must have worked because Florence was the only one to turn up in the twinset she wore in the agency, while the other twenty or so women looked like they were heading out on a day trip to Brighton Beach. The only thing missing from their get-up was a windbreaker and bucket and spade.

At ten on the dot, black leotards were handed out and in groups of four, the women trooped on to the raised platform at one end of the bar, to show off their dancing skills. Florence wasn't expecting this. Dancing was not a thing she had ever done. Ever. She might have tapped a toe to a jaunty tune, perhaps even allowed herself a little head nod if the beat of the music was particularly compelling, but moving her entire body in time to the music the way these women were doing so effortlessly? Never. She didn't even know if her body could. And when it was her turn to go up on the stage, she realised, within half a minute, that it absolutely couldn't. She tried to remember all the moves from the movies she'd seen recently, a little shoulder shrug courtesy of Marilyn Monroe in *Let's Make Love* (she stopped short at pursing her lips up and blowing a saucy kiss to the imagined audience, feeling the crushing weight of her conservative upbringing pressing down on her) then when she felt that the shoulder shrugging had gone on for a little too long, she alternated it with a bit of straight leg, pointed toe flicking while tucking her thumbs into an imaginary waistband à la Elvis in *Jailhouse Rock*.

The three men sat at a table facing the stage, watching with barely concealed shock, but the size of Florence's milk-engorged breasts combined with their ability to have a rhythm all of their own was enough reason not to call time on the whole sorry debacle and they let her finish the whole song, which seemed to Florence to not only last longer than her entire labour with Bonnie, but also be just as painful.

'Girl on the far left,' one of the men called out after conferring with the other two, 'you can't dance for toffee, but you can have a trial as a hostess tomorrow lunchtime if you like? The other three of you, sorry, you're not what we want. Next!'

Florence had no idea what a hostess was, but as long as it didn't involve dancing or wearing a leotard she'd had to tuck her pubic hair into like a swimming hat at the public baths, she'd take it.

'Are you sure you don't mind looking after Bonnie again?' Florence looked at the reflection of Martha in the mirror she was standing in front of, trying to pin up her hair in exactly the same way as the woman in the photograph the owner of the revue bar had given her for reference.

'Of course I don't, but make sure you keep your wits about you,' Martha said, jigging Bonnie up and down in front of the lounge window at a passing Ford Cortina.

'It's a lunchtime shift, I'll be serving cheese sandwiches to bankers, there'll be no funny business in the middle of the day. Anyway, it's a very respectable place, they have more rules than you do.'

As it turned out, funny business was exactly what the bankers wanted for lunch, along with a ploughman's and a bottle of Chianti. The rules of the club stated that a 'cordial distance' had to be maintained between hostesses and clientele at all times, fraternising was punishable by immediate unemployment. So it took Florence completely by surprise a few shifts in, when her bottom was pinched and a hand slid up her leg under her skirt. Particularly as the hand was sporting a thick gold band on its third finger.

'Do you mind!' she haughtily retorted, moving away quickly and pinning a stare of death on the man.

A few feet away, standing at the bar, the manager pinned his own eyes on Florence's, and motioned towards his office door with his head.

'But you said that I'd get fired for letting the men touch me!'

'Yes, but you need to give them the impression that you'd let them if only the establishment allowed it.'

Florence's brow wrinkled in confusion, 'I'm not sure I understand. Are they allowed to touch me?'

'No.'

'But I have to try to make them believe that I want them to?'

'Yes.'

'And you are firing me because I wasn't able to infiltrate their brain with the right subliminal message, while still abiding by every rule you have set.'

'Yes. You can come back on Monday to collect your wages.'

Rosemary was starting her shift as Florence was clearing out her locker in the tiny anteroom off the staff toilets where the girls kept their belongings. She saw Florence was crying and put her arm around her shoulder, 'Hey, what's wrong?'

'Sorry,' Florence wiped her face with her sleeve, embarrassed at being caught crying by her friend. 'I just don't know what to do now, I need to work, and everything I do goes wrong.'

Rosemary was quiet for a moment, then said, 'You couldn't ask Bonnie's father for some help? You know, with money?'

Florence was surprised none of them had asked about him sooner, you can't switch off curiosity, even if you choose not to act on it. She shook her head. 'No, he's not around.'

'It makes me so mad, men like that. Sorry, Florence, look, I can give you all my tips this week to help you out, and I'm sure the other girls have got a few bob stashed away, please don't worry, it'll be OK.'

This act of kindness made Florence's tears flow even more. Since arriving at the house with the green door, a complete stranger to the women within it, she'd made friends that would last a lifetime. She had thought she had that in Hazel too, but she'd had five letters returned unopened to her, and the ten or so times she'd tried to call her at home, Mr or Mrs Taylor had replied coldly that she wasn't available. She'd even tried calling her at the club, but she no longer worked there. When she'd called the club, she'd imagined the phone echoing through the cavernous foyer, into the bar and library beyond. Henry might even have been there, drinking his tea, reading his journals, snapped out of his concentration by the telephone's shrill ring. She liked that thought, that for a fleeting moment their lives were joined again.

That night, like every night, Florence sat staring at the cracked ceiling rose above her bed. She had twelve pounds to her name. Bonnie was almost ready to be weaned onto food that cost money and was also getting too big to sleep in a drawer. Her parents had disowned her. Her landlady was lovely, but even her patience must have a limit.

Through the thin wall, Florence heard the girls in the bedroom next door to her laughing over something one of them had said, followed by the opening chords of 'La Bamba' from the record player as they put on their make-up ready for a night out, taking rollers out of their hair, spraying lacquer on to hold it in place, dabbing perfume on their pulse points and rolling up their nylons.

Florence got up off the bed, and walked over to the basin in the corner of her room where Bonnie's soiled towelling napkins were soaking in hot water and soap flakes. She picked one up and wrung it out so it would dry faster in front of the electric fire. It was fair to say that the other girls in the house were living in a very different London to the one she was.

34

Bonnie

Bonnie's conversation with Florence about telling Stella the truth has been whirring round and round in her brain on a loop since Harry was born, and he is now nearly eight months old. She honestly thought she would get to the end of her days never having needed to say anything about it. Most days Bonnie woke up determined that today would be the day that she would speak to Stella about it, but then she'd see the way her daughter would laugh in awe at something Harry did, and she'd freeze, not wanting to cast a shadow over their happy lives.

Florence is having a ham sandwich on the sofa and looks up when Bonnie comes into the lounge.

'I've decided that I'm going to wait until after Christmas to decide what to tell Stella,' Bonnie says.

'I'd have thought Christmas was a nice segue into it – Jesus didn't know who his dad was either.'

'Christ, Mum.'

'Exactly.'

Bonnie stands in the bay window watching Stella push Harry down the road in the pram. The nappy bag 'that Daddy wouldn't like' is hanging from a hook on the adjustable handles she's not using but bought anyway because she liked the colour.

'But you are going to tell her?'

'Not until one of them have done a test, and as I have no idea where Steven is, it'll have to be Oliver, which is going to open a whole can of worms.'

'But how do you know where he is?'

'He'll be easier to find than Steven, now that the internet's invented. I just can't bring myself to do it yet.' Bonnie thinks about the hours, days, weeks, she spent calling pharmacies up and down the country after Stella was born. It seems incredible that if she types his name into Google right now, she could be seconds away from finding him.

'How are you going to get the DNA sample from Stella?'

'That's easy. I've bought her one of those "trace your ancestor" kits for an early Christmas present, I just won't send the swab off after she's done it, and I'll test it against Oliver's.'

'Do you want me to type in his name on my phone?' Florence asks.

'No, you finish your sandwich. I'll look on mine.'

'Come and sit next to me while you do.'

Bonnie sinks heavily into the sofa next to Florence and lays her head on her mother's shoulder, 'Oh Jesus, Mum, what am I going to say to him if I do find him?'

'You'll cross that bridge when you get to it.'

'*I have a daughter called Stella. She may or may not be yours, here's a swab, open wide, there's a good fellow?*'

'Let's just try to find him first.'

Bonnie's hands are shaking as she picks up her phone, then before she can type a letter, she flings it back down on the sofa. 'What if he's moved to Australia?' she says. 'Or what if he's dead?' The thought physically chokes her. She must have felt it, if he'd died, she would have known. The thought that he's always been out there somewhere has been a comfort for the last forty years; to think he might not have been makes her heart hurt.

Florence rests her warm hand on top of Bonnie's shaking cold one.

'What if he's alive but doesn't remember me?' Bonnie whispers finally. 'What if all these years, he meant more to me than I did to him? What if he and Janet have been so incredibly happy and he has blocked me out? Not thinking about me once since he left? What if that's happened? That would be worse than him dying, Mum, I don't think I could bear it. I don't think I could cope with him looking at me like a stranger, I can't. I've loved him for forty years, I have thought about him every day of those years. I have done the best for Stella because I owed it to him, to make his daughter someone he would be proud of, but what if there's no recognition there at all when I see him? What if it's all been in my imagination? What if he never loved me at all?'

Florence waits for her to stop, stays silent even through the sobbing that follows, just rhythmically moving her hand back and forth on her daughter's, until finally she says, 'But hasn't the idea of the love you once had been wonderful? You have spent most of your adult life certain in the knowledge of this man's feelings, so don't doubt them now. Now come on, wipe your eyes, pick up your phone and let's try to find him.'

They don't need to try too hard. His LinkedIn profile shows that he's been working as the head pharmacist in the Boots in Harrogate for the last fifteen years.

The blood rushes through Bonnie's ears and she lets out a gasp. Springing to her feet, she shakes her hands, trying to breathe, blinking back tears, pacing around the living room. Florence watches her daughter go through a thousand different emotions at once, desperate to console her, bring her back to the room, but Bonnie is miles, and years away.

Florence joins Bonnie at the window, staring out on the road, the same road she's looked at thousands of times over the years, stripping back the years, swapping the Renaults, Fiats and Kias out there now with the Morris Minors, the Ford Cortinas and the Vauxhall Vivas. Such a lot has changed, but then, not much has at all.

The next day is Wednesday, but Bonnie can't bring herself to see him then, so she waits until Thursday to go to Harrogate. When she gets to Boots, there's a queue and she joins the end of it. She can see him, but he hasn't seen her yet. She'd have been able to pick him out of a hundred thousand sixty-five-year-olds in a split second, with no hesitation at all. The last forty years have added a few wrinkles, shrunk him by an inch or two, thinned out his hair, but otherwise time has bounced over him, tapping him lightly before moving on to the next person. She doesn't think she's been quite so lucky, putting her hand self-consciously to her grey hair, and patting it down, biting her lips to give them more colour. She didn't think about putting some make-up on, she should have done. But then why, she berates herself, she isn't here to woo him, she is here to get some of his saliva.

'Next!'

She shuffles up one place in the queue. His glasses are different, but then they would be, wouldn't they, you wouldn't expect someone to be wearing the same frames for forty years. Fashion changes, things break. Nothing lasts long.

'Next!'

It's busier than she thought it would be. Where will they go to talk? There's that little frosted glass consultation room for private conversations that squeamish patients ask to speak to the pharmacist in, but that's a bit too intimate. Just thinking the word 'intimate' makes Bonnie blush.

'Next!'

The person in front of her hands over their prescription and stands to the side, where he points. His fingers are curved like Stella's.

'Next!'

He doesn't look up from arranging the prescriptions.

She takes a deep breath and says, 'Hello, Oliver.'

His face floods with recognition and he has to hold onto the desk in front of him to steady himself. 'Bonnie,' he croaks.

'Can we talk?'

He blinks and nods. 'Yes, yes of course.' He has a quick word with the other chemist and goes out of the door Bonnie hadn't noticed before, coming into the store just behind her without his white coat on.

'There's a coffee shop next door, shall we go there?' he says, putting one arm into a dark blue waterproof, the expensive kind you'd buy for hiking. Unless Janet has completely changed personality in the last four decades, Bonnie guesses correctly that he probably spends quite a lot of time alone.

'This is such a surprise,' he says, his voice laced with genuine happiness that she's sitting opposite him.

'Look, I'll get to the point,' she says, stopping for the young man to put down their matching cappuccinos before getting to the point. 'The reason I'm here is . . . well, the reason is . . .' She can't do it. She can't blow everything apart into pieces.

'What's the reason, Bonnie?'

She has to. 'The reason I'm here is a forty-one-year-old woman called Stella, who I think might be your daughter.'

He's just picked up his cup, which shakes so violently that hot coffee spills onto the table, summoning the waiter over with a cloth. 'Don't worry about it,' he says cheerfully, happens all the time.'

'I don't want anything from you,' Bonnie says in a low voice as soon as they're alone again. 'I just need to know for sure before I tell her. *If* I tell her. I have a DNA kit here, with me, if you could just—'

'Hang on, what are you saying, Bonnie? I don't understand.'

'I didn't know I was pregnant until after you left, and I had no way of finding you to tell you. Look, I don't even know if you are her father, I just need to either confirm it, or rule it out, so please can you swab the inside of your mouth and I'll let you know in a week or so.'

'But, Bonnie, I—'

She shakes her head. 'There's nothing more to say until we know for sure either way, so let's just finish our coffees, you do what you need to do with this,' she puts the paper bag with the kit inside on the table in between them, 'and we'll leave it at that for now.'

He goes to the toilet to do it. She guessed he would rather that than do it at the table, and while he's in there, Bonnie allows herself to breathe properly. She had to do it like this, professional and matter-of-factly, or it wouldn't get done. If she allowed herself to see this as anything other than a genetic puzzle that needed solving, then she'd fall apart. If it's positive, then there will be time for more conversation later. If not, then this was just a nice coffee with an old friend, well that's what she tries to tell herself anyway.

He walks across the coffee shop, his long legs taking long strides, and hands the bag back to her, holding on to it for a heartbeat longer than necessary. 'You'll let me know, won't you? I've written my number on a piece of paper inside the bag. Even if she's not . . . not mine, I'd love to meet her some time, and see you again, for a proper chat if you'd like?'

'I'll be in touch.' Bonnie gives him a polite, quick smile and leaves the cafe before all propriety is thrown out of the window and she rugby-tackles him to the ground begging him never to leave her again.

35

Stella

It's funny, but now that Harry is Harry and not Thing, he's become more his own person, and less an extension of 302. I still think about rollercoaster man, don't get me wrong, and I think I probably always will, wondering if Harry's ability to laugh, sneeze, wee and poo simultaneously is a 302 thing, because it's certainly not mine, but it's not all-consuming the way it was in the early days. It's as though now Harry has his own name, his own identity, he's carving his own route in life.

'We used to get loads of Christmas cards,' Florence says, from the hall, emptying out the wire tray attached to the back of the front door, and taking out a handful of bills and a couple of Christmas cards. 'We'd string them up on ribbons in the living room, do you remember, Bonnie?'

Mum nods, a little distractedly. She's been really strange since the conference she went to last week up north in Harrogate, I hope she's not doing too much. Now that I'm contributing more to the running costs of the house, she shouldn't need to work quite so many hours anymore, particularly so far away from home. But then again, I am milking her for free childcare now that I've gone back to work, so perhaps that's tiring her out.

Florence adds, 'I've had quite a few people say that they're donating the money they would have spent on cards to charity. Which is nice, but it does mean the walls look bare.'

'Nothing for me in the post?' Mum says.

Florence shakes her head, putting the pile on the side table.

'Expecting anything in particular?' I ask, handing Harry over to her.

'Oh you know, Christmas stuff.'

I turn away, but not before glimpsing Florence gesticulate wildly to Mum, pointing to the pile of post and nodding her head, her eyes wide as saucers. I don't know what surprise they're planning for me, but it looks like it's going to be good.

I spread all the decorations out on the floor around me in the living room as though I'm a bee in the centre of a flower. Florence insisted on us choosing the biggest Christmas tree at the garden centre, which completely covers the bay window, the twinkle of the lights reflected in the glass of the window. The greatest thing about being an only child was always being the one to put the angel on the top of the tree, never having to take turns on alternate years to be lifted up, or, in latter years, balance on a coffee table, to place it on. There's a box of decorations from the sixties – or what's left of them, there have been a fair few casualties over the years – but every time Florence catches a glimpse of a tiny painted wooden nutcracker, she smiles, so I make sure to hang the remaining three of them in prominent positions at the front.

I don't hear Mum come in, but she sits alongside me on the floor, and wordlessly picks up the end of a piece of tinsel, pulling it through her fingers.

'Where's Harry?' I ask, plugging in the fairy lights that I've laid in a circle around me on the floor.

'Flo's got him in the kitchen.'

'Oh OK. He'll need to eat soon. Oh good, these all work.'

'In a bit. Just stay here a minute.'

She wants to say something. It's something I'm doing wrong with Harry. She was like this when I offered him one of my McDonald's chips when he was about four months old, and Mum sat there watching, wringing her hands on a tea towel before springing forward and wrestling it out of my hand when it was about an inch from Harry's mouth. 'Sorry,' she said, 'I know I said I wouldn't interfere, but you can't do that.'

'Say it, what have I done now?' I ask.

'It's more what I've done. Or did.'

'Spit it out. It can't be that bad.'

'You know I love you. More than you could possibly imagine. Although now you have Harry, maybe you understand quite how much I do love you.'

'Y-es.'

'And I would never intentionally hurt you in any way. And any pain that I am about to cause you by what I'm going to tell you is completely unavoidable, and I'm—'

'Jesus, woman, tell me what it is, you're getting me really worried.'

Mum takes a big breath in, holds it for a beat and then her words tumble out, 'Your father isn't a man called Steven Morris, he's a pharmacist called Oliver Gillespie and he lives in Harrogate.'

I start laughing, 'Oh my God, Mum, that's hilarious, is Gran filming this?' I look over my shoulder for Florence peering round the door with a phone.

'It's true. I was having an affair, sort of, it's complicated, with Oliver, and I didn't know I was pregnant with you. He moved away before I found out, and so I stayed with Steven. I didn't know for sure until just now.'

She holds out a paper with DNA results on it. I don't understand the numbers; apart from one at the top that says a 99.9% match to someone called Oliver Gillespie. My mouth drops open as I realise she's completely serious. 'But . . . but I thought Dad cheated on you? That's why you left him. But it was the other way around?'

Mum is concentrating on the tinsel in her hands as though it holds the secrets to the universe. 'Steven and I were in a . . . what would you call it? A mutually open relationship, with another couple, Oliver and Janet. Steven and Janet were in love, and Oliver and I were certainly very fond of each other. Janet got pregnant with Steven's baby, he didn't want anything to do with it, so Oliver did the honourable thing and said that he would take care of her and the baby. They moved away and soon after, I found out I was pregnant. I didn't know for sure who your biological father was, and it was easier to just assume it was the man I was married to. Like I say, it was complicated.'

'And you let me assume that too,' I say slowly, as the magnitude of what she's telling me starts to sink in. 'For forty-one years.'

'Stella, I didn't realise Steven would turn out to be so awful, I promise you. For the first few years, he stayed in touch, sending letters and presents, he was an OK father.'

'Oh good, yes, he remembered a handful of times that Christmas falls on the twenty-fifth of December each year, what a superdad, and then completely forgot he had a child at all for the next thirty-five years.'

'Look, I realise now that I made a mistake allowing Steven into your life, I should have cut him out completely and just brought you up with Mum.'

'Did Flo know about this too? Have you both been lying to me?'

Mum shakes her head. 'She didn't know. It was a really difficult time, Stella, I did what I thought best at the time.'

'When you did realise that no dad would be better than the one you lumbered me with, why didn't you tell me then? Why wait until now? Is this my Christmas present? A new dad?'

'I didn't know for certain until recently, that's why I went up to Harrogate, to get a sample from him.'

'How did you find him? Have you always known where he is?'

Mum shakes her head, 'He was pretty easy to find; he's worked at the same chemist's for forty years.'

'So why now? Why find him now? Why not when I was little? When I actually could have enjoyed having a dad? Why keep him from me?'

'Please, I thought it was the right thing to tell you now, what with Harry not having the dad you chose for him. I thought if you knew that genes don't matter, that it's the love you give a child that makes them turn out the way they turn out—'

'Oh, so this is for me? Oh thank you, I thought this might be some cleansing therapy for you? But this bombshell that makes me question every single thing about my childhood is actually said for *my* benefit? That makes all the difference. Well, in that case, thank you, brilliant, when can I meet him? Is he coming for Christmas dinner? Will he bring me a new bike?'

I stand up, leaving Mum sitting there with all the detritus of a family Christmas laid out all around her. The fairy lights are blinking rhythmically on and off, on and off, and she just lets them.

About ten minutes pass, and there's a knock on my bedroom door and I know it's Florence before it even opens. She was always the one to come up here after I argued with Mum as a teenager, smoothing things over with her wise words and conspiratorial wink, making me think she was always on my side. I realise now that she probably did exactly the same to Mum downstairs: the eternal peacemaker.

'This is my fault,' she says, sitting down next to me on the bed.

I raise an eyebrow at her. I wonder if Oliver Gillespie can. 'I fail to see how exactly this is *your* fault.'

'I told her to tell you. To make you understand that whether Harry's father is Donor 203 or 507 or 804 it doesn't matter. What matters is what *you* do.'

'Oh great,' I say, 'so when I completely fuck him up, I can't even blame bad genes.'

'You're not going to muck him up.'

'You know what's the worst thing about all this,' I say, my voice shrill, 'is that all my life I've blamed him, Steven, for all my flaws, the fact I had a shitty job, couldn't hold down a relationship. All of it, I've said, "Oh well, I can't help it, my dad was the same," as though that gave me a free pass to be a complete failure, and now I know that, actually, my real dad is a freaking pharmacist. I mean you can't get a more boring job, apart from Mum's, and he's held down the same career for forty years. Forty years! Some of my jobs haven't gone past the forty minutes mark!'

'That wasn't your fault though, you had no way of knowing that speaking Portuguese was a pre-requisite for the job.'

'Except when I ticked the box on the application form that said, do you speak Portuguese? I bet Oliver Gillespie's never told a lie in his life. Although up until half an hour ago, I'd have said the same about Mum, and this is as big as it gets.'

'She did what she thought was right at the time. Which is exactly what she's doing now. If it's any consolation, Oliver had no idea you even existed until a couple of weeks ago, so he never left you on purpose. He's desperate to meet you, by all accounts.'

'Wow, what a disappointment I'm going to turn out to be. He'll be expecting a professor of neuroscience or something, and then he gets me.'

'When are you going to realise quite how fabulous you are? You're really—'

'Don't say funny. Anyone that gets described as funny as the first adjective invariably is not clever or pretty.'

'That's rubbish; you are clever and pretty. I just value humour above both of them.'

'Wow, sucks to be Mum then.'

Florence laughs, 'Your mother is very funny, just in a very dry way.'

'Do you know what, all this time, I've thought of her as this staid scientist, who thinks that having a white wine spritzer is "letting your hair down", and then it turns out she had this whole hidden past. For my entire life, I've felt that I needed to be more focused and practical, more like her and less like him. If I'd have known that she also had this side to her, the one driven by lust and love, her *heart*, then maybe I wouldn't feel like I let her down so much.'

Florence pats my hand. 'You've never let her down. And she loves who you are.'

'I'm just saying, it would have been easier.'

'What would be easier?'

'Easier to understand her. She's not who I thought she was. Why would she pretend all these years to be so . . . so measured? So in control of everything?'

'I don't think all of it was an act, she is like that, but she's also human, and humans fall in love and forget to be sensible. We all have our skeletons.'

'You don't. Congratulations.'

36

Florence

Sixty years earlier . . .

One of the girls – Florence's money was on June, although it could have been Nancy – dyed their hair using a hook and cap and dripped peroxide, making permanent white dots on the pink carpet in the back bedroom. However much Florence scrubbed them with a wire brush, they wouldn't come out. It was right in the centre of the room as well. If she was Martha, she'd make them pay for a replacement, but Florence knew Martha would just shrug and say, 'Accidents happen' in her Scottish burr. Much like she'd smiled and said, 'That's fine,' when Florence sat her down and admitted gravely that she couldn't pay that week's rent.

'But in return for board and lodging, for a very short while, probably only a few weeks, can I completely clean the house every day, change all the beds, the bathrooms, everything, and once I've read a few recipe books, I can prepare the evening meal too?'

Florence had built up to this conversation for days, practicing her speech on seven-month-old Bonnie, who seemed to think it was very good, clapping her chubby hands together and giggling.

As much as it annoyed Florence growing up, Mrs Weston's dedication to dust removal and surfaces that shone was useful when it came to Florence's new job. There wasn't a corner in any ceiling that Florence didn't attack with a feather duster tied to a broom handle, or an inch of grout between tiles that wasn't painstakingly scoured with an old toothbrush. The inside of the chimneys, the inside of the oven, the inside of the new fridge – Martha's pride and joy – all sparkled. With her final few pennies, Florence had bought some seeds and, as a surprise for Martha, dug out the soil in the patch of earth just outside the kitchen window and planted a row of potatoes, carrots, lettuces and constructed a wigwam for tomato plants. She went to bed each night aching in parts of her body she had no idea she had, but happy she was earning a roof over her and Bonnie's heads and growing food to put in their stomachs.

It was early December, and at Martha's request, Florence was moving the furniture in the living room around to make room in the bay window overlooking the street for the Christmas tree, which was being delivered later on in the afternoon. While the task was keeping her physically occupied, Florence couldn't stop her mind wandering back to Alderton Close, imagining the preparations for Christmas that would be happening – if it even was happening this year. Would her parents bother with the fuss of setting out crackers on a table just for two? Would her mother have already made the Christmas cake and wrapped it in muslin cloth in the larder, feeding it with brandy every week like she always had done, or would she think there was little point this year? Last year, she'd celebrated Christmas with her parents in complete ignorance of what this year was going to bring. The three of them sitting in pained silence around the dining table, each wearing a paper hat, eating Christmas dinner, complimenting her mother on the food, sipping watered-down wine, 'to make it last'.

The presents from her parents last Christmas had been practical, in view of her impending wedding in the new year: four white plates with matching bowls and side plates, a set of four knives, forks and spoons, and a trio of saucepans along with a *Good Housekeeping Cookery Compendium* recipe book. 'How lovely,' Florence had said, flicking through it, 'and so useful.' On Christmas Eve, sitting close together for warmth, on a bench in a park, Henry had given her a simply wrapped box in brown paper, tied with a red ribbon and a sprig of holly attached to a luggage tag which read, *'To Florence, Here's something you want, something you need, something to wear, and something to read, Love always, Henry x'*

The torn-out classified pages of a newspaper lay on top of a copy of the Highway Code and a provisional driving licence in her name, a pair of pale blue lamb's leather gloves, and a hard-backed copy of China Achebe's *Things Fall Apart*. 'Our first home is in those newspaper pages,' he explained, pointing at the classifieds. 'You need your independence, so here's a driving licence and the Highway Code for you to study. Your hands are always cold, and pale blue matches your eyes. And this book is just beautiful and is a great introduction to Nigeria, where I really hope we'll visit together one day. They speak Igbo there.'

She had smiled at his earnest explanations; it didn't occur to her then to see all four as prophecies: the apartment that would never get lived in; the driving licence, valid for six months, which would never be used; the gloves, left behind in the hurry to pack, but too special anyway to cover her now coarse, rough hands; the book, full of promise of adventure, with a title that unknowingly foreshadowed everything that came after.

'Penny for them,' Martha said, carrying a pile of logs in from the shed and dropping them in the basket next to the fireplace.

'Christmas,' Florence answered, summing up in one word all her thoughts.

Martha nodded. 'Ah.'

In the six months Florence and Bonnie had lived there, Martha hadn't once asked how or why they ended up ringing her doorbell that night in June. At first, Florence thought it was just out of politeness but that one day natural curiosity would triumph and she'd casually ask, the question, sandwiched between other casual enquiries like, 'Seems like the rain will hold off, what have you got planned? Who got you pregnant and why are you here? Would you like to borrow an umbrella just in case?' But that never happened. Martha genuinely didn't seem interested in knowing Florence's story; she was here now, and anything that came before that was just history.

'I've been thinking,' Martha said, sitting on the settee and patting the spot next to her for Florence to sit down too. 'You're doing far more around the house than you need to, way more than a cleaning lady would do, and so I think that as well as your board and lodging, I should also be giving you a bit extra, as wages.'

Florence vehemently disagreed, shaking her head, 'You've done so much for us already, I couldn't possibly take any money from you, Martha. No, please, I already feel awful that I'm taking up a room that a paying guest can take, but I promise you that when I get another job, I'll pay you all the rent I owe—'

'Florence, listen to me,' Martha said, patting Florence's hand. 'It is an absolute pleasure having you and Bonnie here.

Having a baby around the house again has brought so much joy, and you are a complete angel doing all you do. I am not a poor woman, Florence, I don't need the income from these rooms, I just like having the house filled with life, so it makes no difference to me whether you're here for free or not. But it makes a difference to you, and that's what I'm saying. I would like to make this arrangement between us more formal, and so I have two proposals for you. One, you and Bonnie stay here for free, including food, and you manage the house for me, as my housekeeper, for thirty pounds a month—'

'Thirty pounds!' Florence gasped. 'That's far too much, I couldn't do that!'

'Wait, I haven't finished. You're a young woman, with a child, and you need to set yourself up with a proper career, to make sure you can always provide for Bonnie, and so I'd like you to think about going to college and training for something. I'll look after Bonnie while you're studying, but you need a vocation, not just a job like the other girls, who'll all marry men who'll provide for them. Your needs are different.'

Florence was about to open her mouth to protest again but realised that what Martha was saying was true. She wasn't like the other girls who knew that their jobs were time-fillers; a way to pay for their cosmetics, new clothes or the first drink in a bar on a Saturday night until the rest of the drinks were bought for them.

'What would I do?' Florence asked. 'I'm not good at anything.'

'How about nursing?' Martha suggested.

'But I don't know anything about nursing.'

'That's what they teach you at college! I've got a friend who works in the admissions department at the local college that has ties with Guy's and I've set up a meeting for you with her tomorrow. I'll watch Bonnie.'

'But—'

'Ten-thirty.'

'Martha, I—'

'Ten-thirty, don't be late.'

If the bedroom had had carpet, it would have been worn down to the boards by the time dawn broke. Florence had talked herself into it, then out of it, then was gung-ho about it being exactly the path she should take, then absolutely adamant that whatever it took she would cancel the appointment, so by the time the first sliver of light poked its way through the curtains, Florence was already washed and dressed in her smartest clothes, coat and hat on, ready to go before she could change her mind again. As an afterthought, before leaving her room, she opened her little jewellery box and took out her mother's wedding ring, slipping it on her left hand.

The interview went well, and instead of hiding Bonnie's existence, it was the first thing she told Martha's friend, and if she was shocked, it certainly didn't register on her face, making Florence think that either Martha collected friends with exactly the same mindset, or, more likely, Martha had forewarned her. A few days later, a letter arrived in the wire tray on the back of the door offering her a place on a three-year nursing course starting four weeks later in mid-January.

The excitement was palpable in the house the week leading up to Christmas. Each night, the five women sat around in the living room after eating dinner off their laps on the settee, cutting coloured paper into strips and gluing them into paper chains ready to string up criss-crossing each other on every ceiling, even in the bedrooms. Bonnie even had pink and red striped ones threaded through the bars of her cot.

The tree in the bay window of the lounge was magnificent, so large Florence had to stand on a chair and snip eight inches off the top so it didn't graze the ceiling. Her father had always seemed to seek out the smallest tree possible, so short it had to sit on a table in their window to make it look bigger from the street so no one could accuse them of being mean.

Martha brought a box down from the attic and planted it on the floor, telling them 'to use anything in there for it', and soon tinsel, glass baubles, little wooden nutcracker figures – a haphazard medley of happiness in a box – made the tree shine with life.

Florence's present to Martha was being delivered the day before Christmas Eve, and every time a van went past the house, Florence raised her head like a meerkat, waiting for the engine to stop and a door to slam. It finally arrived just after four, in that half-light between day and night. 'Come in, come in,' she said, 'take it through to the kitchen.'

Martha came out of the lounge, wiping her hands on her skirt from laying the fire. 'What's going on?'

'It's my Christmas present to you, with my housekeeping money. A proper table for the kitchen. We're like a family, so we need a family table to sit at together.'

That night, the five women sat around the new pine table long after the plates had been washed and put away. They moved the record player into the kitchen and played cards, laughed, and talked until the early hours, only reluctantly going to bed when one of them mentioned the long journeys they all had the next day back to their families for Christmas. All of them except Florence.

Every day of December, Florence had been so hopeful that her parents would send a letter or a card to her. There was a line in the *Magic of Christmas* book that her mother used to read to her and Stu that said, 'Just maybe, because it is Christmas', and Florence had started repeating this to herself like a mantra every time the letter box jangled and cards cascaded into the wire basket. The tray was full every morning with cards, all of them offering joy for Christmas and prosperity for 1961, but none were from Alderton Close. Florence had bought a nice brooch of a nightingale for her mother, 'my little Florence Nightingale', and a book on suburban garden wildlife for her father, and took them to the post office, wrapped up with a black and white photo of her and Bonnie that Martha had taken, tucked inside a snow-scene card. They would have received it two weeks ago now, but sent nothing back in return.

Martha could sense Florence's sadness masked in false jollity, as she stood alongside her in the kitchen rolling out the pastry for the mince pies. Bonnie sat happily on the chequered kitchen lino behind them, propped up with cushions taken from the living room. Every so often, Florence's rolling pin would pause for a second or two before starting up again faster, harder, than before. This should have been her and Henry's first Christmas together, possibly hosting his parents or hers, or both; Florence winced at that thought. Never both. Where was he tonight? Had he met someone else? Was he happy? She had thought about sending him a card, wishing him well, but felt so ashamed at how she'd behaved, it was kinder just to let him be.

'Salt water will ruin the pastry,' Martha said kindly, gesturing at the tear that had fallen onto the kitchen counter.

'Oh God, sorry.' Florence wiped her face, putting a streak of white flour across her cheek.

'Don't be.'

Florence gave her landlady a small smile, 'I can't thank you enough for all you've done for us.'

'Hush. Now I don't know about you, but I think some mulled wine might be in order while we listen to the carols on the radio. Shall I make some, while you make yourself look less like the abominable snowman?'

On Christmas morning, when Florence carried Bonnie down the stairs. Avoiding the eleventh creaky stair that might wake Martha up, she opened the door to the living room and her mouth flew open. Two filled stockings were hanging on the mantelpiece, both knitted in the same rainbow colours, one embroidered with her name, the other with Bonnie's.

'I know this isn't the Christmas you'd thought you'd have, but it's going to be a good one, I promise,' Martha said from behind her. Under the tree were more presents wrapped in colourful paper, left by Nancy, June and Rosemary. Florence blinked back tears when she saw them lying there, with Bonnie's name on the tags. All this time she thought she hadn't got a family anymore, but it turned out they were living under the same roof all along.

* * *

Three years later . . .

'We're all going for a drink if you fancy it, Flo?' one of the other nurses said, taking off her hat and tucking it into her handbag.

'No thanks, Penny, I need to get back.'

'Next time?'

Florence nodded, 'Next time.'

It was a charade, they all knew that, but also they all wanted Florence to know that they'd never stop asking, just in case. She was an anomaly to them, instantly likeable, but shrouded in mystery. The other nurses talked endlessly about their lives, their boyfriends, sharing every detail from their weekends and nights off, but Florence mentioned nothing. She'd laugh along with their descriptions of a disastrous first date which ended in the man's convenient lost wallet when the bill was due, or smile with their giggling recollections of a good date which ended in an entirely different way. But when the questions turned in her direction, she'd bat them away with a, 'Oh I'm dull and boring compared to you', while twisting the slim gold band on her left hand that she had decided it was easier to wear.

Then it had just slipped out one day. She was caught off guard by an elderly patient, telling her that had he been fifty years younger, he'd have asked her out for a drink. She laughed appreciatively and said with a wink, 'I'm very flattered, Mr Rodgers, and had I not been a happily married woman, I'd have said yes.'

'What's the lucky chap's name, nurse?'

'Henry,' she said. 'Henry Fairbrother.'

She didn't see the nurse at the next bed along turning a patient onto his side, eyes wide at a nugget of new information about their enigmatic friend that she could share with everyone else working on the ward.

Once everyone knew, and the seal to the secret was well and truly broken, Henry started to take shape in Florence's life in unexpected ways. 'Best get home, Henry's waiting,' had much more gravitas than, 'sorry, I need to get back for my landlady.' But it wasn't just in work either; the plumber she'd called to unblock the kitchen sink told her to buy a plunger, so next time her husband could do it. Rather than correct him as she would have once done, feeling a weighty sense of guilt if she didn't, then having to face either a sneer of distaste if he caught sight of Bonnie, or, worse, an invitation to the pub with him, this time she smiled, and said, 'Absolutely, he's good with his hands.'

She had no idea why it had taken her three years to do it; it made her life so much easier. Henry became such an omnipresent feature in her life over the next few months, and she relished speaking about him again, hearing his name out loud, conjuring up thoughts of him instead of suppressing them. Then, one day, without thinking, it tripped off her tongue to Martha. 'Henry used to say . . .' and 'Henry used to do . . .' started filtering into her speech. Martha made no comment, but the other girls did, picking up on the reference to Florence's secret past life like beagles catching a scent.

She had to invent parts of his life for him for her co-workers – 'Our wedding was lovely, a three-layered cake with different flavours for each layer, Victoria sponge, fruit cake and coffee and walnut.' It wasn't a complete lie; that was what she'd told the cake maker she wanted for their wedding, it had just never got baked or iced. She'd imagined what their marriage would have been like so many times, it was easy to conjure up details.

But she'd never once imagined what would happen if the two worlds collided.

In June 1963, in the final year of Florence's training, she was on a three-month placement in the accident and emergency department. It was the fifth night in a row of twelve hours of emptying bedpans, cleaning bedside lockers, dressing wounds, making beds with crisp hospital corners and

Florence could hardly stand up. The double doors at the end of the corridor banged open, showing the first strains of daylight, as paramedics ran in with a trolley. Nurse Linney, a petite red-headed nurse with a laugh like a baby seal, put her hand on Florence's arm, 'I'll take this one, you look done in. There's only fifteen minutes left before the shift change, start getting yourself together.'

Grateful, Florence gave the nurse's station one last tidy before the ward sister came for the changeover. She'd just finished when Nurse Linney arrived breathless in front of her, 'Florence, you have to come, I think the new patient's your husband!'

37

Stella

I'm meeting my father at a service station on the M1 between Junction 21 and 21A. I racked my brains trying to think of a different, more auspicious meeting place for our touching reunion but honestly couldn't think of a better place than Leicester Forest East, with its array of eateries – KFC *and* Burger King – and it even has an electric charging point, should my biological father be the green kind. The reviews say that parking is limited to two hours and strictly enforced, so that's a bonus as well if things are a bit stilted and time is dragging, but with both a Starbucks and a Krispy Kreme on site, I doubt that will happen.

I was going to leave Harry at home with Florence and Mum, but then thought that, practically speaking, he'd be a good distraction if it's too awkward, and even though he's only eight months old, he's a great emotional support.

I see the sign for the services coming up, a cup of tea, a knife and fork crossed in the middle – a nice lunch for two. What will he be like? Will he like me? Will we look alike? Would it be immediately obvious we were related? Should I call him Dad? '*I'm just getting a refill, would you like one, Dad?*' Have I got siblings? Has Harry got cousins? '*Why did you sleep with my Mum when she was married?*' Would he give me the answers Mum can't? We've reached a truce, Mum and I, more borne out of geography than anything else, living as we do in the same one-hundred-square-metres. I do get it though. We make decisions every day of our lives: some make no impact at all, and others leave a legacy of a lifetime and there's no way telling which is going to be which.

I pull into a parking space a little away from the building and just sit in my car for a few minutes looking around the car park. Which car is his? From the little I know of him, he'd be a Volvo man, possibly a Nissan. Definitely not a diesel driver or the owner of a gas-guzzling SUV. He might have a UK sticker on the boot, 'I love the Loire Valley.' He's possibly a member of the caravan club, although he wouldn't advertise that. Nobody's business.

There's a sky-blue Nissan Qashqai parked a few spaces along from me, about ten metres away, with an older man at the driving wheel just staring into space and I instinctively know it's him. He doesn't move, just looks ahead as though in a staring contest with the windscreen.

It's not just me who feels like they're standing on the edge of the earth then.

I pick up my phone and type out *I'm here. I love you, it's all OK. Talk later, Sxx.*

Mum replies straight away with a heart emoji.

Now it's time to meet my dad.

Hoicking Harry onto my hip, I walk over to the Qashqai and knock on the driver's window, which is a bit of a risk thinking about it, what if I'm wrong and the portly man with pastry crumbs from his sausage roll decorating his fleece getting into a transit van is really my father?

The driver jumps, and opens his door, his face flooding with recognition, and a red rash immediately starts spreading on his neck.

'Hi, are you Oliver?'

'Stella?'

I nod. He gets out of the car quickly, banging his head on the inside of the door.

'Oh God, are you OK?'

'Fine, fine, sorry, yes. Hello. I'm Oliver.'

We shake hands. Which feels right. A hug would be too much.

'Shall we get a coffee?' he says, nodding towards the brown-brick building, while he puts out his little finger for Harry to grasp.

'Yes,' I say as we walk across the car park together, 'there's a choice of outlets inside.' *Shut up, Stella.*

'You find a seat, I'll get them, what would you like?'

As I weave through the tables to an empty one at the back, I think about how that simple command is such a dad one; a division of labour he would have made every time we went out if he'd have lived with us. 'You get the trolley, I'll get the parking ticket'. 'I'll get the drinks in, you get the table.'

I drum my fingers on the table as I see him picking up his tray and scanning the room for me. I rise out of my seat a little and give him a wave. He's taller than I thought he'd be, and very slim. He actually looks quite a lot like Mum. It's easy to imagine the two of them together, each adjusting their glasses as they pore over a journal together.

'Busy today,' he says, looking round at all the tables filled with families and couples.

'Yes.'

'Did you have a good journey up?'

'Not bad, there were roadworks for a bit around Milton Keynes, but it didn't add much to the journey.'

'Oh that's good. I had a clear run.'

'Oh good.'

'Did you want a cake or a muffin or something as well? I didn't ask you? I can go and get one?'

'No,' I say, 'I'm fine. Thank you.'

'I don't really eat sweet things, that's why I didn't ask. Sorry.'

'No, honestly, I'm not hungry.'

'Oh, OK. Good. Does the little one want one?'

'No, I've got his snacks, thank you though.'

We sit in silence for about three years. I mean, not exactly three years, but as one minute morphs into the next, they start to take on the feeling of calendar months rather than accumulation of seconds.

'So you live in Harrogate?' I ask finally, not sure where I intend to go with this question being as I already know the answer.

'Yes, do you know it?' he says eagerly.

'No, never been.'

'Oh, OK, yes, it's a nice town. A spa town.'

'I like spas. They're very relaxing. Especially facials and hot stone massages.'

'No, it's called a spa town because of its mineral springs.'

'I know, it was a joke.'

'Oh.' He laughs an awkward laugh. 'The first was discovered in 1571. The spring, I mean. The water's full of sulphur, which is meant to be quite medicinal.'

'Lovely. I like water.' *I like water?*

'I like water too!' he says excitedly.

'Well, we didn't really need a DNA test to prove we were related after all!' I say jubilantly.

The mention of the test makes his face drop again, the elation at finding some common ground short-lived, even if it is just that we both drink water.

'So, you're a pharmacist?' I say. 'That must be . . . interesting.'

'Oh it is. No two days the same. And what do you do?'

'I'm the manager of a care home.'

'That's fantastic, gosh, that must be incredibly rewarding.'

'It is. I sort of fell into it by accident, it's a long story, but I love it. I was the assistant manager for years but got a promotion to manager last year.'

'Oh, that's brilliant. Really great. Well done you.'

He picks up his teaspoon and stirs his coffee again, despite the fact that he's already done that, twice, and it must be pretty cold by now.

'Have you had a happy life?' he asks finally.

'You make it sound like I'm at the end of it,' I laugh. 'Should I have told someone I was meeting you here today, just in case I disappear?'

'Doesn't anyone know where you are?' He seems panicked. 'You should always tell someone where you're going. What if you broke down?'

'But I didn't.'

'But you might have done. Or you could on the way back. Why doesn't your mum know where you are?'

'Because I'm forty-one.'

This seems to shut him up.

'Anyway, to answer your original question, yes, I've had a very happy life. Mum and Florence have made sure that I've never wanted for anything, and now I'm a mum myself, I realise the sacrifices they made for me.'

'I had no idea I had a grandchild until you turned up with him. He's so lovely.'

'Didn't Mum tell you?'

'She didn't really say anything apart from here's a swab, put it in your mouth.'

'She's always been quite direct.'

'Yes. That's what I used to love about her.'

His eyes get a bit wider as he realises what he just said, and the rash on his neck now spreads up his jawline.

'Out of interest, what *did* you like about her?' I purposely don't say love, he can't have loved her, otherwise there would be no need to be having a coffee together at a service station forty-odd years after he made me. Unless we were going on a day trip to visit a selection of nursing homes that I might be considering putting him into.

'She made me feel alive.'

To my horror, I notice that his eyes have gone all misty and he looks like he's about to cry, right in the middle of the crowded services, just in front of a slowly moving queue for Krispy Kreme. I should comfort him in some way. I think about putting my hand on top of his, but he doesn't look like the type who would welcome physical contact from a stranger. But I'm not a stranger.

'I was quite a precocious child, I think,' I say quickly, moving the conversation on, steering it into safer, less emotional waters. 'I think I gave Mum and Florence a few grey hairs.'

'In what way?' he smiles, his neck turning paler again.

'I'm quite loud and silly. And spontaneous. And stubborn. I'm definitely ruining their quiet retirements, having moved back in with them, and having Harry.'

'I bet they love it. Do you all live in London still?'

'Yes, the same house I grew up in.'

'Not the one in Wandsworth, the one with the green door?'

'Yes, that's the one. Did you go there? Oh God, are you going to tell me you and Mum had sex in the house I live in? Oh no, was I conceived in the room I sleep in?'

His eyes twinkle for the first time, 'Do you sleep in the kitchen?'

'Oh yuck. You're both disgusting,' I say in mock horror, pretending to vomit.

'So Bonnie never moved? She's been there the whole time?' He looks wistful.

'Yes.' Suddenly everything is making sense: the refusals to ever move out, the vehement row we had when I suggested painting the door that distinguished our house from all its identical neighbours. 'She hasn't said this,' I say, 'but if I know my mum the way I think I know her – although you existing shows that actually I don't know her as well as I thought I did – I would wager she never moved because she thought one day you might turn up at her door.'

38

Bonnie

'I can't believe you thought you could just turn up at my door—'

'We thought it would be a nice surprise,' Stella says. She realises as she says it that she has massively misjudged how this reunion might go.

'I can leave?' says Oliver, looking from Stella's face to Bonnie's, waiting for one of the women to give him a command as to his next course of action.

'You've driven for five hours today already, you can't drive home now,' Stella says.

'Well, he can't stay here,' Bonnie replies.

'I'm fine to drive home, I'll take lots of breaks and drink some caffeine.'

Florence walks into the hallway from the kitchen to see what all the commotion is about, 'Hello, Oliver, nice to see you again. I'm just popping the kettle on if anyone fancies a cuppa?'

Bonnie glares at her mother; you'd have thought Oliver had been on a week-long business trip, not a forty-one-year hiatus the way she just greeted him.

'Or a wine? I'm having a wine,' Stella says.

Oliver smiles gratefully, 'Tea would be lovely thank you, Florence, if I'm driving again.'

'Which you are,' Bonnie says.

Florence and Stella both turn to glare at her rudeness.

'What?' she shrugs. 'Just stating a fact.'

The hallway is starting to feel very small. Bonnie looks around to see if anyone else is feeling that the walls are closing in. Oliver's got that mottled redness again; she forgot he used to get that. Florence and Stella look completely oblivious to how horrific this situation is for her. Look at them, just standing there smiling at him, like he's some sort of prodigal son returning from war.

The five of them sit around the kitchen table. Bonnie and Oliver drinking tea, Florence and Stella have opened a bottle of wine, Harry's having some juice in his beaker. Bonnie and Oliver are suddenly painfully aware of what happened last time they were in the kitchen together. It's as if Stella can read their minds because she suddenly exclaims, 'Oh God, you two did it in here.'

Florence furrows her brow, 'Did what?'

'This is where they made me. In here.'

'In the kitchen?' Florence asks. 'Wasn't that really uncomfortable?'

At the same time, Bonnie gasps to Oliver, 'You told her?'

'I don't know how it came up.'

Stella splutters out her wine.

'I'm taking my tea in the living room,' Bonnie says, walking out in disgust.

Oliver waits an awkward minute before saying, 'I better go and . . .' He finishes his sentence with a nod towards the lounge door.

Bonnie looks up when he comes in, mug in hand.

'Can I join you?' he says, hovering by the door, politely waiting for permission to enter.

She shrugs, which he takes as an invitation. He slowly closes the door behind him.

They start speaking at the same time: 'I don't know why you're here,' she says.

'I should have called to ask if it was OK.'

'I wanted to do the test for her, to give Stella some peace of mind about Harry, not for you to waltz back into our lives.'

'I'm not waltzing, Bonnie, I'm tentatively making the first steps towards getting to know my daughter.'

'If you'd have stayed here, and not left, you'd have had a lifetime to get to know her,' Bonnie says, refusing to meet his eyes, and training them on the bookcase.

'You never gave me a choice.'

'You had a choice, Oliver. You chose Janet.' How could his rejection of her forty-one years ago still sting so much?

'But I didn't know about Stella then.'

'But you knew I loved you. That should have been enough. If you stayed for the baby, but not for me, that's not love, that's duty.'

'I should have been allowed to make that decision though. All these years, I had a child I never knew about who you kept from me.'

Bonnie turns to him, her eyes blazing with the insinuation that she deliberately kept Stella a secret, denied her a proper father. 'I didn't know for sure she was yours until she started growing up, until she walked with your lolloping strides, with your ridiculously long legs, until she started concentrating when writing, sticking her tongue out at the side, until she made me buy the old till from the pharmacy you used to work in because something about it made her feel happy, and I had to watch her playing on it every day, knowing that your fingers and her fingers had touched the same buttons. When she grew out of it, it sat in the hall cupboard for a year or so, taunting me every time I got the hoover out, until I couldn't bear seeing it, making me think of you, and you and Janet, and you and Janet and your child, and so I threw it in next-door's skip.'

'The child's called Stefan.'

Bonnie stiffens. 'You're kidding.'

Oliver shakes his head.

'You raised a boy your wife named after her lover, my husband, and you still stayed with her?'

'I promised.'

Bonnie inhales slowly, 'So where are Janet and Stefan now?' She stumbles over the child's name, how the hell has Oliver managed it for over forty years?

'Back in Harrogate. Stefan married his husband Dean last year. They're very happy. They're on the adoption list for a baby of their own.'

Bonnie can't help but think that Stefan's almost definitely had an easier life having Oliver as his father rather than his real one. 'And Janet?' she says finally.

'Janet's well.'

'You're still together then?'

'No. No we're not, we got divorced the year Stefan left for university.' He lifts his arm and scratches the back of his head. 'She, um, found it difficult to be happy, with just me, when Stefan wasn't there. And I felt I'd done my duty by then, bringing him up, helping him become a good man, so I asked her for a divorce. I've never stopped thinking about you,' Oliver says, searching for her eyes.

She meets his gaze for a moment before looking away. 'You could have come to find me any time. I was still here, behind the green door. I wouldn't even let anyone paint it in case you came back and couldn't find the house. How deluded is that?'

'But what about Steven?'

Bonnie scoffs, 'Steven and Janet are cut from the same cloth. He had another affair. I packed his case for him. We haven't heard from him in years. Since Stella was tiny.'

'So you've raised Stella completely alone?'

'No.'

'So you married again?' His question is laced with sadness.

'No, I had Mum. We raised Stella together.'

'I'm so sorry,' he says sadly, shaking his head. 'If I had known, I'd have come sooner.'

'To rescue us?'

His brow furrows in confusion, 'No, I just mean, to provide for you.'

'I've provided for us just fine, thanks. We didn't need you to swoop in and save the day, we managed very well by ourselves.'

'Why are you so angry with me? I didn't leave you like Steven did.'

'No, but you did leave me. You left me for a woman you didn't love and a baby that wasn't yours. And knowing where I was on your list of priorities took me a fair while to get over. So forgive me if I still harbour a bit of resentment all these years on.'

'I'm sorry,' he says, leaning forward in his chair placing his hands on his knees as if to stand up. 'I shouldn't have come.'

Bonnie's voice softens, 'Of course you should. You just found out you've got a daughter, and a grandson; of course you'd want to spend time with them. Whatever I feel . . . felt for you, is nothing to do with you building a relationship with them.'

'Thanks, Bon.'

'Knee.'

'What?'

'Bon-nie. No-one's called me Bon in four decades.'

'You're really not going to make this easy for me, are you?'

'I don't know what you mean. You just walk back into my life unannounced and I'm being called out for not responding to a pet name you once had for me? Hardly seems fair.'

'We should have called ahead, so you'd have had time to prepare.'

Hearing him use 'we' for him and Stella makes the hair stand up on Bonnie's arms. They weren't 'we'; she and Stella were 'we'.

'You know what?' she says matter of-factly. 'If I had known you'd be coming here today, I'd have probably gone out.'

'Ouch.'

'No, I just mean, I would have avoided doing this,' she waves her hand back and forth between them. 'Digging it all back up.'

'When you and Steven broke up, and you knew that Stella was mine, why didn't you try to find me?'

'Google wasn't invented and you didn't exactly leave a forwarding address with your letter your replacement gave me at the pharmacy. And anyway, like I said, you made your choice, I wasn't going to turn up, baby in my arms and beg you to make a different one.'

'But I might have done.' He moves over to the sofa where Bonnie is sitting and gently sits down beside her.

His proximity unnerves her and her heartbeat quickens. 'And you might not. Either way, one child was going to be fatherless, Stella or Stefan, and by the sounds of it, Stefan might have needed you a bit more than Stella did.'

'She seems a very capable young woman, you've done a fantastic job.'

'Considering?'

'No, not considering anything, just that you're quite clearly a wonderful mother.'

Another biting retort is ready to fire out of her mouth, but then she stops. He didn't ask for this to rock his quiet contentment in Harrogate. He was probably very happy easing into semi-retirement with a golf club membership and being on the waiting list for an allotment; he wasn't sitting at home wishing that somewhere in the world he had a child he'd never met.

'So, how does it feel to have a child that's actually biologically yours?'

'Stefan *is* mine,' he spits with such force it takes Bonnie aback.

He's right. He clearly has a bond that's as strong as blood with Stefan. 'I'm sorry. I didn't mean that. Of course he is. That was really insensitive of me.'

'I never in a million years thought that you'd still be alone,' he says sadly. 'If I knew that, I would have come sooner.' He clocks her rolling her eyes and waits another beat before adding, 'Not for Stella, for you.'

'Don't say that. Don't say it if you don't mean it, Oliver, I couldn't bear your pity.'

'It's not pity. It's despair that all this time I've been in Harrogate lonely and miserable thinking about you, and you've been down here doing the same. For twenty years.'

'I haven't been miserable,' Bonnie says. 'Well, not all the time.'

'Let me in, Bonnie, please. We're old now, with much more of our lives behind us than in front, please, let me in.'

Bonnie closes her eyes and bows her head. 'But what if you leave again?' she says no louder than a whisper, 'I can't mend myself again, Oliver, I'm not that strong anymore. I will break into a thousand pieces and I can't . . . I can't do that.'

Oliver reaches up and strokes her hair out of her eyes. 'Give me a chance.'

Bonnie lets out her breath slowly, 'People don't just walk back into your life and live happily ever after, Oliver. Second chances don't happen in real life to real people, they just don't.'

He covers her hand with his. 'Sometimes they do.'

39

Florence

Fifty-seven years earlier . . .

Her mind whirring a thousand miles an hour, Florence froze to the spot.

'His name's Henry Fairbrother! He's waking up, come on!'

It couldn't be the same man. Surely there were many Henry Fairbrothers in London?

She ran across the ward towards his bed, with no thought to propriety or the other patients, those of whom who could were raising themselves slightly in their beds to see what the commotion was about.

'Henry!' Florence gasped when she saw his face; bruised, and swollen, but definitely him.

Nurse Linney stood at the end of the bed; her hands clasped together, tears in her eyes at this cruel twist of fate. But neither Henry nor Florence thought it cruel; even through the haze of strong medication, Henry managed a smile, and Florence pulled up a chair alongside him, picked up his hand and didn't leave his side. He had broken his hip, his collarbone and his right shoulder getting knocked off his bicycle by a car. She neither affirmed nor corrected the doctor when he told her that her husband was going to need surgery. She sat on a hard chair outside the theatre for most of the day. At some point during the morning, Martha dropped Bonnie to the hospital, as she had appointments and couldn't find anyone else to stay with her. After getting her some lunch from the staff canteen, Bonnie lay across Florence's lap for a nap, Florence's coat over her. Finally, at around 3 p.m., the surgeon came out of the double doors with the large RESTRICTED ACCESS sign written across them. Florence was pinned to the seat by her sleeping daughter but looked up at him, worry etched across her face.

'It went well, but recovery is going to be long and slow, I'm afraid. He'll have limited mobility for months and will need constant care, and not necessarily from children,' he added, pointedly looking down at Bonnie. 'However much they want to play nurse to Daddy.'

'We'll manage,' Florence said, with a steely determination she was slowly getting used to feeling. 'Can I see him?'

Henry was sure the anaesthetic was giving him hallucinations as Florence floated into his field of vision, her soft hand holding his. He smiled, not knowing if she was real or not, but she was here, and that's all that mattered.

The next time he woke up, he was in a different room, his brain wasn't quite so tired and hazy, and she was still there.

'Florence.'

'Hello, Henry. Try not to speak, you need to rest.'

'Please don't leave.'

'I'm not going anywhere.'

For the next three weeks, every shift of hers started and ended on Henry's ward, and she'd invariably try to slip in unnoticed past the eagle-eyed ward sister a few times during each shift as well, taking the stairs between Casualty and

Men's Surgical two at a time to get there quicker. His eyes brightened as soon as she turned the corner into the ward, often bringing with her something to cheer him up: a bunch of daffodils one day, a book of Greek myths the next. While these were a welcome distraction from the bleak monotony of the hospital ward, it was Florence's company he looked forward to most. She read him headlines about the Profumo affair, which was still dominating the news, and hummed the first few bars to the song 'Come On', which a new band called The Rolling Stones had just released, which Nancy played constantly at home. She told him about Martha and the other women she lived with. In all her visits, she never mentioned Bonnie, not because she wasn't burning to, it was a massive effort not to talk about the most important piece of her, but because mentioning her would lead to conversations she didn't want to have.

Although she hated seeing him in pain, plaster casts on different parts of his body, it was as though while he was in here, the rest of the real world didn't exist. Neither of them corrected the doctors when they referred to her as his wife, or told her in front of him that 'your husband's making steady progress'. Henry was worried that she'd be denied visiting rights if they found out they weren't married, and Florence's lie was so deeply embedded in her persona at the hospital, she couldn't have corrected them even if she wanted to, without her whole world crumbling.

'Tell me about the baby,' he said quietly, one Tuesday morning after she'd come off a night shift downstairs.

'Her name's Bonnie.'

'And she's still with you? You didn't need to give her up?'

Florence nodded her head. 'She's with me.'

'So you married her father?' Henry said sadly, putting his head back on his pillow.

'No, I didn't. I told you, I live in a boarding house with other women.'

'So you're raising Bonnie alone?'

Florence laughed, 'Hardly, she has more parents around her than most children. Sometimes I think she'd like to be alone, but she's not.'

'What's she like?'

No one had asked her that before. What was Bonnie like? 'She's quite a serious little thing,' Florence smiled, summoning up Bonnie's screwed-up face of concentration as she held a crayon, or arranged her toys in height order. 'But funny too. She's talking lots, mainly questions, she wants to know everything about everything.'

'Sounds like a girl after my own heart. I'd like to meet her.'

Florence shut her eyes. *What good could come of this?*

'I waited, you know,' he said finally.

She opened her eyes and looked at him.

'At the church. I wore a suit and put a flower in my buttonhole and waited for an hour until a coffin covered in flowers turned up for a funeral and I realised you weren't coming. Why didn't you come, Florence?' There's a sadness in his voice that hits her.

'I couldn't let you do that.'

'I wanted to. No one was making me.'

'But they were making me, don't you see that? My parents, society, you, even you, Henry. Don't look so shocked, I felt like I was the inconvenience that everyone had to fix, but it wasn't your problem to step in and sort out.'

'I never saw you as a problem, Florence, and I never would have.'

'But I had to do it by myself. I couldn't have let my bad decisions affect your life too.'

In the silence of the moments that followed this, Florence realised that's exactly what had happened in the end anyway, and the bad decision wasn't getting pregnant with Bonnie, it was letting Henry wait at the church alone.

Later that night, she hung up her sensible navy coat on the hook in the hallway on top of June's bright orange knee-length one and wearily walked up the stairs, avoiding the creaky eleventh step in the middle so she didn't wake anyone up. 'Come and sit with me a moment, Florence,' called out Martha from her bedroom. She was propped up in bed, a book open on her lap on top of the covers. 'Sit down.' She waited until Florence had sat on the end of the bed before saying, 'Tell me about Henry.'

Florence coloured. In the three and a half years she had lived there, this was the first time Martha had broken her own rule and asked a personal question.

'What do you want to know?'

'Whatever you want to tell me.'

Florence looked in the older woman's eyes and could see that she could remember as clearly as Florence could the night she had arrived in old clothes, with Bonnie strapped to her chest by a torn bedsheet with the initials of the mother and baby home stitched into the corner.

'I loved him. He was a wonderful man,' Florence said truthfully. 'But I made a mistake, and I had to let him go.'

'Bonnie?'

'Yes, Bonnie.'

'She's not a mistake. She's a miracle.'

Florence smiled, 'Yes, I suppose she is. But in 1959, she was very much considered a mistake.'

'Life's not easy for women like us, Florence.'

Women like us? Other things Martha had said over the years came back to her: 'it's lovely having a baby in the house again,' 'changing nappies is like riding a bicycle, you never forget how to do it.'

Martha kept talking, 'He'll need looking after when he gets discharged, and you said he's on the third floor in his own lodgings, which would be impossible with his hip. Since Rosemary's moved out, the downstairs bedroom's free, why don't we set it up for him? I've been meaning to get a downstairs bathroom installed for ages, I'll get a quote to have the larder in the kitchen turned into one.'

'No, it's too much upheaval,' Florence replied, the idea of having Henry living with her behind the green door too terrifying and exciting to think about.

'I'm not getting any younger, so I've wanted a downstairs lavatory for ages. You said he's got another two weeks in hospital? Suggest it to him tomorrow and I'll call the builders in the morning. It'll be nice to have a man around the house, especially if he's as wonderful as you've said he is.'

'But I—'

'Florence. Ask him.'

Two weeks later, with a paramedic one side of him, and Florence the other, Henry walked through the green door for the first time. She'd moved the bed to face the window into the garden, onto the new vegetable patch, so he could have a nice view while he recuperated. Before leaving for work in the morning, she would leave everything he might need for the day within arm's reach: a jug of water, a couple of books, a crossword, a walking stick, a jar of paracetamol, and when she returned, she found his room turned into a den, kitchen chairs back to back with a tablecloth over them, Bonnie sitting underneath, reading a picture book with a torch. She chased her out, to the sound of Henry laughing, telling her to 'leave her be, I like it.' Over the next few weeks, she found broken crayons in his bed sheets where Bonnie had been lying next to him colouring, along with a medley of crumbs from snacks Bonnie had brought in to share with him. Bonnie's rudimentary drawings of animals and flowers were now stuck up around his room. 'Monet she is not,' Florence laughed, when she brought his dinner in on a tray, looking at the latest addition to the gallery, an elephant with giraffe-like proportions and pigs' trotters for feet.

'No, but she could give Picasso a run for his money!' he laughed.

He asked her to marry him on a Thursday evening. She was turning down his bed for him while he had a bath; everyone else in the house was asleep. There was no fanfare, no big preamble, just a simple, 'Marry me?' said from the doorway as he stood in his pyjamas and she still wearing her nurse's uniform from a long day at work. 'You don't need to answer me now. Have a think about it. I'd raise Bonnie as my own.'

She tapped quietly on Martha's door as she passed it on her way to bed, telling her in hushed whispers what Henry had just said.

'Do you think he'll be a good father?'

Florence smiled. 'The best.'

'Well, Bonnie is very lucky.'

'But he isn't her real—'

'Shush. Anything you can do to make it easier for yourself, for her, you should do.'

A few minutes later, Florence tiptoed out of her bedroom, slowly closing the door. Once she was the other side of the wall, she sat on the end of the bed and looked at Bonnie sleeping through the bars of her cot, which she'd found next to a bin and painted white. She was nearly four. She had no idea what a daddy was, but she'd start school in September, and the question was bound to come up then. Could she lie to her? To other parents? Could she commit to keeping this untruth going for the rest of her life? Once she'd said it to Bonnie, it couldn't be taken back. Florence finally drifted off to sleep as the house's water pipes whistled.

Their wedding cake had three layers: Victoria sponge, fruit cake and coffee and walnut. They'd be eating it for weeks as there were only nine people in the entire wedding party: two of his friends, the four women who had become like family to Florence and Bonnie, who wore a cream dress with a sash tied into a big bow. He twirled her and Florence around the room, holding his stick for support, to Elvis crooning, 'I can't help falling in love with you'.

Later that evening, when the front room was made back into a living room, and not used as a dance floor, after they had their wedding photo taken in front of the fireplace and mantelpiece it now sits on, she and Henry sat at the pine kitchen table finishing a bottle of champagne before tackling the washing up. Bonnie sat on a kitchen chair alongside them, pouring the leftover liquids from the different glasses in together, watching as the green crème de menthe of Nancy's cocktail turned Martha's rosé wine purple, before putting some dregs of red wine into an inch of white wine to make a pale pink.

'What are you doing, Bonnie?' Florence asked.

'Doing experiments.'

Henry gave a chuckle, and put his arm around his new daughter. 'Looks like our Bonnie might turn out to be a scientist, just like her daddy.'

40

Stella

Oliver stays the night in the end, on a fold-out bed from the attic, in the living room, which makes him and Mum share an awkward laugh, for some reason. She fusses over him like he's a celebrity who couldn't get into the Savoy so stayed with us instead – 'Have you got a glass of water?' 'Let me get you a towel for the morning.' 'Here's a spare toothbrush.' 'We've had a new shower put in since you were here last, let me show you how it works.'

'He was last here over forty years ago,' I joke. 'To get hot water then, someone would have had to pedal really fast on a bicycle generator.'

'She thinks she's hilarious,' Mum says, rolling her eyes at him.

'I'm getting that,' he replies.

For the first time, I have two parents ganging up on me. It's going to take a bit of getting used to. But I think I like it.

I'm knackered. The jury's out on whether it's because of the five hours spent on the M1 or the family reunion. He seems nice though. As biological fathers go. He's already asked me when my birthday is, and Harry's, and wrote the dates into a little black pocket book he retrieved from the inside of his jacket, so it looks like I'll be getting my first birthday card from a dad in a few months' time, which will be something to look forward to. He doesn't strike me as a funny card kind of guy, so he'd probably pick something with just a cake or a balloon on the front with an unnecessary declaration of 'It's your birthday!' But it would be better than nothing. It'd be really nice in fact.

Dinner could have been odd, but oddly wasn't. The ingredients were there: erstwhile lovers brought together after four decades apart; a father and daughter reunion; an octogenarian who kept grinning like a cat that had the cream, a can of tuna and a filleted mackerel. Florence couldn't be less subtle about how she felt about this turn of events if she tried.

I felt really bad at first when he and Mum were arguing in the lounge; her look of sheer panic when he walked in was not what I expected. I'm not actually sure what I expected, to be honest. I don't think I really thought it through when I blurted out the offer for him to come back with me. I actually felt a bit sick as Florence and I sat in the kitchen trying not to listen to them: flicking the kettle on to boil, turning the radio up. Why didn't I even consider how difficult it was going to be for Mum to see him again? I should have anticipated that. I was so overwhelmed with having an enthusiastic dad, I just got carried away. It was thoughtless of me, but actually, it's turned out rather well.

But I'm not going to lie; having a man in the house is unnerving. The oversized anorak on the hall pegs, the large shoes neatly paired up under them, the low snores coming from the front room as I tiptoe past its closed door to get Harry's breakfast ready in the morning all jar with the familiar surroundings.

I splash the milk into Harry's Weetabix and strap him into the highchair, pulling my chair closer to him. He's gurgling, and trying to eat his little plastic spoon, which he throws delightedly on the floor, his new pastime. I crouch down to get it, but it's under the big Welsh dresser. I contemplate leaving it there, we have other spoons, but then the ethics of communal living bite me, and I reach for a magazine to try to prise it out with. Under the dresser, the magazine touches something and I make a sweeping motion with it, expecting the spoon, forty years of dust and detritus to come with it, but there's a paper bag with something in it inside. I rock back on my heels as I pick it up and look inside. It's Florence's blue notebook I gave her, along with a folded-up piece of paper. What's it doing under the dresser?

If you're reading this, then you've moved this dresser, which is so heavy I know it can only be because you're moving house. And if that's the case, I can only assume it's because me and Bonnie are not around any more, because there's no way we'd willingly leave this house alive. So I'm taking a calculated risk and putting this here for you Stella, or you Harry, to find at some point in the future.

Everything in this notebook is a lie.

Well, most of it.

When I started writing, I thought this would be my chance to finally be honest, but when it came to putting pen to paper, I couldn't. I've lived in this version of the truth for over sixty years, and when it came to it, it was actually impossible for me to write anything else, because somewhere along the line, the lies became fact.

When you read the last entry in this book, please think kindly of me. 1959 was a very different time and place to the one you live in now and I made the decisions I felt were right at the time.

Please never doubt how much I loved Bonnie, or you Stella, or you Harry. You three were my world.

I shiver reading Florence's words in the past tense. She's written this as though she's long dead, yet is actually sleeping in the room above my head. A letter from the grave, when the grave isn't even dug yet. What does she mean, everything she's written is a lie?

I carry the book back carefully to the kitchen table and sit down, stroking Harry's head as I do. I flick to the last entry she's written in her neat slanted script.

Harry, you are going to grow up a strong, confident, brilliant person because of how Stella is going to raise you. At times, you're going to wonder about your father, of course you are, but you are going to realise that you are who you are not because of what your genes are, but because of the stories we will read you, the games we will play, and the conversations we have around the kitchen table as you grow up.

Something happened today which made me realise quite how important honesty in families is, how so much time is wasted if people keep secrets from one another. I never set out to rewrite my story to make it better, it just sort of happened, and I didn't see the harm in letting Bonnie and Stella believe it, not if it made them both happy. As the years passed, nothing would be gained from bringing it all up, but I have given this so much thought, and I feel that I need to tell you the truth. I can only hope that by the time you read this, Bonnie will have joined me and Henry on the other side, so this won't hurt her. Please just remember that I lived in a very different time to you. The world was a very different place, a less forgiving place, and I did what I did to protect us, to make life easier for all of us.

I became pregnant at sixteen by a mechanic called Kenny Buck. He was married and had a child, although I didn't know that at the time. I only found out I was pregnant after I'd met and fallen in love with Henry. We'd even set a date for the wedding. I called it off when I realised I was pregnant with Kenny's baby. I was sent to a mother and baby home in East London, and Bonnie was going to be adopted until I ran away with her in the middle of the night to this house and a wonderful woman called Martha who took us in.

I only met Henry again by chance, when Bonnie was three years old, and he took us both on. She was too young to remember a time without him being there, so she's just assumed he was her father right from the start. I kept meaning to tell her, but he never wanted me to, he begged me not to. He didn't want her to see him any differently, so I didn't, and then after he died, she threw herself into a career in science to be like him, and she'd feel like her whole life has been built on a lie if she knew the truth. So I have kept this secret for sixty years.

I want you to see that what genes you inherit might determine what eye colour you have, or whether you have curly hair, but it doesn't make you a fantastic artist – getting crayons as a child does that and an art teacher who inspires you. A concert pianist might pass on their long fingers to their child, but a love of music comes from the soul, not the blood type you have. You can be whoever and whatever you choose to be, just like I have, and your grandma has, and your mother has. That's what's important.

Florence

I can't compute any of this. I suddenly remember the dates of their wedding song not matching up, her saying that she had her wedding reception in the living room, Florence's confusion over which room Mum was born in, the nursery wallpaper – the pieces all start to slot into place.

I blow out my cheeks and slowly exhale, my hands clasped in front of me as if in prayer while I wonder what to do with this.

'Are we going to have a séance?' Mum says, coming into the kitchen in her dressing gown.

I slam the notebook shut and hurriedly brush my face with my sleeve.

'What are you reading? Is that Mum's notebook?'

I slide it under a newspaper on the table. 'No,'

'Stella,' Mum lifts up the paper and takes it out. 'Does she know you've read it?'

I shake my head.

'Is there something in there that upset you?'

How can I answer that? She goes to open it and I grab it out of her hands, 'No, don't!'

She stops. The book falls open in her hands. 'She's written it in here, hasn't she? About me.'

I bite my lower lip.

'If it's what I think it is, then I know.'

'Know what?'

'About Henry.'

I pale.

'I've known for years.'

I shake my head. 'She doesn't think you do.' I tap the book, 'This is for Harry to read when he's grown up, after Flo's gone, after you've gone. She doesn't want you to know. She hid it under the dresser so we wouldn't find it.'

Mum sinks into a kitchen chair and speaks slowly. 'Dad told me, just before he died. He didn't realise he did, I don't think, he was really confused in the day or so before. He said,

"I've always loved you as my own." Those words, "my own", just stuck with me, it didn't make much sense. I thought about it for years after, and so as soon as I turned eighteen, I ran some tests on myself using some hair from his hair-brush Mum kept in a box in the bottom of her wardrobe. We weren't a match.'

Her voice is level, but I can hear the faint tremor in it, and reach out my hand to put it on top of hers. 'That must have been awful to find that out. Why didn't you talk to Flo about it? Confront her?'

'This whole house was a shrine to him, she adored him, and she was always saying, "you're so much like your father", "your father would be so proud". She'd obviously rewritten the past in her mind, and I didn't want to upset her. And, if I'm honest, what good would it have done? I had thirteen years of him as my dad, where was the other guy when Dad was holding the back of my bike saddle when I wobbled down the street? Or pulling out my teeth with his hanky? I had a dad. I didn't need another one.'

'But weren't you curious about what the other man looked like? What you got from him?' I can't believe that Mum could just file this away in her mind and never think of it, never wonder. Never tell me.

'It's why I got into genetics, if I'm honest. I wanted to understand how DNA works, nature versus nurture, genes versus culture. Why I felt so much like Henry's daughter when I biologically wasn't.'

A thought occurs to me, 'But . . . but . . . you *are* a scientist, like him, how does that work if your real dad wasn't?'

'Because I watched him read science journals all the time, and he helped me catch frogspawn and keep them in a jar on the windowsill to teach me about life cycles. Because he never gave me age-appropriate answers to any of my questions, he'd tell me the truth about evolution and biology. He made me curious through his parenting.'

'Aren't you curious what you got from Kenny Buck?'

'Thankfully not his name,' she smiles. 'If I thought Fairbrother was bad, imagine that being sung at you in the playground. Anyway, that's the first time I've ever heard his name. I don't know anything about him.'

She seems awfully calm for someone that's just found out the identity of her father. 'We could google him?' I suggest.

'Why would I want to do that?'

'Because he's your dad.'

'No he's not. My dad's in Highgate Cemetery.' She places a hand over her heart, and then points at her head. 'And here and here.'

'Honestly I don't know how you can be so OK with this. I literally feel like the rug has been pulled out from under me finding out that Oliver is my father and not Steven.'

'But why does it matter? Steven hasn't been part of your life for years, he might be dead for all we know.'

'He's in Minnesota. He sells insurance,' I say blankly. 'According to Facebook, I've got three half-brothers, except I don't, do I? They're no relation to me at all.'

'I didn't know you'd traced him?'

'I didn't want to hurt your feelings. God, we're a pair, aren't we?'

'More of a trio, really,' she smiles. 'Look, I know you might not be ready to hear this, but Oliver wants to be part of your life. Of Harry's. He's a good man, Stella. A fine, clever, brilliant man.'

'That's another thing that I can't get my head around,' I say. 'I thought my dad was a complete deadbeat who never held down a job, so I thought that gave me permission to be like that too, but actually he was a clever pharmacist and the irony is, your dad who you thought was a brilliant scientist was actually an East End mechanic.'

'Is that what it says in there?' Mum nods towards the closed book burning a hole on the table.

I nod.

'Can I look?'

I shrug, 'It's your story.'

I sit quietly while Mum reads this last entry. I watch as her eyes move side-to-side digesting each line. Her body is completely still. She gets to the end and takes a big breath, which she lets out slowly. 'Well, that's that then.'

'Are you going to speak to her about this?'

Mum shakes her head. 'No. If it's been that important to her to keep this secret for sixty years, then a few more years can't hurt. Anyway, if I mention it, she'll know we've read it, and we really shouldn't have done.'

'But you might have family you've never met just down the road.'

Mum shakes her head. 'I don't need any more. I might feel different if I hadn't had Henry in my life, I might feel a gap that needs filling, but I really don't.'

I spoon some cereal into Harry's mouth, busying myself so I don't have to look at Mum as I say, 'I'd like to get to know Oliver, if that's OK? And Stefan too if that's not too weird for you?'

'Not at all, Stefan may be biologically Steven's, but he's Oliver's son, and therefore, your half-brother, sort of.'

'Jesus, we're a complex bunch, aren't we?'

'Definite talk-show material.'

'Right, I need to put the notebook back under the dresser.' I put it back in the paper bag, along with the note from the future, feeling a lump form in my throat knowing that the next time I read it, the use of the past tense in *You three were my world* will make complete sense.

41
Stella

'Happy birthday, dear Harry, happy birthday to you!'

'Hold him up so he can blow out the candles.'

'He's one, Oliver, he can't do that,' Mum says.

'But for the photo, that's it, just in front of the fireplace, yes, just there, and smile.' Oliver looks at the picture on his phone and says, 'That'll look lovely in a frame. I'll make a copy for each of us. It'll brighten up my new flat.'

'Why don't you take some of the cushions with you as well, we've got loads.'

I slip away from the party into the kitchen; still able to hear Mum and Oliver swap ideas of how he can make his new apartment two tube stops away more like a home. She offers to pop round with some lamps tomorrow and a rug. I see an imminent dash to Ikea in our future to replace all the stuff she's merrily giving away, but this is the happiest I've ever seen her, so what's a few bits of home furnishings between friends?

'Hi, Flo, I thought you'd gone upstairs,' I say, coming in to the kitchen with Harry on my hip. He holds out his hands to Flo for her to take him. She looks tired.

'No, I thought I'd get ahead on the tidying up.'

'We normally leave that to Mum, don't we?' I laugh, taking the tea towel off her and flicking her towards a chair.

'Well, she seems rather preoccupied,' replies Florence with a twinkle. 'I was just thinking how much your grandfather would have loved today. I can see so much of him in Harry.'

I don't know whether she actually believes it, or just wants to. 'Can you?'

'Oh, they're like carbon copies of each other.'

'Well, Harry's a lucky chap then.'

An hour or so later, Florence has gone up for a nap, Oliver has left, laden down like a donkey on the Everest trail with the contents of all our cupboards and Mum's promise that she'll pop over in the morning to help him unpack. I have a feeling that after sixty-five years, she might be almost ready to move out and I have no idea how I feel about that. This house is Mum. Every room has her in it, and I can't imagine being here without her. But since having Harry I understand her so much more, and appreciate every sacrifice she's ever made. She's definitely due some happiness, and while I personally wouldn't choose someone who's a proud wearer of Crocs and has a National Trust membership for my own life partner, Oliver's definitely made for Mum.

I decide to take advantage of the dry afternoon and take Harry across the road to the park. He falls asleep within seconds of leaving the house, so there's no sandpit action or toddler swings today, so I just sit on the same bench I sat on almost two years ago crying my eyes out, Harry snoozing happily in his pushchair next to me. I've become more visible since he came along, at least by association. Everyone that passes first looks at him, then at me, and smiles. I feel like I should be in a TV commercial selling vitamins, leisurewear, or cars. Nothing sells a Volkswagen more than a mother on a bench next to a sleeping baby.

I look at our house across the park. The green door I've gone in and out of thousands of times. The door that opened to Florence when the rest of the world's doors were closed. The door that Steven slammed shut on his way out of our lives forever is the same door that Oliver just went out of telling us joyfully that he'll see us next weekend. The love, the lies, the stories this house has known, and still harbours. Florence's notebook still sits under the kitchen dresser gathering dust and toast crusts. That's what she wanted, so that's what we're doing. Her secret will go to her grave with her. It didn't stop me googling Kenny Buck though. Mum might be able to stem her curiosity, but I can't. Apparently he won £1.3 million on a midweek Lotto draw shortly after the lottery launched back in the nineties, but with three ex-wives and eleven children to support, most of it went in alimony and he squandered the rest on a bar in Torremolinos which went bust within six months of opening. I couldn't find any mention of him anywhere after 2006.

How different would Mum's life have been if she'd had Kenny Buck as her father? She might not even have met Oliver at all, or become a scientist. And would I have pushed myself more at school if I knew my real father was in medicine? None of us can say really, can we? But if I had the chance to do it all again, knowing what I know now, I do know that I wouldn't have wasted months and months on my quest for the perfect donor. I'd have gone to page seventeen and chosen the second one down. Or page five and third one up from the bottom. Either or. It really wouldn't have mattered at all. We're what matters.

* * *

Dear Harry,

Today was your first birthday and it feels fitting that I end the day writing in your book. We had a little party for you with Great-Granny Flo, Grandma and Grandad. You alternated between eating, laughing and sleeping your way through it, which, to be honest, sums up some of the best parties I've ever been to.

We were having tea after the party when Florence reminded me what we needed to do. She grabbed a pen and called us all into the kitchen. We balanced you on your feet, your back straight against the door frame – you couldn't stop giggling, you found it so funny. Mum held you still while Florence held a book level with the top of your head against the wood and I marked a little line on the door frame between Bonnie 1yr and Stella 1yr. The first lines of many more to come. And when you're a bit older, I'll hand you the tools myself to carve your initials on the leg of the kitchen table and the pen to write your own message on the walls of your room.

All too often we get fixated on what we inherit from our parents, but sometimes I think we need to ask the opposite question: what do we get from our children? I used to think that growing up meant moving on, moving out, moving up, but now I know it doesn't. Growing up means being happy where you are and who you are. And I can honestly say that I'm truly happy with both.

I get that from you.

Acknowledgements

I've always ended my acknowledgments by thanking my family, but it seems especially fitting for this book, which is so rooted in family life, to start my roll-call of thanks with a shout-out to my own tribe who I get so much from. To my three children, Millie, Rafe and Theo, thank you for making me a mum. I get my drive to be a better human from the three of you.

To my Dad Tim and Mum Carol, thank you for reading my childhood stories and telling me they were good, I get my confidence to follow my dreams (and my love of obscure sixties music) from you.

My sisters, Hannah and Davinia, thank you for always being there. I get my sense of belonging from you.

My novels always have fierce, fun women at their core, and I'm thrilled to also be surrounded by these women in real life too. Lisa, Netty, Catherine, Kirsteen, Bev, Lorna, Sally, Nina and Tabs, I get my inspiration for all the funny parts from you.

To my agent, my cheerleader, my ally and my friend, Hannah Schofield of LBA, this book wouldn't exist without you, thank you for everything. It's no understatement to say that I get all my best ideas when I'm around you.

Massive thanks to Hodder and the brilliant editorial, art, rights and marketing departments, in particular the unflappable Olivia Barber whose love for Florence, Bonnie and Stella made them all the more real to me. I get this beautiful book from you!

Thank you so much to all the bloggers and book reviewers, who work so hard purely for the love of fiction to spread the word for books they enjoy, you are doing such a fantastic job. I get my ambition to keep writing from you.

And finally, to Ed, who's been flatly refusing to listen to my moments of self-doubt for seventeen years, thank you for giving me everything.

If you loved *You Get That From Me*, discover Charlotte Butterfield's hilarious and heartwarming story of second chances . . .

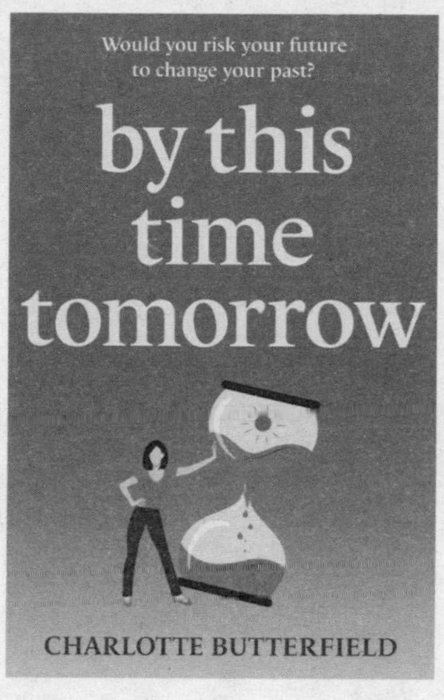

Jessica Bay has it all – and it's all too much. Between moody teenagers, a hectic job and a husband who can recall that the last time they slept together was 632 days ago but somehow can't remember to put the bins out, Jess is close to breaking point.

Desperate for change, she moves the family to a tiny island in the English Channel. An island that has a secret: it can take you back in time to relive any day in your past. To have another go at doing it right.

But as Jess becomes dizzy with the fact that she can, she forgets to consider if she should. Because changing even one moment in your past will change your whole future in unknowable ways. How much of her supposedly imperfect life is Jess willing to gamble? And will she realise the risks before she loses everything?

Available in paperback, eBook and audiobook now!

We love a happy ending. But, almost more than that, we love the promise of a new beginning.

Join us at www.hodder.co.uk, or follow us on Twitter @hodderbooks, and be part of a community of escapists who enjoy nothing more than curling up with a good book.

Whether you want to find out more about this book, or a particular author, watch trailers and interviews, have the chance to win early limited editions, or simply browse our expert readers' selection of the very best books, we think you'll find what you're looking for.

And if you don't, that's the place to tell us what's missing.

We love what we do, and we'd love you to be part of it.

www.hodder.co.uk

@hodderbooks

HodderBooks

HodderBooks